ANGRY HOUSEWIVES

Eating Bon Bons

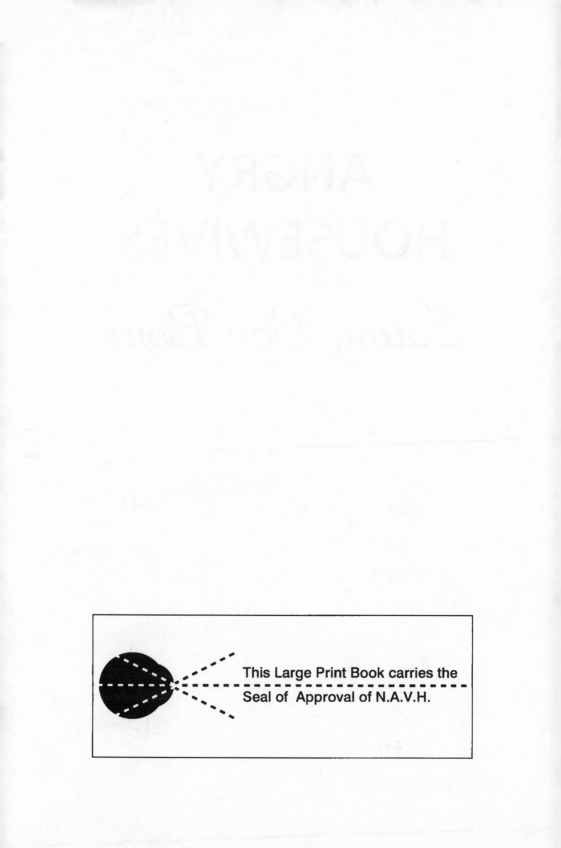

ANGRY HOUSEWIVES

Eating Bon Bons

Lorna Landvik

Thorndike Press • Waterville, Maine

Published in 2003 by arrangement with The Random House Ballantine Publishing Group, a division of Random House, Inc.

Thorndike Press® Large Print Core Series.

The tree indicium is a trademark of Thorndike Press.

The text of this Large Print edition is unabridged.
Other aspects of the book may vary from the original edition.

Set in 16 pt. Plantin by Minnie B. Raven.

Printed in the United States on permanent paper.

Library of Congress Cataloging-in-Publication Data

Landvik, Lorna, 1954–
    Angry housewives eating bon bons / Lorna Landvik.
      p. cm.
    ISBN 0-7862-5406-8 (lg. print : hc : alk. paper)
    1. Female friendship — Fiction. 2. Housewives — Fiction.
3. Book clubs — Fiction. 4. Minnesota — Fiction. 5. Large
type books. I. Title.
PS3562.A4835A54 2003
  813'.54—dc21   2003042300

To Lori Naslund

and

Betty Lou Henson Long

For years of deep friendship and big laughs

Acknowledgments

A big thanks to the many book clubs who've invited me to their meetings and shared their food, libations and conversation — what fun women you are! Thanks to my own book club and its members: Susan, Camille, Julie, Gloria, Isla, Lizabeth, Joyce, Terri and Amy — long may we read, converse, laugh, wine, and dine.

And speaking of sisterhood (I was, you know), I'd like to reach back to my childhood to thank the mighty Mellstrom sisters — Joyce, Carla, Marilyn and Debbie — who taught me about the power of women early on, and the Eggerts — Judy, Candy and Becky — whose Toni perms I coveted and whose Friday night breaded-shrimp dinners were exotic to a Lutheran girl. Thanks to Darcy Allison for all those hours we spent drawing and writing stories. Also thanks to my mother, Ollie, and her band of sisters — Gola, Amy, Vellie, and Orpha — and to the memory of Gladys, Viola, and Beata — wonderful aunts all.

Thanks to Wendy Smith, Kim Hoffer, and Judy Heneghan (when are you going to move back here?) for being such good and fun friends. Thanks also to Mike Sobota for your visits, to Melissa Denton and Dana Farner for that incredible church service, and to Mary Jo Pehl for letting me crash at your apartment, man.

Thanks to Tom Winner, Mark and Kathy

Strandjord, and Dick Farrell for your help in getting us set up in a house with an office.

A deep and grateful thank-you to Leona Nevler and Betsy Nolan — the editor and agent who held my hand from the beginning — and an equally deep and grateful thanks to Maureen O'Neal and Suzanne Gluck, those responsible for holding my hand now.

And to my dazzling daughters, Harleigh and Kinga, and my wunnerful, wunnerful husband Chuck — for everything, thank you.

Prologue

September 1998

FAITH

I knew all about having my life saved. When I was three years old, I broke free of my MawMaw's callused grasp to chase a paper cup skittering across the street at the same time a jalopy full of new army recruits careened around the corner. A sailor coming out of Knapp's Drugs and Sundries, with reflexes I hope served him well in his tour of duty, threw his bottle of Hires root beer to the sidewalk and raced out into the street, scooping me up in his arms. I can still hear the cacophony of squealing brakes, honking horns, and my grandmother's scream, feel the sailor's rough cotton uniform on my cheek and smell the soda pop on his breath. Thereafter, root beer would replace Nehi as my favorite soda, and of course I would forever believe the navy superior to the army because that's what the sailor said, in so many (profane) words, once he found out what field of service the scared young men in the rusty Nash had joined that morning.

When I was eleven, DellaRose Pryne and I had

9

taken a walk along a country road to smoke the Viceroy I'd swiped from MawMaw's pack. When the wind began whipping up and the sky turned green, it seemed a great adventure, until DellaRose spotted the moving black smudge beyond the line of telephone poles and screamed, "Tornado!"

We jumped into a ditch and lay there, arms entwined around each other, as the locomotive of wind roared over us. Even in my terror, I couldn't resist looking up to see the tornado throwing up parts of the earth — and the Dobbses' chicken coop — all around us.

And then there was the time when I was sixteen and drank too much on Student Skip Day and had to be fished out of the Tallahala River after bashing my head against a rock. I woke up to find myself being given mouth-to-mouth resuscitation by Billy Lawler, whose resemblance to James Dean had not gone unnoticed by every girl in the tri-county area. But this was not the way I had fantasized about kissing him, his anxious face mottled with the blood that streamed from my hairline, and I turned my pounding head to vomit in the scrubby grass, embarrassed and ashamed.

I didn't become a teetotaler that day (I hope that I never have to join *that* club), but I did revise my standards as to what social drinking was, and never again drank to the point of passing out. My life may have been saved by that adjustment; certainly excessive drinking had led to my mother's death, and if anything, I did not want a death like my mother's, let alone a life.

I took a sip of the brown swill the hospital claimed was coffee and regarded the four women in the room.

But it's you, I thought. *You who've saved my life more times than I can count. Who forced me to tell the secrets that were eating me up, and still loved me.*

As if hearing my thoughts, Audrey looked up from her knitting, adjusted her reading glasses, and winked.

She was completely silver-haired now, and at least fifty pounds heavier than when I had first thrown a snowball at her, but there was an easy elegance to her that neither age nor weight could diminish. In the days of miniskirts, Audrey could be counted on to wear the miniest, as well as necklines that plunged inches past propriety, but to me, she always looked . . . well, regal. Audrey had laughed when I told her this, had even slapped her thigh and claimed it was nothing but "posture, Faith . . . and an attitude. Good posture and an attitude let you get away with anything."

Audrey, who introduced herself these days as "a former atheist whose wake-up call just happened to have God on the other end," was the type of person who got away with a lot simply because she refused to ask permission for the privilege of being herself. It was certainly not an attitude I came by easily.

"You've got to start living up to your name," Audrey had told me long ago. "Have a little faith in Faith."

It was as if she had asked me to break the sound barrier on foot.

"How'm I supposed to do *that?*"

"For starters, stop trying so hard to be perfect. No one's perfect — except maybe Donna Reed, and she doesn't count, because she's only perfect on TV."

I smiled at the memory of that conversation

11

and of those gentle television sitcoms. We mocked the beautiful mothers in shirtwaist dresses as they poured milk from glass bottles and dispensed wisdom in their showplace kitchens (in high heels, of course), but at least their kids acted their age. Not like today, when the laugh track is cranked up high in response to every sexual innuendo lisped by some wide-eyed moppet. Don't get me wrong, sexual innuendoes have their place — but not in conversation with a second grader. I guess I'm getting old, longing for those days when kids on TV called their dads "sir" and *Shindig* was considered racy.

"Why are you looking at me like that?" asked the woman who still held the honor of being the loveliest woman — including Donna Reed — I had ever seen.

"I was just trying to remember if you ever wore miniskirts."

"Good Lord," said Merit, closing her book. "I hope so."

"Miniskirts," said Audrey with a long sigh. "How I loved my miniskirts. And hot pants. Remember those white vinyl hot pants I used to wear?"

Nodding, I tossed my Styrofoam cup into the wastebasket. "I'm sure every man in Freesia Court remembers those hot pants."

Merit frowned, her slight fingers probing the dimple in her chin. "You know, come to think of it, I don't think I ever did. I don't think I was *allowed*. To wear a miniskirt, that is."

Another memory made goose bumps rise on my arms.

"Maybe Kari can sew you up one," whispered Slip, nodding at the dozing woman.

"How about it?" I asked as she opened her eyes. Everyone took turns snoozing during this vigil and had a knack for waking up whenever the conversation called for it. I was the only one who wouldn't sleep. I was used to staying alert; to be awake was to be armed, and if the Grim Reaper even *thought* about making an appearance, he was in for a fight from me. "How about you make us group miniskirts, Kari?"

"I imagine it would take a lot more fabric than it did in the old days," she said, "but sure, I'll get right on it."

Kari was the oldest of the group by a dozen years, but as far as looks went, she had been blessed with an aging clock that was set slower than the rest of ours. We all got older and Kari stayed the same.

"No, I think my miniskirt days are over," said Merit.

"Never surrender," said Audrey, pointing a knitting needle in Merit's direction. "In fact, I vote that we all wear miniskirts to the next AHEB meeting."

The laughter that greeted her nomination was short-lived, as reality reminded us that the next AHEB meeting was in question. The room fell back into a silence muted by the clicking of knitting needles and the rustle of turning pages.

I studied one of the photographs I was considering using for our scrapbook. It was a picture of Kari holding a tray of cookies at one of her annual Christmas parties.

"How are we supposed to stand things?" I had once asked her at the peak of one of the many crises that conspire against anyone with the temerity to be alive and breathing.

A glaze came over Kari's blue eyes, the glaze of a person ready to tell a story.

"Once my mother and I were having lunch in this fancy hotel in Fargo and the waiter served us walleye that was undercooked — honestly, it was sushi before the days of sushi. We had him take our plates back to the kitchen but when he brought them back, the fish was now not only undercooked, but cold. He left us to attend to his other customers, completely ignoring us as we called, 'Waiter!' He had absolutely no time for us or our complaints."

Kari's got a wonderful laugh — as deep as Santa Claus with a cold. Looking at my face, she let it rip.

"My point is, sometimes life's like a bad waiter and serves you exactly what you *don't* want. You can cry and scream and order him to take it back, but in the end, you're the one who has to deal with what's finally set before you."

All of us women in the room have had our share of surly waiters serving bad entrees, but for over thirty years, we have helped one another up from the table, passed along antacids and after-dinner mints, offered shoulders to cry on, stiff drinks, and desserts whose butter content was exceeded only by its sugar load. But this . . . this *cancer* thing — could we survive something that seemed so grimly devoted to taking one of us away?

"I remember *you* had a miniskirt," I said to Slip. "We bought it together in the kids' department of Dayton's. You told me your dream was to buy adult clothes you didn't have to alter."

I doubt she was the five feet she claimed to be, but still, Slip was the one you called when you needed help moving something heavy, the star acrobat in the neighborhood circus, the one who daily used the chin-up bar lodged in her son's bedroom doorway. Slip had hard, defined muscles before it was fashionable; she ran back in the days when people thought you were either crazy or being chased, and became a vegetarian when the rest of us were sawing into porterhouse steaks and thought a pitcher of strawberry daiquiris satisfied our daily fruit requirement.

Audrey pushed back her reading glasses and shoved her knitting paraphernalia into the wicker bag at her side.

"I've always envied your body," she said, touching Slip with her manicured, ring-studded hand.

"Yeah, right," said Slip. "You who could fill out Marilyn Monroe's *and* Jayne Mansfield's clothes?"

"Jayne Mansfield," said Merit. "I haven't thought of her in years. Poor thing — I heard she had a really high IQ."

"Slip has such a boy's body," Audrey said, uninterested in debating Jayne Mansfield's Mensa eligibility. "So little and flat-chested and hipless. I've always thought it must be so freeing to have a body like that."

"I'd give anything for your breasts," Slip said. "Just for a day — one day on a nude beach."

"But you'd tip over," said Merit, and the idea of Audrey's mammoth breasts on Slip's tiny little body made us all laugh.

A male nurse with a wispy blond mustache and ponytail came in and began his business of checking vital signs and IV drips.

"You ladies sure like to laugh," he said. "I've

15

never heard so much laughter coming out of a hospital room."

"Really?" said Audrey. "You should have heard us when we visited this one in the slammer." She nodded in Kari's direction. It was an old joke of Audrey's to introduce Kari to strangers as an ex-con.

"Slammer." The nurse nodded. "That's funny. It's nice to hear sisters get along so well."

"We're not sisters," I said.

"Really?" said the nurse.

"Nope, just friends," said Merit.

"Really?" said the nurse again. "Because — wow — you sure look alike."

"I'll take that as a compliment," said Kari, smiling.

"I won't," said Audrey, who then looked imperiously, as only Audrey could, at the nurse. "It's just that you're young and male and blinded by a culture that says the only females worthy of attention are eighteen-year-old nubile pinups." She paused to take a breath. "So naturally, you think every woman over the age of fifty looks alike."

"No . . . I . . . my mother . . . it's . . . ," stammered the nurse, whose blush was the color of boiled shrimp. His brow furrowed and he looked at the chart like an actor staring at a script whose lines he doesn't know. "Uh, Dr. Sobota will be here in about a half hour if you have any questions." He hustled out of the room, holding his ponytail as if he feared we'd pull it.

"Holy diatribe," said Slip, trying not to smile. "The poor guy makes a little observation and he gets treated to one of your *rants*."

"Aw, I was just having some fun," said

16

Audrey, picking up her knitting again. She giggled. "I guess this *is* sort of a sisterly scene. Right out of *Little Women*."

"I'm Jo," I said, putting my dibs in first.

"*I* want to be Jo," said Kari.

"You're Meg," said Audrey. "And Merit's Beth."

"But Beth dies," said Merit. "I don't want to be Beth."

Audrey shook her head. "You're the sweet one. Beth was the sweet one. Therefore you're Beth. And Slip, you can be Marmee."

"If I'm Marmee," said Slip, "then that makes you Amy. Spoiled, blond, selfish . . ."

Audrey returned Slip's smile with one of her own. "So I'm not blond."

"I don't want to be Beth," said Merit softly.

We bickered a few minutes over who was most like what character — hardly the only time we'd argued about a book — and then Slip asked if anyone had a quarter.

"I think we should flip for Jo," she said, giving me her famous I'm-right-and-you're-wrong look.

"Let's call in the nurse," I said. "We can ask him who'd make a better Jo."

"As if he'd know," said Audrey. "He doesn't strike me as a man conversant with *Little Women*."

"Yeah," said Slip. "He looks like a man conversant with where to score the best dope."

Merit nodded. "He reminds me of those Deadhead friends of Melody's."

"Get you!" said Audrey.

"What?"

"Well, that you even know what a Deadhead is! You've come a long way, sister."

"Remember when we threatened to burn her Mitch Miller and Mantovani records?" I asked.

"Someone had to drag her into the swingin' sixties," said Slip.

"You guys dragged me into a lot more than that," said Merit, and we all sat for a moment, reflecting on how true the statement was for all of us.

"Hey," said Audrey finally, "while we're waiting for Dr. What's-His-Face to give us the latest verdict, refresh my memory: what's this month's book?"

"*To Kill a Mockingbird*," I said. "My choice for our greatest-hits year."

"I love rereading all our favorites," said Kari. "I can't wait to dive into Jane Austen again."

Slip looked at Audrey. "You're not planning to do *Everything You Always Wanted to Know About Sex* again, are you?"

"That," said Audrey with a smile, "is one subject I can honestly say I know enough about." She looked at the clock next to the TV mounted on the wall. "Say, wasn't Grant going to stop by?"

"He'd better," said Slip. "He said he was bringing chocolate." She yawned into her closed fist. "Hey, while we're waiting, how about a song? A nice cowboy song?"

It was Slip's little entertainment lately — she thought it cheered everyone up — to request group sing-alongs.

"Let's sing something a bunch of cowboys would sing around the campfire. And if any of you wants to throw in a yodel or two, feel free."

" 'Home on the Range'?" asked Merit, and after we shrugged our consent, she hummed a

18

note we all tried to match.

Even though Merit sang for a living now, her voice was always a little too trembly soprano for my tastes; I preferred Kari's clear and strong alto. Slip could carry a tune, but not very far, and Audrey was more a brayer than a singer. I was the Rex Harrison talk-your-way-through type of vocalist, but still, we all sang "Home on the Range" gamely, happily, even joyfully.

Grant tiptoed in and started singing with us, and I wished that there really was a place in the world where discouraging words were seldom heard and the skies were not cloudy all day.

"Faith, are you all right?" Grant asked.

Shaking my head, I brushed away a tear with my finger. "Are any of us?"

"No, but at least we're all here together," said Audrey. "And that's something."

Nodding, I whispered, "I guess," and even in my grief, I didn't have to guess: we *were* all together and that *was* something.

A few years back, when I finally got smart enough to go to a therapist, she asked me how I had held things together all these years.

It didn't take long to come up with an answer. "That's easy. I belong to a book club."

PART ONE

1968—1970

The Members

A Fuller Brush salesman had the unfortunate task of trying to sell his wares to the women of Freesia Court during the fifth day of a March cold snap.

"They were like caged animals," he complained later to his district manager. "I felt like any minute they were going to turn on me."

"Brushes?" Faith Owens had said when he offered up his bright smile and sales pitch on her icy front doorstep. "I'm sorry, but I've got a little more than brushes to worry about right now. Like wondering if spring is ever going to get here. Because I truly believed it might really be coming when *boom* — here it is, twenty below zero with a windchill factor that would bring Nanook of the North to his knees."

"Thank you for your time," said the salesman, picking up his case. "You have a pleasant day, now."

"And what exactly is a windchill factor anyway?"

"Faith," called her husband, Wade, from the living room. "Faith, don't be rude, honey."

"Well what is it?" she asked, slamming the door with her hip. "What exactly *is* a windchill factor?"

"This is Minnesota," said Wade, ignoring her question because he wasn't quite sure of the answer. "What do you expect?"

"Oh, I don't know — *maybe a little damn relief?*"

"Might I remind you," said Wade, "how you cried with delight seeing your first snowfall?"

"I cried with delight the first time I had sex with you, but that doesn't mean I want it nonstop."

"You're telling me," said Wade with a wistful sigh.

"Ha, ha, ha," said Faith, surveying her neat and trim husband as he brushed his crew cut with his palm, a gesture he always made after what he thought was a joke.

It was no surprise to Faith that her husband had less trouble adapting to the frozen north. Hell, he was flying out of it all the time. Right before Christmas, Wade had been transferred to Minneapolis from Dallas, although to Faith, it may as well have been Siberia.

That very morning he was leaving for a three-day trip with a layover in warm and sunny Los Angeles, and as she stomped upstairs to finish his packing, anger seethed through Faith like steam through their loud and clanking radiators — *Los Angeles!* In just a few hours Wade could feasibly be lying poolside as some flirtatious Nordic stewardess (why did every Minnesota stewardess she'd seen have to look like Miss Sweden?) rubbed suntan lotion on his shoulders, while she, Faith, rubbed ointment onto the chapped little bottom of their son, Beau.

She pitched a rolled-up ball of socks into Wade's suitcase with the velocity of a teenage show-off trying to knock down a pyramid of bottles at a carnival booth. There had been a time when she actually *enjoyed* packing for her husband — when she'd fold his shirts into neat rectangles, slipping a sheet of tissue paper between them so they wouldn't wrinkle; when she'd tuck a love note inside a pair of boxer shorts or dab her perfume on the neckline of an undershirt — but routine had long ago tarnished *that* thrill.

Now Faith had an urge to pack a different sort of surprise — perhaps a used diaper from the bathroom pail that reeked of ammonia, or maybe a sprinkling of itching powder.

She smiled then, remembering one of her more innocent teenage pranks. She and Melinda Carmody had ordered itching powder from the back pages of *True Confessions* magazine and, sneaking into the classroom during lunch hour, sprinkled it on their algebra teacher's cardigan sweater, draped over the back of his chair. When tyrannical Mr. Melscher (who rewarded wrong answers with a sarcastic "Think again, *Einstein*") put the sweater on, Faith and Melinda held their breaths in anticipation. Although the man's shirt seemed to have blocked much of the powder's itching powers, he did tug at his collar and squirm a bit, giving the girls far more entertainment than they had trying to figure out if x equaled y.

Closing the suitcase, Faith sighed, realizing how far removed she was from things like best friends and practical jokes and giggle fits.

How far away I am from everything fun, she thought — from rides in convertibles with boys who drove with one hand on the wheel and the other one on her; from parties where couples necked on the porches of fraternity houses; from gently turning down, on the same night, two boys who wanted her to wear their pins.

Who are you kidding? Faith thought, sitting heavily on the bed. *You're starting to believe your own press.* It astounded her sometimes, the ease with which she assimilated into her present life: how she could get huffy about a visit from a Fuller Brush man or about packing her husband's suitcase as if she were some *normal* housewife. As if she weren't Primrose Reynolds' daughter.

She shuddered. It was as if her memories had a geography all their own. In the most recent ones she was on safe and firm ground and was the Faith she wanted and tried hard to be; further back she was the neglected little girl who seemed to be ground zero for lice infestations, the wild teenager who could just as easily have gone to prison as to college. In these memories, she struggled through swamps and quicksand.

Faith's life had been one of constant upheaval, and if she had learned anything, it was not only how to adapt to it but how to go beyond it. But maybe it was to be the great irony of her life that while she survived years of chaos, a few months as a lonely housewife in the frostbitten north had the power to finally do her in.

"Stupid godforsaken frozen tundra," she muttered, refusing to trespass in the dangerous territory of her past. As she dragged Wade's suitcase off the bed, she looked out the window laced with frost to see the Fuller Brush man take a tumble on the slippery walkway of her neighbor's house.

Across the street from the Owens residence, in the big colonial that in Faith's estimation needed a little TLC, Audrey Forrest lay in rumpled sheets, staring at the ceiling. Her five-year-old was bullying her three-year-old, but it was her belief that children settled their differences faster when adults didn't intervene. Besides, she didn't want to get out of bed.

She stretched her arms to the ceiling, admiring the delicacy of her fingers and wrists. At the moment she was on a diet that called for entirely too many grapefruits and boiled eggs, and until she saw progress on a scale, she would admire those few things, such as her wrists and fingers, that were in no need of size reduction.

Thinking about her stupid diet, her good, lazy-cat mood faded — why was Paul so adamant that she lose twenty pounds anyway?

"It'll help you feel better about yourself," her husband had said the other day, handing her the diet paperback he'd bought on his lunch break downtown.

"I feel *fine* about myself," said Audrey, piling her thick dark hair on top of her head and posing like a pinup model. She liked her curvy body, ample seat, and full breasts. "And fine about my body." She leaned over, wrapping her arms around Paul's neck. "*You* usually feel fine about my body." She pressed herself to him, nibbling his earlobe, but what normally drove him crazy now seemed to alarm him, for he pushed her aside as if she were transmitting a germ he did not want to catch.

"Paul," she said, unable to believe he didn't want to ravish her right there on the kitchen floor, "what do you expect? I'm Italian." In truth, she was mostly Dutch and German, but she felt far more affinity toward the Italian

27

grandfather who spiced up her genetic mix.

"No," said her husband, looking at her with the glasses he thought made him look like a more experienced attorney than he was. "Gina Lollobrigida and Sophia Loren are Italian." He pulled the sports section out of the paper and snapped it open. "You're just fat."

"Paul," said Audrey, her voice wounded.

"Oh, baby, I was just making a little joke."

"Well, it wasn't funny."

"I know. I'm sorry. I *do* think you're beautiful, Aude. It's just that, geez" — he swatted the newspaper he was reading — "every one of these models in here looks like that damned Sticky."

Audrey had to laugh. "Twiggy, honey. Her name's Twiggy."

"Well, compared to her, Miss America — which *you* could be, babe — looks hefty."

He certainly hadn't been thinking of where her weight fell in the current fashion curve that morning, when he'd pulled her to him, pushing up the fabric of her nightgown until it was a lacy roll around her waist. Audrey had been in the middle of a dream about her grandfather's back-yard garden, the place of some of her happiest childhood memories, but she was always welcoming of Paul's advances and kissed him hungrily. After he climaxed, he jumped out of bed, his arms held up to the ceiling, and said, "Thank you, God, for letting me marry a sex maniac!"

"There are worse things to be a maniac about, wouldn't you say, big boy?"

Paul didn't turn around to acknowledge her little Mae West impersonation, but skipped off to the bathroom to shower.

"That's mine! Give it back!"

A crash accompanied her three-year-old's plea, and then there was a moment of silence before both her children began screaming. Wrapping her robe around her, Audrey got out of bed, ready to seize the day — or the scruff of her children's necks.

A Sunday-school teacher had once told Merit Iverson that God had held her face in his hands and sculpted it himself. It was true, she had the face of an angel, and had anyone been observing her that morning, it would appear also true that she had the smoking habit of a pool hall hustler. She lit her third cigarette of the hour, dragging on it as if it were oxygen and she were tubercular. If moving to Minneapolis from Iowa had been the first subversive act of her life, smoking was the second. Her father, a Lutheran minister (from whom she hid her habit), thought smoking — at least for women — a vice as well as a mark of low moral character. But waiting for her bus one day, Merit saw a billboard of a woman lighting up, a sophisticated, elegant woman who looked as if she had the world on a string, something Merit decidedly did not. She bought a pack of Kools that day.

Her husband, Eric, didn't mind if she smoked; he thought a woman smoking an occasional cigarette was glamorous. But she knew he'd mind how *much* she smoked. Even she was surprised how quickly a full pack deflated into an empty, crumpled one, but if cigarettes calmed her nerves, what was the harm?

"Are you sure it won't hurt the baby?" she had asked Eric, because if anything would make her give up her beloved habit, it was her beloved baby, growing inside her.

Her husband had given her one of his bemused, dismissive looks, which made her feel like a cute but pesky kindergartner, and said, "I'm a doctor, aren't I?" (Somehow he seemed to think Merit needed to be reminded of this fact — as if she hadn't typed millions of invoices in a drafty accounting office to help put him through med school.) "I'm a doctor and I smoke — would I do anything to endanger my health?"

"But the Surgeon General —"

"The Surgeon General's talking to *heavy* smokers. *Moderation,* Merit. Things done in moderation are fine."

A wreath of smoke hovered over Merit as she began to wipe down the counter. Barbra Streisand belted out "People" on the radio, and she added a little dance step as she attacked the smudge marks on the toaster. She listened to a radio station in whose demographics she did not fit (she knew far more songs by Perry Como than the Rolling Stones), and the waltz step she did in time to the music preceded the Twist or the Pony by centuries.

When she was finally convinced all crumbs and fingerprints had been banished (her husband liked his home as sterile as the hospital he worked in), she sat down at the kitchen table and leaned over to smell the roses Eric had brought home last night. Her pregnancy had been good for a number of bouquets and fruit baskets, one of the latter from the senior Dr. and Mrs. Iverson, who were wintering in Florida. They were thrilled by the news; they'd been pestering Eric and Merit ever since they were married to produce a grandchild. "And while you're at it," her father-in-law would add with a wink, "make sure it's a boy." Sons who became doctors was an Iverson tradition, started five generations earlier.

Merit stubbed out the inch that remained of her cigarette and rubbed her stomach.

"Please be a boy, little baby," she whispered. "It would make everything so much easier for everybody."

Freesia Court was a short dead-end street tucked on a parcel of land a stone's throw north of Minnehaha Creek. Nearly all the houses had been built in the 1920s and '30s, and it was such a pretty neighborhood that once in, hardly anyone left. Like many others in Minneapolis, Freesia Court was a cathedral street, so named because the leafy branches of trees on one side of the boulevard met those on the other side, giving those driving under them the sensation of being inside an airy green cathedral. It was only recently, when the original owners had grown too old for the upkeep of their spacious homes, that they had become available for sale. Now more than half of the retirees had moved out, and the sidewalks were littered with tricycles and wagons and chalk drawings belonging to the children of the young couples who'd replaced them. Today, however, the only evidence of children in this frigid winterscape were abandoned sleds and scrawny, weather-beaten snowmen who, with their missing stone eyes and broken and sagging twig arms, looked like Civil War veterans returned home after battle.

Faith's stucco Tudor (she still could hardly believe she lived in such a nice house) was at the end of the cul-de-sac, and the south side of her yard gradually eased into a hill that ran down to the creek basin. She had splendid views from her kitchen window, hundreds of trees and the creek itself, but it was not this view that was making Faith teary-eyed; it was that of her husband, Wade, backing out of the driveway. Seeing her standing at the window, he gave a jaunty salute, which she returned with a limp little wave.

At least the twins were sleeping, thank God. In January, just after their first birthday, they had taught themselves to walk, giving themselves a gift Faith often wanted to take back to the returns department. If they weren't contained in a playpen or crib or high chairs, Faith was chasing them through the house, plucking them off stair landings and couch backs and other dangerous perches that were so attractive to them.

Faith had been an athletic girl — you can't be a college football cheerleader and not be athletic — but all the jumps and splits in the world couldn't have prepared her for the all-day marathons her twins put her through.

She raced to the living room, where she could watch Wade turn out of the driveway. She blew against the windowpane, and as a foggy circle of condensation expanded, she waved again to her husband, by now halfway up the street. She felt a sadness tinged with panic (she was used to Wade leaving on trips, but unused to being left in a place that still felt alien to her) settle on her like the cold and unwelcome hands of a stranger.

She took several deep breaths until it no longer felt her lungs were seizing up on her, then said, "Bye, Wade," as she sat down on the window seat. Distracted from her misery by what was going on outside, she leaned toward the pane for a better view.

Faith sniffed. She knew she was capable of working herself into a really good cry, but a really good cry would interfere with the surveillance of her neighbor — the same neighbor who had shown up at Faith's door with an older woman, presenting her with a sheet cake and a welcome to Freesia Court. The flu had prevented Faith from inviting them in, and the second time they showed up — this time on Valentine's Day, with a tray of heart-shaped cookies — Faith only had time to apologize: "They look wonderful, but we're on our way to the airport!" (Wade had surprised her with a trip back to Dallas, a Valentine's present that rivaled the engagement ring she got in '65.)

Now, as Faith watched her neighbor break the big icicles that hung from her front eaves, she tried to remember the woman's name.

"Slim?" Faith said out loud. "Slinky?" The older woman's name was Kari (when she introduced herself, she'd said, "It's Kari as in 'car,' not as in 'care'"), but for the life of her, she couldn't recall the funny name of the one her age. She knew it started with *S* — Snoopy, Sailor, Swifty, Skippy? Spot, Sport, Slut?

No, she thought, sinking into the quagmire of memory, slut *was what they called* me.

Slip was the name Faith was trying to think of, and it belonged to a woman whose father, seeing her for the first time, exclaimed, "Why, she's just a slip of a thing!"

His early assessment had proven true: Marjorie McMahon as a full-grown adult barely

33

passed the five-foot mark, and only if she was standing very straight. But what she lacked in size, she made up for in strength; it was one of her adult cousins' shame that at last year's family reunion in Jersey City, she'd beaten him in an arm-wrestling competition (her own brothers were not so foolish as to challenge her any longer, having learned through the years they could just as easily lose as win). No girl had ever done more pull-ups or thrown a ball farther on Athletic Skills Competition Day, and at any social gathering, a request was always made for Slip to do her backflips. She used to be able to do four in a row, but at the same family reunion where she had brought down the arm and ego of her blustery cousin, she had only managed three.

"It must have been all the dessert I ate," she said to her husband later. "I had two of Velma's seven-layer bars and a piece of Orpha's gooseberry pie."

"Any of Beata's fudge?" asked Jerry, who loved attending any gathering of his wife's family because of the company *and* the food.

Slip nodded. "But Ollie's doughnuts were gone by the time I got to them."

"They were good," said Jerry, remembering.

He was as big as Slip was little, as tawny as she was freckled, as mild as she was fierce, but a more perfect match neither of them could imagine.

Jerry McMahon was a research scientist in the meteorology department of the University of Minnesota, a man who found delight in dew points and barometric pressure as well as the really exciting weather that his native Minnesota brewed up — blizzards and severe thunderstorms and tornadoes.

He and Slip had met at the U — she was a scholarship student from New Jersey, and he was smitten as soon as he heard this tiny redheaded girl reproach a teaching assistant in an accent that sounded automatically pushy, "Sorry, bub, but you don't know what you're *tawking* about."

"I know what I'm talking about," Jerry said, approaching her after class. "I know I'd like to take you out for coffee."

"I'm on my way to a lecture," said Slip, "by a nuclear power proponent. Wanna come? We need more protesters."

Always a big believer in social change, Slip was already out of school and a mother by the time the Vietnam War made college protest practically a credit, but she returned to campus regularly to march in picket lines, to sit in sit-ins, to pass out flyers. She also volunteered two nights a week at the McCarthy for President headquarters, leaving Jerry in charge of the kids, a job he loved.

"But don't they drive you *nuts?*" Paul Forrest asked at the neighborhood Christmas party. "I mean, I love my kids, but that doesn't mean I want to *baby-sit* them."

Jerry was about to launch into the joys of child care — just the night before, Flannery, his precocious four-year-old daughter, had read *him* a bedtime story — but then Eric Iverson, who had ignored the rum punch in the crystal bowl in favor of the stronger offerings from the bar, stumbled toward them, demanding to know just what the hell the two men thought of these goddamned draft dodgers. Slip, who was helping the party's hostess fill the peanut bowls, piped up, "I

35

think they're people with a conscience — at least the ones I met at the march on the university were."

"You were at that march?" croaked the young doctor, doing a very good Joseph McCarthy impersonation.

"We both were," said Jerry, putting his arm around his wife. "And we'll be at the next one."

Eric Iverson stood hunched over, slack-jawed, staring at the couple as if they'd just stepped out of the pneumatic door of a flying saucer.

"Commies," he said finally, shaking his head. "We've got commies in the neighborhood!"

This announcement he made while turning in a semicircle, a movement that apparently affected his equilibrium, because he fell down in a heap.

Merit had rushed over to him, mumbling a continuous refrain of "I'm sorry," oblivious to Slip's cheerful reassurance that it was all right, she'd rather be called a commie than a hawk. Then, making more apologies, Merit half dragged and half pushed her cursing husband out the door.

Under the arch that separated the living room from the small foyer, the commie-hater suddenly stopped and, braying the word "Mistletoe!" grabbed Merit, kissing her as if a kiss were food and he were starving.

There had been a hush after the Iversons' departure, and then the hostess put a Tony Bennett album on the hi-fi (Slip had brought the Beach Boys album *Pet Sounds*, telling Kari to put it on when she wanted the party to "really rock") and, holding out her arms, asked Jerry McMahon if he'd care to dance.

That hostess, Kari Nelson, was the same woman who had accompanied Slip twice to Faith's doorstep when they'd welcomed the newcomer to the neighborhood, the same woman Faith now watched walking up the shoveled sidewalk to where Slip stood decimating icicles.

Faith watched the two women talk for a moment, vaporous plumes tumbling out of their mouths. Something funny must have been said, because both women tipped their heads back, laughing.

Faith felt a pang as real as a pinch, jealous of the women's merriment. How long had it been since she'd shared a laugh like that with a friend? She watched as both women began pushing what looked more to Faith like a stalactite than an icicle. It was monstrously big, and when they had dislodged it from its perch, they jumped out of the way like two lumberjacks trying to dodge a falling spruce. They laughed again, and Faith had a deep urge to grab her coat and run out and join them. But then Beau began to cry (even when they were newborns, she'd been able to differentiate the twins' cries), and the urge crumbled under the call to duty.

Kari Nelson, meanwhile, took a rain check on Slip's invitation to come in for a cup of coffee.

"But just a short rain check," she assured her friend. "Say around one o'clock? I told myself I couldn't have any fun until I finished my niece's coat."

Kari's sewing talents were much admired and much employed — if she wasn't sewing a pair of bell-bottoms for one niece, she was making slipcovers for another. She had four nieces, and even though two had moved out of state, it still didn't stop their requests (her three nephews had no desire to wear hand-sewn shirts or pants; they were more inclined to solicit care packages of chocolate chip or almond crescent cookies). Kari really didn't mind; her nieces were always so grateful and sent thank-you notes, occasionally accompanied by chocolates or, when they were really flush, her favorite gift: books.

Up in her small, sunny (when the sun wasn't in winter hibernation) sewing room, Kari pinned a sleeve to a cuff made out of fake acrylic fur, which was all the rage but certainly not a fabric she would choose to work with. Kari was a snob when it came to her material — she loved fine worsted wools and soft silks and Egyptian cottons. Even though she had just celebrated her fortieth birthday, she felt the generation gap everyone was talking about was more a crack than a chasm, and one she felt she easily skipped across, although for the life of her she couldn't understand or appreciate the fashions of the day.

A paisley jacket with green Day-Glo fake fur cuffs? This particular abomination was for Mary Jo, her niece who last fall had left for Berkeley a demure college coed wearing pleats and Peter Pan collars and come back at Christmas break a full-fledged hippie. Kari didn't think they were going to have any luck fabric shopping (Mary Jo opined that the tartan wool was "too Tricia Nixon" and the wheat-colored linen was "something a sorority sister would wear"), but when Mary Jo spotted the fake fur and the wild paisley, it earned a rapturous "Far out."

Not that Kari, like much of her generation, dismissed the whole peace/hippie movement out of hand; no, she had been shaped as a liberal thinker by her Norwegian immigrant parents, North Dakota farmers, who had been instrumental in organizing the Democratic Farmer/ Labor Party.

She agreed with the hippies' antiwar stance but not with their drugs — hated hearing those awful stories about LSD takers jumping out of windows and bright and responsible students all of a sudden dropping out of college to go smoke dope in "crash pads."

"*You're* not smoking marijuana, are you?" she asked Mary Jo as they had pie and coffee after their fabric search.

The long dangly earrings her niece wore jingled as she laughed.

"Well, of course I am," said Mary Jo, who was honest with her aunt in a way she wasn't with her own mother. "Not *heavily* — but yeah, I like a good toke now and then."

Unconsciously, Kari shook her head in small, rapid movements. She was often torn when her nieces confided in her — should she tell their parents or, like an attorney, consider their confessions privileged information? It was times like these when she yearned for the wise counsel of her dear husband, Bjorn, dead now for five unbelievably long years. It wasn't just she who considered his counsel wise; he had been, after all, a district judge, and a more reasoned man she had never met. The only problem that Bjorn Nelson could never solve was why he and Kari could not have children.

Both sets of plumbing, as one doctor had put it, were in fine working order, but after years of trying (trying had been fun and exciting the first couple of years, but when they realized conception might be more of a problem than they thought, their trying took on a sense of game team spirit, then melancholy, and finally desperation) they came to the sad and puzzled conclusion that they were not going to bear children. Then God threw them a reminder that we never know what we think we know, and there was a pregnancy. But it survived only the first two months, and as blood poured out of Kari, she thought all chances of a life with meaning were pouring out too. She was certain of this when, six months later, she suffered another miscarriage.

She truly thought she was living a hell on earth, but in retrospect, she'd take hell any day over what followed.

Passing the adoptive-parents tests a year later, she and Bjorn were given a beautiful week-old baby girl and had her for two blissful days (Kari had known motherhood would be wonderful, but this bliss was hard to imagine) before the hand-wringing woman from the adoption service showed up at the Nelsons' front door, accompanied by a lawyer, telling them she was awfully sorry, nothing like this had ever happened before, but they had evidence the mother had been coerced into signing the release papers, making them invalid. They had come to take the baby back.

A noise began in Kari's head, a great roaring, as if she were holding giant conch shells up to her ears, and she entered a zone that was devoid of all feeling; she was sucked into a gray fuzzy hole of nothingness.

Of course they hired a lawyer, but there were

two nurses who had overheard the birth mother's boyfriend threaten her life if she didn't give up the baby, and even Kari knew that the rightful place for Bettina (named after Kari's mother) was with her seventeen-year-old mother, who had never wanted to give her up.

In anguish, Kari pleaded with God to let her know what she had done so terribly wrong to have such terribly wrong things happen to her.

"Maybe he knows something about me that even I don't know," she cried. "Maybe he's taking these babies away from me because he knows I'd be a bad mother."

"Then He would be a God I couldn't believe in," said Bjorn, "because He wouldn't know anything."

Bjorn was the reason Kari was able to keep her faith; who but God could have given her a blessing of such magnitude?

But then, just as Kari was thinking she was strong enough to go through the adoption process again, Bjorn died in his sleep at the age of forty-five. She lost her life then too — except people made the mistake of thinking she was still alive. They kept coming over with food, kept coming over to sit with her, to hold her hand, to take her on walks during which she wondered why they didn't hear the wind whistling right through her. Grief strangled her heart as surely as a blocked artery strangled Bjorn's, but grief didn't have the grace to finish off the job.

Her family truly became her life support. Her sister Wanda from Grand Forks came down and stayed with her for the first two months, followed by her sister Anna from Bismarck. Her brother, Anders, and his wife, Sally, who lived in

Minneapolis with their three children, were over constantly. They helped her keep alive what was still alive and coax back to life what was dead. This was achieved because of their vigilant care and kindness, and in no small part because of their children, whom they brought with them.

Kari had always been a favorite of her nieces and nephews, and they crawled on her lap, placing their little hands on her face and asking her things the adults were too adult to ask.

"Do you hate God for taking Uncle Bjorn away?"

"Did Uncle Bjorn die because he did something wrong?"

"I heard people turn blue when they die. How blue was Uncle Bjorn?"

"Do you think if maybe we both wished really really really *really* hard that Uncle Bjorn would come back, he would?"

These questions were a tonic for Kari because, in effect, she was answering questions she herself asked. And because she was a teacher by nature as well as by profession, she demanded that her answers be carefully thought out. Trying to explain to a child things that were unexplainable was like being thrown a life preserver — a leaky one, but one that would keep her afloat for at least a moment.

About a year and a half after Bjorn's death, she still lived in grief's house, but the walls weren't so pressing and the ceiling wasn't so low and she felt strong enough to resume some of her old aunt duties, hosting her nieces and nephews for long weekends and rainy afternoons occasionally when the parents took adults-only vacations.

Her sister Wanda and her husband, Butch, took a Caribbean cruise, leaving their two battling boys and fussy daughter with Kari, and came back to find their sons the best of friends and their daughter happily eating meat loaf *and* broccoli.

"You're a miracle worker," Wanda had told Kari, who turned the compliment around, saying, "Well, then they're the miracles I got to work with."

More than half her nieces and nephews were no longer children — in fact, Randy was getting married in the fall and Cynthia was expecting her first baby (Kari had already crocheted a yellow blanket and would have started sewing baby clothes if she'd only known the sex) — but Kari enjoyed them just as much as when they were little and felt a sense of pride in their accomplishments, a pride that was deserved, as her steadfast love and good humor had influenced them all.

But marijuana! she thought now, trying to ease the pesky sleeve to fit the cuff. Would that lead to stronger stuff like LSD or, heaven forbid, morphine? Or was it heroin? She's ask Slip, she decided, trimming the seam. Slip was much younger and knew about these sorts of things.

Slip would have been happy to offer what minimal knowledge she had on the subject of drugs (she and Jerry had tried marijuana at a Pete Seeger concert, accepting the passed joint like old hands, but Slip's inexperience was evident after her first inhale, when she coughed so hard she thought her brain might hemorrhage). It certainly would have been a far lighter conversation than the long-distance one she was having now with her younger brother.

"Fred, you can't enlist — that's insane! You can get a college deferment! Remember how happy you were to get into Penn State? Come on, Fred, finish college, and if the war's still going on, then you can think of enlisting."

She heard her younger brother's easy laughter and then a thunk.

"Sorry, Slip, I'm making a sandwich and I dropped the phone. What were you saying?"

"You know what I was saying," said Slip. She tugged at the towel she had wrapped herself in when the phone rang, interrupting her shower. "You cannot be so stupid as to want to enlist in the army."

"Who said anything about the army? I'm thinking about the marines."

"Oh, *Fred,*" breathed Slip with relief. "I don't find that funny at all."

"You shouldn't. It's not a joke."

In the thick, staticky silence that followed, Slip realized it wasn't.

"Fred, please. It's a stupid war. It's not worth it."

"It's worth it to Miles Coons and Todd Hagstrom, my two best friends in the world."

"But Fred, you said Todd and Miles were drafted! They wouldn't have gone unless they were forced!"

"So I shouldn't go just because I don't have to?"

"Exactly!"

Fred sighed. "Slip, not everyone's a big liberal peacemonger like you."

"Peacemonger? Fred, are you on something?

44

Tell me you're having a bad trip or something, *please.*"

"I feel the need to serve my country," said Fred crisply.

"Well, serve it! Join the Peace Corps or VISTA or —"

"Talk to you later, Slip."

Hearing a click and dial tone, Slip hung up, trembling. He *couldn't* be serious. She looked up and startled, saw her reflection in the dresser mirror. Inside, Slip McMahon was a big, bold woman, an Amazon who rumbled through life like a Sherman tank. So who was this freckled little thing with carrot-colored hair and a twelve-year-old's body, shivering under the terry-cloth sarong of a damp towel? As she often did, when seeing her mirrored self, she stuck out her tongue.

The temperature had lifted slightly that afternoon, but then it began to do what everyone, by late March, was thoroughly sick of: it began to snow. And snow and snow and snow.

Faith, making the twins' supper, was in the mood to mash more than her children's potatoes and carrots. Watching the swirling snow through the kitchen window, she thought how nothing would give her more pleasure than pulverizing her husband's face. What was he thinking, taking her to this twilight zone where winters never ended? She banged the spoon against the saucepan, startling Beau, who yelped, and delighting Bonnie, who banged her own spoon against the metal tray of her high chair, shouting, "Yang, yang, yang!"

It didn't take Beau long to get over his fright,

and soon he was joining his sister in creating an earsplitting, erratic percussion that put the *h* in headache, as far as Faith was concerned. She tried to distract them, humor them, and, stupidly, to reason with them, but they were as wild and frenzied as tribal drummers announcing war.

Finally, she had no recourse but to take their spoons away — which solved one problem but created another when she served their food. How were they to eat mashed potatoes and carrots with no spoons? Reluctantly she went to the sink to retrieve them, but before she'd rinsed them off she felt a warm splat on one of her stockinged feet, heard a delighted giggle, and suddenly was dodging an arsenal of vaguely orange, mushy cannonballs, launched by her fiendish twins.

She stood at the sink, her heart racing, her hands clamped around the sink edge, thinking how she could so easily march over to those bratty little monsters and slap them from here to Sunday.

Instead, like a drill sergeant advising slow-learning privates, she ordered, *"You will stop that now!"* and the raised decibel level of her voice so startled the twins that they clutched their sticky little hands and began to cry.

Time then took on a slow-motion quality, and after Faith got them bathed and into bed, it seemed she had aged several years.

Sighing with weariness, she poured herself a highball and selected a book from the stack she'd gotten at the library. Settling on the couch, under the cashmere throw Wade had given her the day the temperature had plunged to minus forty-two degrees, she felt the familiar mixture of calm and anticipation.

It didn't matter that a storm raged outside, that her husband wouldn't be back until Friday, and that she came awfully close to inflicting bodily harm on her twins at the peak of their vegetable bombardment. What mattered was that for a few hours she could forget her world and enter someone else's.

Books were Faith's easiest friends. They demanded nothing from her but her attention.

She opened the cover and ran her hand over the page, enjoying the paper's smooth, cool texture under her hand.

Chapter One. How many times in her life had those two words invited her to go to a different place, a better place than the one she lived in?

She read the words again before plunging into the first paragraph, and then the lights went out.

Faith's heart clenched. Was there a prowler in the basement messing with the fuse box? Should she run upstairs and get her babies or call the police?

Oh, Wade, she thought, *do I have time to get your pistol?*

Her heart beating in triple time, she eased herself off the couch, but if stealth was her objective, the edge of the coffee table foiled her.

"Ouch!" she hissed as pain shot down her shin. She clamped her hand over her mouth, not wanting to give the intruder/murderer/rapist any more clues as to her whereabouts.

She slunk across the living room toward the staircase but stopped at the large picture window, parting the curtain ever so slightly to take note of whatever getaway car might be waiting.

Through the falling snow, she could see that there was no dark sedan occupied by a lookout man, but what thrilled Faith even more was the absence of lights throughout the entire neighborhood. It wasn't yet eight o'clock, and she knew that everyone couldn't have mutually agreed to go to bed so early.

"The power's out!" she whispered, and relief surged through her so strongly that for a moment she thought she had wet her pants. She pulled the drapes open and then sat back primly on the couch, as if she were waiting for instructions to begin a test. The grandfather clock that the previous homeowners had left behind (it kept erratic time at best) ticked its sibilant ticks. Faith wondered if she should run upstairs and check on the babies — but then the power outage wouldn't have affected them, seeing as they'd been sleeping in the dark anyway.

Faith shut her eyes and dozed for a few minutes — it had been a long day and she was tired — but she was startled awake by questions. What would she do if the power stayed out all night? Would she and the twins freeze? What about all the food in the refrigerator — would it spoil? Would the hot water heater go out? She got up, determined to find a flashlight and investigate whatever there was to investigate.

Through the picture window, she saw movement in the dark snowy night. Pressing her nose to the glass, Faith saw that more than the power was out — so were several neighborhood kids. She could barely see them, let alone identify them, but, squinting into the blurred darkness, she was able to make out three forms the size of teenagers, although the little one was probably

the industrious Hammond girl, who had presented Faith with a card that read, *Baby-sitter for
Hire — Cheap Rates, Good Service.* Faith had accepted the card but never took the girl up on her
offer — no eleven-year-old, no matter how en-
trepreneurial, was going to watch her precious
babies.

Another, taller one joined them, and the ad-
vent of a fourth person seemed to inspire the
group to break into teams and begin pitching
snowballs at each other. One of these snowballs
— hurled by the Hammond girl, Faith was sure
— smashed into the very window she was
looking out of.

She gasped. Normally she might let a little
teenage vandalism slide, but because she was at
the end of her rope — trapped without power in
the middle of Antarctica with no husband and
babies who might be double the pleasure but
could also be double the trouble — she decided
to give those insolent Yankee teenagers a lecture
on manners, or at least proper aim.

Groping her way to the closet, she grabbed her
winter coat and rushed out the front door.
Pulling on her gloves, she marched down the
front sidewalk (which had been shoveled but
now sported over three inches of new snow) and
to the circular turn-around at the end of the cul-
de-sac where the young vandals cavorted. Only
they weren't young vandals. They were her
neighbors, the two women she'd watched earlier
that day and two others Faith saw at various
times leaving or entering their homes.

"Oh, good, you've come out to play!" said the
statuesque dark-haired woman from the un-
kempt colonial.

"Not really, I —"

"Sorry about your window," said the slight woman Faith had mistaken for the eleven-year-old baby-sitter. "I was aiming for Kari, but she ducked."

"I'm surprised you didn't break it," said the older woman, turning to Faith. "She's got an arm like Sandy Koufax."

"You probably think we're a bunch of nuts, having a snowball fight in the dark." The tall brunette scooped up some snow and began packing it into a ball. "But it sure beats being trapped inside with two boys who wouldn't know the meaning of brotherly love if you hit them over the head with it."

"I was vacuuming," said the fourth woman, whose face was so lovely Faith nearly gasped when she saw it. "I thought I'd blown a fuse or something — but I wasn't about to go down to the basement myself and check!" She blinked, dislodging a snowflake from her long eyelashes. "It's not that I'm afraid of the dark," she said, smiling shyly at Faith. "I'd just rather not be in it alone." She flashed a shiny white smile. "By the way, I'm Merit. I know you've already met Kari and Slip —"

Ah. Slip, thought Faith. *Riddle solved.*

"And I'm Audrey," said the tall woman, offering a mittened hand to shake, "as in Meadows."

"Or Hepburn," offered Faith.

"If you insist," said Audrey, batting her eyelashes.

"I'm ashamed we haven't made more of an effort to get to know you, but it's been so cold this winter." Kari nodded at the golden retriever leaping through the snow. "That's Flicka. She said if I didn't start walking her again, she was going to report me to the SPCA."

"People go a little crazy when they're snow-bound," stage-whispered Slip as she spun a gloved finger near her temple. "Not only do they talk to their animals, they start thinking the animals talk back."

"At least I don't threaten poor salesmen who are only trying to make a living," said Kari.

"I had just put on Joe's snowsuit when I realized he had a dirty diaper," Slip explained, laughing. "It was hardly the time to be called on by the Fuller Brush man." She looped her arm through Faith's. "So, what do you say? Join us in a little winter warfare?"

"Well," said Faith, not exactly sure what winter warfare was, "I left my babies sleeping. . . ."

"Then they're fine!" said Audrey, taking her other arm, and for the first time in her life, Faith joined in a snowball fight.

Laughing and shrieking, they half slid, half tumbled down the moonlit hill to the creek basin to continue their battle, Flicka looking more like a big rabbit than a dog as she bounded after them. Surrounded by a white swirl, Faith was exhilarated. The snow, whose appearance had earlier depressed her so, now looked enchanted, filling the night sky with movement, frosting the tree branches that stretched over the creek, settling on pine boughs and whitewashing the layer of old snow that covered the ground.

It didn't take her long to learn the maneuvers — scoop, pack, and throw — and she laughed maniacally when her snowball hit someone or a snowball hit her.

"Faith!" shouted Audrey, who'd paired off as her partner. "Incoming! Incoming!"

Faith ducked behind a giant oak tree, but not before a snowball exploded on her shoulder.

As she bent to mold her own munitions, another snowball hit her on the back. She packed a handful of snow and threw blindly, repeated the process, then repeated it again. It was the first time Faith had ever played in the snow (once in Oklahoma Faith had been in an ice storm, but what little snow she had seen never amounted to anything), and to do so at night was an experience that delighted her senses, that made her feel like a kid because she was doing something so strange and new. Snow clotted under her collar and the cuffs of her sleeves, and each breath she took seared her lungs with cold, but when a torrent of snowballs pummeled her, she laughed as if she were being mercilessly tickled.

She wiped her dripping nose with the side of her mittened hand and threw a snowball at the older woman.

"Uncle!" said Kari, holding up her arms. "I surrender!"

"Good," said Audrey. "I'm freezing my patootie off."

"Oh, please," gasped Faith, "let's stay out a little longer."

Slip laughed. "We might have a convert here, ladies."

When no one else expressed a desire to remain outside, Faith said, "Can we at least move the party inside? I'll volunteer my house," and before she had a chance to rethink her invitation, everyone had agreed that it sounded like a great idea.

As the women made their way up the hill and to the sidewalk, patting the snow off one another's backs, they were as enthusiastic as Shriners assembled for a national convention.

"I'll just bring Flicka home," said Kari as the others turned up Faith's sidewalk.

"Oh, bring her in," said Faith, who was in a more-the-merrier mood.

"Hey, are you all right?" asked Slip. "You're limping."

Faith was glad the dark hid her blush. "Old cheerleading injury. It flares up sometimes."

"You sure you don't mind Flicka?" asked Kari. "She's all wet."

"She'll dry," said Faith, opening the door.

In the entryway, they stomped snow off their boots, unwound mufflers from their necks, and crammed snow-caked gloves and mittens into their coat pockets. Faith held her forefinger to her lips and cocked her head to the staircase. Hearing no sounds of distress from her babies, whispered, "This way."

Holding the flashlight she got off the closet shelf, Faith led the group into the living room. When Merit tripped and bumped into Slip, who grabbed Audrey, a spontaneous conga line formed, each woman giggling as she held the hips of the one in front of her. Someone started up a chant, and they all joined in, the volume of their voices low in deference to the sleeping babies.

"Dada-dada-da-*dah!*"

"If I knew someone was going to be fondling my behind, I would have put on my girdle," said Audrey.

"I'm not fondling your behind," said Slip. "I'm just trying to hold on."

Faith got matches out of the cigarette box on the mantle and lit the many candles that were placed around the living room.

"I haven't seen this many candles since my last birthday cake," said Kari.

"Did you *know* the power was going to go out?" asked Audrey as a soft, shadowy light dappled the room.

"No, I just like candles," said Faith. "Only with kids I hardly ever think to light them."

"I love your accent," said Merit shyly.

"She told me the same thing," said Slip. "And I told her people spend years trying to get Joisey *out* of their speech."

"It doesn't matter what kind of accent it is," said Merit. "I like them all. I like thinking about how big the world is." She smiled at Faith. "But yours isn't really a southern drawl, it's more like a southern twang."

"Whatever the difference between a drawl and a twang is," said Audrey. "So where are you from?"

"Texas," said Faith, who didn't add *by way of Arkansas, Oklahoma, and mostly Mississippi.* "Now, what would everyone like to drink? Is hot chocolate the preferred drink after a snowball fight, or should I plug in the coffeepot?"

Four faces looked at her expectantly, and then Audrey asked, "You wouldn't happen to have anything stronger, would you?"

Faith laughed. " 'Course we do. I just wanted to be proper. I didn't know if y'all liked a little *pizzazz* in your drinks."

Martinis were the unanimous choice, except

for Kari, who asked for a highball — a whiskey Seven, maybe?

"That's my drink," said Faith.

In her haste, or excitement, Faith dropped the first glass she took out of the portable bar parked near the staircase. Fortunately, the carpeting was thick and it landed softly.

"Thank the Lord," whispered Faith. Now that she had such good fortune, she tried to protect it with superstitions, and she was superstitious about her wedding presents. Her sister-in-law Carleen had broken the creamer from her china set the day she got back from her honeymoon, and sure enough, a year later she and her husband were divorced.

"Hey, mind if we build a fire?" Slip asked.

"Be my guest," said Faith. She poured vermouth and gin into the metal shaker and gave it a good shimmy. "So, how long do you think the power'll be out?"

"It could stay out all night as far as I'm concerned," said Audrey, who watched Slip stacking a little triangle of logs. "My boys had this little wrestling match going — it started at seven o'clock this morning — so I told Paul that if I didn't get out of the house, they'd *all* be sorry."

"Eric won't be home till after midnight," said Merit softly. "He has to work such crazy hours."

"What's he do?" asked Faith, serving the drinks.

Merit flushed as she patted her ash-blond hair, tucked into a French roll. "He's a doctor. He's almost finished with his residency — he's going to be a surgeon."

Thinking how she still sounded like a newlywed, Faith smiled at the pride in Merit's voice.

At the same time she felt a zip of envy — was Merit more in love with her husband than Faith was with hers?

"Here you go," she said, handing Kari her drink and joining the others seated on the couch and overstuffed chairs that made up the living room's conversation pit (although truth be told, this was the first conversation that had taken place in it, excluding those Faith had with Wade or tried to have with the twins).

Wade had encouraged Faith to join the Pilots' Wives Association ("You need to make some friends, hon"), but between unpacking and decorating, between the twins' chicken pox and their trip back home and a fear of driving in the winter weather, Faith had had no time for socializing. Other than the paper boy or the diaper service man, these were the first people who'd been in Faith's house, and she was buzzing with the pleasure of hosting actual *company*. There was a high color to her face, and the happy, expectant expression she wore made her look like the college coed she had been not so long ago. Her glossy black hair (it was dark to begin with, but Lady Clairol gave it a dramatic boost) was teased and worn in a flip (after the snowball fight, a *limp* flip). She had just done her nails last night, and the house was clean (the twins threw everything — toys, blankies, and bottles, as well as the occasional supper — but Faith had learned to pick up throughout the day rather than wait until the mess had accumulated into a pile too daunting to deal with), so there were no worries about how she or her housekeeping was being judged by these women. She could relax (as much as Faith *could* relax) and enjoy herself.

Audrey, satisfied that the fire was going, got up and draped herself over the chair like an afghan, crossing her long legs, which were encased in black stirrup stretch pants. "So, when are you due, Merit?"

Faith turned to the woman who could have stripped her old college roommate of her dozens of beauty pageant titles, including Miss Yellow Rose, Miss Star of Texas, and Miss Conventional Drill Bit.

"July," was Merit's answer. "July fourth."

Faith was surprised; at over five months, the woman barely showed.

"Oh," said Kari, "a Fourth of July baby."

Merit shivered. "I hope not. If there's one thing I'm more afraid of than labor, it's fireworks."

"Is this your first?" asked Faith, and because she couldn't help herself, she added, "You are so pretty — has anyone ever told you you look like a doll?"

Merit did have the curvy rounded forehead and cheeks of a doll, the poreless skin, heavily lashed eyes (a deep brown, which made a startling contrast to her blond hair), and rosebud mouth, and Merit had in fact been told that more times than she could remember, but she smiled anyway, as if pleased to be compared to something inert.

"Yes," she said, answering Faith's first question. "We've been trying for over two years — ever since we got married."

"That's the fun of trying to get pregnant," said Audrey as she fumbled in her sweater pocket. "You don't have to make excuses for your raging libido — you can just say, 'But honey, we're trying to have a baby, aren't we? Come on now, unzip your pants.' "

Taking a cigarette out of its pack, Audrey looked at the women who had suddenly grown quiet. "You mind if I smoke?"

Faith shook her head as she, Slip, and Merit helped themselves to the pack of Tareytons Audrey extended.

"Jeez, I start talking about libidos and everybody clams up. Why's everybody so uptight about something as *sin*sational as sex?" Audrey squinted as the flame from her lighter met the end of her cigarette. "I mean, it's how we all got here."

"I don't know about you," said Slip, looking like a juvenile delinquent as she lit her cigarette, "but I walked."

"What does *uptight* mean, anyway?" asked Merit. "I just heard it yesterday in the supermarket — the bag boy was telling the cashier she was too uptight for her own good."

"It means to be self-conscious or overly worried about something," said Kari. "I get all the current slang — all the *groovy* stuff — from my nieces and nephews."

"I think we need some snacks," said Faith, and as no one protested, she took a candle off the coffee table to illuminate her trip to the kitchen.

After dousing her cigarette under the tap and tossing it in the garbage disposal (having kicked her teenage habit, she was now only a social smoker, and since she hadn't been very social, this was her first cigarette in a long time and she was light-headed from it), she arranged crackers and slices of cheddar on a tray, narrowly

58

avoiding a thumb amputation as she cut the block of cheese in the dark room. She reapplied her lipstick from a tube she kept on the window-sill above the sink (Faith had lipstick tubes placed as strategically as land mines throughout the house; without lipstick she felt undressed) and then, carrying the tray and the candlestick, she made her way back to the shadowy living room.

Faith had the sharp eyes of someone who always had to figure out where she fit in, and the quick impressions she had of people were nearly always accurate. Strong-featured Audrey was sprawled across the chintz chair in a way that told Faith she came from money (the rich girls at school were the ones most careless with the furniture, spilling Cokes on the common-room couches and putting their feet up on the coffee tables). Of course, the gold jewelry and huge diamond ring that had taken up squatter's rights on her finger were also a clue.

Merit sat primly (the little bow at the collar of her shirt would definitely have to go) on the edge of the couch, her lovely face hopeful, as if she was expecting something good to happen. When a person looked like that, why not expect something good?

Unlike Merit, whom Faith could tell had been pampered and protected from the hardships of life, there was something about Kari's soft manner (as well as those dark circles under her eyes) that told Faith the woman had seen her share of sorrow.

It was the first time Faith had seen Slip without a stocking cap, and even in the dim candlelight, she looked as shockingly red-haired and

59

freckled as Pippi Longstocking. She sat near Merit, but on the floor, making her seem smaller than she already was. But Faith could see by the way Slip held her body that, small or not, she was not one to be trifled with; she reminded Faith of DeRon Graham, the featherweight wrestler on her high school's team. DeRon might have been the shortest boy in the senior class, but he walked through the school corridors as if he were a king and all the big beefy football players were his court jesters and all the tall gangly basketball players were his handservants.

Feeling relieved, the way a performer does after peeking through the curtain to see a smiling audience, Faith blew out a deep breath and urged everyone to help themselves to the cheese and crackers.

"So what are y'all talking about?" she asked after settling down on the carpeted floor by the coffee table.

Slip made a derisive snort. "One thing you'll learn, Faith: if Audrey's in the room, the answer is sex. Always sex."

With a slight smile, Audrey inhaled her cigarette. "Not true," she said, her voice choked with smoke. Jutting her chin, she exhaled one perfect smoke ring that floated, quivering, to the ceiling. "It's just that I occasionally like to talk about something a little more *fun* than Johnson and this stupid war."

"Me too," said Merit softly. "I'd rather talk about anything than the war."

Slip blanched, thinking of her earlier conversation with her brother.

"Not talking about it is not going to make it go away," she said, looking at Faith with a can-you-believe-this? expression. "In fact, that's what they want us to do — pretend it doesn't exist. But how many lives have to be lost before we start talking about it — before we start *doing* something about it?"

In the uncomfortable silence that followed, Faith scrambled to say something that would somehow disperse the tension in the room — it was her duty, after all, not just as a hostess, but the person she was — but Audrey beat her to it.

"My point exactly," she said, leaning over to stub out her cigarette in the ashtray. "How many orgasms have to be lost before we start talking about sex — before we start *doing* something about it?"

For a second Slip looked as though she wished Audrey were anywhere but in the same solar system, but the second passed and she laughed along with everyone else.

"Now, *your* husband," said Audrey to Faith, helping herself to a large wedge of cheese and a handful of crackers. "He's a pilot, right? He looks so handsome in his uniform — well, what I can see of his uniform when he runs out of the door with his coat open."

Faith nodded, surprised at the thrust of emotion that nearly brought tears to her eyes. "Thank you, he is. A pilot, I mean. And handsome too, I guess."

"He's gone a lot, isn't he?" asked Audrey, and it was beginning to dawn on Faith that this woman was the kind her MawMaw described as "pullin' no punches, even when she'd be better off sittin' on her hands." Audrey washed down a mouthful of crackers with the last of her martini, and Faith wondered if her long nails, like her eyelashes, were fake. "I wouldn't mind Paul and the boys taking the occasional trip — I could use a break now and then from this wife-and-mother thing."

Merit shook her head. "Oh, I wouldn't know what to do with myself if Eric had to go away. I can hardly stand it when he works late into the evening."

"That's because he's so cute," said Audrey. "In fact, in the cute husband sweepstakes, he just might take first prize."

Faith felt a defensive twinge — her Wade, with his dimpled chin and killer smile, could stand up to anyone.

"Audrey, let's just try for five minutes not to talk about men," said Slip, who, sitting on her knees by the coffee table, was playing with a line of wax snaking down a candle. "In fact, let's talk about each other. You're up, Faith."

"Oh, lordy." Faith felt her posture straighten, a reflex to being called on by the teacher. For a few moments she sat with a dazed smile on her face, wondering what to share and what to censor. *Well, the first thing you should know about me — but never will — is I'm a big fraud.*

"Let's see. I went to the University of Texas at Austin," she began, unconsciously twirling her wedding band. *It was a first — no one in my family had ever gone to college, let alone high school.* "That's where I met Wade." *Everyone thought he was quite the catch, and why he picked me I'll never know.* "He was my roommate's brother's best friend — they were both navy pilots. He did have a tour of duty in Vietnam, but long ago, before all the fighting started." She cleared her throat. "Anyway, I have a degree in English, although I

62

haven't done anything with it." She lifted her glass only to find it empty.

"Are your folks still there?" asked Audrey.

Faith pretended to take a final sip from her empty glass. "No, my mother died in a car accident the summer before my senior year at college, and my daddy . . . my daddy died just a couple months after I was married." She swallowed hard. "Of a . . . a heart attack."

"Oh, I'm so sorry," said Slip, and after the others murmured their sympathy, the room was quiet. The women seemed suddenly transfixed by the fire.

"So," said Audrey finally, "how long have you and Wayne been together?"

"*Wade*," said Faith. "Let's see . . . I married the summer I graduated, and had the twins two and a half years later." *Imagine that, I wasn't pregnant at my wedding. Imagine that — I had a wedding.*

"And what's that like?" asked Kari eagerly.

"They're fraternal," said Faith, happy to talk about something she didn't have to censor, "a boy and a girl, and their personalities are as opposite as their looks. Bonnie's got straight dark hair — well, what hair she has is straight — and she's real feisty, and Beau's got light brown curls and he's just the most sensitive little —"

"Bonnie and Beau?" said Slip. "Like the kids in *Gone with the Wind*?"

Faith wanted to deny what sounded like an accusation more than a question, but, flushing, she nodded. "It's one of my favorite books. I wanted to name them Scarlett and Rhett, but Wade wouldn't hear of it."

She waited for the condescending reaction

with which these Yankee women would surely greet this confession, but there was none; instead Slip surprised her, saying, "Oh, I loved that book too. I read it in the eighth grade, and I made a hoop skirt out of chicken wire. My dad helped me." Slip smiled, remembering how she had paraded into the living room to show off the finished product, worn under the tablecloth she had fashioned into a skirt. "Guess what *my* daughter's name is?" she asked Faith, her hazel eyes shining.

"Prissy?"

Slip laughed with the others. "It's Flannery. After Flannery O'Connor. One of my favorite writers."

"My comparative-literature professor went to school with her in Milledgeville."

"No kidding!"

Faith held up her hand, Scout's honor, and its shadow wavered on the candlelit wall. "They used to swap lunches. My professor said Flannery loved the date-nut bread her mother made."

"No kidding!" said Slip again.

"Well, get this," said Audrey, her tumble of dark hair falling over her shoulders as she leaned toward them. "Merit's going to name her baby Anna Karenina if it's a girl and Vronsky if it's a boy."

"I am not!" said Merit. "It's going to be Eric, Eric the third."

"Unusual name," said Kari, "if it's a girl."

Still on the floor, Slip shifted her position and her fingers bumped against something under the couch. She drew out a book.

"Hey, I read this," she said, holding it up to a candle.

"Is it good?" asked Faith. "I was just starting it when the lights went out."

Slip waved her hand in a so-so gesture. "You'll know who did it by the second chapter."

"Not me," said Kari. "I thought the meter maid did it the whole way through."

"Mind if I fill us up again?" asked Audrey, holding up her empty glass.

"Oh, please, let me," said Faith, embarrassed that she was remiss in her hostessing duties.

"I love mysteries," said Audrey, heading toward the portable bar. "Only trouble is there's never enough sex in them."

"Not all of us think *The Kinsey Report* is a great piece of literature," said Slip.

"It'll teach you things you never knew," teased Audrey, filling the shaker. "Really, Slip, you should broaden your reading tastes."

"My goodness," said Kari, "you two remind me of Mrs. Lundvall and Mrs. Seiderbaum. Only they never argued over *The Kinsey Report*, I can guarantee you that."

"Okay, you got me," said Audrey. "Who are Mrs. Lundquist and Mrs. Seiderberg and what would they argue about?"

Kari smiled, which did her plain and unadorned face a big favor. "Well, books, of course. Mrs. Lund*vall* and Mrs. Seider*baum* were in my mother's book club. It didn't matter what the book was — they'd argue about it."

"How could your mother have a book club?" asked Merit. "Don't you just sign up and order a book once or twice a year?"

"Not a mail-order book club. A book club where people read the same book and then get together to talk about it. My mother and her friends met the first Saturday of the month in the basement of Blessed Redeemer. I used to go with and sit under the portrait of Martin Luther and listen as they discussed Eudora Welty or Charles Dickens or Edna Ferber." Kari's smile once again brightened her face. "Dad played checkers with the other husbands in the kitchen, and when it came time for dessert, they served it."

"I want to join a club like that," said Audrey. "A club where I get to do the talking and the men run around serving dessert."

"Oh, believe me, it had its critics. Mr. Moe — he ran the bank — told Pastor Curtis that he didn't approve of church property being used by a bunch of idle women talking about ungodly things."

"What sort of ungodly things?" asked Faith.

Kari tucked a section of her bowl cut behind her ear. "Well, I can't remember what book they were discussing, but it brought out a lot of argument, and not just between Mrs. Lundvall and Mrs. Seiderbaum. Anyway, Mr. Moe — if he wasn't at the bank, he was at church — heard all of this and came downstairs just livid, asking everyone why they weren't home where they were supposed to be instead of making a ruckus in the Lord's house.

"The men came out of the kitchen — Mr. Hanson was wearing an apron, and boy, that really sent Mr. Moe around the bend. 'Men in aprons! Angry women shouting about books! What was the world coming to?'" Kari laughed, shaking her head. "I remember leaving my perch under Martin Luther to sit by my mother, absolutely terrified of what Mr. Moe was going to do."

"What *did* he do?" asked Merit.

"Well, he raved on until Pastor Curtis and some of the husbands settled him down and escorted him back upstairs. There was a big silence after he left, but then Mrs. Gepperson — now, she was a *card* — got up and started mocking Mr. Moe, shaking her finger at everyone and yelling how she was sickened by all these idle women shouting about books. I tell you, I never saw grown women laugh so hard."

"Hey," said Slip, her eyes wide, "let's take up where they left off. Let's start a book club of our own."

A log in the fire popped, spraying an arc of sparks.

"I've always wanted to be in one," said Kari, petting Flicka's broad forehead. "I know how much pleasure it gave my mother and her friends."

"I'd join," said Faith, feeling a warmth that was attributable either to the idea of a burgeoning social life or to her second martini. "I think it'd be fun."

"Damn right," said Slip. "Now, all in favor, raise your hands."

Every hand but one went up.

"Well, I'm not exactly sure what I'm getting into," said Merit. "We won't have to write book reports or anything, will we?"

Faith wondered if she was making a joke.

"Merit, this isn't supposed to be punishment," said Audrey, "it's supposed to be fun."

"Okay," said Merit, and her raised hand made the count unanimous.

With the vote in, the lights came on. No one

applauded this victory for technology; electric lighting, when compared to that provided by candle and fire, was jarring, overly bright, and certainly a destroyer of ambiance.

"Well, that's my cue," said Audrey, standing. "Paul's probably bound and gagged the boys by now."

Her announcement reminded everyone else that yes, it was getting late, but hadn't this been fun and wasn't a book club a good idea?

"So I'll figure out the details for our first meeting," said Slip, "and let you all know."

"What a pretty room," said Merit as the group walked toward the foyer. "I don't think I've ever seen peach living room walls before."

"Sometimes I go a little crazy," said Faith, who felt a pride in her decorating skills as well as a need to apologize for them.

Amid thanks for her hospitality and an offer from Kari to baby-sit the twins, the quartet of women readied themselves for the cold dash back to their own houses.

"I think it's warmed up, ladies," said Audrey as she opened the door and a blast of stinging air blew in. "It must be only thirty below now."

Kari held on to the collar of her dog. "Come on, Flicka, I'll race you back."

"Bye," said Merit, drawing up her coat collar so that its fur framed her movie star face. "I had a nice time."

Faith was just about to close the door when Slip stepped back in.

"Good night," she said, her cinnamon-colored eyes shining, her freckled nose already red from the cold. "See you at book club."

Dear Mama,

Wade's mama, Patsy, has been complaining that she does ten times the writing and calling that we do, so after I dutifully wrote her a letter (why is it that the wife is always the communicator? why can't Wade pick up a pen?) I thought: why not write my own mama? I could pretend you're still alive and that we're as close as Chang and Eng. I could write you *the real truth* because we're each other's best friends and we just love each other to pieces.

Hey, I can dream, right? So here goes . . .

Yesterday I was over at my friend Slip's house. Her mother's visiting from back east, and Slip's kids were climbing over their grandma like happy little monkeys, and along with being jealous of Slip for being so lucky, I thought how nice it would be if I had a mother my kids could climb all over. But even if you were here, I can't see you enjoying being their jungle gym — I can see you swatting them away and then asking me where the nearest "libation station" was.

Slip's mom smelled of hand lotion and coffee, and I thought what a sad little habit it is of mine to try to get a whiff of every mother I meet — always trying to find that smell that reminds me so much of you. Funny, though — I have yet to meet a mother who reeks of whiskey, cigarettes, and clothes that should have been in the laundry bag. Funnier still — how come I miss that smell?

Oh, Mama, I don't know why I'm being so mean. It's just that . . . well, you know yourself, the meanest people are usually the ones who hurt the most.

Hey, guess what? Spring finally got here and it's a beaut. There are lilac bushes all over the place, and just when you think pastels have taken over the world, you see a patch of bawdy red tulips or brilliant yellow crocuses. Imagine the world being frozen for so long and still being able to come up with these surprises.

I did go to a Pilots' Wives luncheon — they served a fancy ambrosia salad and chicken divan and the food reminded me of the kind they served at the Vernell Hotel in Oklahoma City, the kind of food that waiter boyfriend of yours would bring home to us in white paper sacks. Anyway, the gals I met there seemed nice enough, but all we did was sit around all afternoon talking about our husbands' seniority and what routes they fly. The real friends I'm starting to make are here in my neighborhood — and my book club. I can just hear you asking with your hands on your skinny little hips, "Now what the Sam Hill is this book club you're talkin' about?" Well, we pick a book and talk about it and then eat a really good potluck — mostly desserts. I had the first meeting at my house and picked a book by a guy named Bernard Malamud (it wasn't the kind of book I was dying to read, but I wanted everyone to think it was). Anyway, it was a lot of fun. There are four other gals (we might ask others to join later on, but right now we're going to keep it small) besides me, and there's not a dumb one in the bunch, at least not overtly. Merit is so quiet, I haven't figured out yet if she's dumb or just thoughtful. Brains probably never meant too much to her — she's

70

the kind of beautiful that makes you feel sort of mad and churned up in your stomach, but her looks seem to embarrass her, which makes it easier not to hate her! Audrey's the resident sex queen — she feels underdressed unless she's wearing a cleavage — and Slip's the resident firebrand peacenik who'll try to recruit you into any leftist cause that comes along. The two of them argue like Frick and Frack, even when they're on the same side. What saves them is they're both funny. Remember how you used to say, "If a man can make me laugh, he don't need money or looks"? Me, I feel the same way about friends (and lucky for Slip she's funny, because her looks aren't anything to write home about . . . but then again, I *am* writing about them).

Last, there's Kari — she's a couple years younger than you, Mama, and is the type who thinks before she speaks. I'm glad she does, because she'll say something that'll make me *think*. There's something about Kari that makes me feel calm — after listening to her I feel like I've drunk a warm glass of milk.

Being with them has started to make this frozen wasteland feel like home — not that I'm so familiar with what *that* feels like.

As for those twins of mine that you're just so crazy about and send so many darling presents to (hey, I can dream, can't I?): Beau's up from his nap — I can hear him snuffling around in his crib — so I'd better get in there before he wakes Bonnie. I like my time alone with Beau — Bonnie has the big personality that takes over, so it's nice just to play with him alone sometimes and wallow in his sweet little-boy self.

Oh, Mama, how I wish you could read this! But how do I send a letter to purgatory? (Ha-ha — that's a joke, and come on, at least I don't automatically assume you went even lower.)

I'm sorry,
Faith

To say that Faith had had a fractious childhood was to say that *a* began the alphabet. Primrose Reynolds, named after the town she was born in and not the path she took (which in her case led to disaster), was sixteen years old when she delivered Faith in the ripped backseat of a 1938 Studebaker, ten miles outside Little Rock.

"I tried to keep you in till we could get to the hospital," she told her daughter, "but y'all were so damn pushy! Just had to get out and see the wide world!"

This story would inevitably cause Primmy to convulse in laughter; of course, most stories did, seeing as she only told them when she was drunk and feeling good. When she was drunk and feeling bad she'd cry — not quietly into a handkerchief, but loud enough so that the neighbors in whatever run-down, urine-smelling pay-by-the-week dive they were living in at the time would yell out their doors, "Shut your trap or I'll shut it for you!" or "You want something to cry about? I'll give you something to cry about!"

Faith would sit on the thin mattress of the bed her mother shared with her when she wasn't "entertaining" (then Faith slept on a folded blanket on the floor, or on the couch if they happened to have one), patting her mama's shaking shoulders, lying to her that "it'll be all right."

When things got too rough for Primmy, when she lost a job or a boyfriend or the desire to get up in the morning, Faith would be sent to live with her grandmother in the small town of Trilby, Mississippi.

MawMaw wasn't mean to Faith, but removed, as if she had seen that emotion invested in people never garnered a profitable return.

Still, that small house with the blistered gray clapboards (not only on the wrong side of the tracks, but right next to them) gave Faith a stability she never had with her mother, gave her her good friend DellaRose, gave her acres of woods to run in as they reenacted Civil War battles, gave her regular meals and her own bed to sleep in.

She stayed with MawMaw for months at a time, and once for her entire second grade year at school; the day when her mother came to fetch her became not a reward but a punishment.

"Look at how my baby's grown!" Primmy would say, pressing Faith to her until the girl was sure she was going to pass out from lack of oxygen and a surplus of anxiety. "Just look at my baby!"

Primmy would always be dressed up for these reclaiming occasions, always wearing a bright, shiny dress that Faith, even at a young age, knew was not the kind worn by the nice women who walked by the house on their way to church. She rouged her cheeks with a heavy hand and blackened her eyebrows with pencil, and the bluish red lipstick she wore made her mouth look like a wound. Primmy Reynolds was a young and pretty woman, but her clothes, makeup, and reliance on liquor and cigarettes conspired to make her look worn and cheap. Faith would cry in her arms, and not with tears of joy.

When MawMaw died suddenly of a stroke while hoeing rocks out of her narrow, weedy garden, Primmy moved into her house, but the drunkenness and trail of boyfriends ruined whatever security Faith had felt there, and her own life began spiraling out of control, began to mimic her mother's in the drinking and the boyfriends and the sense of desperation.

Faith would automatically start shivering anytime she thought of how close she had come to being Primmy junior — how but for a simple question her life became more than she had ever dreamed possible.

The question, "What colleges are you planning to apply to?" was asked at the end of Faith's junior year by a guidance counselor new to the school, who wore a wide handlebar mustache that reminded Faith of the horns of water buffalo she'd seen in *National Geographic* and a tweed jacket that smelled of mothballs.

Shifting in the hard wooden chair, Faith rolled her eyes.

"Let's see," she said, examining the fine line of dirt underneath her thumbnail. "Besides Radcliffe, there's Wellesley, and oh yeah, I think the Sorbonne wants me too."

"I bet they would," said the counselor, offering a smile that stretched his handlebar mustache even wider.

"Right," said Faith. "Can I go now?"

The counselor leaned forward on his desk, and now, along with mothballs, Faith could smell body odor.

"I don't care how hard you try to hide it, Miss Reynolds," he said, "but you're a smart girl. Your tests scores are high and your grades . . . well, we know they could be a lot better, but as I said, your test scores are high, and with teacher recommendations —"

"Who's going to recommend me?" asked Faith of the teachers with whom she had a tepid relationship at best.

Twirling one end of his mustache, the counselor peered at a sheaf of paper.

"Well, Mrs. Allison seems to think you're a gifted English student."

"She *does?*" asked Faith. Any compliment Mrs. Allison had for Faith was shadowed by criticism: *I liked the way you expressed your thoughts, but honestly, your handwriting is so sloppy I could hardly read your paper.*

"Yes, and Mr. Christopherson says you have an acute grasp of history."

"It's just that we studied the Civil War," said Faith. "I don't know why, but I've always been interested in the Civil War."

Behind his thick glasses, the guidance counselor's eyes gleamed like those of a prospector finding gold in his pan. Faith crossed her arms, sullen again. Why had she bothered to tell this pathetic creep anything?

Lingering after school because she hadn't wanted to go home, Faith had once overheard, through an open door, a conversation the guidance counselor was having with Miss Franklin, the home ec teacher.

"Ernest," she'd said, "no offense, but I wouldn't go out with you if you were the last man alive."

Now this man, who was a pariah to the prettiest teacher at Pawnee High, set aside the papers and, still twisting his mustache, fixed his smudged and magnified gaze at Faith, expecting her to pay attention to him.

"Is that all, Mr. Teague?" she asked, standing up. "Because I really gotta go."

Undefeated, Mr. Teague offered a smile. "That's not all, Faith. Don't let it be all. It doesn't hurt to shoot for the moon."

As if it were a hot and itchy sweater, Faith shook off the advice, or at least she thought she did. But hours after her accident, when Billy Lawler fished her out of the Tallahalla River, she lay on her thin and lumpy mattress, her head throbbing from its wound, belching burps that tasted of sour beer, crying softly, and wishing that her mother were home, if not to offer comfort, then to at least scream at her for her stupid, nearly lethal behavior. What good did it do to nearly drown if there wasn't anybody around to care?

Tangled up in a gray, pilly blanket, Faith felt swaddled in misery itself. The thought occurred to her that maybe it wouldn't have been so bad to stay under those cold rushing waters, to stay under and not come up.

Her life seemed as dark and weighted as the night sky, seen through the windowpane that Primmy had cracked years ago when she threw a shoe at a retreating boyfriend.

I could have been dead. The thought was tinged not with awed relief but with regret. But then the clouds, pushed along by a night breeze, tore apart, revealing a yellow and pitted moon, and Mr. Teague's words came back to her, and for a moment she didn't feel so bruised and broken.

Well, why not shoot for it? she thought. *That moon's there as much for me as for anybody.*

The summer passed, and if she wasn't exactly a new Faith, at least she was an improved one: not automatically accepting every bottle of beer handed to her, not smoking until she got a headache, and, most importantly, not accepting every boy's invitation to climb into the backseat of whatever borrowed vehicle was available.

When she started her senior year, she made a promise to herself that she'd make all A's, and she did, even when she had to miss eleven straight days to take care of her mother, who had come down with a case of jaundice that turned her yellow as pus.

She spent long, conversational afternoons with Mr. Teague during which he helped her research colleges and fill out grant and scholarship applications.

When she burst into his office to show him the letter that informed her she had won an academic scholarship to the University of Texas, the counselor took off his chronically smudged glasses to wipe his eyes.

"Thank you for all you've done for me," she said, feeling a little teary herself.

"Just doing my job, Faith," he said, unused to student gratitude. He twisted the end of his mustache. "Just like you did yours."

They hugged then, because those were the days when affection could pass between teacher and student without fear of overstepping the guidelines listed in the district sexual harassment manual.

In Mr. Teague's thin, musty-smelling arms,

Faith felt as cared for and buoyed as she ever had in her life. As they drew away from each other, she said, "That Miss Franklin is a damn fool."

In Austin, unburdened by her home or her past, Faith reinvented herself, flourishing academically and socially. She made the dean's list and the cheerleading squad, and interested a number of boys (whom she *didn't* sleep with). By the time she met Wade at the end of her junior year, her confidence was such that yes, of course, she deserved him. It was a fairly constant confidence on the outside, but one she battled to maintain on the inside, especially when her mother, making threats to visit, began shaking it. But then her mother died, and even though it was an awful death and one that haunted Faith, it nonetheless freed Faith from what she had been all her life, what now nobody ever had to know: "no-account," "white trash," and "daughter of the town tramp and just as trampy herself."

She became a new Faith, born of a different set of parents, into a different world.

In English class, she laughed silently as her professor quoted Keats. *Believe me,* she thought, *truth is* not *beauty; the Faith I've made is a lot less ugly than the one that's real.*

It wasn't so hard fooling everybody; however, always being careful was exhausting. But Faith knew being tired was nothing compared to being found out.

HOSTESS: MERIT

BOOK: *Hotel* by Arthur Hailey

REASON CHOSEN: "Well, it *is* a bestseller."

When Merit told Eric that she was joining a book club, her husband had laughed out loud. Then, as if someone had abruptly turned a switch, his laughter stopped. Shaking his head, he said, "No way, Mere."

"What do you mean, Eric?"

"What do I *mean?*" he said, smiling a mirthless smile. "I mean I don't see the benefit of you joining a bunch of women who sit around eating bon bons, yakking about some asinine love story."

"We're not going to be talking about a love story," she said, her voice high as a young girl's. "We're going to be discussing *The Fixer*. It's about —"

"I don't give a shit what it's about!" said Eric, picking a copy of *Life* magazine off the coffee table and flinging it across the room. "I don't want you joining a book club!"

Merit, sitting next to him on the couch, willed her body not to shiver, even though it felt as though her blood had been replaced with something cold, because Eric didn't like it when she acted scared; it made him yell even louder and accuse her of trying to make him feel bad for setting the rules in his own house.

"Eric," she said, her voice straining as she tried to keep it even and light, "you're always saying how you wished I'd graduated from a four-year college, and this would be a chance —"

"I thought we were going to have a nice quiet evening at home."

"— to improve myself; I mean, it would almost be like taking a class, and —"

"I don't get many opportunities to have a nice quiet evening."

"— besides, I think it'd be nice to get together with the neighbors, and you wouldn't have to do anything to help me get ready —"

Crack. Merit felt the blow to her cheek immediately, felt the white-hot flash of pain, but it took a moment for her brain to process the terrible information that the cause of the pain now radiating from her cheekbone up into her eye had been her husband's hand.

"Oh, God, Mere," he said, his face suddenly pale as wax. "Oh, God, what happened?"

You hit me, that's what happened! she wanted to scream, but didn't, and as much as she wanted to lurch off the couch and out of the arms he wrapped around her, she didn't. Instead she sat and trembled as tears from his eyes wet her cheeks, sat and trembled as he told her over and over how sorry he was, but he'd been under so much pressure at the hospital and she kept pushing and pushing and he'd never do anything to hurt her, she knew that, didn't she?

After his long, droning apology, a wave of nausea washed over Merit as he pressed his lips against her throbbing cheek. Desperately she swallowed down the bile; she was fairly certain

80

that upchucking in her husband's lap was not the way to ensure his repentance.

"I'm going to get some ice for that," he said, patting her knee as he stood up, and when he was out of the room, Merit cupped her hands over her mouth and screamed. It wasn't a loud scream — she didn't want Eric to hear her. It was more a squeal, and as soon as it filled her ears she realized she might not be able to stop it. A new fear rose in her — what would he do to her if she couldn't stop screaming? — but then the baby inside her pelted her with a *boom-boom-boom* of kicks, her little baby was telling her to knock it off, it would be good for everyone if she just knocked it off, and because of her baby, she was able to take her hands from her mouth and stop her high-pitched wail.

He held the ice bag to her cheek gently, telling her that it was going to be all right, that it would be red for a while but surely there would be no bruise, and if there was, God forbid, she should just tell everyone she banged it on the edge of the cupboard or something, and don't worry, it would never happen again.

She looked into his gray-blue eyes, and more than anything she had ever wanted in her life, she wanted to believe him.

Merit had been the first member of the Mayes family to leave Decorah, Iowa, since her ancestors had settled there four generations earlier. It was a move that was not celebrated with farewell toasts; neither was a bon voyage party thrown.

"It's the devil's path you're taking," said her father.

Pastor Mayes did not reserve sermonizing or

grand speeches or his pithy axioms for the pulpit. Something as simple as buttering toast ("waste not, want not") or asking if anyone had seen the hairbrush ("pride goeth before the fall") incited the minister's rhetoric — rhetoric that Merit, by the time she had finished high school (class of '61; secretary, Future Farmers of America; choir; Community Key Club; Best-Looking Girl) was thoroughly sick of.

She made the decision to move to a big city (she considered Des Moines, but Minneapolis was closer) the night of her senior prom, when she was in the arms of Richard Pelke, a boy who managed, even with a crew cut, to have severe dandruff.

Fortunately, his tuxedo was pale blue, which made his dandruff less obvious, and he *was* a good dancer, which in Merit's eyes excused a multitude of sins. Merit was a good dancer too, which was not an easy thing to be in a household where dancing, while not forbidden (they were Lutherans, after all, not Baptists) was nevertheless thought of as slightly lurid and definitely unnecessary. Rock and roll had taken its time in coming to Decorah, but when it did, it was *embraced,* and now in a muggy gym smelling of Vitalis and Jungle Gardenia, Mennen deodorant and feet, Merit happily followed Richard's lead as the Mello-Tones — college boys from Iowa City — played "Unchained Melody."

"Gosh, Merit," whispered Richard, his breath hot against her ear, "I think I love you."

She stiffened in Richard's arms, desperately trying to think of a breezy comeback. Many boys had expressed similar sentiments (boys she hadn't even dated, boys who'd yell the words at her as she passed them in the halls), but Merit never knew what to say, could only blush and stammer and feel guilty that she didn't return the feeling.

"We've got the whole summer ahead of us," he said, and again her ear was assaulted with heat, "a whole summer to do what I hope we'll do tonight."

By the way he moved his hands down the small of her back and pressed his body to hers, it was evident what he meant.

"Richard!" she managed to squeak, wondering what had gotten into the mild-mannered pharmacist's son for which the senior prom constituted their first date. (Clark Eiderbaum, football captain and a member of the all-state baseball team, had broken up with her earlier that spring, telling her he could understand a girl holding out, but not to the extent that *she* held out.)

Fortunately the band chose that moment to end their song, causing couples to break apart and applaud.

"I'm . . . I'm going to the powder room," said Merit, and as she lifted the skirt of her pink tulle formal so it wouldn't drag on the floor, a dozen boys followed her exit with longing eyes.

"Forget about it, Lyle," said a girl named Jean, poking her date in the ribs with a gloved elbow. "At least with me you don't get blue balls."

Sitting in a bathroom stall, Merit pondered her options, first for the evening (she could call for a ride home, but she was sure Richard Pelke would have calmed down by the time she returned to the gym; he was too mild-mannered to sustain such boldness) and then for her future.

Wasn't she supposed to be excited about it? Everyone else seemed to be excited, everyone else (except for those boys who'd immediately begin full-time work on their family's farm) had made big conquer-the-world plans (Ginger Stanhope was going to Vassar! Dave LaFleur was going to Florida State!) but Merit had nothing more exciting to look forward to than a two-year stint at the junior college in her hometown. She looked down at her pink dyed-to-match shoes, and they suddenly struck her as so hopeful, so silly, that she thought she might cry.

The bathroom door opened, and with a swish and rustle of chiffon and organza and satin, a group of girls entered.

"You going to the pit?" asked one, referring to the gravel pit, which was the preferred place for high school lovers to park.

"You bet," said another. "Will's bringing a keg."

"Who's all going?"

"Everybody."

Merit sighed; she, as usual, wasn't considered part of "everybody." Her shyness was perceived as standoffish (how could a girl that beautiful be shy?), and besides, any chance of a social life was pretty much overruled by her parents' demand that she spend most of her time at home or church.

That her parents had allowed her to date Clark Eiderbaum for the better part of the year was not *that* surprising; after all, Clark went to their church, and their approved dates consisted of walks home after youth group or Saturday matinees in which they supervised their siblings. But then Clark had wanted more, wanted to kiss her longer and drive out to the gravel pit, and while a part of Merit said a loud and resounding yes, the other part, stained by her parents' large shadow, said no, and eventually Clark began dating Alice Swanstad, who was president of the pep club and, rumor had it, a girl willing to go to third base, at least.

Listening to the girls outside the stall giggle and make plans, the feeling that had quietly tip-toed into her head while dancing with the hot-breathed Richard now stomped in, banged walls, knocked down furniture: *I've got to get out of here!*

Toward that goal, she worked that summer cashiering at Pelke Drug (Richard, figuring it was a fluke that she had gone to the prom with him in the first place, was a gentleman and didn't pester her for any more dates) and waitressing at LeMond's Supper Club out on the highway, making tips that did not endear her to the older, more experienced waitresses.

Finally one night, over a dinner of bright red meat loaf (Mrs. Mayes thought ketchup was less a condiment than an all-purpose spread) and lumpy mashed potatoes, Merit told all assembled at the table that the next day she was taking the train to Minneapolis.

"But tomorrow's choir practice," her mother said.

"I won't be going," said Merit softly. "In fact, you'd better find another soprano."

"What exactly is that supposed to mean?" asked the Reverend Mayes as he plopped a ladleful of potatoes onto his plate.

Merit felt her courage flutter inside her like a sparrow struggling to escape. She took a deep breath, tamping it down, forcing the sparrow to stay inside her, to turn into an eagle.

"What it means is I've saved money and I'm moving to Minneapolis tomorrow."

"Moving to Minneapolis!" said her mother, as if she had just announced she was joining the Methodists.

Her father, whose wrath she had been steeling herself for, surprised her by laughing.

"Oh, Merit," he said, shaking his head. "*Minneapolis*? What'll *you* do in Minneapolis?"

Her face burned red as she pushed her mashed potatoes around with her fork.

"I'm going to go to business school."

"Business school?" said her father, the supple joviality in his voice turning brittle. "But you're going to school here."

"No, sir," said Merit, her face so hot she felt consumed by a sudden fever. "I'm going to business school in Minneapolis." She felt her voice catch in her throat, but swallowed down the rising sob, refusing to give her father the pleasure of seeing how scared she was. Pastor Mayes appreciated weakness in other people — it allowed him to show how strong he was. She lifted her head and looked him right in the eye, an act of defiance that, she could tell by his mild flinch, disconcerted him.

"You're not the one to tell us what you're going to do. You've got the order reversed, missy."

"I'm eighteen years old. I can make my own decisions now."

Pastor Mayes slammed down his fist, and the silver and glassware jangled on the table.

Mrs. Mayes brought her hand to her collar button, and Merit's younger brother and sister, who had been witnessing this confrontation with the glee of schoolkids watching the school bully being goaded by the skinny kid, now realized one essential truth: because of his strength and power, the bully *could* be the bully and the skinny kid of course had no chance.

But Merit was not done with her surprises. As her father railed about honoring one's parents, she pushed back her chair and said, "Excuse me, but I've got to finish packing."

Slack-jawed, the Mayes family watched as Merit left the room.

So stunned by his sister's derring-do was fifteen-year-old Donald that he had no time to censor himself.

"Jesus Christ," he exclaimed, which of course was the wrong thing to say to a minister already inflamed by one of his children's actions.

In Minneapolis, everything, for the first time in her life, clicked for Merit. A young woman whom she met while staying at the YWCA had just found an apartment and needed a roommate; she got a job waitressing at a downtown steak house where the tips were good; and she began a secretarial course at business school. She and her mother shared a weekly correspondence, and while there were occasional notes from her brother and sister enclosed, there was no word from her father.

"Your dad still thinks you owe him an apology," explained Mrs. Mayes, but Merit, having no idea why making a life of her own was grounds for apology, never paid that debt.

In her mother's letters was always a P.S.: "Hope you've found a parish of your own!"

Merit hadn't; she was, for the first time in her life, sleeping in on Sundays. She went home for Christmas that first year, but her father was sadly incapable of practicing what he preached and virtually ignored his daughter her entire visit. His hypocrisy (how could he exhort his parishioners to "love and cherish each other as Jesus loves and cherishes us" and yet leave the room every time Merit entered it?) turned Merit away from him as well as from his church, but the following year, alone for the holidays, she decided that what she needed to lift her gloom was to sing some carols, and so on Christmas Eve she found herself in the church nearest her apartment (Episcopalian), singing "Joy to the World" like the former soloist she was.

The whole row ahead of her turned around to see who belonged to the high, pretty voice, and one man in particular didn't want to turn back around.

"I thought, *I believe in angels!*" he liked to tell her, reminiscing about the day they met, "because I knew I was looking into the face of one."

After the service, he managed to move through the crowd of people to wish her a merry Christmas and then ask her if she had plans for the evening.

"It's Christmas Eve," she said, as if that explained everything.

"I know what day it is. I also know that sometimes people are away from their families on the holidays, and if that's true in your case, I think you should come and spend them with mine."

His parents, with whom he'd been sitting in church, seemed to think there was nothing odd or out of place about their son's invitation.

"I'm glad you're coming," said Mr. Iverson, taking her arm. "Now I'll have two beautiful women under the mistletoe."

"Oh, Eric," said his wife in a voice that asked, *Isn't he just the most lovable cut-up?*

The Iversons' grand house, with its Lake of the Isles view, was decorated not only with mistletoe but with evergreen boughs and poinsettias and a miniature English village that was arranged in a bay window, complete with fake snow and a running train whose track looped around tiny porcelain homes and shops.

"Oh, my," said Merit, taking in everything, including the twelve-foot tree laden with ornaments and lights.

"I like to go all out for the holidays," said Eric's mother. Then in the next breath she asked, "Sherry?"

For one rubeish moment, Merit thought Mrs. Iverson had called her by the wrong name, but before she could correct her, Eric junior said, "That sounds wonderful, Mother. One for Merit and one for me."

It was the best night of Merit's life, she thought as she stretched under the fine linens of the bed the Iversons insisted she use ("It's snowing too hard for safe driving, and besides, our Christmas brunch is something you wouldn't want to miss"). With classical music playing on the hi-fi and in front of a crackling fire, they had sipped sherry (the first liquor, other than Communion wine, Merit had ever had) and helped themselves to the trays of cookies and sandwiches Mrs. Iverson passed around, telling stories about themselves. (As to the question about her own family, Merit replied

89

truthfully that her father was a minister in Decorah, Iowa, and untruthfully that she hadn't been able to get time off from work to go back for the holidays.)

"We know what it's like not having children home for Christmas," said Mrs. Iverson, offering Merit a cigarette. "Our Douglas is in Cambridge — he's studying medicine at Harvard — and our Joanie's spending the semester in Copenhagen, studying Danish."

"Oh, my," said Merit, thinking how different the lives of their Douglas and Joanie were from her own parents' children.

How different their celebration had been, too; there hadn't been one reading of the Scriptures, one prayer, one recitation of the Bethlehem story, and yet Merit couldn't remember a more special Christmas, and that was including the one in which she had been Mary in the pageant *and* gotten her baby doll, Betty Lou, who to her delight really did wet.

A year later, Pastor Mayes was officiating at the wedding of his daughter (whose honor and good standing in the family had been fully restored now that she was getting married — and to a medical student, no less), and Merit marveled at her own good luck. She truly understood, for the first time in her life, what her father had meant by the bounty of God's blessings.

The idyll lasted nearly six months. Then one night as she was taking a bath, Eric came in and asked her if she ever aspired to be more than a secretary. Or had she always known that she wasn't smart enough for anything that required real thought?

"I wouldn't say you're borderline retarded," said Eric, turning to regard his handsome face in the mirror, "but I'll bet you're not as far away from that distinction as you think."

Something like a chicken bone seemed to catch in Merit's throat. Then she laughed, because surely he was joking, but when she saw the look of fury in his eyes as he turned away from the mirror, her laughter died as quickly as it had started.

"Well, maybe I'm being too generous. Only a retard laughs when someone tells them they're retarded."

Merit drew in her breath and was glad a layer of bubbles coated her bathwater; she couldn't bear to be naked in front of him right now. Still, she crossed her arms over her breasts and drew her feet, resting on the tub's edge, back into the water.

He left then, muttering to himself about being saddled with an idiot wife. As if she were being pushed by an unseen hand, Merit slowly sank down in the tub, until she was underwater.

She never knew when one of Eric's moods might come or what had provoked them; she only knew that he would say things that made her feel thoroughly, completely worthless (he often questioned how she had gotten the name Merit, "because you certainly don't have any"). She had trained herself to tune out the I'm-right-you're-wrong preaching Pastor Mayes directed at her and her siblings (and the world for that matter), but Eric's taunts and insults were too harsh to tune out, and he often held her face be-

91

tween his hands as he told her one horrible thing after another.

If she cried or protested, he accused her of being a baby, and sometimes he would pull her to bed, or onto a table or floor, and pound himself into her until he screamed in release and Merit screamed without sound.

It wasn't constant cruelty — weeks could pass without incident, and Merit would be lulled back into a peaceful existence. Then all of a sudden Eric would be firing away, unconcerned about breaking the armistice.

Once while sitting on the toilet (her sanctuary from him), Merit thought maybe she should leave her husband, but the thought caused clammy sweat to bead on her forehead and her heart to forget its regular rhythm. Where would she go? Going back to Decorah was as feasible as relocating to Timbuktu.

"This is your *marriage*," Merit whispered to herself; implicit in the word were all the vows she thoroughly believed in. She just hadn't known that the "for worse" parts were going to be this bad.

Intellectually, she knew that Eric's outbursts were *his* fault, but emotionally, she thought she had to be doing *something* to inspire them. It became her mission to please him: wearing her hair the way he liked it, in a French roll, just like his mother's; dressing in only the clothes he picked out (she had a closet full of outfits that made her feel like either a little girl or a church organist); watching what he watched on TV (and laughing when he laughed); cooking what she knew were his favorite foods, ad infinitum. It got so that she couldn't remember if she really liked what a candidate stood for or voted for him because that's who Eric liked; that she'd drink a Tom Collins with him even though the taste of gin made her shudder; that she stopped telling him that she thought his father was going a little overboard in his flirting ("your behind," he had told her just last week, "is what we men of science call a perfect specimen"); that she wouldn't do a smidgin of anything that might remotely upset him.

But her mission had not been successful. By wanting to go to the book club meeting, she had upset him enough that he had hit her. This, however, was abuse that even he was shocked by, and his guilt apparently was going to work in her favor. That night in bed, after he rolled off her, he told her he'd been thinking over this book club business, and really, what was the harm?

No harm at all, thought Merit, allowing herself to smile in the darkened room. *No harm at all in letting a bunch of women get together to eat bon bons and yak about some love story.*

She had gotten out of the habit of reading (Eric always pouted when Merit's attention was diverted by anything other than himself) and so agonized over what to choose for the book club's discussion that she sought help.

The librarian, whose braided bun and eyeglass rims were the color of a steel filing cabinet, said, "Well, Thackeray always makes for good discussion, or Hardy," but a young library assistant tiptoed up to Merit as she stood in the A-H aisle and pressed the book *Hotel* into Merit's hands.

"This is one of the most popular books in circulation right now," she whispered. "I think it might be a little more fun than *Jude the Obscure*."

Now Merit stood in front of her dining room table, stubbing out what seemed to be her thousandth cigarette of the day, holding her own private pep rally as she tried to convince herself that the night wasn't going to be a dismal failure.

She was only a serviceable cook (she had been her mother's helper in the kitchen for years, but her mother's belief that cooking was a chore rather than a pleasure hadn't gone far in spurring Merit's culinary imagination), and baking seemed to stump her; things usually ran the gamut from underbaked to burned. The apple crumb cake that sat in the center of the table looked done, but she knew she could cut into it and be surprised. The rest of the group would be bringing food — but still, at the first meeting, Faith had made a sheet cake decorated to look like an open book (its icing calligraphy read Chapter One — We Begin) and had set such a pretty table, with pastel napkins and place cards printed with names like "Slip Salinger," "Kari Kafka," and "Audrey Austen." (She had tucked her place card, "Merit Maupassant," in her jewelry box and was oddly proud of it, even though she wasn't quite sure who exactly Maupassant was.)

In choosing where the next meeting would be, why had they agreed to Slip's idea ("Why don't we just go in the order of where we're sitting tonight?"), and why had Merit been sitting next to Faith?

Rubbing her lower abdomen, which was tightening up in an uncomfortable squeeze, she entertained the thought of calling the whole thing off, but then her plans were foiled by the ringing doorbell.

Audrey stood rifling through the record collection, shaking her head.

"Merit, Merit, this golden strings elevator music crap has got to go. Don't you have any Miles Davis or Thelonious Monk or even some Beatles?"

"I . . . I don't know. Most of the records are Eric's."

"My God, even my parents have a hipper collection than this."

"Audrey, can you save your review for the book?" asked Slip, kicking off her shoes and tucking her feet under her.

"Ah, yes," said Audrey, turning away from the stereo, "the book. Well, it was a little too simplistic for me. I look for a little more character development in writing — if I want to know about hotels, I'll just read a Holiday Inn brochure."

"I thought it was interesting, learning how a hotel is run," said Faith, helping herself to the package of Tareytons on the coffee table.

"Some books serve different purposes," said Kari. "This wasn't great literature, but it was a fun peek behind the scenes."

"Yeah," said Slip, "and besides, Audrey, Holiday Inn is a *motel*, not a *hotel*."

Merit's eager delight over how well the meeting was going was tempered by her nervousness that it could all suddenly change. No one had asked her to remix their drinks, *yet* (Eric teased her that her drinks tasted as if she measured liquor not in jiggers but in thimbles); even though Audrey hadn't liked the book, no one had criticized her for choosing it, *yet;* her cake, even though competing against a dessert pot-luck, was being eaten and nobody had choked on its dryness, *yet*. There was only one area in which Merit's confidence was not subject to evaporation, and that was in her housekeeping, which everyone complimented.

"Oh, I get it," said Audrey, looking around the spare, spotless living room. "It's part of the theme. Clean as a hotel room, right?"

Merit only smiled, not knowing if Audrey was teasing her or not.

The book discussion was lively and at one point — when Audrey told the story of getting locked out of her Paris hotel room on her honey-moon — hilarious, and Merit marveled at every-one's willingness to disagree. Disagreement was always a symptom of mutiny in Merit's child-hood home, as well as her current one.

And it wasn't just Slip and Audrey; Faith had opinions, Kari had opinions. The beauty of it was that no one seemed to resent anyone else for having them.

When Merit did speak, it was either to ask hostess questions or to agree with opinions al-ready shared, and so the yelp that came out of her mouth struck the others as completely out of character.

"Sorry," she said, her eyebrows furrowed into check marks above her brown eyes, "but that one really hurt."

"You had a contraction?" asked Slip.

"I've been having them all night," said Merit.

"How far apart?" asked Audrey.

"They're not very regular," said Merit, "but that one hurt like hell."

"She's in labor," said Slip, recognizing immediately that when a woman who could barely say boo chose to curse, things were definitely happening.

"I don't think so," said Merit, taking a deep breath. "I've had them before — the doctor calls them Braxton-Hicks contractions."

"False labor," explained Kari the teacher.

"Is Eric at the hospital now?" asked Faith.

As Merit nodded, she grimaced, her palms pressed against the neat mound of her belly.

"Which is where you should be," said Slip. "Come on, I'll give you a ride."

"But we're not done talking about the book. . . ."

"*Hotel* can wait," said Audrey, standing up and brushing apple cake crumbs off her pink capri pants. "Babies can't."

They all sat in the waiting room paging through sticky back issues of *Good Housekeeping* and *Ladies' Home Journal* and reliving their own labor stories.

"Well, I had a C-section," said Faith, "so of course I didn't feel anything. Except when I woke up."

"I was so drugged I wasn't supposed to feel anything," said Audrey, "but both my boys weighed almost ten pounds. Believe me, I felt *plenty*."

"I'm not going to have any drugs the next time I have a baby," said Slip, and she was about to launch into the benefits of natural childbirth when she caught sight of the look on Kari's face. Her friend wore a pinched smile, the kind a mother wore when the teacher was telling her what a reprobate her kindergartner was; the kind a man wore when his proposal of marriage had just been turned down.

"Hey, who's got a cigarette?" asked Slip, but there was no need for a subject change, as Dr. Iverson entered through the swinging doors, holding Merit by the arm.

"Braxton-Hicks contractions," he announced. "Apparently Merit wants to get in a few practice innings before the real game.

"I'll see you at home tonight," he said, touching his wife's face. "If they start up again, make a nice pot of tea and sit with your feet up."

"Hubba hubba," said Audrey, watching as the tall, dark doctor strode briskly through a swinging door. "Cancel my appointment with Dr. Kildare and put me on *his* examining table."

"You're a degenerate," scolded Slip as the others laughed.

They were gathering up their purses when a nurse bolted through the door, and for a moment Merit thought she was going to be called back and told to hop onto the delivery table, as tests had showed she was in labor after all.

But the nurse raced by them, one hand holding her white cap, her white sweater swooping out behind her shoulders like a cape.

"My gosh," said Kari, "where's the fire?"

"Robert Kennedy's just been shot," she said, turning her head, her stride unbroken.

They watched after her dumbly, and amid the gasps and cries, Audrey said the only understandable words: "Holy Mother of God." A fluorescent tube inside the ceiling panel flickered and went out as if responding to the terrible news.

Merit's belly was clenching hard, and for the

first time she was grateful for her false contractions, because even though they hurt, they were not pushing her baby toward birth. She was already thinking like a mother and, wanting to protect her baby, did not want him to come out into the world at this moment in time. It was better that he stay inside her, where it was safe.

July 1968

HOSTESS: SLIP

BOOK: *Soul on Ice* by Eldridge Cleaver

REASON CHOSEN: "Because we white Americans don't know diddly."

Holy wet noodle, I am not a heat person. Heat brings the similarities between my hair and a Brillo pad all too close plus, unlike dewy Merit, I am not a delicate perspirer. It surprises me how much sweat my body produces; the volume of water is not at all consistent with my size.

Jersey City can be humid, but maybe Hudson River humidity is different from lake air humidity. Trust me, Minneapolis is *muggy,* muggy like you could grab a handful of air and wring it out like a washrag.

Anyway, heat makes me crabby, and with humidity added, I'm about as good-humored as Lizzie Borden with cramps. Factoring in my belief that the whole friggin' world was coming to an end — well, even my own four-year-old daughter couldn't stand to be around me. I'd yelled at her all morning over nonexistent infractions until finally she grabbed her *Pokey Little Puppy* book and plunged out the screen door in tears. But *come on:* even in temperate climates, how could any American citizen not be on the verge of insanity? First Martin Luther King Jr., then Bobby Kennedy. As if we didn't have enough to worry about with this stupid war (thank God I hadn't heard any more enlistment/death wishes from Fred lately), now anyone who offered any hope of peace was getting mowed down on motel balconies and in hotel kitchens.

"Mommy, why did they shoot him?" Flannery had asked in April, sitting at the breakfast table as I read the paper with the awful picture of King's friends pointing in the direction the shot had come from.

"Oh, Flan," I said, "I don't really know."

She had asked the same question at the same breakfast table just a few weeks ago, when Kennedy was shot, and again I had no answer for her. Or the answer I had was one I didn't want her to hear: *Well, Flan, the world is full of truly evil people who want to make things truly awful for the rest of us. And now that you've been given that sobering dose of reality, how 'bout another pancake?*

When I was little, my dad had Indian nicknames for all us kids. Mine was Warrior Bear.

That he hadn't chosen some pretty, condescending name like Little Feather or Dancing Fawn was proof to me that he appreciated the person I was: strong, fierce, tough. It was only when I got to junior high and some idiots heckled me as I gave my student council president campaign speech that I realized there was a certain burden in being a Warrior Bear.

"They laughed at me when I said I thought we should overthrow the principal and rewrite the constitution!"

"Oh, Slip," said my mom, holding out her arms. (I think it's size more than age that prevents kids from climbing into their parents' laps;

101

because of my smallness, I let them take me in their arms up until the time I left for college.) "Slip, it's asking a lot of ninth graders to overthrow the principal *and* rewrite the school constitution."

"Not the school's," I said, "the *American* constitution. The one that says all men are created equal but doesn't say a thing about women."

My mother drew her lips in; I could tell she was trying hard not to laugh.

"That's a pretty big task for junior high kids."

"Mom, it's the principle of the thing! Why should we bother with stupid things like whether or not there's chocolate milk in the lunchroom when our own constitution says women aren't created equal?"

I felt my mother's chest rise in a sigh. "Slip, honey, it's just a student council election."

"Change has got to start somewhere," I said, pushing myself off her lap.

I lost the election (and, I might add, the winner's presidency was absolutely ineffectual — he couldn't even get his chocolate milk initiative passed), but a Warrior Bear isn't named that for nothing. I continued to battle for justice in high school (where injustice is king) and in college (I was part of the group of students who got Professor Lermond, the biggest woman-hater on campus, brought up for review, and I wrote a column for the *Daily* called "Proletarian's Progress"). Being a wife and mother didn't slow me down at all — it made me realize I have to work even harder for the sake of my kids — but man, these assassinations were making me wonder what a Warrior Bear can do in the midst of such craziness.

With the world on the brink of self-annihilation, I still had to host book club that night and was trying to find a dessert I could make without turning on the oven. But paging through the cookbook, the words blurred and all I saw were the faces of Coretta Scott King and Ethel Kennedy.

"Promise me you'll never get shot," I had said to Jerry when we sat on the couch watching the news after the kids had gone to bed. It wasn't often I enjoyed my size, but I did when my big husband's arm was around me.

"No one's got much of a vendetta against meteorologists."

We both smiled wanly at the truth of Jerry's statement, and as I watched the news clips of Robert Kennedy's funeral train, I wondered how wives of men with dangerous jobs (of course, being a preacher or politician shouldn't inherently be a dangerous job) managed to live any kind of normal life.

I tried to focus on some recipes under the inane heading "Light 'N' Easy Treats" and swatted at a giant mutant fly that had managed to slip through the fortress of window and door screens. It must have gotten in when Flan went outside. *Flan.* My poor little girl who had a banshee for a mother.

With a glass of lemonade as a peace offering, I went into the backyard. It was even hotter outside, and as I walked to the big oak tree, I felt I was in the clutches of a big, hot, and sweaty hand.

"Flan, honey, look what I brought you," I said, shading my eyes with one hand to look up at the roofless tree house I knew she was probably hiding out in.

The piece of canvas that served as a curtain was pushed aside, and Flannery's strawberry-blond head (I'm forever grateful to Jerry for tempering the red genes I passed down with blond ones of his own) appeared in the cutout window.

"I'm not thirsty," she said in a tone of haughty disgust, as if I were offering her a glass of sewer water to drink.

"Oh, come on, Flan. How can you not be thirsty in weather like this?"

"E-a-s-y." My dear, precocious daughter thinks her strong feelings are emphasized when she spells them out. She disappeared back into the tree house.

I set the glass on the sidewalk and tugged at the damp neckline and hem of my sleeveless shell, hoping to get some stagnant air circulating.

"I could come up and visit you," I said as a drip of salty sweat rolled over my upper lip.

"No thanks," she said from inside the tree house. "I'm *reading*."

Kicking my feet up, I sprang forward with my hands on the grass. I got my balance and began walking around the tree on my hands. Usually my kids can't get enough of this little trick, but today Flan wasn't interested in her mother's acrobatics.

"All right," I conceded, back on my feet. "But I'm taking the lemonade inside. Otherwise the flies or the ants will get it."

My concentration on dessert ideas totally shot, I wandered into the living room and saw the book that I hadn't quite finished (I prided myself on always finishing the book we were discussing) on the coffee table. I decided to join Flan up in that sun-baked tree house.

"Mommy," said Flan in that delighted tone only children seem capable of when you surprise them, "are you going to read up here too?"

"Yup," I said, crawling through the lopsided square that served as the tree house door. "So scoot your scooter over."

Despite the heat and the mosquito attacks (why is it so satisfying slapping a biting mosquito into a bloody smear?), I felt a semblance of tranquility as I sat pressed against the rough wood, *Soul on Ice* balanced on my bare knees. Flannery sat in the exact position, and after ten minutes or so had passed we looked up at the same moment, taking a slight reprieve from the world we'd entered to check on the one in which we lived.

I winked at my daughter. "How's the pokey little puppy doing?"

Flan blinked back. "He's pretty pokey. How's your book?"

I frowned. "Scary. And sad."

"Anybody home?"

"Uh-oh," I said. "Trespassers."

We both looked out of the window to see Faith at the back door.

"We're up here," I said, and as Faith looked up, a hand shielding the sun from her eyes, I asked her if she'd misplaced my son on the way over.

"Wade's home today," she explained. "He's got the kids all running through the sprinkler. Flannery's welcome to join them if she likes."

Flan bit her lip. "Is that okay, Mommy? It is pretty hot up here."

"Sure, honey. Run and get your suit on."

Flannery scampered down the tree.

"I thought I'd come over and see if y'all needed any help for tonight," said Faith, her head still tilted back, looking up at the massive tree. "Unless you're planning to spend the afternoon up there?"

"Maybe I am," I said. "And maybe you'd better come up here and join me."

"Okay!" As she began to climb the slats nailed to the tree, she said, "I've never been in a tree house before." She stood looking at the small rectangular room through the tree house door. "Hey, this is really neat."

"Well, don't just stand there gawking," I said, moving over as Faith crawled through the door. "Come on in. But watch out for those acorns."

Faith moved her foot to avoid the mound of nuts piled in the corner.

"Flan's trying to catch a squirrel," I explained, "and tame it. So she hoards acorns in here."

"Has she had any luck?" asked Faith as she sat against a wall, facing me.

"With the squirrels? Nah, but she's convinced all she needs is patience."

I tossed an errant acorn into the pile, and it was as if a buzzer went off: playtime was over, the medication had worn off, and life had reared its big ugly head. Holy hepped-up emotions, all I could do was rest my forehead on my knees and start to cry.

"Slip?" said Faith. "Slip, what's wrong?"

I kept crying into my folded arms.

"Would you like me to go?" asked Faith, and when I shook my head, she scuttled over to me, putting her arm around me. Like a child, I

106

turned my head into her shoulder.

I don't know how long I cried — all I knew was that it felt too good to stop, even though I was risking dehydration, adding pints of tears to my gallons of sweat.

"I'm sorry," I said when I was drained of all bodily fluids, "but I just keep asking myself, whatever happened to the Summer of Love?"

"I beg your pardon?" Faith looked like she'd just been asked to explain the theory of relativity.

"You must think I'm some kind of nut, but it's just . . . I don't know, it's just that I can't take what's happening in the world. I can't take all these people getting shot. I can't take this war. I just thought we were supposed to be better than that. I really did believe we were on the dawn of a new age."

"The dawn of a new age?" asked Faith.

"You know, peace and love and . . ." My voice wavered. "Damn it," I said, wiping my faucet of a nose. "Damn it, I am not going to cry again. I am not going to spend one more minute thinking about assassinations or Vietnam or race riots or how we're polluting the world for our kids."

The heat bore down on us through the lacy canopy of oak leaves. Faith swatted a mosquito feeding on her arm.

"What about poverty?" she asked.

"Huh?"

"Well, you probably don't want to think about poverty either. Or the threat of nuclear war, for that matter."

I narrowed my eyes, regarding Faith, who looked back at me like a helpful, expectant sales-clerk.

"Thanks," I said, offering up a smile. "I

needed that. It's just so easy for me to get carried away sometimes."

"I admire that you do. There's a lot to get carried away about."

"Please. Don't get me started." I lifted the back of my Brillo-pad hair and fanned my neck. I was PO'd that she looked so cool and collected, and I guess it came out in my voice. "Don't you ever sweat?"

Faith smiled sweetly. "So now you want to pick a fight about perspiration?"

"Sorry," I said, thinking I just should just take a dive out of the tree house and end this whole miserable day. We sat for a while in silence. Then, trying to salvage some sort of normal conversation, I asked, "You've really never been in a tree house? I would have thought you grew up playing in a miniature plantation nestled in the boughs of your magnolia tree." I slowed my voice into a deep drawl and batted my eyelashes.

"You forget," said Faith, "I'm from Texas. Where we have ranches, not plantations."

"So you didn't have a ranch house built to scale in your giant cactus or mesquite or whatever kinds of trees you build tree houses in over in Texas?"

"Hey, look," said Faith, looking out the window. "I can see Audrey from here. Oh, my gosh — she's sunbathing *topless!*"

"She is not," I said, scrambling over to the window and poking my head out. "She wouldn't — oh, my god, she *is*."

Audrey was spread across the chaise longue like a studious centerfold, one hand pillowing her head, the other holding a book. Her long, pretty legs were crossed at the ankle, and one of her feet swayed back and forth, steady as a pendulum.

"Mommy, I'm ready!" said Flannery, emerging from the kitchen door in a swimsuit patterned with pink fish.

"Why don't you run over by yourself," I called down, "and I'll see if I can see you from the tree house."

"Okay!" said Flan. "Wave to me if you can!"

"I sure will, honey."

"You can't see my backyard from this tree house," said Faith as Flan disappeared around the house.

"Come on, Faith, I'm on watch. I can't leave my post."

We returned to our surveillance.

"Have you ever sunbathed topless?" asked Faith.

A funny gurgle, almost like a burp, rose in my throat.

"No, although it wouldn't matter. Everyone would think I was just an eleven-year-old boy whose liberal parents let him grow his hair out."

Faith whistled as she looked across the yards. "As the boys back in school used to say, she is *stacked*."

"I would have expected those southern boys to be more poetic than that — you know, saying things like 'Her breasts hung pendulous, like ripe grapefruit from a tree that begged to be picked.' "

"How many times do I have to tell you, Slip?" said Faith. "I'm Texan. Texan doesn't mean southern."

"Sure it does." I rearranged my legs under me. "There's the classic, belle-of-the ball southern —

you know, South Carolina, Virginia, Georgia, Alabama. Then there's Mississippi and Arkansas, the hardscrabble South. Then there's Louisiana, which is kind of a Gothic South onto itself. And finally we amble over to Oklahoma and Texas — the cowboy South."

Faith hiked up her accent. "I had no idea a Yankee could have such a deep grasp of the land of cotton."

She looked at me, all crisp and fresh in her lime plaid Bermudas and white sleeveless shirt, knotted above her navel, her hair neatly flipped and teased and ignoring the weather like mine could not. Faith and I had gotten to be pretty good friends, but sometimes I couldn't help feeling that while I'd been invited onto her property, there were fenced-off places I wasn't allowed to go.

Then again, not everyone is as comfortable as I am breaking down and bawling about the sorry state of the world.

"Oh, shoot," Faith said, looking back out the window. "She's gone inside."

"She probably needs to get some more suntan lotion," I said. "I imagine she goes through quite a lot."

"What would you say?" said Faith, laughing. "A bottle a breast?"

"No . . . a jug." I smiled. "A jug a jug."

"A tube a boob."

We laughed harder than the humor deserved, which goes to show you no matter your age, you're closer to adolescence than you think.

The sun bore down like a solar vise, mosquitoes were holding a jamboree in the tree house, and I didn't need a mirror to know that my frizzed-up hair was looking like something a car-load of clowns would covet. But as we talked about wonderfully inconsequential things, like what I should make for the book club dessert or what we thought about the Glen Campbell TV show, the bad mood I felt I'd been entombed in cracked, and holy breath of fresh air, that felt good.

"Hey, you perverts, I'm coming up."

Looking out the window, we saw Audrey begin her ascent up the tree trunk. She had put on her bikini top to make the trek from her backyard to my house, but there wasn't much decorum gained; her breasts spilled out of the bra cups like bundt cakes trying to fit into muffin tins.

When she crawled through the door, the small space got even smaller.

"You know, I could have you arrested for window-peeping," she said, and as she sat against the wall, her long tanned legs stretched across the width of the room.

"We weren't window-peeping —" began Faith.

"You were peeping through a window, weren't you?"

"Well, sure," I said, "but a person's allowed to look out their window. It's when you look through someone *else's* that you're actually window-peeping."

"I'll check that with my husband. My husband *the attorney*."

She glared at us for a couple of seconds, and then her mouth crooked up into a smile.

"Aren't you afraid," began Faith, "of other people . . . I mean people other than us seeing you without your clothes on?"

"Look, I like the feeling of the sun on my body, that's all. Usually I don't have to worry about nosy neighbors — old man McDermitt's nearly blind, and then there's my lilac hedges. How was I to know you were so desperate for kicks you'd climb a tree house just to eyeball me?"

"For your information," I said, "I was up here reading with Flan and —"

"Oh, you're not done yet either?" Audrey picked up the book we were to be discussing that evening.

"I'm just reviewing it," I said.

"I've only got about twenty pages left," said Audrey. "My mother-in-law took the boys to the kiddy pool, so I was sure I was going to have some time to finish it, but then" — here she put on an airy English accent — "my beautiful idyll was interrupted when I realized some perverts were spying on me."

"We *weren't* spying," reiterated Faith as Audrey, propelling herself with her hands and feet, scooted over to the window.

"Hey, you can see a lot from here! Look — there's Kari giving the mailman a hand job! Ha! Made you look," she said as we squeezed in beside her.

I would have rather seen Kari in a compromising position with the mailman than what I actually saw.

"Oh, no," I said, "there's Leslie Trottman."

"Who's Leslie Trottman?" asked Faith as the Pastel Queen (wearing a pink gingham dress and matching headband) strolled down the sidewalk.

"The neighborhood do-gooder," I said. "She lives across the alley from me."

"Oh, yeah — the one who's left all those leaflets in my door with a sorry-I-missed-you note attached. I guess I've never been home when she's come around."

"Lucky," said Audrey. "We hate her. Not only does she color-coordinate her accessories to her outfits, she collects for the Heart Fund, the Cancer Fund, UNICEF —"

"And makes the rest of us feel like a bunch of slobs for not doing our share."

"But she's the type of person who doesn't *want* anyone doing their share. Because it detracts from her doing *her* share. Remember how mad she got at you, Slip, when you went door-to-door campaigning for Kennedy?"

Audrey's words became a finger just ready to switch on another sobfest, but I clenched my jaw like a soldier and nodded.

"See, Leslie's above politics," I said. "She leaves the political fund-raising to her husband, Mr. Young Republican. Natural disasters are her specialty — she prays for natural disasters so she can get out and collect for the Red Cross."

"And she'll make sure you know how many blocks she's walked and how many blisters she's bandaged, but by golly, it's her privilege to do her part for those poor flood victims in Argentina —"

"Or the tragic earthquake victims in China —"

"Or the doomed hurricane victims in Haiti. Just find her a victim, and she's happy." Audrey picked up an acorn and lobbed it in the direction of Leslie Trottman, who, not having any luck in front, was approaching my back door.

"Viva las víctimas!" I said, and my thrown acorn hit its target: Leslie Trottman's sprayed

and shellacked hairdo.

"Ouch!"

We dove to the floor, but the pink-ginghamed do-gooder had figured out her assailants were up in the tree house.

"Flannery, I'm going to tell your mother."

"I hate a tattletale," I whispered. Grabbing a handful of acorns, I flung them over the top of the tree house.

"Ow! Watch it!"

Not about to let me fight the enemy alone, my comrades in arms grabbed handfuls of nuts and threw them over the plywood wall.

"Ow! Stop it!" cried Leslie as a shower of acorns rained down on her. "Damn it, Flannery, wait till I get my hands on you!"

"Did you just threaten my child?" I asked, rising from the giggling heap to stick my head out the window. "Threaten her *and* use the *d*-word?"

"Marjorie! If you think it's funny to throw walnuts at people, well, then you've got another thought coming."

"They're acorns, Leslie. Walnuts come from walnut trees. Acorns come from oaks."

"I don't care if they come from rosebushes! I could have lost an eye!"

Audrey's concerned and solicitous face joined mine at the window. "We would have helped you find it, Leslie."

"Honestly, don't you two have better things to do than assault people?" asked the irate fund-raiser, kicking aside the shrapnel of acorn shells.

"Actually, we thought you were one of those teenagers from your side of the block," said Audrey. "They've been spying on us all afternoon, just because we like to do a little topless sunbathing."

"What?" asked Leslie, echoing the same question I whispered as I sat back down with Faith.

Audrey unhooked her bikini bra, and before you could say "Free the mammaries," she stood up, rising above the four-foot walls and giving Leslie an unsolicited peep show.

"Oh, my stars," said Leslie in a hushed voice.

"Would you like to join us?" Audrey asked sociably. "The milkman and the mailman certainly seemed to have a good time up here."

Faith sat crouched with her hand over her mouth, laughing her head off.

"Say, how many people have you got up there?" asked Leslie.

"Along with the butcher, the baker, and the candlestick maker? Well, there's Slip and Faith —"

"They're not *topless*," said Leslie indignantly.

Faith told me later she had no idea what came over her, but suddenly she was unbuttoning her blouse and unhooking her bra and standing up, baring her breasts to the great and muggy world. Holy exposed flesh, I felt like I was looking up at the prow of one of those Viking ships with the nude Valkyries carved into it.

"Oh, my goodness," said Leslie, bringing one hand to her agitated brow to shade the sun. "This is obscene."

"No, it isn't," I said, wriggling out of my own top and double-A cup and jumping up. There we stood, as Leslie gaped up at us, looking like the illustrations of body types in a high school health book.

Then, like pioneers scoping out the unsettled

115

prairies ahead, we gazed ahead for one beautiful, unrehearsed moment until Leslie declared she didn't find what we were doing one bit funny.

We, on the other hand, did. We laughed as we watched her race around the house and to the sidewalk, her body as rigid and sanctimonious as the class tattletale I'd bet money she used to be. I could have spent the rest of the afternoon up in that overheated plywood playhouse, laughing like hyenas after a kill, but then Audrey saw her mother-in-law's car, returning with her boys, and Flannery came running across the street yelling something about a towel, and our responsibilities were the wet blanket thrown on that odd but definitely exhilarating party.

July 1968

Dear Mama,

I wish you could have seen us, flashing our titties to the world — it's something I could see you doing. Come to think of it, you did do it; remember, the new Baptist minister had come to MawMaw's house to try to recruit us and at first we were all being nice to him but then he pointed at me and said, "This young girl needs church more than anyone I've ever seen," and you said, "Oh, really?" and I think you were right to take offense, I mean he was pretty self-righteous, but to take so much offense that you'd pull up your shirt and say, "More than me, Pastor? 'Cause I've got an awful bad flashing habit I can't seem to get rid of."

Oh, Mama, thank you for letting me remember that — I'm laughing now, although I remember at the time being so shocked and

116

mad at you I could hardly breathe. MawMaw laughed, though — I knew she didn't want to, but she did. Good for her. I like to imagine how much we would have laughed if you hadn't drunk so much.

On the local news front . . . I went shopping with Slip downtown. It was sweltering outside, but the air-conditioning in Dayton's was cranked up — probably a sales tactic, as they've got all the fall clothes out. I felt sort of embarrassed for Slip — we had to shop for her clothes in the girls' department.

"If reincarnation is true," she said, looking into a three-way mirror, "I'm coming back with Brigitte Bardot's face and Wilt Chamberlain's height."

"Now there's a picture," I said.

I bought a midiskirt, but I think I'll take it back — Wade said, "What's the point of having good legs if you wear the kind of skirt my great-aunt Reevie wore?"

I finished painting the upstairs bathroom — in my swimsuit, it was so hot! — and I have to say, it'd take first place in any prettiest-bathroom contest. The walls are a dusky blue and the ceiling is navy — Merit came over and asked me how I came up with the idea for those colors. I told her I'd be happy to help her choose some paint for her own house.

"And speaking of paint, aren't you glad Audrey finally got the outside of her house painted? My gosh, I thought it was going to be condemned by the city!"

Merit laughed. "Oh, it wasn't that bad. I just don't think Audrey cares how her house looks."

"Well, that's obvious," I said. "Now, about your house — how about a nice crimson for the dining room or an apricot for your kitchen?"

"Oh, my gosh," Merit said, "Eric would never agree to anything like that! Off-white is about as bold as he'll go."

On the way downstairs, she stopped to admire the portrait I had taken of me and Wade and the kids, and she commented on how much Bonnie looks like me but how Beau didn't really look like either me or Wade, and then she asked, "Do you have any pictures of your parents? Maybe he takes after your mother or Dr. Reynolds."

I tell you, Mama, I almost s-h-you-know-what my pants.

"Most of my pictures are back in Texas, packed away in Wade's parents' closet," I said, the lie rolling off my tongue as if it had every right to. "I have just got to have them sent up here."

Merit nodded, as if that was a perfectly logical explanation.

It got me to thinking — maybe Beau does look like my father, but the sad thing is I'll never know. I remember asking you as a little girl if you had a picture of him, and you said, "I don't, and I'm glad I don't because I hope I never see his ugly chicken face again."

What'll I do when my kids climb on my lap and ask me about you, Mama? I'd like to think that the lies stop in my own house, but I've told Wade only a fraction of the truth, and by fraction I'm talking slivers, not chunks. It wasn't until a week before our wedding that I

118

confessed that not only was my daddy not a doctor, but I had no idea what he was, as I'd never met him before.

"Baby, I don't care about your family," he said, taking me in his arms. "I only care about you."

He makes it easy for me not to share stories about you, Mama; he gets so mad and upset at you anytime I tell him anything that I find myself defending you and resenting his anger. I can be mad at you, but Wade can't.

Anyway, you rarely come up in our conversations, and as much as his mother would like to pry information out of me, she's learned that when I say, "I don't want to talk about it," I really mean I don't want to talk about it. Still, I'm always leery of Patsy — it's so easy to get comfortable with her, I could find myself telling more than I want to.

Maybe I'll tell Beau and Bonnie about the woman you might have been, because who knows? In the right circumstances you could have been anyone or anything. Professor Primrose Reynolds. Senator Primrose Reynolds. Loving mother, devoted grandma. It could have happened . . . in the right circumstances.

I'm sorry,
Faith

August 1968

HOSTESS: KARI

BOOK: *Middlemarch* by George Eliot

REASON CHOSEN: "I wanted the first book I chose to be one they read in my mother's book club."

"I hereby call the Freesia Court Book Club to order."

"What?" said Slip. "Who authorized you to give us a name? Especially a name that sounds like an old ladies' garden club."

"I'm just trying it out," said Audrey. "Nothing's official."

"Who died and appointed you boss of the meeting anyway?"

"Well, Slip," said Audrey with a toss of her head, "our host seems otherwise occupied."

Kari made herself look up from the baby in her arms. "I'm sorry." To Merit, she asked, "Is she hungry?"

"Probably," said Merit of the baby who was making noises that sounded vaguely like a language student practicing a vowel sound.

"You're hungry, aren't you, Reni?" said Merit, and as she unbuttoned her blouse, the women watched her with eaglelike attention.

"Maybe I'll nurse with this next baby," said Slip.

Merit looked surprised. "You didn't with your other two?"

"I tried to with Flan, but it was such an *ordeal*. Really, it was as if I was torturing her — she'd scream and bawl. My doctor thought the problem was that I wasn't producing enough milk." Slip pulled at the darts of her seersucker blouse. "Another curse of being flat-chested — can't make our milk quota." She shrugged, but her eyes were sad. "After about a week I just gave up . . . and when Joe came along, I was too afraid to try again."

"My doctor told me I'd wear myself out if I tried to nurse the twins," said Faith. She didn't add that she had no intention of nursing anyway; that was something only the poor whites and Negroes back home did.

The baby drew back for a moment and sighed so rapturously that the women laughed. A thin arc of milk splashed onto her cheek, and she bobbed her head as she turned back to the nipple.

"Eric didn't want me to nurse," said Merit, so quietly that Kari asked, "What'd you say?"

Merit caressed Reni's perfectly round head with her hand. "I was saying Eric didn't want me to nurse. It was our first big fight."

"Why didn't he want you to nurse?" asked Slip.

Merit tilted her head, looking at the baby in her arms. "Oh, he had a bunch of reasons. He said modern science has perfected the best formula for babies, and I said, 'Well, modern science could have saved itself the trouble because the best formula is mother's milk *and it's free.'* And then he said that my breasts would lose their shape."

"And don't you worry about that?" asked Audrey. "I thought about nursing, but I didn't want to get all saggy." She laughed. "I mean, I *really* enjoy my breasts — and so does Paul."

Merit shook her head. "So do babies — I mean, that's really what they're there for, isn't it?"

Slip and Kari exchanged looks; strong opinions were not something one associated with Merit.

Her unwavering resolve had surprised Eric too, who usually had no trouble persuading his wife to his way of thinking.

"You can hit me if you want," Merit had said in the midst of their arguing, "but I am going to nurse my baby."

Eric had held his mouth in such a way that his lips turned white.

"I only hit you that once," he said, "and that was an accident."

Merit flinched, certain he was now going to demonstrate the difference between an accidental blow and a planned one, but instead Eric shook his head, his look of anger shifting slightly into one of disgust.

"Jesus Christ," he muttered, "go ahead and nurse her. What the hell do I care?"

Merit had had her baby right on schedule, but in the predawn hours of July 4, so her fear of labor didn't have to compete with her fear of fireworks. She was thrilled not only to have given birth but to have survived it, and her postlabor euphoria was marred only by the look — was it disappointment or disgust? — she had seen on Eric's face when he saw his hoped-for son was a girl. She tried to put that look out of her mind, but its memory had burned into her brain, and she knew that, like a scar, it would always be there.

"Oh, well," he had said with a jocular smile as he hoisted the beautiful and healthy eight-pound girl, "we'll try again next year, right, Mere?"

It was a fertile time for the book club; both Slip and Audrey were pregnant, and their due dates were only two weeks apart.

"So you still do have a sex life, eh, Slip?"

"I guess that's obvious, Audrey. What I *don't* have is your adolescent need to talk about it."

What no one knew — what Kari could hardly believe herself — was that her distraction that evening was caused not only by Merit's baby, but by the incredible, mind-boggling news that she might soon be a mother too.

It's not a dream, she told herself. *The next baby I hold might be mine.*

"Okay, you guys," said Audrey, realizing that if any discussion was going to take place, she'd have to initiate it. (What in the hell was wrong with Kari, and why did she look so *dazed?*) "Are we going to stare at Merit's boobs all night or are we going to talk about *Middlemarch?*" She lit a cigarette and waved out the match with a quick snap of her wrist. "Now, who wanted to take Dorothea aside and give her some free advice?"

Mary Jo sobbed so hard she threw up.

"Oh, sweetheart," said Kari, putting her arm around her niece, who was slumped over, hands on her knees.

"Oh, my God," said the receptionist, "is she puking in my ficus?"

"Could you get us a towel?" asked Kari.

"Because I have had that ficus since it was a seedling, and I do not appreciate it being puked on —"

"A wet towel," snapped Kari. "Please!"

After Mary Jo had cleaned herself up and Kari reassured the receptionist that her niece had only thrown up a little bit of liquid, and if anything, the plant would probably thrive with its new concentrate of nutrients, they followed Larry Rosenberg, a supposed lawyer (did he argue cases like that? wondered Kari, dressed as he was in an embroidered muslin shirt and embroidered bell-bottoms, his hair as long as Veronica Lake's in her prime) into his unlawyerlike office. Psychedelic posters covered the cheap paneled walls, and a thin stream of smoke rose from a stick of incense burning in a tiny filigree pagoda.

"Have a seat," said the lawyer, motioning to the green vinyl beanbag chairs surrounding the low polished driftwood slab that served as his conference table.

Seeing her aunt settle herself warily in the shifting chair, Mary Jo managed one of the few smiles Kari had seen since she had arrived.

Kari couldn't remember a stranger time in her life. Upon getting off the plane, she'd been met at the airport by her niece, who looked as if a shower, sleep, and general grooming were alien concepts.

"Mary Jo," Kari had said, feeling too much bone and too little flesh as she hugged the bedraggled girl, "what happened?"

"I'll tell you everything when we get to our appointment. But for now, let's not talk; just hold my hand the way you did when you'd take me downtown and we'd window-shop at Dayton's."

They had been silent on the shuttle bus ride to San Francisco ("It'll get us there just as fast as a taxi and costs about a third as much," said Mary Jo, and Kari was reminded of her niece's innate practicality). Her head pressed against the smudged window, Mary Jo had gazed out at the square little houses perched on hills in Daly City while Kari cast surreptitious looks at her. What had happened to her? When she had called her aunt with the unbelievable news that Kari needed to fly out to California *now*, that she'd tell her the specifics when she got to San Francisco, that she had found a baby that needed adopting, Mary Jo had sounded, well, *gleeful*. But now, as Kari replayed the conversation in her head, maybe Mary Jo hadn't sounded gleeful; maybe she had sounded manic. Had she been high? Was there a baby at all, or was this some elaborate, drug-addled plot to get her aunt out here? But for what reason? Kari played with the teardrop-shaped knob that fastened her purse, trying to ignore the pain that clenched her stomach. As soon as she'd heard the word *adoption*, all rationality had flown out of her head like a freed bird; sitting in a bus that smelled of cigarettes and Ben-Gay ointment, she'd wondered if what she was on was a wild-goose chase.

But whatever happens, she said to herself, looking again at her niece in her poncho with the matted fringe, *I'm glad I'm here for Mary Jo, because obviously Mary Jo needs me.*

"Well, then," said Larry the lawyer, settling into a beanbag chair himself, "how much have you told her?"

Mary Jo shook her head, her blond hair falling

over her face, obscuring it.

"I was . . . I thought . . ." A sob rose, ending whatever revelation she had planned on offering.

"Oh, dear," said Kari, trying to get up to comfort her niece, but the chair seemed to have swallowed her up. Larry the lawyer, more practiced in the ways of maneuvering off a bag stuffed with beans, was at Mary Jo's side in seconds, sitting on his haunches, stroking her hair (which needed a good washing), and telling her, "Everything's okay, man, everything's cool."

"Well, obviously everything is not cool," said Kari. Just because she was a slow burner didn't mean she didn't have a boiling point. "Now, I would like some answers. I would like to know why my niece can't seem to stop crying, why she called me and told me to come out here with little explanation except there was a baby available for adoption — since when has Mary Jo been in the adoption business? — and why I'm asking these questions of a lawyer who's got dirty toenails. I shouldn't even be seeing those, for crying out loud — lawyers should wear wing tips or brogans. And come to think of it, how do I even know you're a lawyer? Where's your law degree? There's nothing on these walls but posters with pictures and words that look like they're melting. And if I wanted to get a headache from incense, I'd have gone to a high mass!"

Her aunt's outburst was enough to stop Mary Jo from crying; this was tantamount to witnessing Old Faithful blow when you had no idea you were even in the vicinity of a geyser.

Larry the lawyer scratched his beard and chuckled.

126

"I'm not laughing at you," he said, seeing the look of wounded fury in the woman's eyes. "It's just that my mother is as hung up about me wearing sandals in the office as you are."

"I'm not *hung up*," Kari assured him. "I'm only —" She stopped, tears flooding her eyes. She didn't know what she was, other than confused, anxious, worried, and tired.

The beanbag chair Mary Jo was on made a squinching sound as she shifted her weight so that she was close enough to take Kari's hand.

"I'm sorry, Aunt Kari. I should have told you right away what was going on, but I —" She looked at Larry the lawyer, whose beard scratching was increasing in pace. "Well, the thing of it is, I had a baby three days ago, and I want you to raise her."

Kari blinked and swallowed. It was as if a hot wind had raced through her body, drying out all her bodily fluids. Her mouth fell open, but no words followed.

"For the longest time," said Mary Jo as tears slid from her eyes, "I just sort of blocked everything out. I thought about getting an abortion, but I just never could seem to go down to the clinic. I know it sounds stupid, but it was easier for me to pretend I wasn't pregnant . . . until I couldn't pretend anymore." She shook her head, not wanting to think about it.

"You didn't tell your parents?" asked Kari rhetorically, knowing that if she had, Kari would have heard about it.

"How could I?" Mary Jo scoffed. "I'm their National Merit Scholar! Their dean's list girl! I'm the one who got a full scholarship to Berkeley, remember?"

127

Kari nodded, knowing how proud her brother and sister-in-law were of their bright, beautiful daughter, who had never given them a shred of trouble.

"What about school?" asked Kari, so full of questions she found herself asking the ones that mattered to her least.

"I hardly showed before summer break," said Mary Jo. "Everyone thought I'd just put on a few pounds. I've spent the whole summer at Larry's in Marin County — he was nice enough to put me up — and, well, when school starts in two weeks, I plan to be back. That is . . . if everything works out."

"Meaning if I take the baby?"

As Mary Jo nodded, shivers coursed through Kari's body.

"What makes you think I will?"

"Oh, Kari, because it would make everything just perfect! Everyone knows how much you've wanted a baby! And I can't think of anyone who'd be a better mother!"

Kari sank back in the beanbag chair as if the wind had been knocked out of her.

"For how long?" she asked, the awful memory of Bettina being taken away from her rearing up.

"Forever," said Larry the lawyer. "That's where I come in. Mary Jo told me what happened to you before, Mrs. Nelson. The adoption papers I've prepared ensure that upon your signature, the baby is irrevocably yours."

"But what if you wanted her back?" Kari asked her niece. Hearing the utter poignancy in her voice, Larry the lawyer felt his heart thump in his chest.

"I would never do that to you," said Mary Jo.

"Look, I could have had this baby and given her up for adoption here and no one would ever have been the wiser. But as soon as she was born — and only until she was born did it all seem *real* — I had my answer: give her to Aunt Kari. Out of all the people in the world who want to be a mother, I know you'd be the best one."

"Oh, Mary Jo," said Kari, "what if you change your mind? Not now, but next year or the next?"

Mary Jo shook her head. "I won't, Aunt Kari. You've got to trust me on that. And by signing the papers, I give up all legal claim. Forever."

Larry the lawyer stood up and took something out of a file cabinet drawer.

"My law degree," he said, handing the framed document to Kari. "So you might have confidence in my ability to prepare a binding legal document."

Kari read the fancy calligraphy that stated Larry Rosenberg was a graduate, summa cum laude, of Stanford Law School.

"I'm not saying this guarantees I'm *not* an idiot," said Larry the lawyer, "but I give you my word: I'm not."

"What about your parents?" asked Kari, turning to her niece. "Why would they agree to let me raise their grandchild?"

"You're right — they wouldn't. And that's why we're not going to tell them."

The hot wind leached the saliva from her mouth.

"I know what you're thinking," Mary Jo continued. "How can we *not* tell them? But that's part of the deal. If you take the baby, my parents are never to know it's mine. Believe me, it's a lot less complicated this way."

Kari swallowed. "But . . . but Anders is my brother. And Sally and I are good friends. How can I keep something like this from them?"

A hardness settled on Mary Jo's small, fine features. "You can if you want the baby."

Kari pushed herself up — how could anyone *think*, sitting on that ridiculous mushy chair — and went to the window, pushing aside a plant that hung in a macramé holder. It swung like a pendulum, and one of its leaves drifted like a molted feather to the floor. Hoping to stop her trembling, Kari hugged her arms to her chest and watched the traffic below on Grant Street. It was absurd — there she was in the middle of Chinatown, in a law office that was decorated in Early Beanbag and reeked of incense, and she had just been offered the one thing she wanted most in the whole world: a baby.

She watched an old woman dressed in a white tunic and short, baggy pants navigate the streets on a rickety bicycle, its basket stuffed with vegetables. Two men stepped out of a restaurant, toothpicks jabbed between their teeth. A man in an apron stood behind a grocery window that displayed plucked chickens hanging from the ceiling like bizarre light fixtures. Finally she turned around.

"You do realize I'm forty years old? That means I'll be sixty when she's twenty."

"And eighty when she's forty," said Mary Jo with a shrug. "They're just numbers."

Kari raised an eyebrow. This was coming from someone of the generation who didn't trust anyone over the age of thirty?

"Well, what if something happens to me?"

Larry the lawyer stopped scratching his beard.

"I'm sure you'll have the foresight to make arrangements for whatever contingency occurs."

Kari offered a wan smile. "That's the first lawyerish thing you've said all day."

Larry smiled back. "Don't tell anyone."

"Where's the baby now?" asked Kari, feeling the enthusiasm rise in her like effervescence.

"Up at the house," said Larry. "My old lady's watching her."

"Well, then," said Kari, "what are we waiting for? Let's go see this baby girl."

"Oh, Aunt Kari!" said Mary Jo, embracing her.

"Wait a second," said Kari, drawing back, holding her niece by the elbows. "I haven't said yes yet. What if I did and your parents guessed where she came from? What if the baby looks just like you?"

Mary Jo, her beautiful, spirited niece, offered Kari a smile of such radiance that Kari automatically smiled back.

"I don't think they could see past what she's inherited from her father to see what she's inherited from me."

Kari frowned. "What do you mean?"

"Well, Tafadzwa's African, so the baby is too. Well, half."

The knots in Kari's stomach, which had been aching since the plane ride, pulled tighter.

Seeing Kari's face, Mary Jo wanted to kick herself. She had handled the whole thing so poorly, so secretively — who'd she think she was, the CIA? — and even though she knew her aunt was cool, to spring this on her now . . .

For an edge of a moment, Kari thought there was an earthquake, but then realized the seismic activity was coming from her kneecaps. She licked her lips — that dry internal wind was making everything arid again — as the image of a blond, blue-eyed baby disappeared like smoke.

"Well, what are we doing standing around here for?" she said finally. "Let's go see her."

As soon as Larry's "old lady," Andrea (who was all of twenty-five, as far as Kari could tell), handed Kari the baby, she felt the mighty tower of clear and rational thought topple against the weight of the infant in her arms. She *had* to take her, had to raise her, had to be the one for whom the baby would eventually press her lips together and say "Mama."

Mary Jo, Larry the lawyer, and Andrea had seated themselves on the couch draped with thin Indian fabric, sat with their hands in their laps, watching Kari rock the baby. Silence hung like the mist that had risen up in the bay, interrupted only by the creak of the rocking chair and the occasional jingle of the porch chimes when a breeze riffled through them.

The baby was beautiful. Her skin was the color of coffee when it's made caramel by extra cream, her lips were full and well shaped, her hair — well, of course what little hair was there would grow.

Kari's heart had hammered with such an intensity when she first held her that she was certain the noise would wake her, but the baby was a contented, sleeping bundle, and as it relaxed into her arms, so did the rhythm of Kari's heart.

"Have you named her?" she asked quietly, tearing herself away from the baby's face to look at Mary Jo.

Her niece shook her head. "We've just been calling her 'baby.' I wanted you to be able to name her."

"Larry," said Andrea, standing, "why don't we take a nice little walk?"

"Sure," said Larry, recognizing himself that it was time to make themselves scarce. "I could use a little exercise."

The bead curtain that separated the kitchen from the living room rattled as they passed through it.

"Mary Jo, what about the father?" said Kari in a low voice. "What does he say about this?"

Sighing, Mary Jo pulled off the ratty poncho, and for the first time Kari saw the soft roundness of her niece's stomach and breasts, so incongruous compared to her thin, bony frame.

"Aunt Kari, first of all, Taf assured me he was wearing a rubber. I know it's hard to believe that I couldn't tell, but we were both pretty stoned —"

"Do I really need to hear all this?"

Mary Jo shrugged. "I'm just telling the story, Aunt Kari. Now, do you want me to make it all nice and pretty, or do you want to tell me how it happened?"

Kari swallowed. "How it happened."

Mary Jo nodded, her fingers playing with a necklace that looked like it was made out of twine. "I was only with him a couple of times — Taf was *very* popular with the ladies. I mean, I practically had to take a number. We always had a good time together — he always had great dope — but I never thought it was more than what it was. I mean, I didn't love the guy or anything."

"But what does he think about you giving the baby to me?"

Mary Jo laughed, or tried to. "First of all, he doesn't know I had a baby, and second of all, he never will. He split about six months ago, back to Africa — Rhodesia, I think." She shrugged. "And I only know that because I ran into a mutual friend at the Fillmore last spring."

"Oh, Mary Jo," said Kari, shocked at her blitheness.

"Aunt Kari, it was just a fling. A fling I got caught in. But I'm trying to make the best of it."

The baby stirred in Kari's arms, her eyelids fluttering, her mouth pursing.

"Have you . . . have you been nursing her?"

Mary Jo blushed, shaking her head. "I thought that might complicate things. I've been taking pills to dry up my milk."

"Well, I think she needs a bottle now," Kari said as the baby began to softly whimper.

"Back in a flash," said Mary Jo, returning a few minutes later with a warm bottle.

Smiling as the baby earnestly began working on the nipple, Kari asked, "Are you absolutely positive that if I take her, you'll never want her back?"

"Auntie Kari," said Mary Jo, sitting on the old steamer trunk that served as a coffee table, "I don't want to be a mother now — I want to be a college student. I want to major in political science and maybe spend my senior year abroad. After that I want to travel even more, and then there's always the possibility of going on to grad school and then . . . oh, Aunt Kari, maybe someday I'll want to be a mother, but that day and that baby are far away!"

Color swarmed to her pale face, and Kari was struck by how hopeful and excited her niece looked. Mary Jo deserved to be hopeful and excited about her life, just as Kari deserved to be a mother. It was a realization as simple as that and one that made Kari say, "Did Larry bring the papers with him? Because I'd like to sign them now. That is, after I burp Julia."

"Julia?" asked Mary Jo, tears filling her blue eyes.

"After my MorMor — my mother's mother."

"Julia," whispered Mary Jo.

September 1968

HOSTESS: **AUDREY**

BOOK: *On the Road* by Jack Kerouac

REASON CHOSEN: "Because the first time I saw Kerouac's picture on the dust jacket, I thought, Now, there's one sexy-looking writer."

At three months, I had already gained twenty-two pounds.

"Are you planning to keep up this rate of growth?" asked my obstetrician as he looked over my chart.

"You talk to me as if I were an annuity or something," I said, not returning his benevolent doctor smile.

I was irritated by this man in whose hair I could see comb marks and whose earlobes were the longest — at least on a human being — I had ever seen.

Morning sickness wasn't a part of my pregnancy, but general overall irritation was. My doctor's dangling earlobes, the turgid garden watercolors that decorated his office (they *had* to have been painted by a relative or something — no one would hang those up because they *liked* them), the woman in the waiting room who wouldn't give up the current *Newsweek* when it was obvious I wanted to read it — *everything* irritated me.

This included, believe it or not, sex.

"Can't you at least fake it?" Paul asked the other night after a listless (okay, near-dead) performance by me in the sack.

"Paul, give me a break. I'm pregnant. I can't be a sexual dynamo every single night."

"Every single night," he said, slapping his pillow into shape. "We didn't have sex last night *or* the night before. It all starts adding up, Audrey."

"Adding up to what?" I asked, my voice rising to a level a screech owl might find attractive. "What exactly are you saying, Paul?"

If his pillow were steak, it would have been pulverized into ground beef by now.

"I'm not saying anything. I just wish you could be a little more attentive to me."

Attentive to me. The words were flies, late-bill notices, stockings with runs — tremendous irritants to my already bothered-beyond-belief self.

I hefted myself up against the headboard. "Hey, who's the pregnant one here? Who should be waited on and pampered and asked at least a dozen times a day, 'Is there anything I can get you, sweetheart?' "

"You're right," he said finally. "I apologize. Now how about a nice back rub?"

"Ooh, that sounds great."

I rolled over on my big stomach, anticipating his strong hands plying through the tight muscles of my back and shoulders. A minute or more passed.

I lifted my head. "Paul? The back rub?"

He turned to face me. "Yeah, I'm ready."

He smiled, and I realized that he was expecting to *get* a back rub, not give one.

I smiled back, appreciating his little joke. "Too bad," I said, offering a little joke of my own. "After the back rub, I was going to reward you with any sexual pleasure you requested, including certain acts that are still illegal in some states."

To Paul's credit, he laughed.

When he found out I was Lloyd LeMoyne's daughter, Paul's eyes had widened and his whistle sounded like the one they use in cartoons when someone's falling off a cliff.

"Geez, Audrey, I've been trying to get an internship there for the past two years."

Copenhaver, Kronfeld, Schmitz & LeMoyne was the kind of law firm whose partners attended galas and openings and $1,000-a-plate fundraising dinners, then read about their attendance or saw their photographs in the Chicago papers the following day. Everyone from Arabian sheiks with American business holdings to theatrical producers and former presidents used the legal services of CKS&L.

And when Paul learned I was Joseph Rippa's granddaughter, he had a fairly common response: *"Holy shit."*

My grandfather, the love of my life as a child, was a mechanical engineer whose inventions have helped make the industrial world go round. He was also the guy who made sure I was never a poor little rich girl.

"Money's just a ticket, Bella," he used to tell me, "and it does let you into a lot of places and lets you do a lot of things — but it's not as redeemable as people think it is. You've heard the saying that money can't buy happiness?"

I nodded.

"Well, you also can't use it to make someone love you or to buy a better personality."

"So the lady you're seeing would like you if you didn't have any money?"

Poppie's bristly eyebrows formed an awning over his eyes as he narrowed them. "What's your mother been saying now?"

"That Miss Dermott's a gold digger."

He shrugged, and we laughed. My mother, his daughter, was never happy with his choice of companions.

"She probably is," said Poppie, who'd never married after my grandmother died. "But she's a good dancer and gets my jokes." He stroked my hair. "And I'll let you in on a little secret, Bella — money is a ticket for old men like me to pretend they're not so old."

So it hasn't been easy for a guy like Paul — he's the first one in his family to graduate from college, let alone law school — to be married to a girl like me. I know he likes being with such a prestigious firm as CKS&L, but I also know he resents me for not allowing him to prove he could have done just as well without being married to the daughter of the company's boss (thank goodness Daddy's in the Chicago office; at least he's not under his *physical* shadow).

Paul's still got that little boy, puffed-out-chest, show-off quality ("Watch me! Look what I can do!"), a quality I love and one that drew me to him. You'd think my parents would understand and respect his need to prove himself, but Lloyd

139

and Delores LeMoyne are the type who think money is a ticket that can and should buy our devotion, sense of obligation, obedience, blah blah blah. For instance, they offered to buy us a house about three times the size of this one with a backyard that ran into our own private lake, for cripes' sake, but Paul turned them down, wanting to buy what we could afford on his salary. I was thrilled by his strength of character, and by the reduction in square footage, which meant fewer rooms to keep clean.

"Life is like a bowl of spaghetti, Bella: it's still good even when it's all tangled up."

This hokey but nevertheless true adage of my grandfather's popped into my head while I sat in a church pew with Faith and Merit, watching Kari's baby get baptized. Merit was holding Reni, who not only was a beautiful baby but knew how to behave in church — which was more than I could say for myself. I had forgotten to wear a slip under my wool dress, and the itching was driving me nuts. As I scratched myself yet again I thought of how church for me was like a wool dress without a slip — one big irritant that made me squirm.

It was the ceremony we were assembled for and not the pastor's droning sermon that was making me reflective; I was pregnant; Merit had just had a baby; Slip, sitting in the front row with Kari, was pregnant; and Kari herself was about to offer up her new baby to God (if that's what baptism was). As far as I knew, Faith wasn't pregnant, but I stole a glance at her lap anyway, half expecting to see a slight bulge there. But no, Faith was flat-stomached in a way that has never been a part of my body structure.

I do feel birth is miraculous, but it's my belief that to explain all the miracles of nature, someone — some *being* — had to be invented to take all the credit. Human beings like explanations, and God is a good explanation for unexplainable things.

I stared at the old woman ahead of me and the brown velvet hat she wore, wondering what decade she had dug it out of. Its shape was between a pillbox and a cloche, and a smattering of dried-up silk leaves and flowers hung tenaciously from one side. It was the first time I'd had a desire to weed a hat.

The words of the minister were an indistinguishable blur, and I remembered the time I had told my mother, "This is boring — why do we even have to go to church?"

"Because that's what good families do," had been my mother's answer. Not for the first time, I'd yearned to be a member of a bad family.

I scratched my itchy thigh with a claw of curled-up fingers and looked up to see Faith's mouth pursed — in amusement or impatience, I couldn't tell. She was dressed in wool too — a rust dress that looked very autumnal and harvesty — but apparently she hadn't forgotten her slip, because I had not seen her scratch or squirm once. Furrowing my brow, in an effort to concentrate, I looked at Kari.

I had hardly expected the new mother to come to book club last week, but not only had she come, she'd read the book.

"I thought you'd be all worn out from two a.m. feedings," I said, taking Julia in my arms.

"I thought I would be too," said Kari, taking off her raincoat, "but honestly, I can't remember the last time I've had this much energy. I've read three other books beside this one since Julia came, plus I repapered my bathroom."

"She also sewed Flannery's costume for Halloween," said Slip. "Five and a half weeks before Halloween, and Flan's already got her costume — that's a first."

"That sort of behavior could make you very unpopular with your peers," I said. "Are you on something?"

"I'm high on motherhood," said Kari, laughing, and really, she had that glow they usually ascribe to brides.

What I had come to love about book club (besides the fabulous desserts and free liquor) was how in hearing so many opinions about the same book, your own opinion expanded, as if you'd read the book several times instead of just once. Only Merit had yet to offer an opinion that made me think, *Wow, I never thought of that,* and if we'd been some mean and petty sorority forced to blackball anyone, it would've been her. Fortunately, we could leave the meanness and pettiness to the sororities (where it rightfully belonged); we were a more egalitarian group. And truthfully, I liked Merit, even if I didn't think she was much of a reader (or a cook — whatever she brought to the potlucks I had learned to ignore). She brought eagerness to the group, which was a notch up from our own enthusiasm — we were all happy to belong, but Merit seemed thrilled, the way Bryan is when Davey has friends over and includes him in their big-boy play. For whatever reasons, Merit seemed to really need this club.

Another thing I really loved (did I mention the

brownies we demanded Kari always bring, and the booze?) was that our discussions never followed a single tack. One sentence could lead to a discussion of a whole new topic, which then would branch into another one. For instance, I was talking about how *On the Road* had inspired me and Jane Wellhaven (the smartest girl in my English lit class — besides me) to hitchhike to Florida during spring break. We'd both told our parents separate lies, and they probably would never have found out if Jane hadn't called hers tearfully to ask for train fare home, as all our money had been stolen in a truck stop outside Chattanooga, Tennessee.

We'd been the opposite of dharma bums on that train back to Chicago — two rich girls who relied on their parents' money instead of their wits — and we sulked in the club car, fugitives from the fugitive world.

It was only when we'd gotten into the dining car and ordered two big steaks that we began to think that maybe we were less the opposite of hip than victims done in by a misogynist society.

"Sure," I'd said, spearing a big bloody piece of meat with my fork, "it'd be easy to hit the road if the road weren't so full of degenerates."

"Exactly," Jane had said. "I guess we're lucky to get off with just a little theft. It could have been a lot worse."

"When you're a girl and you're hitchhiking, every ride is a potential rapist."

Jane had nodded and licked a spot of sour cream off her upper lip. "You think Jack Kerouac or Neal Cassady ever had to worry about that? *No.*"

"So that's what I did the first time I read it," I

143

told the book club. "This time I wasn't inspired so much to hit the road as to wonder about the one I'm on now."

"What do you mean?" asked Merit in her awed-child way.

"I mean," I said, trying not to let the irritation show in my voice, "that it made me wonder what I'd be doing if I hadn't married and had kids."

"Gosh, I'm scared to even think about that," said Merit, rubbing her arms as if she were cold.

"So you're saying," said Slip, "that the novel reminded you of the poem." She looked around to see if any of us were following her and then said, "*On the Road* . . . 'The Road Not Taken.' "

"When you think about it," I said, "any book can remind you of that poem. That's the beauty of a book — through its characters, you can imagine your life *outside* your life."

"But I mean this book in particular," said Slip impatiently. "This is a hit-you-over-the-head-look-how-different-our-world-is-from-yours kind of book."

"I agree," whispered Kari, so as to not wake the slumbering baby in her arms. "With both of you. I always love reading about people with lives unlike mine because I get to live in their world for a while. But the funny thing about reading *On the Road* is that I didn't feel their world was so alien . . . probably because I'm an outlaw too."

"If you're an outlaw," said Faith, "then I'm Granny Clampett."

We all laughed, but then Slip said, "I'm with Kari. I feel like an outlaw too."

"Well, you are," said Merit earnestly. "You get arrested on picket lines."

"Actually, I've never been arrested," said Slip, and I thought I heard regret in her voice. "But what I mean is that there are outlaws inside all of us — ready to break rules that need to be broken."

"Right," I said. "But society doesn't want its wives and mothers and PTA presidents to be outlaws, so most of the time we repress that voice that tells us to break rules, to —"

"Be who we really are," said Slip, almost shouting. Slip was like the Aimee Semple McPherson of feminism, getting all excited when she thought one of her congregants was seeing the light.

"That's not what I meant," said Kari, interrupting our fervor. "I think I know what you mean, but I really am an outlaw because I have, as the clerk in Three Sisters told me today, committed a crime: the crime of interracial breeding."

Slip was the first to recover her voice. "She didn't. Tell me she didn't say that."

Kari nodded, biting her lip.

"I hope you decked her," I said.

Kari laid the baby on the couch next to her, as if she didn't want the child to feel her rage.

"I would have liked to," she said, blinking her summer-blue eyes, "but I was holding Julia. So instead I said, 'If you believe in God, then you should know He's ashamed of you,' and then I said, 'I'd like to see your manager, please.' "

"What'd she say?" Faith asked.

"She said with this sneer, 'I am the manager,' and I said, 'Oh, in that case be advised that you've just lost a customer, because I don't shop in such an ignorant atmosphere.' "

"Oh, Kari," breathed Merit, "you said that? That was so . . . brave."

Kari shook her head. "It's nothing you wouldn't do — what any mother wouldn't do." She dabbed at her nose with the crook of her finger. "I was shopping for a dress to wear to Julia's baptism — it was our first shopping outing together — and then this awful woman had to —" Her words were broken with a little gasp followed by a surprising lusty sob, which woke up her baby and Merit's, sleeping in a little carryall on the floor, and so while mothers comforted babies, I got up to bring out the sandwiches, which in deference to the book were wrapped up in bandannas attached to sticks, like hobo packs.

Using one of those little pencils that hung on the back of the pew next to the pledge cards, I scratched the back of my leg, hoping I wouldn't snag my nylons.

Along with the minister, Kari and Slip, holding Julia, stood at the baptismal font, while the congregation sang "Children of the Heavenly Father." It was a beautiful song that brought tears to my eyes, even as I didn't believe any of the words:

Children of the Heavenly Father
Safely in his bosom gather . . .

Were that we could gather in anyone's bosom safely!

I guess I didn't notice when I lost my faith — I don't know that you can lose something you're not sure you ever had. My grandfather had a tremendous faith, which, unlike my mother's, wasn't tied up with any particular church.

"I believe God can be found just as easily in a bowling alley as in a pew," he said once during a family dinner.

"Really?" I asked, delighted as a picture of Jesus ready to roll a strike came into my head.

"Audrey, your grandfather's just trying to be funny," said my mother, and if looks could kill, he would have slumped forward into his soup bowl.

Grandpa winked at me, and I understood his decision not to get into an argument with my mother. She always won, and if she didn't, she'd make sure you were miserable in your victory.

Still, knowing that the person I loved most in the world believed in God didn't help my own belief, not even after He paid me a particular visit.

I guess even with the most enthusiastic letter of recommendation, faith won't come to you if you're not ready to meet faith.

I stole a look at my pewmate. What would it be like having the same name as something so valued by so many?

I'd known a girl named Joy in high school; her prevailing mood was morose bordering on suicidal, so I guess she didn't feel compelled to live up to her name. If Faith was an atheist, would she change her name because it so totally misrepresented her? Maybe Joy had changed her name to something more appropriate, like Angst or Depressa.

When the song ended and Faith closed her hymnal with a little thump, I looked toward the front of the church, scolding myself to stop daydreaming and start paying attention.

Kari's relatives, the majority of them towheaded, sat in the front row. Knowing how close she was to them, I wondered why she hadn't chosen one of them to be Julia's godmother.

But if anything ever happened to Kari, Slip would do a great job bringing Julia up; she was as fierce in motherhood as she was in everything else. My brother, Lewis, was my oldest son's godfather, and God forbid he should ever be called upon to fulfill that role. Lewis keeps a sign on his apartment door that says Le Bachelor Pad — Open All Night, and he has a black book the size of an unabridged dictionary. Paul's sister is Bryan's godmother — she's a nice woman, but she's already got four kids of her own. I hadn't given much thought to whom the new baby's godparent will be; maybe it's good to pick ones you wouldn't want raising your child, because it makes you more determined not to kick the bucket till they're fully grown.

Julia expressed her outrage when she felt water on her head, and you could just feel the congregation smiling. I found I was smiling too, and that irritated me — I didn't want to be carried along in the emotion of a rite I didn't even believe in.

I was planning to clear out right after the ceremony, but then Kari came up to us and told us there was cake and coffee in the undercroft (whatever an undercroft is). I'm not one to turn down free sugar and caffeine, so I followed the rest of the opiated masses downstairs. I was right behind Merit when she suddenly lost her footing and tumbled. She managed to grab on to the coatrack, breaking her fall, but not before she bashed her shoulder against the wall.

"Merit, are you all right?" I asked.

"Fine," she said, rubbing her shoulder. "Just clumsy is all."

"You are not," said Faith, and it was true — you could tell by the way Merit moved that she probably knew how to cut up a dance floor.

As we stood in line waiting for our white-frosted cake and church-basement coffee, I half listened to Faith and Merit talk with the woman in the brown velvet hat about the weather and what were the chances of this nice Indian summer lasting. What occupied my thoughts more than their polite conversation was the picture of Merit tripping. It was the oddest thing; it had looked like a staged fall, the kind an old comic makes to get a laugh. And another funny thing was, she had given Reni to Faith. Two seconds after her baby was safe in Faith's arms, Merit tripped.

Digging my fingernails into the small of my back and vowing to forevermore let sheep keep their damn itchy wool on their own backs, I shook my head at my silliness. But that's a mystery reader for you — always hoping to fall into a real one.

October 1968

HOSTESS: **FAITH**
BOOK: *Main Street* by Sinclair Lewis
REASON CHOSEN: "I thought it might help me to understand Minnesota more."

Bonnie wasn't even two yet and had already potty-trained herself.

"Ina big girl," she reminded her mother as she sat on the toilet, her feet dangling a foot off the ground, pigeon-toed.

"Yes, you are," Faith agreed, calling Beau in, as she always did, so that he might catch on that there was another receptacle, other than his diapers, to do his business in.

Beau stood by the sink, thumb in his mouth, watching his sister, but when his mama asked if he wanted to try going in the toilet like a big boy, he widened his eyes and shook his head, as if declining a spanking.

"Don't worry," said Wade's mother, coming in to stand in the bathroom's threshold. "Wade wasn't trained until he was nearly three. It's somethin' about little boys, I think."

Wade's parents had taken advantage of the airlines' family-flies-free policy and had come up for a short visit before they flew to Idaho to attend the retirement party of Dex's brother, Lex (twins ran in Wade's family).

"If you're sure we'll be no imposition," Wade's mother Patsy had asked over the phone.

"None at all," Faith had said, even as her heart sped up. "We'd love to see you, and the kids'll be over the moon."

"Oh, I'll bet they don't even remember their grammy," said Patsy with a little pout in her voice.

"They were just asking about you yesterday," Faith had answered, and immediately grimaced at her lie. Twenty-one-month-olds don't remember grandparents they haven't seen for almost a year. "See, we keep your and Dex's picture on the mantel, and yesterday Bonnie pointed at it and said, 'There's Grammy and Grandpa!'" *Oh, great,* thought Faith, *now I'll have to remember to put their picture on the mantel before they come.*

"We sure wished y'all lived down the block like Carleen," Patsy had said. "We hate missing out on the babies growing up."

"Well, we'll make sure you spend lots of time with them while you're here," Faith had said soothingly, she who had always felt Patsy blamed her and not Wade's job for taking her precious son away from the bosom of his family.

After hanging up the phone, she'd gone straight to the broom closet to get the mop. Her in-laws weren't due for another week, by which time Faith would have mopped the floor a dozen times.

"Okay," said Patsy now, bending over, hands on knees, to better talk to her grandson. "If you're not gonna go pee-pee in the potty for us, let's go get our jackets on and get some air."

Beau burst into tears; he wasn't used to this

151

lady with the swirly blond hair and tanned face who always spoke to him in such a loud bossy voice.

"Go 'side!" said Bonnie. "Me wanna go 'side!"

"See," said Patsy with a big encouraging grin, "your sissie thinks it'll be fun!"

Not caring what his sister thought might be fun, Beau wailed and rushed to his mother, grabbing her legs as if they were guardrails separating him from a thousand-foot drop.

"This is a pretty town," said Patsy as they walked along the creek, on a tarred pathway littered with red, maroon, gold, and yellow leaves. "I really had no idea a northern city could be so pretty. Beau, honey, don't put that in your mouth."

Beau took the twig out of his mouth, waited for a moment, and put it back in again.

"Bonnie, honey, don't run so far ahead of us! My land," said Patsy, "that girl's gonna be a track star, mark my words. Now, is this typical weather for October or should it be snowing by now?"

"Well, this is my first October here too," Faith reminded her. "But I think it's a little early for snow, even here." She smiled and watched as Beau threw down his teething twig and galloped after his sister.

Wade and his father, fishing partners from way back, had decided to try their luck on the Mississippi ("The *Mississippi?*" Patsy had said. "I had no idea the Mississippi came up this far!"), and as they headed out the door, Wade whispered a guilty apology to Faith for leaving her alone with his mother.

"Go on now, Wade," said Faith, giving him a gentle elbow in the side. "I like your mother. We'll have a good time."

"Yeah, but she'll talk your ear off."

She did, but Faith didn't mind; rather, it lightened her own load. In a conversation with Patsy Owens, all Faith had to do was listen.

"Do you think Bonnie's gonna stay taller than Beau?" asked the twins' grandmother as they stood looking up at a huge black crow nagging its neighbors from its perch in an elm tree. "And I do wish they could change hair — Beau's got the prettiest curls I have ever seen and there's poor Bonnie, her hair straight as a stick. Isn't it funny how they came out the same time and yet are so different?"

"Mmm-hmmm," Faith said.

Sensing she might have been critical of her grandchildren, Patsy added hastily, " 'Course, you can't find two cuter kids, so I suppose it doesn't matter what their hair looks like." She stopped and looked at the creek. "Say, listen to this. It's coming back to me: 'By the shores of Gitchee Gumee / by the shining big sea waters / stood the wigwam of Nokomis / daughter of the moon, Nokomis.' " Patsy's coral-pink lips split into a smile. "That's about this place, isn't it? That lake we had our little picnic by yesterday, that was Nokomis, wasn't it?"

Faith nodded.

"My goodness, I don't know the last time I saw a place that had a poem written about it. 'Course, Dex and I visit the Alamo about once a year, and there've been movies about that . . . but still, a poem means more, don't you think? And imagine me remembering that all those years. I can still see myself in my little blue sailor dress, reciting it to the entire assembly. Who wrote it again? Walter Whitman or William Wordsmith or —"

"Longfellow," said Faith. "Henry Wadsworth Longfellow. In fact, there's a library here named after him — it's built to look like his house back east. Would you like to go there?"

Patsy shrugged. "Where I'd really like to go is a bakery. I have a hankerin' for a chocolate-covered doughnut like all get-out."

"That does sound good," agreed Faith. "There's one just a couple of blocks away. We could walk . . . only we might wind up carrying the twins."

"I could use the exercise," said Patsy, who did have a nice trim figure. Cupping her hands around her mouth, she hollered, "Bonnie, Beau — guess who's gonna buy your sweet selves a doughnut!" She laughed as the twins ran toward them, shouting about doughnuts, and then, looking thoughtful, said, "Longfellow. I reckon he must have had some pretty tall ancestors to get that as the family name."

Sitting in a booth in the bakery, the air warmed and softened by the smells of baking bread and cinnamon and the frosted Danishes that had just been placed in the display case on a white-papered tray, Faith felt a calm like a liniment work its way into her body. She didn't realize how tense she usually held her body until it was relaxed, and the sensation always surprised her; she felt like a prison guard who had successfully completed her watch and, at least for the time being, no convict had escaped.

The twins were sitting next to each other, their

little legs tucked under them, trying to get whatever chocolate that wasn't smeared on their faces into their mouths. Patsy, with crooked fingers, tore off little pieces of her glazed doughnut, and just as she brought it to her mouth, she issued a satisfied "mmm, mmm, mmm."

"Mmm, mmm, mmm," mimicked Beau, pulling apart a piece of his doughnut.

"Why, you little dickens!" laughed his grandmother. "Are you copying your old grandma?"

"Mmm, mmm, mmm!" said Bonnie, joining in on the game.

"You too?" said Patsy, as if wounded.

"Mmm, mmm, mmm!" answered the twins.

Smiling, Faith got up and poured herself a cup of coffee from the urn on a stand by the cash register. One thing the Yankees got right was coffee: pay for a cup and the following thirty refills were free.

"Oh, my gosh," said Faith.

"Beg your pardon?" said a young man with long curly hair.

"Your . . . your newspaper," said Faith, nodding to the folded rectangle tucked in the crook of his arm. "That's Jack Kerouac's picture. In the obituary section. We just read his book in our book club." Faith felt herself flush. Why was she raving on, and what could this young man possibly care?

But he did. Nodding, he bunched up his mouth and then said, "We lost a good one." He held out the newspaper. "You want to take it home?"

"Oh, no, thanks. I've got it at home. I just haven't had a chance to read it."

Looking over at the twins, the man smiled and

155

said, "I guess you're pretty busy."

"Who was that?" asked Patsy as Faith sat down, wincing as the coffee sloshed over the edge of the cup. "Or should I say, *what* was that?"

"Huh?" said Faith, pressing a napkin onto the spilled coffee on the tabletop.

"Well, is that a boy or a girl? Look at that hair — and those shoes. My goodness, I don't believe I have ever seen an uglier pair of shoes in my life."

"It's a boy," said Faith. "And those are Earth Shoes. They're supposed to be really good for your feet."

"They better be, 'cause they sure ain't good for your eyes! Why would anyone want to wear shoes that look like big turds? Excuse my French. And why would a grown man wear a necklace? Halloween ain't here for another week!"

"Shh, he'll hear you," said Faith, leaning over the table to wipe a chocolate mustache off Beau's face.

"Well, honestly," said Patsy in a stage whisper, "I just don't know why boys don't dress like boys and girls don't dress like girls. I mean, what's the point?"

The young man with the shoulder-length hair saluted Faith with his white paper bag as he walked toward the door.

"Have a good one," he said.

She nodded.

"Have a good what?" asked Patsy, but Faith was too surprised by the people coming in to answer her.

"Hey, Kari! Hey, Slip!" She greeted her

friends with a big smile even as she felt a little twist in her chest. She didn't like feeling left out.

"Joe!" said Bonnie.

"Show!" said Beau.

Slip's son raced over to the booth, followed by his mother and Kari, whose baby was buttoned up inside her mother's jacket, her little head framed by corduroy lapels.

As the children scampered away to the display case, Faith introduced her mother-in-law to her friends, and even though she extended an invitation to join them, she was glad when they said they couldn't.

"We're going to see Flannery in a little program she's in at school," said Slip. "I volunteered to pick up some cookies."

"Oh," said Faith, the familiar feelings of being left out and jealousy twisting again inside her. Why hadn't Slip invited her to see the program?

"Say, as long as I'm here, maybe I should get something for book club," said Slip. "What do you need, Faith?"

"Huh?" asked Faith, and a second before Slip reminded her, a bell of realization clanged in her head: she was hosting book club tonight.

"Maybe we should postpone it," said Kari, seeing a look akin to panic in Faith's eyes, "what with your in-laws here and all."

"Don't cancel anything on my account!" said Patsy. "Wade and his daddy — my husband, Dex — went fishing, and their usual pattern is to stay out until Johnny Carson comes on — y'all get Johnny Carson here, don't you? Anyway, Faith and I sure don't have anything planned tonight, as far as I know. So come on by, it sounds fun — I'll make my famous butterscotch pie and

157

we can all get to know one another."

Walking home, as the twins kicked up the fallen leaves with a violent glee and Patsy chattered on about God knows what, Faith fumed.

She kept a meticulous calendar; the more organized she was, the more in control she felt, and that she could forget about book club baffled her. She certainly would have postponed it — how could she prepare the way she liked to in just a few hours? — but *no,* her big-mouthed mother-in-law thought it sounded *fun.*

"So how did she wind up with that little pickaninny?"

Patsy's words punctured Faith's thoughts.

"What did you say?"

Her mother-in-law smiled her brightest smile.

"Well, your friend. My gosh, she's as fair as Heidi, and I —"

"Patsy, no one says *pickaninny* anymore," said Faith, her voice sharp.

The older woman's eyes filled with tears, and she drew her mouth in until her lips completely disappeared.

"Mommy, look!" shouted Bonnie.

"Yes, honey," said Faith absently, not seeing the chipmunk that had zipped across the leaves and into a hole in the ground.

"I'm sorry if I offended you," said Patsy, whose girlish little chin was quivering. "I know Negroes don't like certain terms these days — Lord, they don't even like *Negroes.* What is it now, *blacks?* Excuse me if I'm not up on all the current lingo."

"*Pickaninny* has never been the current lingo. That phrase went out with carpetbaggers and Reconstruction."

Patsy's mouth was a thin coral line again, and Faith was glad that she had been able to quiet her. As they walked the rest of the way home in the warm autumn sun, the only voices heard were Bonnie's and Beau's.

Faith managed to set a theme table (as much as she liked time to prepare, she was the type of person who was good in a pinch, able to create atmosphere with a pair of scissors and some paper, to whip up soufflés to someone else's scrambled eggs): she placed torn-up grass in the center of the table, and during the twins' nap time, while Patsy was making her famous butterscotch pie, she made a Main Street, drawing a row of buildings on a shoe box and making several other storefronts out of stiff white paper. She taped a sign up in the living room that read, GOPHER PRAIRIE, POPULATION: IT SURE FEELS SMALL.

When each member of the book club arrived, Faith handed her an apron, explaining that the strings represented constraints.

"Ooh, that's deep, Faith," laughed Audrey, tying the apron around her thickening waist. "But I'm surprised you didn't rent straitjackets."

It was a good meeting. The discussion was rousing (surprisingly, Kari thought Carol was pathetic, whereas Audrey thought she was "sort of a hero"), Patsy's butterscotch pie was a hit, and Merit actually made cookies that weren't burned and didn't threaten the integrity of anyone's molars.

Patsy, not having read *Main Street*, was quiet during the discussion, but she did exactly what

159

she was supposed to do during social hour: she socialized.

"Oh, yes," she told the group, "I was raised in Georgia — on a peach farm, no less — but when Dex and me got married, he dragged me off to Texas. In fact, he likes to tell everybody his bride was a southern belle, but his wife's a cowgirl. And it's true — I wear cowboy boots more'n I wear heels!"

"So what did you think of Faith when Wade brought her home?" asked Audrey, lighting a cigarette now that she had finished her second piece of pie.

"Well, I just loved her right away, of course," said Patsy, raising her brown penciled brows as she smiled at Faith. "Wade brought us to watch her cheerlead at a big football game — it was homecoming, wasn't it, Faith? — and if there's ever been a cuter girl in a short pleated skirt and letter sweater, I'd like to know about her."

"Merit," said Faith, "more pie?"

Merit held her hands up as if she were being held at gunpoint. "Oh, I couldn't. I'm stuffed."

"Faith," said Audrey with a smile, "maybe you'd like to show us one of your cheers."

"Maybe I wouldn't," said Faith, pushing a smile of her own on her face. "Now, would anyone like another drink? More coffee?"

"What about her wedding?" asked Slip. "Did the minister really chase after the maid of honor at the wedding reception?"

"I never said that," said Faith, her face red.

Patsy stared at her daughter-in-law for a moment. "Well, you wouldn't have been lyin'." Shaking her head, she rolled her eyes. "Chased her like a mad dog! Dex finally threw 'im into the car and drove him home — I heard later he ran off with the children's choir director!"

"Surely someone wants more coffee," said Faith, her voice almost a plea.

"So," said Merit, "were you there when Faith's father — Faith, what's your maiden name again?"

"Reynolds," said Faith, as defeated as a GI giving his name, rank, and serial number to an enemy interrogator.

"Were you still there when the best man fell on the dance floor and broke his wrist and Dr. Reynolds set it with a table napkin?"

Patsy leveled her stare at Faith, whose face looked as if all the blood in her body were pooling there, and then at Merit (it was her firmly held belief that southern women were the prettiest in the country, but this gal sure shook that belief).

"No, we had already left by then," she said after a moment. "Lady Bird had invited us to the ranch the next day, and we wanted to get rested up for that."

"Lady Bird *Johnson?*" chorused the women.

Patsy shrugged. "We were only there that once. They were throwing a party for Dex's partner's brother — he and Lyndon were good friends from way back — and we somehow finagled an invitation."

After everyone made their impressed exclamations, Audrey said, "You know what they say about Mr. Johnson's johnson, don't you? It's *huge.*"

"Audrey!" said Merit, who took a beat longer than the others to understand what Audrey was talking about. "He's our president! Show a little respect!"

Slip volunteered to help clean up, but Pasty said no, that's what mothers-in-law were for, and why didn't she run along and get back to her husband and children.

"I really enjoyed meeting y'all," she said, seeing Slip to the door. "I'd start a book club of my own, only I'm not that big a fan of fiction."

Faith felt her last word as if it were a dart thrown at her. She began emptying ashtrays and stacking cups, taking precise care not to look at her mother-in-law.

"Pee-yew," said Patsy, standing by the staircase, waving the air, "it's as smoky as a tavern in here."

Torn between gratitude toward Patsy for covering for her and shame that she had forced her to, Faith wanted to run to her mother-in-law and hug her, but she only nodded and, gripping a cluster of dirty glasses with curled fingers, went into the kitchen.

Patsy was at the sink a minute later with her own collection of lipstick-smeared cups and crumb-splotched plates.

"Faith, honey," she said as Faith squirted dishwashing liquid into a stream of water, "we need to have a talk."

Biting the inside of her mouth, Faith watched the soapy water rise in the sink.

"Listen, I know you've had a hard life —"

"You don't know the half of it!" It was true; she wouldn't, even if Wade had repeated verbatim what Faith had told him about her past.

"I know your daddy wasn't a doctor," Patsy said softly.

Shame heated the tears that sprang to Faith's eyes.

"And even if he was, he didn't set any best man's broken wrist, because your best man didn't break his wrist on the dance floor. As I recall, you didn't have a dance reception."

"So I lied!" said Faith, spinning around to face her mother-in-law. "And what about you? What were all those stories of yours? The minister ran off with the children's choir director? Lady Bird invited you to the ranch?"

Patsy chuckled. "Well, I figured as long as I was embellishing, I might as well *really* embellish."

Faith's face crumpled as if she were going to either laugh or cry, and, being a betting woman, Patsy would put her money on the latter. She was right.

"Oh, now, Faith," she said, taking her daughter-in-law by the arm and leading her to the kitchen table, "it's all right. Everybody jazzes up a story now and then."

"Not like I do!" blubbered Faith.

"Well, then, you must have your reasons," said Patsy, setting Faith down and sitting opposite her on the silver-flecked vinyl chair. She patted the back of her lacquered hair and then rearranged the salt and pepper shakers in the center of the table. "Did I ever tell you about Wade's girlfriend — the one he had before you?"

Faith shook her head.

"Her name was Missy Geroux," said Patsy, making a face that gave a very broad clue as to what she thought of this particular young lady. "Missy came from a family that had lots of money and lots of position, and you know what?

163

She couldn't have been more boring if she'd just been declared brain dead."

Faith laughed in surprise, and Patsy smiled at her.

"When Wade brought you home, I thought, *Now here's a girl with a little fire in her.* And where there's fire, there's usually smoke."

Patsy smiled again, satisfied with her little parable. Unfortunately, Faith had no idea what she meant and said so.

"What I mean is," Patsy said, impatience rushing her words, "is so what if you've got a past? Most everybody does — at least the people I want to know."

Faith looked at her hands. Patsy made the word *past* sound exotic, and hers certainly wasn't.

"Let me tell you something, Faith," said Patsy. "You don't need to jazz up your story as much as you think you do."

"What do you mean?" asked Faith, misery pressing down on her so that she felt she might fall off her chair.

"I mean no one's going to like you any less knowing that your daddy wasn't a doctor but a —"

"But a what? What do you know about my daddy? How can you know anything about my daddy when I don't? When he ran off before I was born?"

Patsy opened her mouth to speak but after a few seconds closed it again. Finally she took her daughter-in-law's hand in her own.

"Listen, Faith, you're a fine young woman. Now, don't sit there shakin' your head — you are. Your friends like you because you're *you*, not because they think your daddy's a doctor."

"Thanks for not giving me away," said Faith.

"You're my son's wife. My grandchildren's mother. I love you, Faith."

"You do?" asked Faith, squeezing the words past the lump in her throat.

"Sure. And if that means telling a whopper to protect you, I will."

"The LBJ ranch thing," said Faith with a smile, "that *was* a whopper."

"I couldn't believe it came out of my mouth," admitted Patsy after they laughed. "I think that's the trouble with lying — once you get started, you can't really take away. You just have to keep adding."

Faith nodded, understanding perfectly, and the two women sat quietly for a moment.

"I'm sorry I called Kari's baby a pickaninny," said Patsy finally. "I didn't mean any harm by it."

"I know you didn't," said Faith.

"Times are sure changing."

"They sure are."

"I'm sorry about your daddy, Faith."

Nodding, Faith sighed. There was so much to be sorry about.

HOSTESS: **SLIP**

BOOK: *The Prime of Miss Jean Brodie*

by Muriel Spark

REASON CHOSEN: "A woman at the

McCarthy rally recommended it to me."

When my dad called, I thought it was to wish me an early Thanksgiving.

"How's my Warrior Bear?" he asked.

"Ready to go shopping. I'm getting a twenty-pound turkey this year."

I expected him to ask me what else was on the menu or how Jerry and the kids were, but he said nothing and his silence scared me.

"Dad? Dad, what's the matter?"

He exhaled a long stream of air. "Slip, your brother Fred enlisted in the army today."

"What? He what? Put him on the phone!"

"He's not here. He just called to tell us he wouldn't be here for Thanksgiving — he's staying down at Penn — but he wanted us to know he'd enlisted."

"Doesn't he need permission from you or Mom?" I asked, feeling like I'd just run a hundred miles. "Can't you stop it, Dad?"

"I wish we could, Slip. But he's over eighteen."

"Well, let's call the recruitment board! Or our senators, or the president!"

"My Warrior Bear," he said with a tired chuckle. "We can't do anything."

"Let's all be pilgrims / Sharing and caring / Let's all be Indians / Caring and sharing / Let's all be pilgrims / Let's all be Indians / Let's all be friends / Amen."

I looked at Flannery across the table, across the steam rising from the dressing and creamed onions, looked at my daughter in her green plaid dress and thought what you're supposed to think on Thanksgiving: *Thank you.*

"My goodness, that was a beautiful prayer," said Jerry's mother.

"It's not really a prayer," said Flannery, "it's more a poem. I just added the 'amen' because it sounded good."

"It did," agreed Jerry's father.

I tried to keep hold of all my gratitude and good, smooth feelings, but after Jerry carved the turkey and we began to load our plates, I couldn't help thinking that all this food could feed a starving family for a week. Not just any family, either: a Vietnamese family whose farmlands had been burned, whose ox had been napalmed, whose little boy had blown up when he stepped on a land mine.

I looked at my plate and the piles of glazed carrots and syrupy yams, the crater of gravy in the volcano of mashed potatoes, and felt a flutter of dizziness.

"Slip, are you all right?" asked my sister-in-law, Wendy.

"Just a little morning sickness," I lied.

"But it's two o'clock in the afternoon, Mommy," said Flannery.

I smiled. "Pregnant women can feel morning sickness any time of the day, honey."

"Then they shouldn't call it morning sickness," said Flan. "That's dumb."

"I didn't get any turkey, Mommy," said Joe.

And there are children who get nothing, I thought, spearing him a ragged wedge of dark meat.

Jerry was looking at me in that way of his that makes me know he understands perfectly, and I summoned up a smile for him, telling him I'd be all right.

"Slip, I understand your brother enlisted in the army," said Wendy, offering us all an unpleasant view of green bean casserole as she spoke. "I wouldn't be too worried — I think the whole thing will be over by Christmas."

I shot Jerry a dirty look — I hadn't told him not to tell anybody about Fred, but I still felt betrayed that he had.

"Auntie Wendy," said Flan, "you shouldn't talk with your mouth full."

"And you shouldn't correct your aunt," I said. "I hope you're right, Wendy, but I can see this thing going on and on."

"Well, we've got to be a presence there," said Jerry's dad. "Or else the communists will keep taking small countries — ones we normally don't even pay attention to — and the next thing we know we're renaming Washington, D.C., 'Marxland' and saluting the hammer and sickle."

Jerry's look said, *I apologize for my father a million times over,* but I didn't let him off the hook with a shrug and my own what-can-we-do look; I was still mad at my husband for announcing the news of Fred's enlistment.

"What's a hammer and sickle?" asked Flannery.

"It's a travesty, is what it is," said Jerry's father. "It's the opposite of our flag — it stands for *no* liberty and *no* justice for all."

"Why'd you get him started, Wendy?" asked Jerry's mother.

"I didn't!" whined Wendy. "I just asked Slip about her brother."

"She's talking with her mouth full again, Mommy."

" 'Nother biscuit, please," said Joe.

At book club earlier that week, trying to merge two themes, we talked about what teacher we were particularly grateful for.

"Mrs. Simick was my favorite," said Audrey, pressing a corner of her false eyelashes with her pinky. "Definitely. She was my fifth-grade teacher, the teacher I went to during recess when I realized that I was bleeding and I hadn't cut myself."

"Your period?" asked Merit, and when Audrey nodded, she asked, "You got your period in the fifth grade?"

"At recess. I found Mrs. Simick standing by the jungle gym reading a paperback — all the other teachers gathered together to talk, but Mrs. Simick was always off by the jungle gym, reading — anyway, I said really matter-of-factly even though I was panicking, 'Excuse me, Mrs. Simick, I think I might be dying.' "

"You didn't know what it was?" I asked.

In a quick, impatient movement, Audrey lit a

169

cigarette. "I *should* have," she said, her voice colored with anger. "I had already started to develop, and you'd think my mother might have wanted to prepare me for what was ahead — but no, I was absolutely without a clue.

" 'You're not dying, honey,' said Mrs. Simick, and she cupped my chin with one hand and got a hanky out of her sweater pocket with the other. 'Wipe your leg with this and then follow me.'

"She took me into the school, making sure we passed as few people as possible, and then she took me into the nurse's office. The nurse was at lunch, so Mrs. Simick got me a pad and some pins and told me what was happening. Then she called my mother to come pick me up. The next day she asked me to stay after, and when all the kids had left the room, she pulled a pink box out of her desk drawer and inside were two cupcakes. She put candles in them and said, 'Some people think when a girl gets her period, it's a rite of passage to celebrate. I'm one of those people.' Then she lit the candles and told me to make not one, but two wishes, 'one for taking your first step toward womanhood and the other for being so brave about it,' before I blew them out. I remember sitting in that classroom with the afternoon sun shining through the windows we'd just decorated with portraits of the presidents, eating cupcakes with Mrs. Simick and talking about everything from Margaret Truman's musical talent and how neat it would be to see African violets not growing in a pot but in Africa to what we supposed the world might be like when I got to be Mrs. Simick's age — which was all of thirty-eight, which of course I thought was as ancient as dawn." Audrey looked at her cigarette and flicked the ash that had grown long as she talked. "She always made me feel like such a . . . *person*. Plus she had us sing our multiplication table to 'Mairzy Doats,' which made even math fun."

"To Mrs. Simick," I said, raising my shot glass.

"On the farm we learned about the facts of life pretty early," said Kari after we had had a reflective moment saluting the good and kind Mrs. Simick. "When I got my period, I knew exactly what it was; in fact, at fourteen, I was getting a little anxious for it."

"Me too," said Faith, "I was thirteen, and all my friends already had theirs. To have your period was a status thing, like getting the right charm for your bracelet on your birthday."

Merit shook her head. "When my mother told me about menstruation, I told her I didn't want to have a period. She laughed and said we didn't have a choice in the matter. One summer morning when I was twelve, I woke up with my pajamas and sheets all bloody, and I remember crying for three days and then sulking for about a month. I thought it was so unfair that girls didn't get to do so many things — that was the year I wanted to try out for the school basketball team and was told of course I couldn't — on top of that, we had to bleed every month."

"For some reason, I can't picture you wanting to play basketball," I said.

"I was pretty good," said Merit with a resigned shrug. "But I gave up athletics after that. It didn't seem worth all the trouble."

"Well, I didn't get my period until I was sixteen, so I was more than anxious for it — I was sure I was barren," I said. "I had convinced myself it was okay — I would adopt underprivileged babies from around the world — but when it finally came, I was so thrilled I ran into the living room, where everyone was watching Edward Murrow, and announced, 'I can have my own children!' "

We all laughed and toasted our menstrual lore, which reminded me of our first toast. "Hey, weren't we talking about favorite teachers?"

"Miss Monroe," said Kari. "My eleventh-grade English teacher. I was in high school during the war, and when all the talk was about the evil Nazis, she had us reading Goethe and Hermann Hesse and Erich Maria Remarque. She said, 'The Nazis *are* evil, but that doesn't mean Germans are.' She made me think in bigger ways."

Faith took her plate of peanut brittle (now it was mandatory that Kari bring her brownies and Faith her peanut brittle to every meeting) off the coffee table and passed it around.

"I actually had two favorite teachers," I said. "Miss Gladstone, my first-grade teacher, because she taught me how to read *and* because she wore open-toed shoes, which I thought were the absolute height of glamour. And then there's Professor Emory — he teaches the theology class I'm taking at night school — because one day he compared religions to a baseball team, with Catholicism as the catcher, crouched down and willing to take the most punishment, giving secret signals; Baptists as the umpires, always judging who'd erred; Buddhism as the pinch hitter, who would hit a home run if he can just get up to bat, but if he only gets to warm the bench, that's fine too. And then after he had us laughing over this facile interpretation, he brought in a Zen master who talked to us about quieting our mind, and we spent the rest of class sitting there in absolute silence. His class is like riding a roller coaster — constant thrills and spills."

Audrey lifted her glass. "You gotta drink to that."

We agreed.

Faith talked about the home ec teacher who had taught her to make "the very peanut brittle you're stuffing your faces with now," and Merit said she had been very grateful for Mr. Marsh, her junior high music teacher.

"He used to play opera records for the class. He'd sit at his desk with his eyes closed, his hand sort of swooping to the music, and we'd laugh, but he was never bothered by that, and eventually we'd all be quiet and listen to the music too. He really helped me hear more."

"I see he meant a lot to you," said Kari. "You're getting all teary."

Merit's nostrils flared as she nodded. "He did. He thought I had a nice voice and used to feature me in the choir concerts and . . . I . . . I . . ." Her features crammed together in anger and then shifted slightly into pain. "I just don't know why he had to kiss me!"

Audrey perked up for a second — I think any mention of sex, in any context, was like a jolt of adrenaline to her — but her brain seemed to process quickly that this was not a nice story.

"He did what?" she asked, along with the rest of us.

173

"In the band room," she said, tight little percussive breaths working up her throat. "He was leaving to teach in Nebraska that summer, and I'd come in after school to thank him for all his help, and all of a sudden he just grabbed me, pushed his leg between mine, and kissed me."

"Bastard," I said.

"I . . . I tried to get away, but he kept telling me I'd been asking for it all year, and he was pushing me up against the desk and I was too scared to scream, and then Jered Johnson — thank God for Jered Johnson — started banging on the door. He'd forgotten his tuba and he'd promised his mother he'd take it home over the weekend." Merit drew in a deep breath and tried to laugh. "I was saved by a tuba."

"Oh, Merit," said Kari as we all reached out to Merit. "I hope that bastard — Slip's right; there's no other word for him — I hope that bastard got fired and never was allowed to teach again."

Merit blew her nose on a tissue Faith passed her. "I never told anyone. For all I know, he's still teaching."

"Merit," said Audrey, half scolding, half sympathetic.

"I know I should have told, but then . . . well, I didn't want to get him in trouble, and since he was moving anyway, I wouldn't have to see him again. And . . . and I just felt too . . . ashamed."

I reached for Merit's pack of cigarettes on the coffee table and shook out two, lighting one for her and for me. "We should track the bastard down," I said, squinting against the smoke. "Track him down and file charges."

"Oh, Slip," said Merit with the kind of laugh a

dead-broke person musters after getting another bill in the mail. "For kissing a fifteen-year-old-girl who came to wish him goodbye? Who asked for it?"

I remember thinking, *If this was a teacher you were grateful for, what were the other ones like?*

At the table as Jerry's father ranted on about the threat of communism and Jerry's mother kept warning him to calm down or he'd have a stroke or give her one, as Jerry's sister explained to Flannery that the man she'd brought to dinner last Thanksgiving was no longer her boyfriend — "Thank God, because he was perfectly happy with his plumbing business while I've hitched my star a little higher" (Flan, bless her, asked, "How high?") — I can't say I was oozing gratitude either. I'll bet if there were a national poll taken, ninety percent would answer yes to the question "Would you rather spend Thanksgiving with people other than family members?"

And every time I thought I might have some fun and start arguing with Jerry's dad, I thought of my little brother going to Vietnam, and fear, like a draft, would make me shiver, and I'd have to take a bite of mashed potatoes or cranberry sauce, just so no one would hear my teeth chattering.

It wasn't until after the table had been cleared that I realized that all through dinner Jerry had kept his hand on my knee, and I felt a deep, Thanksgiving-worthy sense of gratitude for my big solid husband, whose relatives might be crazy but who knew when his wife needed a steadying hand on her knee.

December 1968

HOST: **MERIT**
BOOK: *Slouching Towards Bethlehem*
by Joan Didion
REASON CHOSEN: "I thought it had something to do with Christmas."

At Kari's annual Christmas party, as Slip and Audrey did the frug to "Jingle Bell Rock," Leslie Trottman sidled up to Merit by the punch bowl.

"Look at those exhibitionists," she said, sipping at her drink, her pinky extended like an accusation. "And both of them p.g., too." She shook her head, rattling the mistletoe ornament she had pinned to her red grosgrain headband. "You heard about them flashing me in the tree house, didn't you? Todd says I should have called the police and had them arrested for indecent exposure."

Merit bit her lip, her teeth restraining the smile that wanted to bust loose. She'd been delighted when she heard that story and had hoped desperately that if she had been up in the tree house with them, she would have taken off her top too.

"Good grief," said Leslie, noticing the ornamentation on Merit's dress. "What's with the buttons?"

Smiling, Merit looked at the campaign buttons — Pat Paulsen for President, Alfred E. Neuman for Education Secretary, Betty Friedan for Director of Sanity — pinned across her chest. "They're my Secret Santa gift," said Merit, smiling. "Although I'm pretty sure these are from Slip."

The book club members had gotten to Kari's house early to open up their anonymous (and preferably jokey) presents from one another.

"They're going to leave pin marks all over your dress," said Leslie.

"Merit, if you're pouring, I'll take some punch, please."

Merit released her smile and directed it at Faith, who she thought looked dazzling in her maroon crushed-velvet tunic and bell-bottom pants.

"Me too," said Audrey, her face dotted with perspiration. "Why, *hello*, Leslie."

"Girls," said Leslie with a tight nod toward Faith and Audrey. "I trust you're keeping your clothes on tonight?"

Audrey wagged the end of her feather boa, her Secret Santa gift. "I personally don't make promises I'm not sure I can keep."

"Please eat some of these Christmas cookies," said Kari, holding a plate on which an elaborate pyramid of sugar-dusted and sprinkled cookies was stacked. "There are dozens more in the kitchen."

"Oh, my gosh, the baby's kicking up a storm," said Slip, holding her abdomen as if it were a basketball she'd just caught. For such a small woman, she had a big pregnancy. "How's yours, Audrey?"

"I'm hoping some of this rum punch will calm him down."

"Him?" said Leslie. "You think your baby's going to be a boy?"

"I don't think it, I know it."

"She's been right about the other two," said Paul, standing in a little world of men by the hi-fi.

"And she was right about mine," said Merit.

"Has anyone tried any of this rumaki?" asked Helen Hammond, whose daughter, Jody, was being paid to baby-sit all the children in the finished basement. "It's delicious." She offered the tray to Merit. "Say, how's your book club going?"

"Great," said Merit, feeling a blush warm her face; she was so proud to have something so important to talk about. "We just read Joan Didion."

Helen shook her head. "I don't know how you gals do it. Who has time to read these days?"

"You have to make time," said Kari, passing the cookies to the men. "You should think about joining, Helen. It's a lot of fun."

"I say you're smart to stay out of it," said Paul. "God only knows what goes on there — I think they sit around reading feminist propaganda and bitching about their husbands."

"You're not far off there, sweetie," said Audrey, and threw him a kiss.

"Really?" said Eric, his bright smile as perfect and insincere as a catalog model's. "I thought it was just a bunch of angry housewives sitting around eating bon bons and yakking about love stories."

"Sure," said Paul, laughing, "love stories

today, manifestos on how to overthrow the male-dominant government tomorrow."

"Or primers on how to think like a lesbo," offered Todd Trottman.

As the men laughed heartily and the women offered them courtesy smiles, Bing Crosby started singing about a Hawaiian Christmas, and without asking her, Eric took Merit's hand and led her to the cleared-away space in the living room that served as a dance floor. Todd and Leslie Trottman followed suit.

"You look beautiful tonight, darling," Eric said, taking her in his arms. "Although I don't know why you have to wear those stupid buttons."

"Thank you," said Merit, choosing to accept the compliment and let his other comment pass. The past few weeks had been festive and happy — last night they'd trimmed the Christmas tree with Reni, propped between pillows on the easy chair, watching wide-eyed — and Merit was luxuriating in the normalcy of her marriage. "You look pretty dashing yourself."

He nuzzled her neck. "But what's up with your friend?"

"Which one?"

"Audrey, of course. The indecent one." Eric looked over by the punch table. "The only pregnant woman I know who thinks it's okay to wear a miniskirt."

Merit looked over at Audrey, who along with her boa was wearing a cream silk shirt over a short red skirt. It was a thrilling departure from the sort of maternity clothes Merit had worn.

"I think she looks wonderful," said Merit, and by Eric's slight frown, she could tell it was the wrong answer.

"Time to switch partners," said Leslie Trottman, holding her arms out to Eric.

"Bye, honey," said Merit as she took her new partner's hand.

A few of the other husbands — Paul and Jerry and Wade — decided to play a game of darts in the basement.

"You don't have to run out," Audrey called after them. "I didn't want to dance with you anyways."

"A bunch of *angry housewives*," said Slip with a trace of awe in her voice. "Angry housewives eating bon bons and yakking about love stories."

"What's that supposed to mean anyway?" asked Helen.

"I think it's a joke," said Faith. "Oh, I think old Mr. McDermitt wants you, Helen."

"It isn't a joke," said Slip, watching Helen Hammond cross the room to continue her rumaki service. "It's our new name."

"Our new name?" said Kari, rubbing a beige smear of French onion dip off a bodice pleat of her navy blue dress.

"Our new book club name," said Slip. "We're Angry Housewives Eating Bon Bons. I think it about says it all."

"Yeah," said Faith, nodding. "Since all we do anyway is read feminist propaganda and bitch about our husbands."

Audrey grimaced. "I think my dear husband was kidding. At least I *hope* he was kidding. Now, him," she said, looking to the dance floor where Eric was dipping Leslie Trottman, "I don't think *he* was kidding."

"He reminds me of Mr. Moe," said Kari. "The man who was so upset — and I guess intimidated — by the church women's club."

"So is it agreed?" asked Slip. "Are we Angry Housewives Eating Bon Bons?"

"I love it," said Audrey, "and we can call it AHEB for short, which sounds sort of like Ahab, which is an appropriate name for an angry housewife."

Kari nodded. "Either way, Angry Housewives Eating Bon Bons or AHEB has got a lot more power than the Freesia Court Book Club. You've got my vote."

Audrey and Faith assented, but then Faith asked, "What about Merit?"

"Since when has Merit ever had a dissenting vote?" said Slip. "Still, it's only fair we tell her before we make it official."

Meeting later on the stair landing on the way to the bathroom, Slip did tell her.

"But what are we angry about?"

"Merit, it's just sort of a joke. You heard how the guys were teasing us about the book club — why not take their words and use them? It's like we're giving them and their chauvinism the finger."

"Angry Housewives Eating Bon Bons," said Merit, looking down at the revelry in the living room and in particular at Eric, who had appropriated Helen Hammond for a rhumba. She turned to Slip, smiling. "I like it."

January 1969

Dear Mama,

"Yippie-ki-yay, it's New Year's Day." Remember how you always said that, Mama? Every year you believed that you were going to start over, that you really were going to "quit

181

drinking, settle down, and not attach myself to worthless men." Isn't that funny, Mama, that I can recite your New Year's resolutions? They were always the same ones, and always broken, especially the first one, on the same day you made them.

When I was fifteen and spent New Year's Eve losing my virginity to Jeff Patchett (an event he made sure every single person in school knew about), I made these resolutions as my head pounded from all the beer I drank: "I'm going to be exactly like my mama, I'm going to drink every day of my life, be crazier than I already am, and have sex with people who only care about what's between my legs." I figured resolutions were made to be broken, so why not make ones I'd want to break?

Oh, there I go again. I hate the way bitterness is like a black, bubbling tar pit in me, and I hate the way so many memories of you are in that pit. My big trouble is, I try, but I just don't know how to seal it up.

I talked to Wade's mama a couple weeks ago (we didn't get to Texas this Christmas 'cause Patsy and Dex went to Mexico). Anyway, she asked me for a favorite Christmas memory — *as if I have one.* Maybe I should have told her about the time when we were in Arkansas — you had followed that guy, Lamar, the one with that bald spot the size of a grapefruit right in the middle of his big round head? Anyway, you told me he had a good job in Greenville and we were gonna move in with him and be a real family. And we did move in, right before Christmas, only it wasn't just his house, he lived there with his sister, and I got to know her pretty good, seeing as you and Lamar took off and I didn't see you again for days. I was, what? — five, six? — and spending Christmas with a lady I didn't even know. A lady who only spoke to me to tell me my mama was a tramp but if her brother wanted to get together with her, that was none of her business. And on and on in that direction she talked, when what I should have been listening to was " 'Twas the Night Before Christmas" or a Bible story or something. Yeah, that's a memory I could have shared with Patsy, or maybe I should have regaled her with the New Year's Eve memory I just shared with you. You think she'd like to hear how her son's wife rang in that New Year?

Wade's on a three-day trip, so I spent New Year's Eve with Beau and Bonnie, my neighbor Kari, and her new adopted daughter. The twins had party hats, and Bonnie (who — excuse me for bragging — is a little genius) kept wishing everyone "a vewy happy new yeaw!"

The twins fell asleep before the baby, which gave me time to hold her without them throwing a fit. Here's how I could make a million dollars, Mama — by figuring out how to bottle that contentment, that *sweetness* you feel holding a happy baby. After about five minutes, though, I could tell Kari was itching to hold her again, so I gave her back. It touches me, watching Kari with her baby — you can tell that nothing matters more to her than being a good mother. I admit I was pretty shocked at first when I saw this mixed baby in Kari's arms, but now I can't imagine a better place for that baby to be.

Remember DellaRose Pryne? I don't know that I've ever had a better friend — our favorite game was Civil War and she always played General Grant or Abraham Lincoln, while I had to be the freed slave. Anyway, she used to wait for me outside El-Ray's Sweets because she wasn't allowed in. I always gave her more than half of my Moon Pies and chocolate drops because I felt bad Miss Ellie or Mr. Ray wouldn't let her come inside herself. Still, why didn't I ever say anything? Slip would have gotten a whole group of protesters together and said, "What you're doing is wrong and we're not going to stand for it." Why couldn't I? Well, maybe a person's not so eager to stand up for somebody else when they're always worried they're going to have to stand up for themselves.

I was thinking of this when Kari was telling me about all the ignorant or just plain mean things people say to her about Julia, and I said that sure must wear a person down, and she shrugged and said, "It's all worth it."

Remember the first time you pawned me off to MawMaw because your latest boyfriend didn't like kids and you only came to get me when MawMaw threatened to put me in a foster home?

"Tie me down, that's all you're good for," you said when you picked me up, and I can still feel my hand wrapped around the door handle of that car that stank like whiskey and hair tonic and how close I came to opening it and tumbling out. "Tie me down" — how could you say words like those to your own daughter, Mama?

Kari and Julia left a little after midnight — I told her they were welcome to stay the night, but she said Flicka (that's her big sloppy dog) would be lonesome for them, and so I watched her wade through the snow with the baby wrapped up in five pounds of blankets. So it's just two hours into 1969 — can anything sound more modern? — and I'm sitting here in front of the fireplace, tucked under my cashmere afghan but still feeling as cold as stone, feeling jealous of the love Kari has for that mixed-blood baby! How can I feel jealous when I've got my own two babies, who people never say mean things about and whom I can't imagine loving more? It makes me sick, Mama, this way I think — that everybody's better than me, that somehow they love better, feel deeper, have something that I can't describe but know I lack. But no one would ever guess I feel this way — if there's one thing you taught me, Mama, it's how to act.

Okay, I was sitting here crying — how many New Year's Eves have I brought in with tears? — but then I got a funny little picture of Mr. Teague in my head. Dear Mr. Teague, smelling of BO and mothballs; the first person who believed in me enough to make me start believing in his belief.

Anyway, Mr. Teague always said the same words to me whenever I started complaining too loud about something: "If you don't like where you're at, move." So, remembering that, I just got up off the couch and went over to sit on the easy chair. Ha ha ha. But I do feel a tiny ounce better.

I used Mr. Teague's advice a lot my senior

year, Mama, when you were with that creep who topped all creeps, who taught creeps how to be creepy, the Great King of Creeps. Sandy. He thought he was a cowboy and was so proud of his cowboy name, Sandy. I used to call him Curly or Hoss, just to tick him off.

One day he was sitting in the kitchen while I was making my school lunch. I have no idea what he was doing up so early — maybe he still hadn't gone to bed. Anyway, there he was, wearing only his underwear and cowboy boots, sitting backward on the kitchen chair flipping playing cards into his stupid cowboy hat he'd set in the middle of the floor. Once or twice I felt a card flick at my leg, but I tried to ignore the creep, as I was trying to make something appetizing out of bread that was a day away from being moldy and cheese hard as linoleum.

"Y'ever been with a cowboy, angel?" he said, and I said, "No, Curly, have you?"

His lip curled up — I guess it was a smile — and he said, "You know what happens to sassy girls, like you?"

I didn't even bother to make a guess, just rolled my eyes like I was making it clear I had no time for him, and all of a sudden he lunged out of the chair. He was fast enough to grab my arm, but not strong enough to hold on — I yanked myself out of that miserable creep's stinking hand and shot out the back door like I was a girl catapult. I could hear the creep's stupid snickery little laugh as I raced through the backyard, dropping tears on the ground like bread crumbs, only I knew they wouldn't lead me safely back home; they'd just dry up in the dirt.

I was thinking of just going to the river; maybe there'd be other truants down there, drinking whatever liquor they had managed to steal and making out with whomever they happened to be sitting next to, but then I thought, no, that's what my mother and stupid Sandy probably did — at least before they quit school altogether. I remembered good old Mr. Teague and even though I couldn't physically move away yet, I could go anywhere I wanted to in my head.

So I did. I was walking to school, because my father, the doctor, was called to the hospital early. We loved our rides together. We talked about absolutely everything; he'd tell me about his cases, and then we'd discuss current affairs and he'd be very impressed by my insights. Sometimes we'd sing duets together, and he wasn't a country hick either; nope, my daddy liked singers like Perry Como and Rosemary Clooney. When we got to school, he'd always give me a five-dollar bill and tell me to buy sodas for everyone on the way home, and then he'd give me a kiss on the cheek, and all the other girls whose daddies were too lazy or hungover or just plain uninterested to drive their daughters to school would stare at me with their bottom lips pushed out, wishing they had a daddy like Faith Reynolds did.

Oh, Mama, by the time I got to school, I was like a balloon, blown up with good feelings, and even Mr. Hilgerman, the snotty principal who always stood on the steps watching the kids come in as if they were germs, said, "Why, hello, Faith, you look like a ray of sunshine," and I said, very proper, "Why, thank you, Mr. Hilgerman."

Mama, I have moved away so many times from places I haven't wanted to be in, taken so many trips in my head, that sometimes I forget where I really am. And yet when I find myself in this nice neighborhood where the women are married to lawyers and doctors and scientists, the kind of neighborhood I fantasized about, I think: what the hell am I doing here? Where are the men staggering out the front door, zipping up their pants? The scrawny chickens stepping around the broken bottles that decorate the dirt yard like sinister lawn ornaments? The old, dented cars bleeding rust onto the cement blocks they're perched on? How'm I supposed to feel at home?

But then I see your face, see your face the way it looked the last night of your life, and I remember exactly where I am and who I am. And then I want to ask Mr. Teague, "People like me will always want to be moving, won't we? Because things never really will get nice enough to stay."

Hey, could I get any bluer? Could I feel any lower? But then guess what? Wade called from Denver, wishing me a happy new year and telling me he would like to resolve to love me more, but how is that possible?

How come I can't hear words like that and not feel like the luckiest woman in the world? How come I can't hear words like that without hearing awful little echoes rising up from the tar pit? "Tie me down, that's all you're good for."

Oh, Mama, I'm sorry,
Faith

April 1969

HOST: **KARI**

BOOK: *The Song of the Lark* by Willa Cather

FOOD: "Kari made the kind of dessert Willa had on the farm: yellow cake with chocolate icing and molasses candy."

It thrilled Kari, who was a long-standing member of the Democratic Party and the teachers' union, the PTA and the Lutheran Church, to be part of a group with the provocative name Angry Housewives Eating Bon Bons. To her it sounded like the code name of a subversive group Gloria Steinem and Sara Lee had put together, whose plans included taking over if not the world, then at least the world's chocolate supply.

She remembered asking her mother why Mr. Moe had gotten so upset about the church women's book club, and her dear mother (how Kari wished she were alive so that she could see Julia!) had said, "Women with minds scare some men. We make them wonder if they're as on top of things as they think they are."

She wanted to do something special as tonight's hostess — or, as she corrected herself, as tonight's *host*.

They had decided to drop the word *hostess*.

"It's a useless feminine ending," said Slip. "People don't call female doctors doctoresses or female lawyers lawyeresses; so when *-ess* is used, I think it's diminishing. See how less substantial *authoress* sounds than *author* or *actress* than *actor?*"

"I *like* the word *actress*," said Audrey, "and I like the word *hostess*. What I don't like is when feminism tries to do away with what's feminine."

"I'm just saying when we do the same job as men, our titles should be the same."

"I never thought about it much, Slip," said Merit. "But I get your point."

"Me too," echoed Faith. "Wade told me some of the stewardesses don't want to be called that anymore, that the name trivializes their work."

"Well, come on," said Audrey, "what kind of work is serving drinks and sleeping with pilots on layovers anyway?"

A surge of anger warmed Faith's body. "I hope you're not implying that my husband sleeps with stewardesses."

"I'm not implying anything. I just think people are getting all bent out of shape over semantics."

"Can you imagine how men would be out-raged if they had a masculine version of *Mrs.* or *Miss?*" Slip frowned, her copper-colored eye-brows meeting her eyes. "I just get so . . . so fed up with all this repressive shit."

"Okay, okay, let's call each other hosts," said Audrey, laughing. "Anything to avoid Slip saying things like 'repressive shit.' "

"It's true; we must fight for justice," Kari re-minded Julia, who was carefully inspecting the Cheerios scattered across her high-chair tray. "If you think someone's being poorly treated, you say so! Don't ever be afraid to speak up! Now . . . what do you say we make three kinds of brownies?"

Julia smiled broadly, showing off several new white teeth.

Or maybe I'll just sit and watch you eat Cheerios all day, Kari thought as Julia put the small ring of cereal into her mouth, *and be absolutely, perfectly content.*

Julia spent her first night in Kari's house sleeping in the fine-washables drawer, in the center of Kari's bed.

The new mother had taken a taxi home from the airport and slipped inside her house with Julia tucked inside her unzipped carryall. It was dark outside, but she wanted to make sure no one saw her; she wanted to have one night with the baby all to herself before she introduced her to the world.

"Well, there *is* someone I want you to meet right away," she said after she had changed Julia's diaper. (Mary Jo had packed a bag full of diapers, plastic pants, and doll-sized T-shirts, but Kari was struck by how woefully unequipped she was for a baby in the house.)

When the phone rang, Kari jumped as if someone had thrown a firecracker at her.

"Well, howdy, stranger," said Slip. "I saw the lights come on, and I was hoping it was you and not some burglars. Anyway, you want me to bring Flicka over?"

"Yes," said Kari, "but . . . but I'm not feeling very well, and —"

"I can make you some hot tea."

191

"Oh, no, please, I'm ready to collapse into bed."

"Kari, I've got to bring Flicka back. She *knows* you're home."

The new mother placed Julia in the center of her bed and surrounded her with pillows.

"I'll be right back," she said when she heard the doorbell ring.

Hunching over and mustering a cough, Kari opened the door a crack.

"Thanks for watching her," she said in a croaky voice as Flicka bounded in.

"The kids loved having her around," said Slip. "Flannery dressed her up like a reindeer, and Joe tried to ride her like a horse —"

"I've got to get to bed," croaked Kari, and, thanking Slip again, she shut the door and raced back to the bedroom to find Flicka pacing around the bed.

"It's okay, girl," she said to the dog, who thumped her tail and whined in agitation and excitement. She took Flicka's head in her hands. "It's a baby, that's all. Now, you're going to have to show me you can settle down and be gentle or I won't show her to you."

Kneeling on the bed, she carefully took Julia up in her arms. Flicka gave her such a thorough sniffing that at one point the baby's little arms shot out and her face puckered.

"It's all right," she whispered to the baby, who fell back to sleep. "It's all right," she said to the dog, who was still a little skittish. "You'll love this dog, Julia, and you'll love the baby, Flicka."

It was in the middle of the night, when Kari was burping the baby that a realization hit her.

"Oh, my," she said, not in response to the nice

belch Julia had just let rip, but to the thought that had come into her head. "Oh, my."

With the baby in her arms and Flicka following her, she climbed the narrow staircase to the attic and at the top pulled the chain of the bare bulb.

"Oh, my," she said again, and this time in awe, for there amid boxes marked Camping and Books — Law and Text, amid Bjorn's legal files and a broken typewriter, was the bassinet they had gotten for Bettina. And next to that was a stroller and a box Kari knew was filled with baby clothes and another filled with toys.

"We've got some hand-me-downs for you," said Kari as the sweet, tiny baby nestled closer to her chest. "From your sister."

The words made her feel both happy and sad, and she sat down on a trunk for a moment to think about them. Flicka rested her head on Kari's knee, and with her free hand, Kari patted her.

"We are a patchwork family, and certainly not the family I imagined having," she said to infant and retriever, "but I'm very happy and very blessed to have it." She looked around the dimly lit attic, spotting Bjorn's fishing rod, Bettina's stroller, her grandmother's old sewing machine. "And all who came before and all who'll come after."

Slip called the next morning inquiring about Kari's health.

"Actually, I'm much better, but I was wondering if you could do me a favor."

"Shoot."

"Could you round up Audrey and Merit and

193

Faith and come on over, oh, say, about ten o'clock?"

"You're throwing a coffee party?"

"Something like that."

Kari fretted over how to best present Julia. Should she have her on the couch, where everyone would see her as soon as they came in, or should she keep her in the bedroom and bring everyone in on the pretext of looking at her new curtains? Should she be holding Julia when she answered the door, or would that be *too* big a surprise for them?

She opted for putting her in the bedroom, and there was a mild excitement as her friends gathered in the living room. There was always mild excitement whenever they got together, especially when they hadn't planned on meeting, and especially because it was Saturday and the women (except for Merit, who brought her baby with her) were able to leave the kids home with their fathers.

"So," said Audrey, "if this is a coffee party, where's the coffee? Where're the treats?"

"It's not really a coffee party," said Kari.

"Sheesh," said Slip with mock offense, "talk about getting us here under false pretenses."

"Yeah," agreed Audrey. "I thought I was getting at least one of your homemade cinnamon rolls. What gives?"

Kari pressed her lips together, trying to hold back the smile that wanted to burst all over her face.

"Look at you," said Faith. "You look like the cat who swallowed the canary."

Laughter burbled out of the older woman.

"Oh, Kari," said Merit breathlessly. "Did you meet someone?"

"That's it!" said Audrey, clapping her hands together. "Kari's fallen in love!"

Kari laughed again and nodded. "It's true, I have fallen in love."

"Holy love and intrigue!" said Slip. "That's why you were acting so funny last night — he was here with you!"

"Well, not exactly."

"Is he from California?" asked Faith. "Is that why you went out there?"

"Why don't you all just come with me to my bedroom?" said Kari, her bright blue eyes never brighter, never bluer.

"What, you're going to introduce us to your boyfriend *in your bedroom?*" said Audrey. "That's kinky, Kari."

"Won't he be embarrassed?" Merit whispered as they made their way toward the bathroom.

"Won't we?" asked Slip. " 'Uh, hello, mister, we're Kari's friends, just here to gawk at you.' "

Opening the door, Kari could hardly contain herself.

"Jeez Louise," said Slip, "you're shaking."

There was a moment of stunned silence as the women stood huddled inside the door, staring at a bed that held not a man in a bathrobe but a sleeping infant.

"There's a baby in that bed," said Merit.

Audrey, resisting the urge to comment on Merit's powers of perception, said instead, "Whose baby is it, Kari? What's she doing in your bed?"

"She's my baby," said Kari. "And she's sleeping."

"Your baby! What do you mean?"

"Where'd she come from?"

"How old is she?"

"What are you talking about?"

"Why, she's black!"

"Yes, she is," said Kari, hearing Faith's statement in the jumble of everyone else's words. "Half black and half white."

The women had formed a semicircle around the bed and stared at the little hump on the center of the mattress, Neanderthals staring at the first fire. All of them were so full of questions they couldn't speak. Finally a space opened up in Slip.

"Kari," she said, "tell us everything."

But Kari couldn't. Instead she told them the story she'd rehearsed about a fellow teacher who'd been transferred to California and a teenager she'd had in her class who was pregnant and wanted to give her child to a loving family.

"But you're not a family," said Faith. "You're a widow."

Kari plastered on a fake smile; inside she winced at Faith's bluntness.

"Well, this was a private adoption. Arranged by the girl's family's lawyer. Their only requirement was that they find someone who really wanted to love and raise a baby."

"Well, that's certainly you," said Slip. She paused for a moment, brushing a tear out of her eye. "But you're sure everything's on the up and up? Nothing can happen . . . like it happened before?"

"No, Julia's mine," said Kari. "For ever and ever."

Merit set her sleeping daughter next to Kari's. At two months, Reni looked huge next to Julia.

"I bet they'll be best friends," said Merit

softly, and Kari wanted to hug her. In fact, Kari wanted to hug everyone.

"I'm going to run home and get my camera," said Audrey. When she returned she brought both a fancy Nikon (whose many lenses she had never used) and a bottle of champagne, and as they toasted the new mother and baby, Audrey snapped pictures. Eventually the laughing and jostling woke Julia up (Reni slept on), and for the first time in their lives her friends got to watch Kari pick up a baby and address it as her own.

"Okay," said Kari, who, even in the midst of the sweetness of her daughter, could be swept away in one of the sweet memories Julia had already given her, "I really have got to get to work now." She began assembling the ingredients for chocolate, blond, and peanut butter brownies. Unconcerned whether she had an audience or not, Julia continued to concentrate on which Cheerio passed muster.

If she and Julia were out and about in the world, she could count on at least one rude remark and several ignorant/stupid ones, but Kari wasn't as ready to pick a fight in defense of her daughter anymore; it wasted too much time and energy. *Let the idiots figure things out for themselves,* she thought, ignoring questions like "Didn't they have any regular babies to adopt?" or "Is she a mulatto?"

It's one thing I'll have to teach Julia, she thought. *Pick which idiots to fight and which ones to ignore.* Sometimes the idea of all she'd have to teach her daughter was a daunting prospect, but if Kari had learned one thing, it was to not borrow trouble. Trouble would find her if it wanted to; there was no sense worrying about the whens and ifs.

The thing that really unsettled her so far didn't happen in the grocery store or strolling Julia in the park; it happened at her brother Anders' house last weekend. She and Julia had been invited over to help celebrate his wife Sally's fiftieth birthday.

Everyone, after alternately complimenting the food and complaining about eating too much of it, was lounging in the living room, their stockinged feet up on ottomans, their belts loosened, talking about nothing more important than who got to hold Julia. Kari loved these get-togethers, relaxing so completely in her family's presence that she could have easily fallen asleep, except that she didn't want to miss out on any of the conversation, jokes, or rounds of dessert.

"Okay, my turn," said Kari's nephew Scott. "All I get to hold at school are coeds and beer bottles."

"Uffda," said Sally, swatting her son's leg. "Your report card better not show that."

"I doubt it will," said Kari of her nephew, who was valedictorian of his senior class.

"Thanks for your vote of confidence," said Scott, and Kari handed him Julia. Dressed in a pink dress and tights, Julia looked as if she had been the inspiration for the word *precious*. She held her arms out to the young man; that she wasn't a fearful baby was yet another aspect of her personality that caused Kari's heart to swell with pride and love.

Julia had been welcomed by Kari's family as the gift she was, but they had plenty of questions

— the same type of questions the Angry House-wives had, ones she accepted as curious rather than accusatory.

When Anders and Sally had first come to see Julia, Kari was almost sick from nervousness.

"Oh, Kari," Sally had said, taking the baby in her arms, "she's absolutely beautiful."

She's your grandchild! Kari had screamed inside.

"She looks a little like Bjorn," Anders had said.

It's you she could look like! but it was such a sweet and generous thing for Anders to say that she had felt some of the nervousness melt away.

"You know, I think you're right," she'd said, studying Julia's face.

Anders was telling Scott it was time for Uncle Anders to hold the baby when the phone rang.

Sally answered and then, cupping the receiver, announced, "It's Mary Jo!"

While Sally chatted happily about Scott coming up from Ball State bearing his laundry — "but a present too, a lovely teapot" — and her other son, Randy — "oh, he and Beth both have the flu, but they're taking me to the Guthrie next week" — Kari felt everything disappear inside her body but heat.

She was about to excuse herself to the bathroom, where she could splash cold water on her face, but then Sally said, "And of course Kari's here with Julia — honestly, Mary Jo, she's the cutest little baby." There was a pause, and then Sally held out the receiver.

"Kari, Mary Jo wants to say hello."

"I . . . I . . . ," she said, flustered, before taking the phone.

"How are you, Aunt Kari?" came Mary Jo's bright voice, and Kari was able to answer, "Fine," without her voice belying her terror.

Many times Kari had picked up a pen with every intention to write, to share with her niece the phenomenal progress this phenomenal baby was making — "She rolled over!" "She's sitting up!" "She's got teeth!" — but fear made her cap her pen and put away her stationery. She and Mary Jo had shared a warm and close relationship, and as much as she missed that, Kari felt that if she communicated with her niece, it would remind Mary Jo of what she had given up. And if she was reminded of what she had given up, wouldn't she start yearning for it? How could she not?

So Kari had sent Mary Jo none of the letters and care packages of cookies she'd sent her other nieces and nephews, hoping she'd understand and/or welcome her silence.

"I hear Julia's just a wonderful baby!" enthused Mary Jo, to which Kari murmured that yes, she certainly was.

"Well, that's great, Aunt Kari. I'm so happy it's all working out!" And then, to Kari's surprise, her niece went on to talk about her incredible art history professor and campus demonstrations and her new appreciation of physics, and when Kari finally handed the phone back to Sally, she thought: *I've just had a conversation with a college girl. Not the biological mother of my daughter, but a young woman thrilled by her class schedule as well as the sex appeal of one of her professors; a young woman participating in sit-ins and be-ins in front of Sproul Hall.* Relief rained on the parched dryness inside Kari, and she said a silent prayer, thanking God for letting Mary Jo be happy to be a college girl, making it easier for Kari to be a mother.

HOST: **MERIT**
BOOK: *Dr. Faustus* by Thomas Mann
REASON CHOSEN: "It made a lot of banned-books lists."

True to his word, Eric didn't hit Merit again after that first time. At least not for a whole month. And it wasn't really a hit, more of a slap, inspired by Merit's inability to recognize how hard Eric worked during the day and was it that difficult to have a drink made the way he liked it when he got home? Another slap followed a couple weeks later — this because the baby's diaper needed changing and Merit (who was cooking dinner) had the audacity to suggest he change it.

But it wasn't until they had walked home from Kari's Christmas party almost a year ago, Merit holding her baby with one arm and her drunken husband (he was normally so careful with his behavior, and yet he felt no compunction in getting absolutely blotto at Kari's Christmas parties) with the other as he struggled to find traction in the snow, wasn't until she had laid Reni down and then gone downstairs and found Eric sitting on the couch, still wearing his overcoat, wasn't until she kneeled down to slip off his wet shoes, that she found out there were worse things than getting hit. With his foot against her chest, he pushed her backward, hard.

As she gasped for air, her mind tried to make sense of how she had been kneeling two seconds ago and how she was now lying on the living room carpet. Then another blow, delivered by Eric's foot, pounded into her side, and at the same time her mind exploded with disbelief and terror.

"I told you to take off those stupid buttons," he said, ripping the Pat Paulsen for President button off her dress. "And what was all that flirting going on with you and Todd Trottman? You think I'm blind — you think I can't see what you're up to?"

"Todd Trottman?" Merit said, or tried to say, not knowing if the words had come out before he kicked her again, this time on her upper thigh, before stomping out of the room. For at least half an hour, she lay on the beige carpet, her arms wrapped around her knees, her knees drawn up to her chest, staring at the legs of the coffee table her in-laws had given them, wondering how they were made to curve out like that, wondering how much weight they could stand before they finally snapped.

She had seen Faith at the grocery store the next day, and Faith asked her why she was moving so stiffly.

"My gosh, you're walking like an invalid — are you all right?"

Merit had smiled and said she had fallen down the steps while carrying the laundry basket to the basement.

"Merit," said Faith, "you're lucky you didn't break a leg!"

"I know," said Merit. "It's the last time I'll carry a full laundry basket down the steps." Shame swarmed through her, and she was relieved when Faith said she'd love to talk but Wade was getting home from a trip and she'd promised she'd make him a pecan pie.

Merit was not used to lying, didn't like the feel of a lie inside her, and yet felt at times her whole life was a lie. She lied every time she made herself trip or appear clumsy so that in case someone saw a bruise, saw her "walking like an invalid," she could excuse it away — "Oh, you know me, Clumsy Clara." She lied when asked how she or Eric was, smiling and answering, "Great." She felt like a bad actress in a play she never wanted to be in.

Merit hadn't noticed a pattern yet, but she could count on at least one "rage" a month (*just like my period,* she thought, although, having recently discovered she was pregnant again, she wouldn't be having one of those for a while). The hitting, slapping, and kicking were bad, awful, terrible, but afterward was by far the worst, when Eric would plead for her forgiveness, kissing the bruises that were already rising on her body, when he'd force himself on her, all the while telling her that from now on things would be different, she'd see.

She learned how to hold her breath midway in her throat, which stopped the rising bile; she learned how to pretend she was asleep afterward so that he'd finally turn around and go to sleep himself; and she learned how to convince herself that she didn't hate the man she married, she only hated what he did, and that of course would stop soon, had to stop soon.

Once Slip had said that Jerry had gotten so mad at her he told her he was going to kill her, and Merit had looked up expectantly, horrified that someone else's husband wasn't what he seemed, and horrified over how happy she felt about it (she wasn't alone!), but then Slip told how she and Jerry had been talking hypothetically about what awful thing they would have to do to make the other want to divorce them.

"I told him I'd tithe half of Jerry's salary to Richard Nixon and the other half to George Wallace, and Jerry said not only would he give me a divorce for that, he'd have to kill me," and Merit realized that the threats that were real for her were just a joke for Slip.

Eric used his surgeon's precision when it came to hitting her, only doing damage to parts of her body that wouldn't be seen by anyone (he knew her next appointment with her obstetrician wasn't for three more weeks). She drew her shame tight around her; it was a coat that had no buttons, no zipper, so she couldn't get out of it, but most importantly, nobody could get in.

She knew from her father's sermons based on biblical sacrifice that there were a lot of people in the world less fortunate than she, and the trick was figuring out how to deal with one's particular (mis)fortune.

Motherhood was her biggest trick. She had known she'd love her children, but she was stunned at the force of her love, awed with the knowledge that if the world needed to be wrestled to benefit her baby girl, she would not only wrestle the world but pin it to the mat. She, who was the queen of the cowed, wouldn't accede to Eric's wishes to bottle-feed Reni; she wouldn't accede to her mother-in-law's advice to put her on a schedule or to not pick her up when she cried "because you're teaching her she's the boss and you're not." She rationalized — she had to rationalize when it came to her husband's abuse — that what Eric did to her was a separate issue, and as long as he wasn't hurting the baby already born and the one inside her, she would find a way to deal with it.

And so she had come to practice small rebellions.

Eric liked her to go to bed in a particular negligee — it was pink and lacy and, in Merit's mind, something a child bride would wear. Gradually, sitting on the toilet, she began pulling out the seam stitching, inch by inch, night after night until one night, as Eric pulled her to him, the side of her gown ripped open. Despite Merit's assurances that she could repair it, Eric, who believed new was better than mended, ordered her to "throw it away," and a tiny star appeared against the dark nightscape of Merit's marriage.

When Eric first asked her to wear her hair in a French roll the way his mother did ("It's so elegant, so feminine"), Merit was happy to oblige him. She was tired of it now and had talked of cutting her hair, but Eric wouldn't hear of it. So one morning, sitting at her vanity, she tore a piece of tissue she had just used and began rolling it up in her hair. Throughout the day it made her giggle to think of the wadded-up, dirty tissue hidden in her elegant, feminine French roll. Another day she rolled up a used Q-tip; another day a teething biscuit Reni had gnawed on.

Of course, she never told anyone that she purposely unraveled her nightgown or that she harbored dirty personal hygiene items and food products in her hair; never told anyone that sometimes when she made Eric coffee, she liked to put in it a grain — only a grain, so that he could never taste it — of salt or pepper, or the tiniest drip of spit. These were her secrets, these little crazy things she did that helped keep her sane.

She had also learned that the less Eric knew of Angry Housewives (she loved the new name; she had finally figured out she *was* an angry housewife) the better; if he found her curled up on the couch with a book, he was just as likely to fly into a rage ("You sit around all day while I'm in surgery for ten hours straight?") as to ask, "Whatcha reading?" She had learned to read while he was at work or on the sly (nursing in the middle of the night, folding clothes in the laundry room), and to read fast, training herself to see like a hawk, swooping over the page, not missing a thing. Books became her comfort, her sanctuary, and she got scared when she thought of her life just a year and a half ago, when they weren't a part of it. She had always checked out their book club selections from the library, but now she went to bookstores, buying them with the household money Eric gave her every week. Each purchase was another twinkling star.

In another of Merit's rebellious acts, she decided her book club selections would only be banned books. It didn't matter when or where they had been banned; what mattered was that someone had hated a book enough to try to ensure that no one else got a chance to read it (and possibly hate it too). She remembered her mother's sister, her aunt Gaylene, coming to baby-sit. Merit's brother and sister had been put to bed, but Aunt Gaylene had let eight-year-old Merit stay up and play with Lincoln Logs while she lay on the old-fashioned and lumpy horsehair couch that had come with the parish home. The radio was on, and Merit luxuriated in the peacefulness the oldest child of three is rarely privy to, but then her parents came back from their "date" (they had chaperoned the Luther League bowling party) and Pastor Mayes, upon seeing the worn library copy of *Dr. Faustus* on his sister-in-law's lap, threw one of his famous conniption fits.

"How dare you bring that sacrilegious book into this house!"

"Sacrilegious?" laughed Aunt Gaylene. "Have you ever *read* it, Stanley? It's a classic!"

Merit's heart thumped — she would have been spanked and sent straight to her room for speaking to an adult in that snippy tone of voice.

"Well, it's not going to be a classic in my house," said the pastor, grabbing the book out of the woman's hands.

Merit saw the flash of anger in her aunt's eyes, but instead of jumping into the argument her father seemed anxious to push her into, Aunt Gaylene merely smiled and then, really surprising Merit, laughed.

"You're a piece of work, Stanley," she said, shaking her head as if remembering a good joke. She rose, held her hand out for the book, and repeated, "A real piece of work."

Reading *Dr. Faustus*, Merit was reminded of the promise she had made to herself, that someday she was going to be as brave as her aunt

Gaylene. More than fifteen years later, someday was long overdue. But Merit knew there was a price to pay for everything, including bravery; in her last conversation with her mother, Mrs. Mayes had described her recent visit with her sister in Sioux City.

"Well, you know, Gaylene's never found a man for herself, Merit, and that sort of kills a woman's spirit. Now, she *says* all she needs are her friends and her cats and her books, but I'm telling you, she's living half a life."

A part of her wanted to laugh; she knew Aunt Gaylene would have laughed, but the part that shamed Merit believed her mother.

November 1969

Dear Mama,

2:00 a.m. and I think I drank too much coffee — I feel as wired as a fuse box. We had book club tonight and talked about *Dr. Faustus.* When we asked what sort of bargains all of us would make with the devil, Audrey said she'd sell her soul for a chocolate eclair.

"That's a pretty cheap sacrifice," said Kari.

"Well, what does it matter if I sell my soul for a chocolate eclair to someone I don't even believe exists?"

"You don't believe in the devil?" asked Merit.

Audrey fluffed her hair with her hands. "I think he was just invented as a scare tactic."

"Oh," said Merit, and honestly, those eyes of hers were like saucers. "I think the devil is real."

"And what does he look like?" I asked. "Red and horned like Beau's Halloween costume?"

"No," said Merit softly. "He could look like anybody."

"What's that supposed to mean?" asked Slip.

Pink spread across Merit's beautiful face, and if there were a thousand ships around, she'd launch 'em.

"It means," she began, "that I think that's where the devil shows up. In people. He sneaks into them and that's why they do such evil things."

"Give me that old-time religion," said Slip.

Merit shrugged. "That's what I believe."

"So what would make you make a deal with him?" I asked.

Merit sat quietly for a moment, looking down at her lap. "I think we make deals with him every day."

All of us looked at each other like "What the hell (no pun intended) is she talking about?"

"Merit," I said, "I think your preacher daughter roots are showing."

"Probably," she said, and smiled. Then, turning toward Slip, she asked, "I'll bet you wouldn't make a pact with the devil. I'll bet the devil would even be afraid to ask."

Slip looked pleased, and Audrey looked as irritated as I felt. Just because Slip likes to carry a picket sign, Merit thinks she's Joan of Arc or something.

"Well, I think I would," said Slip. "If it were between my children's safety and my soul, I'd give up my soul."

We all nodded, except for Kari.

"That's a hard one," said Kari, her face pale. "Because if you had no soul, you'd have no chance of seeing your loved ones after you die. And I couldn't stand not to see Julia or Bjorn in eternity."

"Now *you* sound old-timey," said Audrey.

"And I can't really believe that you'd give up Julia in the here and now just for the chance of seeing her in what may or may not be an eternity," said Slip.

"I believe there is," said Kari. Her voice was steely, even though there were tears in her eyes. "I can't say as I know what it will be like — but I believe it exists. And I don't think a person should give up their soul for anyone or anything. They would gain nothing."

"They might gain their children's lives!" I said.

"But without a soul, your children would mean nothing to you," said Kari. "All would be nothing."

"It wouldn't matter!" I said. "They'd still be alive!"

"Without meaning there is nothing but nothingness," said the big philosopher.

So how do you like that, Mama? The woman who acts like Julia is God's gift to the world wouldn't even give up her own soul for her. Either I don't understand the depth of her faith or she's not the übermother I thought she was.

Aw, what's your soul anyway? If it's the core of you, the real you — hell, I give up pieces of that every day.

I'm sorry,
Faith

PART TWO

The Seventies

May 1970

HOST: **SLIP**
BOOK: *The Electric Kool-Aid Acid Test*
by Tom Wolfe
REASON CHOSEN: "Because I think
Tom Wolfe should be president."

When a cop grabs you up off the ground, your impulse is to scream and/or wet your pants. At least mine was. Instead, I looked to my fellow protesters for behavior guidelines.

We were a sight, some of us drenched in fake blood, others dressed as National Guardsmen. Dori, a college sophomore, was asking her personal policeman why he didn't just shoot her. Edith, a woman who earlier had shown me pictures of her grandchildren, asked the officer pulling her to her feet to please take it easy, she had arthritis in her knees. There was no screaming, and as far as I could see, no one had wet their pants.

"So what are you arresting me for?" I asked, trying to put a toughness in my voice that I didn't feel.

"I'm not arresting you," said the policeman placidly. "We've just been asked to escort you off the stage. The band wants to start playing."

A handful of people on the sidelines were

booing and shouting, calling out "pig" along with any number of colorful adjectives. A much larger group of people, some dressed in traditional Norwegian costumes, sat quietly on the benches surrounding the bandshell.

Holding me by the arm, my badged escort took me down the steps and released me next to an old man holding a fiddle.

"More power to you," he said in a strong Norwegian brogue.

"Thank you," I said with a catch in my throat. It always touched me when someone I didn't think would back me backed me.

"Sometimes you got to vonder vhot's da verld coming to," said the fiddler, shaking his head.

"I know," I said, shaking mine.

Kent State. It was what had brought me and a handful of protesters to the Norwegian Independence Day celebration at Minnehaha Park, interrupting their festivities to reenact the unbelievable horror that had happened at the Ohio college.

"You want me to pretend I'm a student getting shot?" I'd asked the organizer who called me the night before.

"Yes. We want to do something visually shocking. We want people to be jolted."

"But why the festival?"

"Well, usually at least one TV station does a feature on it," she'd said, and I couldn't argue with that logic. I know the real worth of a protest lies in how many people see or hear about it. Unfortunately, there must have been a big fire or a train derailment, because we had waited for hours for a camera crew that didn't show up.

All the protesters had been cleared off the

stage, and the city councilman who was acting as emcee stepped up to the mike.

"Sorry about that little incident, folks," he said. "They must all be Swedes."

This got an appreciative laugh; I had been in Minnesota long enough to know that anytime a Swede was denigrated to a Norwegian or vice versa, it was considered a good joke. But was that what we were to these people, a little *incident,* a joke?

"Now let's give a hand for the song stylings of the Four Norsemen." Amid applause, the quartet of older gentlemen, including the fiddler, stepped onto the stage.

Usually I felt jazzed up after an action, high on the belief that I was doing *something* to better the world, but now, standing alone in my (fake) blood-soaked shirt, I felt not only conspicuous but ineffectual. I saw two of my fellow protesters buying a box of popcorn, but where were the rest? A group of cops stood by a drinking fountain, where they were listening intently as one regaled them with stories — probably about the time he'd busted heads at a "real" protest like the Democratic National Convention in Chicago.

Feeling foolish, like a host who threw a party no one wanted to stick around for, I put on the sweatshirt that was tied around my waist, covering up my "wound." I was debating whether to walk the couple miles home or check out some of the food stands to see if there was any lefsa around (Kari had turned me on to that particular treat) when I heard "Slip!" For a moment I thought maybe I was being summoned by a fellow protester — maybe this thing wasn't over yet — but the person calling me was wearing a belted pantsuit with absolutely no traces of fake blood splashed on it.

"Hi, Faith!" I said as she and another well-dressed woman came toward me. "What are you doing here?"

Faith introduced me to her friend Nancy, whom she'd met at the Pilots' Wives Association. "And her husband's family is Norwegian, so —"

"So," interrupted Nancy, "I thought Faith might be amused by this rather arcane event. I'm certain they're not used to this level of folksiness back in Dallas."

Holy pretentious nose in the air — was she serious?

"Arcane?" I asked. "What's arcane about a group of people celebrating their heritage?"

Faith blushed for her friend, since fancy-schmancy Nancy didn't seem embarrassed by me calling her on her fancy-schmanciness.

Nancy smiled at me as if I inspired pity in her. "Hmmm. You must be Norwegian too."

"No, I came here as part of a demonstration."

Nancy looked as if she'd swallowed pickle juice. "You weren't part of that . . . that blood-stained group of nuts?"

I pulled my sweatshirt over my head to show her that yup, I sure was.

"We just got here as the police were taking people off," said Faith. "What was it all about?"

"We were protesting what happened at Kent State."

"Oh, that was awful," agreed Faith. "I couldn't believe something like that could happen in the United States."

"Still," said Nancy, "I fail to see what good it does to pour food coloring over yourselves — I'm assuming it's food coloring — and interrupt a celebration people have been looking forward to for weeks."

"Well, we thought it was so *arcane* that it needed something topical. And what's more topical in this day and age than a protest?" I gave her my brightest, beamingest smile, which she did not care to return.

"I really don't understand you people," she said. "I don't quite understand what it is you hope to accomplish."

Faith looked like she'd rather be standing between Hitler and Stalin than us two.

"Well, I personally don't like to sit back as all these *atrocities* occur. I figure I have to do *something* to express my outrage."

"Outrageous is more like it," said Nancy. "Most people think you protesters are nothing but a bunch of —"

"Nancy, please," said Faith, finally getting off the fence. "Slip is very dedicated to —"

"Faith, I'm sorry, I don't care to discuss this anymore." With that, she turned on her stacked heel and began walking toward the pavilion.

"Sorry," said Faith glumly. "I don't know what her problem is."

"I've heard worse," I said, appreciating her apology. "Hey, you don't have to stay with me. Why don't you catch up to her? You came with her, after all."

"You . . . you won't be mad?"

"Of course not. I just feel sorry for you having to spend more time with her. She makes Leslie Trottman look like a font of liberalism."

Faith smiled. "She has her good points . . . I'll bet."

I watched her catch up to her misguided friend and decided I'd head for home but was stopped in my tracks by the fiddler of the Four Norsemen.

He had stepped to the microphone, holding his bow and fiddle at his side.

"Bee-yoo-tiful day, isn't it?"

The crowd signified their agreement by applauding.

"Ya, and it's pretty nice to sit back and listen to da music, isn't it?"

Again, the audience clapped.

"Vell, I yust hope you're grateful dat you can listen to music on a bee-yoo-tiful day, because dose kids from Kent State can't. And I tink dose people dat vere up here hed da right idea. Dose kids need to be remembered. Let's all take a moment out of dis bee-yoo-tiful day to sit in silence for a moment and remember dose kids."

Quiet fell over the crowd, and as the fiddler bowed his head, so did I, thanking him and hoping that his amplified words somehow reached Nancy and all the other Nancys in the world.

Jerry was sitting on the front steps when I got home.

"Hi, honey," I said, eager to report on my day in the trenches and to hear how he had held down the fort. (The kids had accompanied us to several demonstrations, but we thought this one might be a little too dramatic for them.)

"Slip," he said, standing up, and immediately I could tell something was wrong.

"What's the matter?" I asked, my heart racing. "Where are the kids? Are they all right?"

"The kids are fine, Slip," said Jerry, "but your mom called. Fred —"

"Oh my, God!" I said, and the words felt like stones I could choke on. "Fred — is Fred dead?"

"Oh, Slip, no." Jerry took me in his arms. "God, no. He was wounded — not bad, not bad, Slip — he got some shrapnel in the arm, enough to be sent home."

"He's alive?" I asked, pressed against my husband so my heart wouldn't fly out. "Fred's alive?"

"Yes! Yes, he's coming home!"

I can't say that I had been constantly worrying about Fred, but the fact that he was in Vietnam had been like having a bad tooth; you could go on blithely with your business until you took a bite of something and nearly screamed with pain. I had lost four pounds, which doesn't sound like a lot, but on me it's the equivalent of a normal person's dozen; I chewed my fingernails until the quick bled and it hurt to dial a phone or scratch my arm. But I was going to get what thousands of others did not: a brother who was coming back from Vietnam, alive.

I clung to Jerry, sobbing, until Flannery came out of the house, her face puckered with worry.

"What's wrong, Mommy?" she asked. "Didn't they like your protest?"

That night I hunkered down in the bathtub, a half-foot-high layer of bubbles covering me like a suds comforter (I always use plenty of bubble bath in the tub — if there's one thing I need an obscured view of, it's my naked body). The water was just on the verge of being too hot — just the way I liked it — and my nose was only a half inch above the bubbles.

"Ahhhhhhh." My body felt weightless, and as I closed my eyes, all thoughts of the protest, of Fancy Nancy and the fiddler, of my brother Fred coming home drifted away in the fragrant steam cloud that rose above the tub. I was a mermaid; no, I was a being less complicated than that — I was an amoeba, floating along in water and bubbles that smelled of hibiscus.

There was a quick rap on the bathroom door. "Honey, where's the powder?"

My one-celled amoeba mind evolved in seconds to the mind of a mother trying to track down an object. "On the bassinet."

The door cracked open and Jerry poked his head in.

"No, it's not. I looked there."

"Mommy," said Joe, pushing the door wide open. "Gil pooped."

"Babies'll do that," I said.

"Yeah," said Flannery, "but not like Gil. Really, Mom, I've never seen a baby who can poop so much. Why's it so foggy in here?"

Without invitation, my entire family had joined me in the bathroom. As any mother of small children knows, while time alone is a rare and precious commodity, bath time alone is almost a religious experience. Gil was clinging like a little monkey to Jerry, his eyes wide, as if he couldn't quite grasp that the wet-haired thing submerged in bubbles was his mother. Plus he absolutely reeked, nullifying the hibiscus scent of the bubble bath.

"Jerry, please, can't you change the baby?"

"Well, that's what I'm trying to do, but I can't find the powder."

"Mommy, do you want some of my toys in there?" asked Flannery, opening up the linen closet. "They're right in here."

"No, Flan, I'm fine, I —"

"I want that!" said Joe, grabbing a plastic boat out of the old dishwashing tub we kept the bath toys in.

"No!" said Flan, grabbing the toy out of her brother's hand. "These are just for when you take a bath!"

Joe reached out to take something of Flannery's, which in this particular case was a hunk of her hair, which made her scream, which startled the baby, who probably wanted nothing more than a nice clean diaper, which made me yell, "Will everyone please get out of here, now?" which made everyone leave with hurt feelings, which wrecked my warm bubbly religious experience, which made me cranky for the rest of the night, which is why I must get a lock for that bathroom door.

So of course when I finally got to bed, it was a not unfamiliar scenario: husband and wife were travelers with two different destinations in mind: I wanted nothing more than to visit the Land of Nod, and Jerry was hoping for a quick trip to Sex World. Don't get me wrong: Jerry does more around the house than any other husband I know (he had been with the kids practically all day) but, pardon the expression, that's still jack shit. Of course, he has a full-time job, but so do I; I just don't get to leave the house to do it, I don't get to dress up for it, I don't get paid for it, and the world at large seems to think it's pretty inconsequential. Oh, and did I mention that calling in sick is unacceptable?

See? Mess around with my bath, and this is the mood I bring to bed.

"Mmm," said Jerry, nuzzling my ear. "You smell good."

"Jerry, I'm so tired," I whispered, as if even talking was too much of an effort.

"Mmm," said Jerry, continuing his nuzzling. This was not the answer I'd been hoping for, but he didn't seem to mind when I rolled over; he just pressed his body against mine and started stroking my hip bone. I must admit, I like when he strokes my hip bone; I feel like I'm being sculpted by a sculptor who really loves the medium he's working in, like my skin is the clay he's going to turn into something curvy and amazing. So in spite of the fatigue that made me want to sleep into the next week, I found myself responding to Jerry, found my body moving along with his, found my lips wanting to meet his, and just as I rolled over to really get things going, the baby cried.

We froze and for a few moments we were nothing more than ears; straining to tell what kind of cry it was and more importantly, would it be short-lived. It wasn't.

"We could ignore him," I said, kissing Jerry's upper lip. "He shouldn't be hungry."

"Sounds good to me," said Jerry, kissing me back.

But this was not a baby who was going to somehow calm himself back to sleep; this was a baby who wanted someone else to do that job.

"He's going to wake the whole house up," I said, finagling my way out of Jerry's embrace and reaching for my robe at the foot of the bed.

"No," said Jerry, "I'll go see what he needs. You stay here."

The thing is, this was no halfhearted gesture; I knew Jerry really would get up and see what Gil wanted. And that's why I loved him.

"No, I'll go," I said, tying the robe. "I'll calm him down and then I'll see what I can do for you."

"Mmm, can't wait." Jerry reached out and cupped my rear end as I got out of bed. "Hurry back."

Gil's pacifier had fallen out of his crib, and after blowing away all traces of germs, I stuck it back into his grateful mouth. With some pats on the back and some reassurances that he was my good little boy, he was asleep.

I raced back to the bedroom, all bright-eyed and bushy-tailed, but the detour this traveler had been willing to take was now blocked off. Jerry lay on his back, his jaw sightly unhinged, sleeping. I climbed into bed, hoping to wake him with my throat clearing and little tugs of the blanket, but he was not only in the Land of Nod, he had staked a claim there, had been elected mayor there. And I knew that it didn't matter how exhausted I was — some taunting force would keep me awake, would punish me for wanting to see to the needs of husband and baby. I lay there in the dark for a while, sighing great put-upon sighs, but then I reached for the nightstand and the thing on top of it that might not guarantee me quick passage to Nod, but at least would entertain me until I got there: my flashlight, and underneath that, the book we would be discussing at tomorrow night's meeting.

Sister Ignatius taught me in Sunday school that "in the beginning there was light," but to me, it was always an incomplete sentence, which God should have known to amend: in the beginning God created light . . . to read by.

HOST: **AUDREY**

BOOK: *Everything You Wanted to Know*

About Sex But Were Afraid to Ask

by Dr. David Reuben

REASON CHOSEN: "I think it's obvious."

Merit had practically swooned when I announced my sexciting selection, saying she wasn't sure Eric would like her to be reading a book like that.

Then hide it from the a—hole, I'd wanted to say, but contrary to popular belief, I *am* capable of censoring myself, especially with regard to Merit's husband, about whom Merit never joked or allowed others the courtesy.

"Oh, come on, it'll be fun," Kari had said. (I don't know if it's motherhood or what, but Kari keeps surprising me by her willingness to jump into anything.)

"Well, how are we supposed to discuss a book like that?" Faith had asked, pulling at one of her earrings. "I mean, it's not as if we can identify with a particular hero or discuss the symbolism of the missionary position."

"I for one wouldn't mind discussing the symbolism of the missionary position," Slip had put in. "Think about it — the man on top, dominant and in control, converting the woman, i.e., the native, by whatever means possible."

A laugh had burbled out of Merit.

"I was just thinking what my father would say about that," she had explained.

Faith was the most imaginative when it came to hosting a meeting — she always decorated and served food that tied in with the book we were discussing, but tonight, I was truly inspired. In keeping with the *Everything You Always Wanted to Know About Sex* theme, I had made several artful yet tantalizing arrangements; on one platter long spears of bananas nestled between peach halves decorated with a frill of parsley; on another, pineapple rings encircled bratwursts. There were hard-boiled eggs in one bowl and sunflower seeds in another. No doubt about it — I had set a table that would be banned in Boston.

My two older boys (Davey and Bryan had a brother now, ten-month-old Michael) were at Paul's mother's for the evening, and Paul had called from work.

"As long as you're having a girls' night in, I thought I'd have a boys' night out," he said, "unless you'd rather have me there to mix drinks and fetch hors d'oeuvres."

I laughed at the improbability of that occurring.

"I don't know, we probably could use a bouncer. I mean, when you're discussing a book about sex, anything could happen. . . ."

"Hmmm, maybe I should come home after all."

"You'd probably learn something," I said, and after I hung up I thought how nice it was to be joking with my husband again. We had had some rocky times — the first few months after Michael was born it seemed our words were aimed at each other rather than spoken — but the easy teasing that had always been a mainstay of our marriage had finally come back.

I checked on the snack mix in the oven (pretzel sticks and Cheerios) and just as I grabbed a pot holder, the knowledge that Paul was having an affair rushed through me.

"Oh, my," I said, thinking that rather than the hot flashes my mother had complained about, this was a cold flash, as if an ice storm had suddenly stirred up in my heart and blew its frozen winds through my body.

A little puff of air escaped from the red vinyl cushion as I collapsed on the kitchen chair. It was no use trying to talk myself out of what I knew to be true, and my absolute certainty scared me almost as much as the idea of Paul's affair.

"Why'd you make me see that?" I whispered, speaking to my sixth sense or ESP or whatever freakish thing it was that enabled me to know or see things that maybe I wasn't supposed to know or see. "Why couldn't I have been left in the dark, like most other wives?"

I had to laugh then, a thin and brittle laugh, before I got up to take the snack mix out of the oven.

The day after his burial, my grandfather had come to visit me in my bedroom. I was eleven years old, a big girl whose breasts had passed the budding stage and gone into full flower, a girl who already had her period. Still, unlike poor

Trudy Himmler, whose hormones had kicked in almost as early as mine and who always hunched over, trying to hide all evidence of her maturity, I wasn't beaten down by these two events; in fact, my confidence was as much a part of me as my big feet or my wide brown eyes and just as likely to always be there.

"Poppie!" I had whispered, not in fear, but in surprise.

My grandfather was dressed not in his burial suit but in the clothes he wore to garden in, and he tipped his straw hat as he sat on the edge of my bed.

"Poppie, what are you doing here?"

His bright white dentures were revealed as he smiled, and even though I didn't hear his voice, I *heard* him.

He told me everything was all right, that he was in a place of such peace and wonder it made earth look like the "cartoon compared to the feature."

I was delighted at the analogy; Saturday matinees had been our regular date.

When I asked him why he had to die, he told me — without speaking — that it was his time and he had come back only to tell me that he was in a better place and not to feel *too* bad about his dying.

"A little bit bad is all right," he said, the twinkle still filtering through his rheumy eyes, "but not *real* bad." He also told me I had a gift and not to be afraid of it.

"What kind of gift?"

"You'll know."

I wasn't sure if he put his arms around me, but I sure felt as if I'd been hugged, and then he was gone.

The next morning, my mother nearly choked on her poached egg when I told her about Poppie's visit.

"Is that supposed to be some kind of sick joke? Because it's not funny!"

"It's not a joke — he did come to visit me and he told me he was in a better place and that I had a gift."

"I'm warning you, Audrey," and I think it was only when I flinched that she realized she was holding up her arm, as if to strike me.

She knelt down and took me by the arms, pressing her fingers into them. "I'm sorry, Audrey, I wasn't going to hit you," she said, her voice hoarse, "but what do you expect me to do, hearing such nonsense?"

"It's not nonsense, he really —"

"Audrey, please, I just lost my father! This is not helping me, so please — *stop talking like a crazy person!*"

And I did. I kept to myself all the odd things that happened to me; didn't tell anyone about the day when the principal came to the classroom and before he said anything I knew that Blake Rothman's brother had been killed that afternoon (in an archery accident, it turned out); didn't tell anyone about the time I was going to Bell's Double Bar Ranch for my riding lesson and knew, before I opened the door, that old Jim, who cleaned the stables, would be lying on the floor, dead (I didn't know the cause, an aneurysm, and didn't even know what an aneurysm was — all I knew was that I'd find him dead); didn't tell anyone about all the many little things that I knew were going to happen before they actually did.

I was so good at not telling anyone that eventually I was able to convince myself that I too didn't believe in such nonsense. By my teens I was no more prescient than the next person — I might occasionally know who was on the telephone before I picked up the receiver, but so did a lot of people; I might know what was inside a wrapped present before I opened it, but that was only lucky guessing. I believed I had keen intuition and nothing more and was relieved of the burden of knowing more than I wanted to . . . but this past spring I had woken Paul up out of a dead sleep and told him to call his sister Marilyn in Oconomowoc and tell her to get everyone out of the house.

"Wha—"

"Just do it!"

Cursing me for my ridiculousness, Paul had nevertheless dialed the little Princess phone we kept by the bed, and when his sister answered he launched into an apology but was abruptly cut off.

His face was as pale as the moonlight that shone against the wall.

"Paul?"

He turned to me and in a low, strangled-sounding voice asked, "How did you know?"

"I . . . I had a dream."

"A dream about a fire?"

I nodded, although I hadn't yet fallen asleep when the prickly feeling, as if all of my limbs had fallen asleep, had come over my body and I saw the picture of a burning house, my sister-in-law's house.

"Because," continued Paul in his strange low voice, "because right after she asked me what I was doing calling so late, she yelled, 'Paul, I can't talk, I smell smoke!' "

A shiver spasmed through me. "Call them back!"

He tried several times, but there was no answer.

Even though the covers were pulled up to our chests, the two of us sat shivering with our bodies pressed against the headboard, staring at the phone, as if willing it to ring.

"Tell me about your dreams," Paul said finally, and I did. I told him everything. I talked until the moonlight began to fade in deference to the flush of morning, talked until the phone finally rang with news from Paul's sister that the space heater they kept in the three-season porch had been knocked over — probably by the dog — and started a fire.

"She said the whole porch is destroyed, but everyone got out safely, thanks to my phone call," said Paul.

Relief pumped through me and I couldn't hug my husband tight enough, but instead of hugging me back, Paul pushed me aside.

"I need a drink of water," he said, flinging the covers aside as he got out of bed.

"Could you bring me one too?" I asked, but he had darted out of the room like an animal who's just smelled a hunter.

"Girls," I said as we all settled in the living room, "I think tonight we're going to have to get a little stoned."

"You're not serious," said Slip. Watching me take a joint out of my breast pocket, she said to the others, "Oh, my God, she is serious. Not

233

only does she want us to talk about sex, she wants us to be high on drugs while we're doing it." (How can Slip be so hip and yet so *unhip?*)

I laughed, assuming she was joking. (It's a trick I've learned — whenever someone disapproves of or disagrees with you, laugh as if they're just joking.)

"I think it would enhance the conversation," I said, firing up the joint my brother had given me. I drew in a big cloudful and held the skinny little cigarette out toward the general public.

"What about the kids?" asked Kari.

Her baby and mine, the only ones not left at home with a husband or sitter, had been put to bed before the meeting started.

"The kids are sleeping." Still holding my breath as I talked, my voice sounded like that of a Borscht-belt comic.

"But what if Julia wakes up? What if she needs me?"

"You'll be fine," I said, and then exhaled the sweet-smelling smoke. "Now hurry up before it burns down."

"Well, I can't say I haven't been curious," said Kari, taking the joint. "I'll just take one little puff." She pursed her lips, and the end of the joint glowed red as she inhaled.

"Oh, my," she said, sputtering out smoke like a defective chimney. "Oh, my."

Slip laughed. "So I'm not the only one who can't hold my marijuana."

"You smoke it too?" asked Merit, her voice as wide open as her eyes.

"I've tried it," said Slip, taking the joint. "But I always seem to cough out every trace of hallucinogen."

"Hallucinogen," said Merit. "You mean if I smoke that thing I'll see pink elephants or Satan or something?"

"Only if it's really good dope." Seeing her stricken face, I reassured her I was just kidding. "Most likely you'll just find everything hilarious."

Boy, did we. I have to hand it to old Merit — she took the joint and held it as if she had a live animal by the tail, but then inhaled like an old pro, only coughing a little. Faith was the one we had to badger; she sat shaking her head, her arms folded across her chest, acting as if we were committing a felony or something. I mean a deservable felony.

"Come on, Faith," said Merit. "If I can do it, you can."

Faith's nostrils flared and she was perched on the edge of her chair as if she were contemplating escape, but after biting her bottom lip, she said, "It's not a question of if I can do it, it's a question of wanting to do it. But if y'all are going to gang up on me, then give it here."

By her second inhale, she was laughing as hard as the rest of us . . . especially when we began the book discussion.

"What I'd like to know," she said, waving her hands like she was drying her nail polish, "is how many times y'all said, 'Oh, that's disgustin',' while readin' this book."

"Your accent's coming out," said Merit.

"Well, I know something is," said Faith with a giggle. "But I thought it was all rational thought." She fanned her fingers in front of her face. "Anybody else see sparks when I do this?"

"Faith," I said, "you didn't drop acid, you just

smoked a little grass."

"Well, it's not like I'm seeing a meteor shower," she said haughtily, "just a few little sparks is all."

Merit watched her hands intently as she flicked her fingers. "I don't see any sparks, but I do think I can see the blood rushing through my veins."

"Merit," said Kari, "you know who you look like? One of Chopin's études."

I laughed. "You guys are *stoned*."

"People, I was about to say something," said Slip, and she looked up at the ceiling as if her answer hovered there. Apparently it did. "In response to the question you asked about a mile ago, Faith; I think I said 'Oh, that's disgusting' about a hundred times. And I think I said it the loudest when I was reading about fellatio."

"Are you kidding me?" I said. "You don't like giving blow jobs?"

They shrieked like a bunch of old ladies whose purses had just been snatched, and then in unison they all cried, *"Blow jobs!"*

I stared at my friends; as far as I could tell, their indignation was real.

"Really, you're kidding, right?" I lit a cigarette now that the joint had been all smoked up. "Are you telling me you don't give them . . . that your husbands don't like them?"

Faith stared at me for a moment, her mouth open, before her upper body collapsed under a big tidal wave of giggles.

Of course the rest of us were knocked over by it. If anyone had come in at that moment (*like the cops,* I thought, but pushed aside the thought, not willing to let a really good high get spoiled

236

by a little paranoia), they would have seen five women sprawled across the furniture, holding their various-sized middles, helpless with laughter. When it seemed the wave had crashed and we were bobbing along in calmer water, someone would say something and away we'd go.

"Well, I've tried it a couple times," Slip said, "but I never get very far."

"Why not?" I asked.

"Either Jerry says ouch or I say, 'Air! I need air!' "

The tidal wave crashed in again and we laughed until our faces were wet with tears.

"Wade pesters me to try it," said Faith, hugging a pillow to her stomach, "but he always stops me right in the middle. He says the sound of my gagging turns him off."

We were dying. Caught under a tidal wave and dying in my living room.

"How about you, Kari?" I asked, emboldened by the dope. "Were you willing to service Bjorn?"

"My lips are sealed," she said, shaking her head, and it took just a second for the pun to sink in and the storm of laughter raged again.

"Oh, my gosh," said Merit finally, her eyes sparkly with tears. "If Eric could hear us now. Oh, my gosh."

"If *any* of our husbands could hear us talk," said Faith.

Slip, wiping her eyes, asked, "Holy strange scenario, could you imagine them getting together and talking about the kinds of things we talk about?"

"Actually, I *could* imagine them talking about

sex," I said. "I mean, don't men love to share their tales of conquest?"

"Maybe in high school or as frat boys," said Slip, "but once a man is married I don't think he talks about his sex life to his friends. I think Jerry would think it was an invasion of our privacy." Cupping her hands to her face, Slip shouted in the direction of her house, "God, I love you, Jerry!"

"I don't think I can move my legs," said Merit. "Should I be able to move my legs?"

"Only if you have somewhere to go," I said.

Merit frowned. "I don't think I do . . . do I?"

We body-surfed on another wave of laughter.

"I think Slip's right," said Kari.

"Right about what?" said Slip. "What'd I say?"

"Right about men not talking about themselves with other men. In fact, Bjorn once said that he thought women were the more evolved species because they felt much freer in sharing their stories with one another." She laced her fingers and stretched her arms out in front of her. "So yabba dabba doo."

"Did you just say 'yabba dabba doo'?" I asked, the laughter welling up inside of me like bubbles in boiling water.

Slip shook her head. "No, what she said was 'yabba dabba *doo*.'"

"Isn't that what Huckleberry Hound says?" asked Merit.

"Merit, you are so far off, you're not even on the map," said Faith. "Fred Flintstone says 'yabba dabba doo,' not Huckleberry Hound."

"I thought it was Anne Boleyn," I said, "when she saw Henry the Eighth for the first time."

"I thought it was Gauguin," said Slip, "when

he first stepped on the white sand beaches of Tahiti."

"Hey, I just moved my foot," said Merit. "I moved my foot!" She looked around, her face awash in rapturous beauty.

"My God," I told her, "your face is awash in rapturous beauty."

"Hey, I just moved my other foot!" said Merit, and, then, smiling at me, she said, "Yabba dabba doo!"

We laughed for about a lunar year, and then Kari said, "This reminds me of how Bjorn and I used to laugh sometimes," and then we were all quiet. It was only recently — only since the arrival of Julia, really — that I felt comfortable asking Kari about Bjorn, only recently that Kari seemed capable of talking about her dead husband without sounding like she was standing on the corner of Heartbreak and Pain.

I said as much and then, hearing the words out loud, added, "Wow, I *am* stoned."

"No, you're right," said Kari. "My heart broke when I had my miscarriages and then it broke a little more when Bettina was taken away, but when Bjorn died, it shattered. I mean it; there was nothing left but shards and dust."

"Shards and dust," said Slip reverently, nodding.

The atmosphere of the room changed then; it was like all those waves of laughter went back out to sea, and we were left floating by the shore, not exactly sad, but spent.

"But you know what I have found?" Kari asked, and I was startled by her smile and how it could transform her plain face. "I have found I'm very glad I tried marijuana — my gosh, you don't get that combination of hysterical laughter and peacefulness very often — but I'll never smoke it again, or at least not until Julia's all grown up."

The blood in my face took a hike in temperature. "If you think I'm endangering my children or something, if you think I'm a pothead, don't hint around, Kari; come right out and say it."

"I wasn't saying that at all, Audrey," said Kari right away. I regretted my paranoia; I could tell by her voice that she meant it. "I was just saying —"

"You were saying something about shards and dust," said Slip. "I want to hear more about that; it sounded like a poem."

"Shards and dust," said Merit, "crumbs and rust. That's all that was left. Left of my heart."

We stared at Merit as if she'd just revealed the secret of the pyramids.

"I can't tell if that was really bad or really good," said Slip finally, and then, turning to Kari, she said, "Now, what did *you* mean by that?"

Kari smiled as she touched the hollow at the base of her throat. "How you can keep a train of thought is beyond me." She stroked her neck. "Oh, yes — what I learned about hearts. I learned they're like lizards — they can regenerate. Lizards are the ones whose tails grow back if they're chopped off, right? My gosh, Audrey, I wish I could wear short skirts like you — your legs are about a mile long!"

"Only a half mile," I said, flexing my foot to admire my ankle.

"Well, mine are half a foot," said Slip, standing up to model her legs, which were stocky and

muscular. Sucking her cheekbones in, she pirou-
etted, her hands resting on the chain belt that
held up her corduroy miniskirt.

"Kari," said Merit as we laughed, "tell us
about the lizard and your heart."

"There you go again," said Kari, "expecting
me to hold on to a conversational thread. Let me
think." She stared at her wedding ring for a long
while. "Oh, yes. Well, I thought there was
nothing left after Bjorn died, but then I got a
baby — *I got a baby!* — and my heart put itself
back together." With her bright blue eyes, she
looked at each of us as if she wanted to include
everyone in the celebration of this discovery, and
we all sat there waiting for her to say more, because everything was sounding so very profound,
but all she asked was, "Isn't it time to eat yet?"

"Well, that was an interesting evening," said
Faith as she brushed crumbs off the coffee table
and into her open hand. "I don't think I've ever
seen Merit so . . . animated!"

"She had to have been stoned out of her
mind."

"What she did with that bratwurst! I thought I
was watching a burlesque show."

I laughed. "Well, it was Slip who was egging
her on. Don't make me think about it again, I'm
already sick from laughing so much." I helped
myself to yet another one of the brownies Kari
had brought to offset my sexually explicit but
gastronomically tepid refreshments. "What I
can't figure out, Faith," I said, catching with my
pinky nail a blob of chocolate that fell out of my
mouth, "is why you were so Carrie Nation about
even trying it."

Twin roses bloomed on Faith's cheeks. Merit's the classic beauty of our bunch, but to me, Faith's face brings to mind that wonderful nineteenth-century word *fetching*.

"Well, I hate to be the one to tell you, Audrey, but smoking marijuana" — this she pronounced as "mary-wanna" — "is illegal."

"Yeah, but come on, Faith, you're usually the first one in line to have some fun. I mean, you certainly like your liquor."

The roses deepened in color. "What's that supposed to mean?"

She had the same defensiveness in her voice that I had when I thought Kari was accusing me of being a pothead. I shrugged, stacking a few of the dessert plates in front of me. "It means nothing, Faith. All of us enjoy a nice drink. I just thought you might have had a bad experience or something, the way you were so adamant at first."

Faith's flared nostrils were perfect little O's.

"Audrey, I have never smoked marijuana in my life — what makes you think I have?"

I shrugged again — was she touchy or what?

"Is that what you think of me?" she asked, the twang in her voice cranked up. "That I've had some wild pot-smokin', drug-takin', lawless past?"

"Faith, why would I think such a thing? Geez, calm down. Take a deep breath. Some people get a little paranoid when they smoke, and I think you might be in that category."

"Well, maybe so," she said, and took in a big gulp of air. "I do feel sort of —"

But I didn't hear how she felt because I was suddenly on my feet, racing through the dining room and up the stairs.

Horror filled me as I flew into the bedroom and to the crib where Michael was sleeping.

"The sheet's wrapped around his neck!"

I raced to unwind the bunched-up sheet and picked my baby up. A gasp and then a wail erupted from his little mouth, and the awful blue color of his face faded to a milky white and then to pink.

"Oh, thank God!" I cried, collapsing on the rocking chair with Michael in my arms. "Thank God!"

From the doorway, Faith stared at me, her mouth an Edvard Munch oval, holding on to the doorjamb as if she needed the support.

"He says he doesn't see a need to bring him in," I said after talking to the doctor on call at my clinic, "as long as he's breathing fine and doesn't seem to be lethargic or different in any way."

"Thank God," said Faith, her face pale against the frame of her shiny black hair.

"Feel my arms."

Faith leaned over to touch a trembling bicep.

"That's probably why Michael's so smiley now," I said, wishing I could smile myself. "Babies like vibrations."

"Can I get you anything?" asked Faith. "Some coffee? A drink?"

"Would you light a cigarette for me?" I asked, and as she did I murmured to the sweet baby boy in my arms, "How did that sheet slip off the corner of the mattress? How did you get all twisted up in it?"

Mikey smiled behind his pacifier, and one

little arm reached for my pendant.

"Oh, my precious little boy," I said, tilting his head as he pulled on the chain. "My big strong precious little boy."

I took the cigarette from Faith and inhaled, blowing the smoke toward the ceiling.

"How did you know he was in trouble?" Faith asked quietly. "I didn't hear him cry. Just all of a sudden, whoosh — you're running up the stairs."

Clamping the cigarette in my mouth, I reclaimed my pendant from the baby's grasp and replaced it with the watch I slipped off my wrist. Mikey seemed happy with the trade, focusing his mighty baby attention on the ticking second hand.

"I . . . I just saw a picture in my head. A picture of him not breathing."

Faith's shoulder twitched in a shiver.

"Do you see . . . pictures often?"

"Well, today seems to be a banner day for them. I guess it's true — when it rains it pours."

"What do you mean?"

I sighed, so tired, yet wide awake. "It's just that sometimes I see pictures, and sometimes I just *sense* things."

"So these pictures or these sensings aren't because of the marijuana?"

I shook my head. "Right before book club tonight I sensed — in a *big* way — that Paul's fooling around."

She exhaled a slow breath. "Oh, Audrey, what are you going to do?"

"I haven't figured that out yet." I felt tears pooling in my eyes. "Right now I'm just going to revel in the fact that my baby's all right."

For a long time we sat quietly finishing our cigarettes and watching Mikey play with my watchband.

Finally I asked the question I didn't necessarily want an answer to. "You don't think I'm a freak, do you?"

Faith shook her head. "No, I don't think you're a freak, Audrey. I had a friend whose grandmother could see things."

"You did?" I asked, feeling my heart quicken.

"My friend DellaRose," she said, nodding. "Grandma T — I don't know what the T stood for, but that's what everyone called her. Anyway, she called it her gift, or her third eye. We used to play a game, looking through her hair trying to find it. Part of me half expected to find an eyeball buried in her scalp somewhere, but other than that, I don't know how seriously I took it, even though DellaRose told me Grandma T always knew when someone had died or when someone was going to have a baby." Faith looked at the Manet print on the wall with a funny look on her face. "Can you see into the past too, or do you just see the future?"

Mikey scowled at me as my laughing jostled him. "Faith, it's not like I'm a mind reader or a fortune-teller, for God's sake. I just get these pictures, these feelings."

"Yeah, but these pictures or feelings — do you get them about everyone? I mean, could you look at me and get a picture or feeling about what happened to me this morning or last year or when I was a kid or something?"

I laughed again, and Mikey once more lowered his little brows at me before closing his eyes. "Faith, you sound so serious."

The funny look on her face — like a kid's who'd just realized she hadn't made it to the bathroom on time — didn't budge.

"And why do you want to know?" I asked, my voice teasing. "Is there something you don't want me to see? Are you hiding something, Faith?"

Her face mottled with color, and then her laughter (which sounded awfully polite) joined mine.

"Yeah," she said, "I'm terrified you're going to discover that I'm a secret agent for Interpol, working to break up all the subversive activities on Freesia Court."

"Otherwise known as Operation Stop Angry Housewives Eating Bon Bons."

Faith nodded. "Exactly." She looked around at the still messy dining room. "Well, I guess we should finish this cleanup so I can get home and see if Wade ever got the kids to bed."

She began picking up dishes as I looked down at Mikey, who had fallen asleep. Bile rose in my throat, thinking what might have happened had I not run upstairs. After a moment, I looked up to see Faith staring at me.

"Thank God he's all right," she said.

I nodded, tears welling up in my eyes.

"Whatever you saw," Faith said hesitantly, "whatever made you go to Mikey — well, like DellaRose's grandmother said, it's a gift."

"Or my third eye," I said in my best Bela Lugosi voice. I swallowed hard. "Still," I said, "don't tell anyone about it, okay? I'd feel weird if it were, you know, public knowledge."

"Your secret is my secret," said Faith.

"And vice versa," I said, not exactly knowing why.

Dear Mama,

For tonight's book club meeting, I had a centerpiece of red, white, and pink carnations. The twins "helped" me make a pink heart-shaped cake (three-year-olds are not particularly skilled at cracking eggs) as well as heart-shaped sugar cookies (three-year-olds are not particularly skilled at sifting flour).

Looking at the table, Audrey said she was going to go into insulin shock, and then Kari said, "That's exactly how I felt reading the book."

"I thought it was a good love story," said Merit (you'd never guess her second baby is due in a couple months — she barely even shows). "*Love Story*. He couldn't have named it any better."

"Oh, yes, he could have," said Kari. "He could have named it *Puke Story*. Because that's what I wanted to do after I read it."

Oh, Mama, we have so much fun. We sat outside on lawn chairs drinking rum and Cokes, and Slip went inside to go to the bathroom, and when she came back she was *walking on her hands* and we all laughed like crazy. Kari said Slip should join the circus and Slip said that was a boat she just happened to miss in life and then I said, "Well, then, let's bring the boat to you," and now we've decided that on Labor Day we'll all get together for a neighborhood circus. (Won't the twins make cute little clowns?) Audrey said she wants to be the ringmaster — she says it's a fantasy of hers to wear satin hot pants and crack a whip. Kari reminded her it's a family affair.

I think how much good it would have done you to be in a book club, to talk about books (and everything else) with your friends, and then I remember that you didn't have any friends. I'm sitting here, thinking hard, but not one single face comes to mind, not one single face of a friend of yours. Surely you must have had one friend, didn't you, Mama? I am racking my brain, but all I see are thousands — okay, dozens — of boyfriends, and I'm sure you didn't talk about cramps or feeding a picky child with *them*.

When I was about eight, I saw a report card of yours, Mama, I think it was from the seventh grade. I found it in MawMaw's darning basket when I was looking for some thread, and when I showed it to her, she asked, "Now how'd that thing get in there?" I stood next to her as she took it out of the envelope. You know MawMaw had two expressions, sad or grim, and looking at your report card, she had this big smile on her face.

"Look at that," she said, the cracked yellow nail of her pointer finger running down a column. "Four A's and two B's."

"Is that good?" I asked.

"That's very good," said MawMaw. "Your mama was a smart little girl."

"She was?" I asked, not used to having my grandmother say nice things about my mother.

"She taught herself to read," said MawMaw, staring at that report card. "Weren't but four years old and she taught her own self to read. Primrose always loved a good book."

"She did?" I asked, thrilled because I did

too, and that meant I shared something with my mother.

MawMaw looked at me then, and the smile on her face shrank until her face was hard and grim again. "Yuh. But then she found something she liked better than books: boys. And after that she found something she liked even more: booze."

I wanted to talk more about the Mama who got four A's and two B's, but MawMaw had used up her conversation for the day. Well, almost all of it — she did have one piece of advice for me as she got up to do whatever joyless task summoned her.

"If you pick one thing to be in life," she said, rubbing her lower back, which always seemed to be in need of rubbing, "pick not to be like your mama."

I never thought of you as lonely, Mama — you were always making such a ruckus, but maybe that's how you fought off your loneliness, by always making noise. If you'd just had one friend. . . . you might have been a different person if you'd just had one friend.

Erich Segal says, "Love means never having to say you're sorry." So I guess you did love me, Mama, because I can't remember you ever apologizing for anything and yet look at me, I can't stop telling you how much I'm sorry.

Faith

October 1973

HOST: **MERIT**
BOOK CHOSEN: *Fear of Flying* by Erica Jong
REASON CHOSEN: "Because it's bound to make hundreds of banned lists."

The day before Pastor Mayes died of a heart attack, he called Merit to apologize for "my inadequacies as a father."

Merit was rendered speechless for a moment by this extraordinary announcement. "Dad," she said finally, "are you all right?"

Pastor Mayes laughed. "Feeling fine, Merit. Your mother and I just did our walk around the golf course, and now I'm sitting here in my office, going over my notes for tomorrow's sermon."

When words failed Merit again, Pastor Mayes gallantly stepped in.

"My sermon is about forgiveness — I must have given at least a thousand on that topic, wouldn't you say? But this time something hit me, and I thought, for the first time, that I don't need to *talk* about forgiveness, I *need* it. I thought, why was I always so hard on my own children?"

Merit felt the tears begin. "Oh, Dad."

He laughed, again, a sound Merit didn't associate with her father. "So, I wanted to know two things, Merit. One, will you forgive me for thinking your fear and obedience were more important than your love and respect?"

"Oh, Dad." They were the only words Merit could formulate.

"And two, despite my inadequacies, did you turn out all right, Merit? Are you happy?"

Merit made a noise, in response to the question and a power kick by the baby inside her.

"Sorry, Dad, the baby just kicked me."

Again, that warm, unfamiliar chuckle. "Two more months, is it? I bet Reni and Melody are excited."

"Oh, they are, Dad, they —" A thought suddenly popped into Merit's head. "Dad . . . why don't you baptize this one?" She and Eric had had the girls baptized in the Episcopal Church, but this one, this one would be baptized by her newly repentant Lutheran father.

Pastor Mayes didn't answer for a while, and when Merit heard a snuffle, she realized he was choked up.

"Dad."

"That . . . ," he said, his voice wavery, "that'd be an honor, Merit."

There was silence on the phone again, but it was a friendly, unhurried silence, as if both parties were content to sit and think about what had just transpired.

"Oh, and Dad — yes, I am happy. Yes, things did turn out."

It was more a half-truth than a lie; she *was* happy with her children, with her friends, and she didn't want to, *couldn't* burden her father with the weight of her marriage troubles.

"I'm glad, Merit. I love you."

251

"I love you too, Dad," and when she received the call the next day from her sister that he had keeled over just as he was pouring his morning coffee, amid her shock and grief was one grace note: that those had been her last words to him.

"Do you suppose he knew he was going to die?" she asked Eric, who had held her while she cried. "Do you suppose that's why he called me to ask my forgiveness?"

"Merit, please," he said in a voice of such bothered impatience that Merit immediately regretted the question, immediately felt childish and vulnerable on his lap. "You think he had a little premonition like your friend Audrey, who gets visits from dead people and can tell what's going to happen before it does? Yeah, right. That's a bunch of bullshit and you know it."

Merit stiffened — occasionally she still made the mistake of telling her husband things, of *sharing* with him, and inevitably he used this information against her. *Never again,* she vowed to herself, *will I think I can trust you.*

Under the pretext of reaching for the tissue box on the coffee table, Merit slid off his lap, her teeth working furiously on the inside of her cheek.

"And no offense," he said, smoothing the wrinkles on his pants, "I mean, I'm truly sorry the man is dead, but baptizing the baby? Eric the fourth will be baptized in the same church I was. What were you thinking, Merit?"

She yanked tissues out of the box as her throat swelled with the thickness of tears. *I was thinking that it would be a really nice thing,* she thought, biting the inside of her cheek harder until she tasted blood. *I was thinking maybe it was my turn to choose where the baby got baptized. Sometimes I'm so silly, Eric — I forget that you don't play fair, that you don't take turns. I forget that you couldn't care less about what matters to me. I forget that I don't get what I need from you — and today I needed a little comfort. Isn't that a stupid thing to want from my own husband on the day my father died? Well, I'm very sorry I'm so stupid!*

The main reason Merit didn't get her hair cut for so long was that she didn't want to give up her I-hate-Eric shrine. Where would she put the dirty tissues and Q-tips, the gnawed-on baby biscuits, the little notes, written on strips of paper as narrow as the ones found in fortune cookies, that said things like *Go to hell where you belong, Eric* or *Dr. Eric Iverson is an incompetent quack in all areas* or *I wish you'd die, Eric.*

Every time she rolled something up in her hair, she felt as if she'd won a small victory, felt as if she were a tiny East European country that for twenty-four hours, at least, had staved off the Iron Curtain from closing in on its borders.

She was never caught. She secured her French roll with enough bobby pins to arm a cat fight, and she always fixed her hair while Eric slept or after he'd left for work.

Inspired by Faith, who was always experimenting with her hair (she had just gotten her hair styled in a cute boy cut), the time came when Merit was willing to suffer any consequences that might come from bringing her hair into the twentieth century, and so while the girls played at Kari's, she went to a beauty salon with a picture she had torn out of a magazine and asked the hair stylist, "Can you do that?"

The stylist could, and Merit practically skipped out of the salon, she felt so modern and free, so happy with her shag.

Eric slapped her face when he saw her; she expected as much.

"You better tell me that's a wig!" said Eric, after — not before — he slapped her.

"I'm sorry you don't like it," said Merit, holding her burning cheek.

"You bet I don't like it," he said, grabbing a handful of her hair. "Who do you think you are, Hanoi Jane?"

"Eric, please," said Merit, holding her head at an awkward angle. "Please, you're hurting me."

She knew, of course, that that was his objective, but her pleading words always came out anyway.

He loosened his grip on her hair and pushed against her head so that she stumbled forward a few feet, catching herself on the edge of the kitchen sink. "You better get used to staying inside," he said, "because you're not going anywhere until that grows out."

"Daddy!" Melody squealed as he burst through the swinging door and into the dining room where she and her sister were playing. "Daddy, look at the fort me and Reni built!"

Her heart pounding, Merit stood behind the swinging door and pushed it open a crack, wondering, as she did every day, how Eric was going to react to the girls.

"Oh, Melody," he said, and Merit watched as he knelt down, taking the little girl in his arms. "That is just about the best fort I have ever seen."

"You mean it, Daddy?" asked Reni, her head

appearing from a gap in the blankets that hung over the table.

"Do I mean it? Of course I mean it. I have never seen a better fort in all my life."

"Thanks, Daddy!" said Reni, scrambling out from under the table, but as happened so often, she had miscalculated the staying power of her father's affections and just as she got to him, he was standing up, shedding Melody.

"It's a good fort," he said, walking to the stair-case, leaving Reni staring after him. "Even though it's really only a blanket over a table."

Merit waited for a moment until she heard water in the pipes — Eric always took a shower when he got home from work — and then, as she had done countless times, she went to her girls to pick up the pieces of their heart, which their father had broken.

"Anybody up for a tea party?" she said, kneeling down (not an easy thing in her ninth month of pregnancy).

Reni and Melody pushed aside the blanket to see their mother and the tray of cookies and milk she had brought.

"Oh, yes!" said Reni.

"Oh, yes!" echoed her sister.

Merit pushed the tray under the table and then, with considerably more effort, pushed herself in. And for a half hour they were happy, sheltered under the heavy walnut dining-room table draped with blankets, eating Fig Newtons and drinking milk out of little china cups.

All of the angry housewives loved her hair.

"You look like a completely different woman!" said Kari.

"Yeah," said Audrey, "you don't look like your mother-in-law anymore!"

"I feel . . . different," admitted Merit. "Lighter somehow." She rubbed her billowing stomach. "As if that's possible in this condition."

"When's your due date again?" asked Faith.

"Three weeks from yesterday," said Merit, a grimace twisting her lovely features.

"Hey," said Slip, "we're not going to have to drive you to the hospital like we did before, are we?"

Merit shook her head as sweat beaded above her upper lip.

"It's these stupid Braxton-Hicks again. You'd think I'd get to go through at least one pregnancy without them." She fanned her face. "So," she said brightly, "what did everyone think about the zipless you-know-what?"

Audrey laughed. "Did you get the edited version, Merit? Because my copy very clearly stated 'zipless *fuck.*' "

"You shouldn't scold someone because they don't feel comfortable using the same words you do," said Kari.

"I'm not scolding her," said Audrey, helping herself to a lemon bar. "I'm *teasing* her."

Merit drew in her breath as a vise grip squeezed her belly.

"Excuse me," she said, hoisting herself off the chair. "Keep talking — I just have to run to the bathroom."

In the bathroom off the kitchen, she splashed cool water on her face.

"You're fine, you're fine, you're fine," she whispered to her red and sweaty reflection. Thinking a little exercise might help her, she decided to go to the basement and check on the kids.

Jody Hammond, the neighborhood baby-sitter, was reading a *Seventeen* magazine on the couch in the basement rec room while the children ran amok. The bigger boys were chasing the bigger girls, inhibited somewhat by the younger children trying to keep up. Only Beau sat quietly, next to Jody, reading *Curious George*.

"Hi, Mommy!" said Melody, racing into the laundry room.

"Everything okay down here?" asked Merit — more a rhetorical question, as she could see by the flushed, happy faces of the kids streaking by her that of course everything was fine.

Jody nodded, but her gratuitous teenage smile was interrupted by a look of genuine concern. "Mrs. Iverson, are you all right?"

"I just get these fake contractions," she said, gasping as another one seized her uterus.

"Should I get someone?" asked Jody, and Merit almost smiled, seeing Beau mimic exactly the concerned look on the baby-sitter's face.

"No, no, I'm fine." She mustered a sally-forth smile, and when she got to the enclosed staircase, she grabbed hold of the handrail as if it were a tow rope.

Halfway up the stairs, a contraction squeezed her with such force that she nearly toppled backward.

She stood paralyzed, willing the pain away, but the will of her body paid no attention to the will of her mind.

"Just get to the top of the stairs," she whispered, and like a mountain climber heeding the advice of her Sherpa, she obeyed — each step

257

another thousand feet, until she was at the top. But no celebration awaited her; instead she knew deeply and clearly that she was going to split wide open.

When she staggered into the kitchen, Faith, who had been getting ice cubes, gasped.

"My gosh, Merit, are you sure you're not in labor?"

"I — oh, no, I — oh, God!"

"Oh, dear," said Faith, and even as fear was upon her like a storm, she knew Merit did not need to hear the panic she felt. "You're fine, Merit," she said inanely but calmly.

"No, I'm not!" Merit's voice careened into a squeal. "God, the baby's coming!" She paced the kitchen erratically before pushing through the swinging door.

Sounding like the Paul Revere of obstetrics, Faith chased after her, announcing, "The baby is coming! The baby is coming!"

The three women sprung out of their seats like a rehearsed act.

"Let's get her in the car," said Slip.

"There's — there's no time!" said Merit as a gush of water spilled out of her.

"Oh, my God, her water broke," said Audrey, dropping her lit cigarette into a martini glass.

"You don't think you can make it to the car?" asked Kari, and when Merit moaned, shaking her head, she said, "Bring her here to the recliner. Faith, call the ambulance!"

Part of the prayer she had recited as a child came into Merit's head in a paraphrased version, *if I should die before I break,* as she spread her legs and, with her hands at her crotch, cried, "It's . . . I can feel its head!"

"Well, push it back in!" said Slip, and then, realizing what she'd said, she amended, "No, no, don't do that." She looked wild-eyed at the other women. "Help me get her onto the chair!"

Three pairs of hands helped ease Merit onto the recliner, and then Audrey unbuttoned Merit's skirt and tried to pull down her underpants.

"Can you put your legs together for a minute, honey?"

Moaning, Merit brought her knees together long enough for Audrey to yank down her underpants.

"It's crowning! The baby's head is crowning! Someone boil some water!"

"Should I call the ambulance first or —" asked Faith.

"Call the ambulance," said Slip, "I'll boil the water."

Merit lifted herself up in the chair as her moan heightened in pitch to a scream.

"It's going to be all right," said Kari. "You're going to have your baby here, but it's going to be all right."

"God, I'm going to die!"

"No, you're not, Merit," said Audrey. "It just feels that way, remember? Now just —"

"Agghhh!" cried Merit through clenched teeth, her fingernails digging into Audrey's arm.

"That's right, push," hollered Audrey as pain zipped through her arm. "Push!"

The chair had jerked all the way back to its fully reclined position, but Merit pushed forward and the chair became upright. She sat so close to the edge of the cushion that she would have fallen off had she not had the support of Kari and Audrey, who held on to her arms and offered soothing words and calm assurances as she screamed or panted or moaned.

"I called the ambulance," said Faith, breathless, running in from the kitchen. "They're on their way."

"And the water's boiling," said Slip. "I've got some clean dish towels too." She knelt to place one under Merit, but there wasn't room on the chair. "Holy laboring mother," she said, her voice hushed. "Somebody better be ready to catch that baby because it's coming."

"Well, you've got the towels," said Audrey.

"Okay," Slip said to Merit, who after panting through a break in contractions was now keening again. "I'm your quarterback, Merit. Hut one, hut two . . ."

"No," said Faith, kneeling by Slip. "You'd be the receiver. Merit's the quarterback."

Merit's face scrunched into a red mask of pain.

"Help me!" she cried. Baring her teeth like a dog ready to strike, she issued a deep, low growl.

"It's coming! It's coming!" said Slip, and in one amazing rush, the baby slid into Slip's arms and the embroidered dish towel that said Thursday.

"It's a girl," said Slip as the perfect little baby released her first cry to the world. Merit collapsed in the chair and held her arms out for her daughter, the love that washed over her unfortunately tinted with dread: this was not Eric the fourth.

"We're done kidding around," Eric the third had told her throughout her pregnancy. "I do *not* want another girl. This one's a boy — *all right?*

This one's my son!"

By the time the ambulance arrived, the placenta had been delivered and Kari had tied off and cut the cord with twine and with scissors that had been sterilized in boiling water.

It was only when they were gently putting Merit on the stretcher ("Why do I have to go to the hospital?" she asked. "The baby's here and I feel fine.") that she thought to have her girls brought up from the basement to see their baby sister.

"I'll get them," volunteered Faith.

"Well, we haven't got all day," said the ambulance technician.

"We've got time for that," said the other one.

Her leg stiff from kneeling, Faith limped toward the kitchen. As she passed the dining room table, she yelped in surprise.

"Oh, my goodness, Beau, you scared me. When did you get up here?"

But he didn't need to answer; Faith could tell by his round saucer eyes how long he had been upstairs.

She knelt down, holding her son by his shoulders.

"Did you see Merit's baby getting born?"

The six-year-old nodded, and Faith wanted to cry, thinking of her little boy all alone, hiding in the dining room, watching a woman give birth. Her mind scrambled as she tried to think of words that would lessen his trauma.

"Then you just saw a miracle."

Disagreeing, Beau shook his head. Then, as if to set his confused mother straight, he said slowly and deliberately, his eyes wide, "Mama, that baby came out of Reni's mommy's *butt*."

HOST: **FAITH**
BOOK: *The Heart Is a Lonely Hunter*
by Carson McCullers
REASON CHOSEN: "I think it's one of the
most beautiful titles in the history of books."

Sometimes Faith wondered what had happened when the twins were in utero. Had Bonnie hogged all the space or taken more of the important nutrients out of the placenta? Why did she have all the bravura, the confidence? Why wasn't she afraid of anything, whereas Beau thought monsters and danger were everywhere?

Slip's daughter Flannery was like Bonnie; in fact, their three-year age difference did not pose a big obstacle to their friendship. They were two smart, bossy girls who thought the world should revolve around them and loved trying to convince their brothers of this essential truth. But Joe and Gil weren't cowed by their sister's demands and fought them, unlike Beau, who as far as Faith could see was practically Bonnie's handservant.

"Beau, honey, what are you doing?" she had asked that morning after finding her son in Bonnie's room, making her bed.

"Bonnie told me I could play with her troll

dolls if I made her bed," he said, tucking the chenille bedspread underneath the hump of pillows.

Faith's stomach took an elevator ride. "Well, Beau, honey," she said, trying to keep her voice light, "you shouldn't have to make Bonnie's bed just to play with some of her toys."

"I don't mind," said Beau, scampering off the mattress to smooth the last wrinkles out of the spread. Satisfied, he placed Bonnie's stuffed parrot in the center of the pillows. "I like to make beds."

Faith pushed down an impulse to grab Beau by his shirt collar and holler, *No, you don't! Little boys don't like making beds!*

She scraped her upper lip against her teeth, tasting the perfumy taste of lipstick. "Listen, Beau," she said, kneeling down and taking the boy by the shoulders, "why don't you run outside and play? All the kids are out there. Bryan and Mikey built a fort in their backyard and —"

"Can't I play troll dolls, Mommy? I made a little house for them out of two shoeboxes. There's windows that open and shut, and a little —"

"Beau. Beau, I want you to play outside." Even as Faith's voice was stern, she grabbed her son to her chest, holding him so tight he began to wriggle. To get out of her suffocating embrace, he promised he'd go outside and play.

Faith couldn't imagine a child with a sweeter disposition; while Bonnie's one great concern — like that of most kids — seemed to be herself, it was Beau who climbed into Faith's lap when she was feeling sad, who presented her with dandelion bouquets and crayon portraits and vows that he would marry her when he grew up.

The twins' faces matched their personalities too. Bonnie looked like the tomboy she was, with a little snub nose and eyes the color of her straight brown hair, and Beau — well, Beau was beautiful, with his tumble of sandy curls and eyes a startling pale blue-green color.

Up until he was four, Faith never worried that he was different from the other boys; on the contrary, she thought herself lucky to have such an affectionate little boy. But then she began to notice things: how the other boys had no interest in playing dolls or dress up, how he cried so easily, how when he ran, he held his elbows to his sides, his arms flailing back and forth. The more she noticed, the more scared she felt.

"My God," said Wade after trying to play baseball with him in the backyard, "the kid swings the bat like a little fruit."

Faith had forced herself to laugh, to show Wade how ridiculous she found his comment.

"He just needs a little practice," she said. "It's not as if you're out there every day pitching balls to him."

Wade muttered something, and Faith swallowed down her fear. But she began to watch Wade watch Beau, and she could see the look of disgust that would pass his face when Beau fluttered his hands in excitement or when he sat on the ottoman, softly talking to Bonnie's Barbie dolls as he changed their clothes.

It's just a phase, she told herself, *just like Bonnie's tomboy stage. He'll probably grow out of it by the time he gets to kindergarten.*

But he didn't, and Faith changed her projected deadline to first grade. Much to her surprise, she did notice a change in his behavior; it was as if his personality was less flamboyant, had been tamped down.

"Beau, honey, do you like your teacher?" she asked casually one day as he sat at the table, eating his after-school milk and cookies.

"Miss Carlson?" asked Beau, and after licking his milk mustache, said, "Sure, Mama. She's real pretty and she reads to us every day."

"Well," said Faith, lifting cookie crumbs off the table by pressing her finger against them, "do you like the kids in your class?"

"Mom, Gina and me'll be outside," said Bonnie, racing into the kitchen with the friend she'd brought home from school. They stopped at the table to take another cookie before running out the back door.

Beau smiled, watching the girls. "Gina's nice."

"Yes, she is," agreed Faith, and then, searching her son's face for clues, she asked, "Do you like the other children in your class?"

Beau's long lashes fluttered as he stared up at the ceiling, thinking.

"Well," he said finally, "Sunshine's nice to me."

What are you, a plant? Faith thought before remembering that Sunshine was a little girl whose parents no doubt had conceived her on a commune or an acid trip.

"Well, why wouldn't she be nice to you?" asked Faith. "You're a very nice little boy."

Beau nodded even as tears filled his eyes. "I am. I am nice, but only Sunshine likes me. Gina likes me, but she's in Bonnie's class. Everybody else calls me bad things and pushes me down on the playground."

Outrage, like adrenaline, surged through Faith's body.

"*They push you down? They call you bad names?* What kind of names?"

Beau shrugged, a picture of misery. "Sissy, mostly. Sometimes Tie-a-Pretty-Beau. Sometimes Fruity-Tooty. Those are bad names, right, Mommy?"

"Yes, those are bad names." Suddenly Faith was angry at everyone, including Bonnie, who should be protecting her brother against these thugs. "What's your sister doing while you're being pushed down?"

"If Bonnie knew they were pushing me down, she'd help me," said Beau, his head jiggling in a nod. "But she always plays by the swings."

"Where do you play?"

Beau bowed his head and the sun glanced off his sand-colored curls. "I usually don't play 'cause I don't want to get pushed down. So I go and sit by the tree. There's a woodpecker in there, Mama!"

Faith wondered if her heart could hurt any more if someone grabbed it out of her chest.

"Beau, have you told your teacher what these bad kids do?"

The little boy's blue-green eyes widened. "Oh, Mommy, they'd do even worse things if I did that."

Faith called for a meeting with the principal and Miss Carlson the next day.

"You've got to do something about these hoodlums!" she said, rapping the purse in her lap with each word.

Chuckling, Mr. Talbert, the principal, pushed his glasses up the bridge of his narrow nose.

"Mrs. Owens, kids'll be kids. A certain amount of name-calling, while we don't encourage it, is bound to happen."

"Well, you shouldn't let it!"

"Mrs. Owens," said Miss Carlson, "believe me, I do not allow any name-calling or bullying in my class. However, I cannot always control what happens on the playground — have you seen the size of our playground?"

"Of course I've seen the size of your playground," said Faith, wondering how her son could find this lantern-jawed woman pretty. "But if it's too big to supervise the children properly, maybe you —"

"Mrs. Owens," said the principal, "you need to calm down. Now that we're aware there's a problem with Beau, we'll keep a closer eye on him."

"The problem isn't with Beau!" Faith said, her voice raised to a level that Mr. Talbert's secretary, sitting in the next room, could hear. "The problem is with the other kids — with those evil little brats who need to be given a taste of their own evil medicine!"

Faith drew in a quick breath and bit her lip. She was so angry she wanted to hit both of them, and yet even in her anger she was embarrassed by her outburst, was aware of how her accent came out.

"Mrs. Owens," said Mr. Talbert, standing up behind his desk, "we'll do everything we can to ensure the safety of your little boy. Now if you don't mind, I have another appointment."

Appointment my ass, thought Faith, but she got up, offering her hand to the surprised principal and teacher (that was something she had learned

267

from Slip — Slip always offered her hand to men and women, explaining, "People know you mean business when you shake their hand instead of just standing there, nodding and smiling"), and left the office vowing that she would find ways to protect her son because she sure couldn't count on anyone else to.

And she did. She played endless games of catch with him, pitched him balls until her shoulder cramped, taught him how to run faster by "not moving your arms around so much; see, clench your fists instead of leaving your hands open." Her goal was to never give Beau any indication that the way he did things was wrong, but that they could be done in an easier way.

And Beau was a smart little boy; he picked things up. He learned it was easier to ask Joe or Bryan if they wanted to play pirates or bank robbers rather than house (no real skin off his nose, as he loved to play make-believe); he learned that his dad didn't throw his newspaper down and yell to his mother, "Don't we have some damn trucks he can play with?" if he didn't play dolls in the living room; he learned to not cry so easily, at least not in front of people. Most of all, he learned that he had secrets that he had to hide. He was his mother's son, after all.

It didn't take long before Wade started making comments like "Thank God, Beau seems to be coming around," or "He doesn't seem to be so girly anymore." When asked about school, Beau told his mother, "No, the kids don't push me down anymore," and he actually came home one day beaming, having been picked for a kickball team. He wasn't the first pick, the second, third, or even fourth, but he hadn't been picked last, and that was a first for him. And because he was her precious, sweet little boy, Faith promised herself that she would always find ways to make him feel wanted and needed, to make him beam.

July, 1975

HOST: SLIP

BOOK: *The Total Woman*

by Marabel Morgan

REASON CHOSEN: "I was drawn to it the way you're drawn to a horrible car accident."

While my eleven-year-old daughter has her piano lesson, I wait for her in Mrs. Klanski's doily-infested, camphor-smelling den. It's a half hour I thought I'd use as uninterrupted reading time, but it turns out Mr. Klanski likes to converse, and I oblige him, seeing as he's old and I don't seem to have much choice. In fact, the conversations (accompanied by faint piano scales or halting attempts at "Greensleeves") are generally one-sided and concern his daytime form of entertainment now that he's retired: soap operas. He likes to update me on the happenings of the people who live in towns with names like Rose Haven or Port Rogers or Eden Prairie.

"And then Dr. Marshall revealed to Teryn that not only had he delivered her of her baby, he was her real father!"

"Wait a second. Are you saying Dr. Marshall is Teryn's father, or Teryn's baby's father?"

"Well, Teryn's father, of course! Wouldn't you

think she'd know who her baby's father is?"

Sometimes I want to tell him, *Wait a minute, if you want soap opera, come on down to Freesia Court.*

For example, in a plot twist none of us saw coming, Todd Trottman ran off with a nineteen-year-old teller at his bank.

"He went in to make a deposit and instead took out a big withdrawal," Leslie Trottman explained gamely when AHEB decided to make a charitable contribution (a pan of brownies and an afternoon's worth of sympathy) to the Collections Queen. "And the thing that really gets me is she used to wait on me! She was always so nice, writing in my balance, telling me how she liked my outfit, how cute my kids were. I even complimented her to the bank manager — I said, 'You ought to give that Miss Jenson a raise, she's just the most polite teller.' Oh, I'll bet she and Todd got a big laugh out of that!"

Even though Leslie Trottman was my personal syrup of ipecac, I was able to stop gagging long enough to feel sorry for her. I think she really did believe in the life she was living; she really did believe that Todd was her Prince Charming, that the 2.3 children (their snarly Pekinese is included because Leslie always treated him like a baby) they had created would be heirs to their entitled Republican kingdom, that by wearing headbands that matched your clothing you somehow made a stand against chaos.

Leslie moved back to Missoula — Audrey says her father owns half the state of Montana — and Helen Hammond got a postcard whose message was pure Leslie: *It took some teeth-pulling, but I'm engaged to an orthodontist!!!!*

Then it turns out our friend Audrey has a psychic gift, although I just think it's women's intuition revved up a notch (which of us *hasn't* known when something's not right with our husband or one of our kids?). She doesn't really talk about it, not like she talked about what was happening between her and Paul (who now look headed for divorce court). See, Mr. Klanski — scandal, ESP, divorce, *and* we even have a gay couple on the block, now that Stuart and Grant bought old man McDermitt's house. Not only is Stuart gay, he's Japanese! I mean, we're covering all kinds of demographics here.

Seeing as she lived next to him, Audrey had known Mr. McDermitt the best, and so I asked her, "When did the old man get so liberal?"

"Topping the list of things that old man McDermitt really hates is kids," said Audrey, laughing. "And I'm sure my boys did their share in reinforcing that particular bias. Remember when they were trying to dig to China in his tomato patch?"

"I could hear him hollering, and I was down in my *basement* doing laundry."

"Exactly. I think the idea of more kids trampling through his backyard or, heaven forbid, through the house where he and his beloved Mrs. McDermitt had shared so many happy, childless years was just too much for him. When Stuart and Grant appeared, he couldn't put up the Sold sign fast enough."

So there you have it, Mr. Klanski — all the drama on Freesia Court, except of course my own, which I certainly haven't seen addressed in any soap opera. I mean, their intention is to attract viewers, not repel them.

When Fred got out of the VA hospital, I flew home to see him, and he seemed like the old Fred, minus an arm that could bend effortlessly at the elbow. He laughed and joked and made plans to go back to Penn State, and at the big party my parents threw for him, he held up his glass (with his good arm) and toasted "life, and boy am I glad I've got mine."

His letters those first months he was back at school were cheerful and funny and often accompanied by music tapes he custom-made (featuring Neil Young, Emerson, Lake and Palmer, The Doors, and, inexplicably, Jimmy Dean). He had decided to major in math, formerly a subject that held no interest for him. His reason should have sounded a little warning buzzer: "because it's orderly."

The first time I got an SOS call, I thought he was joking.

"Fred, it's one in the morning," I mumbled after the jangling telephone had snatched me out of a deep sleep. "It's all right," I whispered to Jerry as he gathered his pillow under his chest and pushed himself up on his elbows. "It's just Fred. Go back to sleep."

Our bedroom phone has a long cord, so I was able to walk out into the hallway, where I was sure I would listen to Fred tell me about the girl he'd fallen madly in love with or the one he'd just broken up with. What else could be so important to him that he needed to rouse his sister halfway across the country?

"Slip, they keep coming."

"What keeps coming?" I asked, the last time I was blissfully ignorant of Fred's troubles.

"The flashbacks."

For a moment I was confused. "Fred, have you been taking LSD?"

"I wish," said Fred, sounding as if he were on the verge of tears. "No, Slip, these are *real* flashbacks of what happened in 'Nam."

Holy battered psyche. It was as if all my senses were suddenly adjusted, fine-tuned: my breath sounded amplified in my ears; the objects in the hallway, fuzzy in the darkness, suddenly became clear, and I could see the toy truck Joe had been looking for tucked under the radiator; I could feel each vertebra of my spine pressed against the linen closet door, feel how nubbly the carpet felt under my bare feet.

"What . . . what kind of flashbacks?" I asked, even though I didn't want an answer.

Fred gasped, the way someone who's been underwater for a long time gasps when he finally breaks through the surface. "All kinds," he said. "I see my buddy Phil, who stepped on a land mine — he was walking right in front of me, and he blew up just like a firecracker, Slip. *Just like a firecracker!* And then he's screaming in my ear, not really screaming, but moaning, 'Where're my arms, Fred? Where're my legs? Where am I?' "

"Oh, Fred —"

"And then I'm back in this village again, Slip, we came to it just as the sun went down, when people were probably thinking, 'Ahh, safe for one more day.' But they weren't. They were harboring snipers, Sergeant Myers was convinced of it — and they were, Slip, we caught one — but why did we have to burn down everything? Why'd we have to burn the whole village, Slip? That's what the old lady keeps asking me, Slip,

the old lady with the burned baby in her arms —
for a second I thought it was an old charred log
in her arms, Slip; she keeps screaming and I
can't stand it, because I don't have any kind of
answer, Slip, and she keeps asking me and I —"

"Fred," I said, my voice like a slap — I had to
get his attention. "Fred, listen to me."

"Slip, I need — I need —"

"I'll tell you what you need," I said in the firm
voice of authority my children always paid attention to. "You need to calm down, and I'm going
to help you do that, okay, Fred?" I cradled the
phone receiver under my chin and drew my knees
to my chest, encircling them with my arms, trying
to fight the cold that had come over me.

"Slip, I —"

"Okay, you need to listen to me now, Fred.
Tomorrow you're going to go down to the VA
hospital and talk to someone, okay, Fred? I need
to know that you'll do that, Fred."

My brother groaned. "What about *now*, Slip?
What am I going to do *now?*"

My mind reeled. "Well, now you're going to
listen to a story, okay?"

"Okay," said Fred, his voice sounding as
young as Joe's.

Wanting to lighten the mood, if that was at all
possible, I laughed, a little chuckle I hoped
wouldn't sound fake to Fred. "You remember
when you thought your sock monkey watched
you when you slept?"

A pause and then, "The one Grandma Sophie
made for me?"

"Uh-huh. You hauled it around everywhere
and you wouldn't go to sleep unless it was in bed
with you."

"*He,*" said Fred softly. "Danny was a *he.*"

"Oh, yeah, Danny. And no matter how James and Drew teased you about playing with a dumb old sock monkey, you wouldn't give him up."

"Danny was my buddy," he said in a tone that I swear was almost cheerful.

"Until he started watching you while you slept," I reminded him. "You said you couldn't sleep anymore because the minute you closed your eyes, Danny sat up on the pillow and started watching you."

"Scared the shit out of me."

"And do you remember how I offered to stay in your bed all night so that you could sleep and I could tell Danny to stop looking at you?"

"You always were a good sister."

"Thanks. You were always a good brother." A tear fell on my knee and I felt it through the flannel. "And do you remember I was going to tell you what Danny had told me, but you said I didn't need to, because he already had?"

"I don't," said Fred, his voice apologetic. "I don't remember that part."

"Well, you don't need to," I said. "Because I remember. You told me that you woke up in the middle of the night to find Danny sitting up staring at me, and you told him, 'Hey, stop that. Go to bed, Danny, and quit bothering people.' And you never had any problems with Danny after that, did you?"

For a long time I heard nothing but Fred's breathing. Then he finally asked, "So?"

"So," I said, "you hadn't needed me at all. You were brave enough to get Danny to stop staring all by yourself."

"So are you saying you won't help me now?"

said Fred, again in his little-boy voice.

"Oh, Fred, I'll help you all I can. I'm just reminding you how much you can help yourself."

And I had helped him, that night, but my cute little story about a sock monkey could go only so far. It wasn't big enough or powerful enough — could any words have been? — to fight Fred's demons.

At the end of the semester, he decided to drop out — a moot point, as he was already flunking out. For the first time in my life, I began to dread the calls I got from my family.

"You should see him, Slip. He's a freak," said James, second oldest next to me, and the most conservative in the family. "His hair's past his shoulders, and all he does is hang out at the Diamond Lanes."

"Maybe he just likes to bowl," I said, hoping for a laugh — if James laughed, then things couldn't be that bad.

He didn't laugh. "He doesn't bowl, Slip. He sits there and drinks. Sits there and drinks with all the other losers in Jersey City."

"My girlfriend saw him standing in a phone booth screaming," said Drew, older than Fred by just a year and a half.

"Well, maybe he was mad at whoever he was talking to."

"Slip, he wasn't even on the phone."

Both James and Drew had been ineligible for war, thank God, James because of his asthma, and Drew because he wisely stayed in school. Because they had been lucky, you would have thought they'd be grateful for their luck and more compassionate toward their own brother, who wasn't so lucky.

"Try to be a friend to him," I counseled.

"That's easy for you to say. You don't have to see him mumbling at the dinner table at Ma's or standing in a phone booth screaming."

"I thought it was your girlfriend who saw him screaming," I said, "not you."

"That's not the point!" said Drew. "God, Slip, don't you think we all feel terrible? Don't you think we try to help him? But don't you think it gets a little *tiring* when you try and try and nothing seems to help?"

My mother and father offered their own grim commentary.

"Honestly, Slip, he's not Fred anymore," said my mother, and I could hear the tears in her voice. "He was always the happiest little boy, the happiest teenager, and now — now he's like one of those bums that we used to see at the Port Authority whenever we went into the city."

"Remember his Indian name?" my father asked in another phone conversation I'd just as soon hung up on.

I swallowed. "Laughing Spaniel?" I said it like a question, even though I knew it was the correct answer. A lump bloomed like a flower in my throat.

I heard a rasping sound and knew my father was running his hand over his bristly, always-present five o'clock shadow, a gesture he used whenever he worried about something. "I called him that because he was like a happy puppy, always ready to play." There was that raspy sound again. "Well, Marjorie, he's not Laughing Spaniel anymore."

I burst into tears. My dad only called me Marjorie when delivering bad news.

Still, you can't discount the power of distance as far as troubles are concerned; it wasn't my table Fred was mumbling at, or the phone booth by my library that he was yelling in. Even though my heart broke with each conversation I had with someone back home, especially those scary and fractured conversations with Fred, I had the luxury of forgetting about him for hours, sometimes days at a time. My family was given the same luxury when Fred decided he needed to get out of New Jersey, and we all felt hopeful: maybe that's what he needs, to go somewhere new, maybe that'll make him feel better.

One of us would hear from him — a postcard from Florida, a letter from Colorado, a phone call from Seattle. This went on for a couple years until a week ago, when, checking to see if the weekly coupon circular was rolled up and stuck into the mailbox, I opened the door to find Fred sitting on my front steps.

Granted, this man looked nothing like my fresh, freckle-faced brother, who was so particular about the back pleat of his Gant shirts being pressed straight, so diligent in polishing his loafers, in making sure that the hem of his khakis came down as far as where the penny went and no farther.

This man was about thirty pounds heavier than the slim boy I remembered and was wearing a green fatigue jacket with dirt ground into it so thoroughly that it gave off a sheen. His hair, not as red as mine but as kinky, was in a matted ponytail, and a beard sprang off his face like copper wiring.

"Hey, Slip," he said, taking a cigarette out of his mouth with dirty hands.

"Fred!" I said, throwing myself at him so that he almost fell off the steps and into the rhododendron bush.

He laughed, and for a moment I was filled with joy: Laughing Spaniel was back.

He'd been here a week, bunking down in the basement on the pull-out couch, and joy had been an infrequent visitor.

It wasn't that he was a demanding guest; it was just that he was an omnipresent one, even though he slept until noon and only came upstairs when he was hungry. His uncommunicative and surly presence changed the whole tone of the house.

He played a rambunctious game of tag with the kids the day he got here — Flannery and Joe were screaming with delight and Gil was just screaming — but it didn't take long for the kids to learn that Uncle Fred only wanted to play when *he* wanted to play, and that was most often "not now." Every invitation was pretty much greeted with that same answer. For the first two nights, he did deign to eat with all of us, but he told me the clamor of a family dinner gets on his nerves, and would I mind if he came up after the kids went to bed and ate whatever was left over? I felt like one of those women in the Depression, leaving food out for a visiting hobo. Although a hobo might have been more sociable than Fred; trying to engage him in a conversation was like trying to force someone with laryngitis to scream.

I came to dread the sound of his footsteps on the basement stairs (which I heard for the first time each day after I washed my lunch dishes and sent Gil off for afternoon kindergarten), came to dread the company of the sour, distant man my brother had become.

He said he would be leaving, that he had a war buddy in Detroit who was going to fix him up with a job at General Motors, and I hoped to God he was serious. About leaving, I mean; I didn't really care about the General Motors job. I felt awful about it, but if there is a season to everything, then that was my season of being a lousy sister. Fred taught me that if you feel sorry for a person and angry at him too, the anger usually overrides the pity.

I didn't know what to expect when he came lumbering into our book club meeting, where no man had ever dared to tread.

"Ladies, my brother Fred," I said as he stood scratching his sloppy belly, while inside I screamed, *Get out, get out, Fred! Just leave!*

Introductions were made, and then I expected Fred to flee (being polite and sociable was not high on his things-to-do list), but, surprising me, he said, "So these are the infamous Angry Housewives. What book are you discussing?"

Audrey exhaled a smoke ring and cocked one eyebrow. "*The Total Woman.*"

"Oh, I read that book," said Fred. "Mind if I sit in?"

It took me a while to shut my unhinged mouth. "*You* read *The Total Woman*?"

Fred nodded, sitting down on the couch next to Merit. She flinched a little but tried to turn it into a smile.

"On a ride from Boise to Rapid City. With a trucker, no less. He bought a copy for his wife, and it was sitting on the console in his cab."

"So what did you think?" asked Kari, a twinkle in her blue eyes.

"Why, she was dead-on right, of course," said Fred.

When the groaning died down, he nodded at the wineglass I held and said, "You mind pouring me one of those, sis?"

"So, Fred," said Audrey, leaning forward in her hot-pink sundress so that he might wallow in the cavern of her cleavage. "For the amusement of all of us, why don't you elaborate?"

My brother smiled, and through his mess of red beard and sunken eyes, I saw a glimpse of Laughing Spaniel.

"Well, come on. You girls are always yapping about not having this right or that right, when you already *have* everything. Men are out in the dog-eat-dog world, having heart attacks while they try to earn just one more promotion so the wifey at home can keep her hair appointment and her ladies' lunch appointments and her weekly trip to the department store."

There was a moment's silence, and then Audrey threw a brownie wrapped in cellophane at him. (I wasn't as good as Faith and Audrey at carrying out a theme, but I must admit, I thought my idea of wrapping all the finger food in cellophane — à la what the author liked to wear to surprise her husband — was a pretty inspired one.)

"Hey, thanks," said Fred, unwrapping the brownie and putting the whole thing in his mouth.

"*You* are a male chauvinist pig," said Audrey.

Chewing the brownie, Fred shook his head. When he spoke, his teeth were brown. "No, just a realist. And please, let's not stoop to name-calling. Because two can play at that game, you bra-burning man-hating feminist." He wiped the brownie slime off his teeth with his tongue and smiled.

We all started talking at once.

"Surely you're not serious," said Kari.

"Do you really think that?" asked Merit.

"Excuse me," said Audrey, "I know you're Slip's brother and all, but would you like to step outside?"

"You remind me of some of the boys back home," said Faith.

"Fred," I said, "is this some sort of a mind game?"

It was the last comment he chose to address, *after* he drained the wineglass and held it out for me to refill.

"You're right, I'm just messin' with you," said Fred, and we all laughed, me the hardest, relieved that he was not, after all, such a *pig*.

"I hate to tell you, ladies, but I've traveled cross country — hell, I've been overseas — and what I've heard men say about women would first scare the bejesus out of you and then make you lose your lunch. You've got to realize that to a lot of men, you're the enemy, and it does no good when women like this Morgan chick break rank and give more ammunition to the other side."

"Wise words for such a young man," said Audrey.

"Thank you," said Fred, and I saw his eyes linger for a moment on Audrey's chest. "Might I bother you for a cigarette?"

"Be my guest," said Audrey, handing him an Eve, her new brand.

"You expect me to smoke a cigarette with *flowers* on it?" said Fred.

"Real men aren't afraid to take walks on the other side," said Audrey, leaning over to light his cigarette.

Fred sat up straighter, and I thought I saw a slight flush rise above his beard. It bugs me that Audrey needs to bring a little seduction into every interaction she has with men, but I appreciated it now, because Fred appreciated it, was responding to it.

"I would imagine any family that had Slip in it would be a feminist family," said Kari.

Fred exhaled a thin stream of smoke, considering this.

"Well, she wasn't really into equality," he said. "She made sure we knew she was our *superior*. And I tell you, when she beat my dad at arm wrestling, it wasn't hard to believe her."

"He probably let me win," I said, suddenly feeling shy.

"She's being modest," said Fred to the others. "For a change."

His second glass of wine was nearly empty, and he held it out for a refill.

"I'm all out," I said. It was the first time I had served wine instead of cocktails at a meeting, and I hadn't known how much to buy.

"A beer'd be fine," said Fred, and when Merit offered to get it, I didn't protest.

"That is the most beautiful woman I have ever seen — and I've been to Thailand, so I know beauty," said Fred as Merit went into the kitchen.

"Are you sure you've looked carefully at all the competition?" asked Audrey, uncrossing and crossing again her long bare legs.

Fred smiled, his eyes fixed on one of her feet and the row of toes tucked inside a strap of her platform sandal, their nails as curved and frosty pink as shells.

"Don't mind her," said Faith. "She's a divorcée without shame. Hey, Slip, got a cigarette? I don't like Audrey's."

I shrugged and held up my palms. "I quit, remember?"

"You did?" said Kari, the only nonsmoker in the group. "That's wonderful — since when?"

"Since three weeks and four days ago," I said proudly.

"What do you mean, 'a divorcée without shame'?" Audrey asked Faith. "First of all, I'm separated, not divorced, but when I *am,* why should I have shame?"

"Here we are," said Merit, cradling a half dozen bottles of beer. "I've got the opener in my pocket." She bumped her shin on the coffee table as she set the beer bottles down. "Ouch," she said, sitting on the couch. "Now let's all have another drink while Fred tells us what it was like over there in Vietnam."

I expected the color to vanish from Fred's face, and it did; I also expected him to bolt out of his chair, but he didn't. Instead, he very methodically jacked the cap off each beer bottle and handed one to each of us. "Ladies," he said, toasting us with his bottle, "I realize you're all story lovers — who isn't? But you must also recognize that storytellers are people who tell stories — probably because they like to, right? I mean, who likes to tell a story they themselves never want to hear again, stories they tried for

285

years to forget?" He took a long draw of beer, and I watched as his Adam's apple, underneath the tumbleweed of his beard, bobbed up and down.

"But since Slip is my wonderful redheaded sister and since you are all her wonderful blond and brunette friends" — boy, I could hear the liquor kicking in — "and since you probably will never find yourselves on a battlefield — although I think *you*," he said to Audrey, "would kick ass in combat; women should be drafted, don't you think?" He took another swig of beer, finishing it. "Anyway, since I have packed up the old kit bag and will be heading out for Motown tomorrow and it's unlikely I'll see most of you again . . . well, maybe I will tell one little story. One little story of war."

He picked up the remaining bottle of beer on the table and proceeded to make fast work of it. Watching him, my heart thrummed in my chest and I wondered if I should call it a night right there. I was worried about Fred, worried about his story and what it might do to him, and yet I was also excited, as excited as I'd been the first time I stood on the high dive of the Jersey City municipal pool. Fred was going to do what he'd failed to do with my parents, my brothers, with anyone: he was going to talk!

He examined his thumbnail for a long enough moment that I thought he might have changed his mind. Finally he chewed off a little flag of a hangnail, looked at me, his eyebrows raised in sort of an apology, and began.

"There was this guy in my squadron. We called him Mitty, as in Walter, and you know why?" He didn't bother to answer, just put his feet up on the coffee table, crossing them at the ankles. "We called him Mitty because he was always telling these crazy stories about how he was a Hollywood stuntman — he said practically any western made in the early sixties had him in it. He also said he could play any instrument ever made and that he'd taught Dennis Wilson of the Beach Boys how to drum and the Mamas and the Papas how to harmonize. I mean, the guy was total bullshit. When he wasn't in Hollywood riding bareback or giving music lessons, he was in the Florida Keys studying dolphins or in the Swiss Alps testing out his newly designed aerodynamic ski poles or bindings or whatever. We all loved the guy even though we knew he was full of bullshit because his crazy stories made the time pass, made us forget that we were getting shot at and might not even be on the fuckin' planet the next day, let alone the next hour."

Fred paused to swallow the rest of his beer, and the rest of us took his cue, taking long draws from our own bottles as if we were parched.

"Excuse my French, by the way," he said to Merit.

"That's all right," said Merit.

"Anyway," continued Fred, "I always thought he knew his role as the bullshit artist was just that; a role. Just like Simmons was the guy who was always cool under fire, Slomovitz was the guy who could fix anything that was broke, Donnelly always had the good dope. Mitty was there to entertain us.

"But one day — and I can feel the air on my skin still; it was so hot and damp, steam was rising from the jungle floor — Mitty and a guy named Webber and I were goofin' off, trying to catch this little wild pig that had been hanging around camp. I think we were supposed to be on some kind of reconnaissance mission, but we were so stoned, we didn't know what the fuck was going on. We were standing under this tree, making sounds we thought a pig might find attractive — Mitty of course saying things like 'When I was practicing veterinary medicine, I made a study of the mating rituals of the Hampshire pigs, and I found that a low oink means "let's be friends" ' — and we're cracking up when all of a sudden there's this sound of thrashing, of someone running through the jungle, and then right in front of us are two Viet Cong. Only they weren't the wily tunnel dwellers who could disappear and reappear like chipmunks. These were just two kids, probably not more than fourteen years old, a boy and a girl, playing war."

The summer night air that wafted in through the open windows (we still didn't have — or want — air-conditioning) suddenly felt cold and drafty, and I rubbed my bare arms. I saw Merit do the same thing.

Fred raked his fingers through his beard, and his eyes stared ahead at what looked to me like the floor lamp I had gotten on sale; but to Fred — who knows what he saw. None of us spoke as he stared off. It was like all of us were hypnotized, waiting for either the master to speak or to tell us that we could.

A spasm rippled through Fred's shoulders. I knew he couldn't be cold in that heavy fatigue jacket, and seeing that shiver that had nothing to do with cold seemed to snap me out of my trance. I was about to say, *Fred, it's okay, you don't have to say any more,* when he sighed and, cupping his bad elbow, started talking again.

"They raised their hands in surrender just as Webber fired, and the boy flew through the air — really, it was like his body didn't stop the bullet but took it for a little ride. The girl cried out, and *bang,* Webber fired at her, but she didn't fly through the air. She dropped, just crumpled to the ground, her eyes as round as her mouth. We ran over to her, and blood was spurting out of her shoulder like a little red geyser. Mitty leaned down toward her, blood splattering on his flak jacket, and then this girl, this girl bleeding to death on the jungle floor, looks into his eyes and she *spits* on him. And Mitty says, 'Well, that's a fine how-do-you-do,' and the next thing I see, he's reaching into his pocket and pulling out a rubber. He always had the craziest shit in his pockets — a tube of his girlfriend's lipstick, Cracker Jack toys, a little address book he said had Ho Chi Minh's private home number in it, clumps of leaves.

"Mitty unwraps the rubber and zips down his pants, and Webber says, 'What are you doing, man?' and Mitty says, 'You can hardly expect me not to use protection — as a doctor, I do *not* intend to go home with a case of the clap,' and then he straddles this girl whose breathing is getting all raggedy and we just stand there watching as he pounds himself into her."

I wished with every fiber of my being that I hadn't heard this story, and judging from the silence that choked the room, I wasn't alone. Finally Audrey said, in a voice that sounded like she was being strangled, "Oh, my God."

I touched my forehead. It was slick with sweat.

289

"What . . . why? Why would he do such a thing?"

Fred closed his eyes. "What you should ask, Slip" — here Fred opened his eyes to look at me — "is why Webber and I didn't stop him. What you should ask, Slip, is why Webber — honest to Christ, one of the nicest guys I ever met — climbed on top of that poor girl when Mitty was done with her. And what you should also ask, Slip, is why I didn't do a thing about it." Fred clawed at his beard. "When Webber pushed himself off her, the blood had stopped spurting from her shoulder, and the red stain had grown until there wasn't an inch of her white shirt that wasn't red. She jerked once, and I knew she was dead. So what you finally have to ask, Slip — although the goddamned problem is that no one ever wants to know — is why she had to be alive through that."

Again that awful choking silence filled the room. Merit's hands were cupped over her mouth, and Kari looked like she'd just taken a carnival ride that spins you upside down.

"That poor girl," she said finally. "Poor you."

Fred snorted out a laugh. "Yeah, poor me, watching my brothers in arms rape a fourteen-year-old girl. Poor me, who was so scared he couldn't think of a way to get those crazy motherfuckers off that dying girl."

I thought I might be sick. Why had I thought it was important for Fred to talk about what happened over there? What was I thinking?

"Oh, man, I've really brought this party down, haven't I?" said Fred, as lightly as if he were apologizing for a mild off-color joke. "But remember, that's only one story of *many* I could tell you."

290

The rest of us sat there, stunned, trying to comprehend what he said when he slapped his thighs and stood up.

"Well, ladies, I believe there's a bar stool somewhere in this fair city with my name on it."

"Fred," I said, my horror coalescing into outrage, "I think you owe all of us an apology. How could you tell us something like that?"

As soon as the words were out of my mouth, I wished them back in. My brother's eyes were pools of sadness, and in them I saw reflected my sanctimonious outrage. "Fred, I —" I began again, but he held up his hand. I watched him leave the room, my mouth still open, the words ashes inside it.

For a long time, none of us had any words. Too stunned to smoke, too stunned to drink, we just sat there in the horror that had entered my living room.

"You know how you always hear war is hell?" said Audrey finally. "Well, I always imagined the *movie* hell; the black-and-white blood and guts, the private dying in his sergeant's arms and using his last breath to ask the sergeant to please give his dog tags to dear old Mom." She lit a cigarette and I saw her hands tremble. "I had no idea war was *this* kind of hell."

I bent my head, and the thought that made tears ooze out of my eyes was this: I really knew nothing at all.

HOST: **KARI**
BOOK: *Roots* by Alex Haley
REASON CHOSEN: "Because it's time we honor everyone's history."

Halcyon days. The thought came into Kari's mind at least once a day: These are my halcyon days.

Two days before school started, Freesia Court held its annual Almost Labor Day Circus, and Julia had been given the prized role of ringmaster. At eight years old, she was a rangy child, long-legged and knobby-kneed, with a nimbus of fluffy brown curls. Her eyes were a pale, buttery hazel, her skin a delicious caramel color. She was taking ballet, to the delight of her teacher, who called her a natural dancer, and she was a perfect mimic who could pick up the traces of Faith's southern accent as well as the voices of her favorite cartoon characters. Her Snagglepuss was particularly accurate. Kari thought she was the most fantastic child in the history of children, and the only regret she had about her daughter was that she would never know Bjorn and vice versa.

"You would have gotten along like gangbusters," Kari told her when they sat looking through her wedding album.

"Is that good?" asked Julia.

"That's very good."

The girl pressed her finger on Bjorn's face, in the picture where he and Kari were leaving the church in a shower of rice. "So that's my dad," she said, and Kari didn't correct her. "Did he like tapioca pudding?"

Kari nodded. Tapioca pudding was Julia's favorite. "He loved it."

Julia knew she was adopted; Kari had taken the opportunity to tell her the first time Julia, at that time four years old, asked why they didn't look alike.

"Because another mommy grew you in her tummy."

"She did?" asked Julia. "Why didn't you?"

"That's just the way things turned out," said Kari. "The mommy that grew you in her tummy couldn't keep you and wanted to find the right mommy for you, and she found me."

"How? How did she find you?"

"God helped her, sweetheart," said Kari, which seemed to be all the answer Julia needed.

Julia now knew her father was black and her mother was white, but she didn't press Kari for details of her adoption. Kari knew the day would come, but just as she knew she would someday die and that someday the earth would be swallowed by the sun, she wasn't about to lose sleep over it.

After the hot dog and potato salad supper, an assemblage of lawn chairs was set up in Slip's backyard and the adults sat in them, chatting about plans for the holiday tomorrow, swatting at the occasional late-season mosquito, and waiting for the show to begin.

A recorded drumroll quieted everyone, and then Julia, strutting in front of them, announced, "Ladies and gentlemen, welcome to the greatest show on earth, a show that will thrill you, chill you, and one for which we will bill you!"

Flannery had written the script, but Kari doubted anyone could have delivered the lines as well. The ringmaster was a coveted role, and some of the older children (Bryan Forrest and Joe McMahon in particular, although she wasn't going to mention any names) thought it was their given right, even if they'd already played the role. But Slip was an organizer who believed in democracy first and talent second, although sometimes she got lucky with her casting, as she had with Julia.

"Our first act," said Julia, adjusting the satin lapels of the tuxedo jacket Kari had whipped up, "has been called the toast of Europe. Ladies and gentlemen — the Dancing Danceroni Sisters!"

Slip's stereo had been set up on the small brick patio, and Dave (he no longer wanted to be called Davey) Forrest placed the needle on the album. (He had decided he was too big to participate in the circus but grudgingly agreed to be the sound man.)

"Jeepers Peepers" blasted its stirring first bars as Reni, Melody, and Jewel Iverson, in their matching pink leotards and tutus, raced out of the family-size tent that had been set up near the clothesline (in this circus, the performers performed *outside* the circus tent, which served instead as the dressing/green room and would later house the children who didn't want to sleep under the stars for the best part of the whole night — the circus camp-out). The adults burst

294

into applause, and Kari nudged the beaming Merit, who sat next to her.

Reni did an expert shuffle-ball step, followed by Melody's just-as-expert one, followed by a hesitant and arrhythmic tapping by Jewel. There was a soft whir as Merit snapped her Polaroid camera and the picture slowly spit out.

"Hi, Mommy!" said Jewel, with a wave of her pudgy little arm.

"God, she's a doll," said Audrey, and Kari nodded. She loved all the neighborhood children, but Jewel, the little girl she and the Angry Housewives had helped deliver, was everyone's pet.

Merit's daughters had inherited their mother's beauty, but what Kari found most compelling about them was their sisterhood; she had never seen such a tight-knit trio of sisters.

Julia and Reni were best friends and in the same class at school, but Julia didn't like playing at Reni's house because the sisters were always included.

"I mean, I like them, Mom," explained Julia, "but Melody isn't even six yet and Jewel's three, and well, sometimes I just want to do bigger-kid stuff."

"I can understand that," said Kari, nodding.

"Well, Reni can't. She doesn't mind at all that they play with us. In fact, once we had her bedroom all to ourselves and we had the dress-up box out and then all of a sudden Reni says, 'Oh, Mel and Jewel love dress-up,' and she goes to the hallway and calls them! And we never have her bedroom all to ourselves!"

Kari loved summer evenings, standing and talking with other parents as the kids ran around playing games of Starlight Moonlight or Kick the Can, and she couldn't help notice how if one of the three sisters was It, the other two would help her find the rest of the kids.

"Let's give the dancers a big hand," urged Julia in her scripted show-biz lingo as the sisters finished their final steps and took a bow.

Kari flinched, hearing a loud, shrill whistle behind her. She turned around to see that Eric, two pinkies in his mouth, had joined the audience. Merit's posture suddenly changed — it seemed as if a weight had been pressed on her shoulders, and her hands clutched and unclutched each other.

"All right, you're probably wondering — what's a circus without lions?" asked Julia, pacing in front of the row of parents. "A circus without lions is no circus at all — that's why we have them! Ladies and gentlemen, all the way from deepest Africa, the most dangerous lions of all and their trainer, Vladimir!"

Kari laughed, wondering if Flan, the scriptwriter, thought Vladimir was an African name or just generally exotic.

Audrey's eleven-year-old son Bryan, who in Kari's eyes seemed to have grown five inches over the summer, swirled his cape and cracked his whip, which was a long ribbon attached to Bonnie's old baton.

"Back! Back!" he ordered as Flicka, wearing one of Julia's tutus around her neck to suggest a mane, bounded out of the tent, followed by Bryan's brother Michael and Slip's son. In painting the boys' faces, Faith had heeded their requests to make them look "really scary" instead of "babyish," and they wore the costumes

Kari had made out of terry cloth and loops of yarn.

"Up! Up!" said the lion tamer, and two snarling lions obeyed, holding their arms up, paws hanging. The other lion thumped her tail and panted.

"And now jump! Jump!"

The lions jumped, at first without incident, but then Michael stepped on Gil's tail and Gil swiped his paw at Michael's face.

"Lions! Lions! Cut it out!" cried Bryan, cracking his whip as Flicka ran in circles around them, barking.

The lions suddenly collapsed in a snarling heap.

"Lions! Lions!"

Kari wondered if this was unrehearsed or part of the act. Dave didn't seem to care; he was bent over in his chair by the record player, laughing.

"Lions — back in your cages!"

Suddenly the lions turned on their trainer, chasing him up the aisle, past Dave, and around the side of the house, snarling and roaring and, in Flicka's case, barking all the while.

As the pleas of the lion tamer grew fainter with distance, Julia stepped out, urging the audience that everything was under control and no one would be hurt by the killer lions.

"Unless you make them *really* mad," she amended.

The clowns were next on the bill, and Flannery, Bonnie, and Joe, with clown faces courtesy of Faith and costumes from Kari's magic sewing machine, bounded out, Flannery riding a tricycle sizes too small and Bonnie bouncing on a pogo stick.

It was Joe who had the real appreciable skill, though; the boy had been teaching himself to juggle and did so now, with three red balls he was able to move through the air with few slipups.

This earned rousing applause, but the audience favorite was yet to come.

"Ladies and gentlemen," said Julia, "now's the moment you've all been waiting for — no, but we'll get to the ice cream soon — ladies and gentlemen, the Amazing Slipperini and, appearing for the first time, her new partner, Beaulioli!"

From behind the circus tent, a sprite in a shiny green leotard executed two backflips. Behind her, in a costume like Superman's without the cape, Beau did the same.

"Oh, my gosh, Faith," said Kari, turning to her. "I didn't know Beau could do that."

"He's been practicing like crazy," said Faith.

"And now he's saying he wants to join the circus — the real circus — when he grows up," said Wade with a smile.

"Slip still threatens to do that," said Jerry. "Although she's down from four backflips in a row to two."

Kari watched Slip, feeling the same awe everyone else did. How could an adult body still do those things, twist and bend and fly through the air? When Kari had first gotten to know Slip, she'd mentioned how much Slip reminded her of a leprechaun, a comment at which Slip took great offense.

"No, no," Kari had blustered, "I mean it as a compliment. You know, with your red hair and energy and high spirits and —"

Slip's raised hand ordered Kari to stop.

"I'd like to know why I never get compared to redheads like Lucille Ball or Arlene Dahl. Why is it always ugly little leprechauns? Please, if we're ever going to be friends, don't ever *ever* compare me to *anything* that might be called upon to be a mascot in a St. Patrick's Day parade."

Kari honored that request, but it didn't mean the comparison still didn't come to mind.

Beau struggled for a moment, but then, getting his balance, followed Slip as she walked nonchalantly, albeit on her hands, toward the audience.

"I always wanted to do that when I was a kid," said Helen Hammond, "but my mother said it wasn't ladylike."

"Sounds like your mother," said her husband.

Beau was able to do everything Slip did — several front flips, a few round-offs — but the topper of the evening was when he got up on her shoulders and then did a somersault in the air as he dismounted.

The crowd applauded wildly, and as Julia called out the rest of the acts to take a bow, flashbulbs shot little blue explosions in the air.

The western sky was flushed with the setting sun as everyone began folding up chairs and cleaning the yard. Slip began whistling the song "Whistle While You Work," and the adults and all the kids who could whistle joined in. Again the words came to Kari: halcyon days.

Jerry and Wade had agreed to supervise the camp-out. That is, they would spear the marshmallows that were roasted over the coals of the grill, tell a few ghost stories, and, when the kids had fallen asleep, stretch out on the chaise longues with a cooler of beer between them. It was the fourth year they had hosted the camp-out (Paul Forrest had joined them the first year), and Faith knew Wade adjusted his schedule for the event.

He and Jerry weren't the kind of close friends the Angry Housewives were (the women discussed this, deciding it was the rare man who *could* have such close friendships), but they enjoyed each other's company and could sit companionably talking about weather (Jerry's choice of topic) or flying (Wade's) or how the Twins or Vikings or North Stars were doing — Jerry had taken Wade to his first ice hockey game, and now Wade was a convert, convinced that it was the sport of the future. And on camp-out night, although it was unexpressed, they felt a sort of privilege in watching over these wild and exhausted lions and ringmasters and acrobats and clowns. Both men couldn't help but smile up at the late summer sky, beers balanced on their bellies, listening to the crickets and the whispered scatological jokes of the kids who hadn't yet fallen asleep.

"What did the sailor find in the toilet?"

"What?

"The captain's log!"

Both men laughed; a kid's dumb joke laughed at on a late summer night in a yard that was still littered with circus popcorn and tutu netting was a tonic that neither of the men could quite articulate. Later, Jerry would tell Slip, "It's just such a peaceful way to end the summer," but those words conveyed only a fraction of the bigness that filled his chest.

Slip knew exactly what he meant. Many times

she had sat outside with her friends, watching their children play in the sandbox or examine something incredibly interesting — a rock, a stick, and once the carcass of a blackbird — and thought, *This is the whole wide world, right here, and I'm in it.*

So with the children under the watchful eyes of two dads drinking beer, the mothers decided to cap off their own summer with a drink themselves at Kari's house.

"I've got to hand it to you, Slip," said Audrey, pushing back on Kari's porch swing, "that was one hell of a circus. I'd say the best yet — even though my firstborn decided he's too old for such 'kid stuff.' "

"Audrey," said Faith, who sat on the swing with her, "you sound like you're ready to cry."

There was a sound of a match striking, and a flicker of flame illuminated Audrey's face as she lit her cigarette. "I think I'll be ready to cry for the next ten years — or however long it takes for my boys to get through puberty."

"Tell me about it," said Slip. "Flannery's already taller than me — not that a lot of sixth graders aren't — but she's starting to get a little sassier, and practically everything I do either embarrasses her or inspires her pity."

Kari laughed. "Will you tell her, by the way, what a great job I thought she did writing those lines for Julia?"

"Sure. She *will* still accept compliments from me." Slip took a sip of her apple wine and tried not to shudder. She had given up hard liquor for good, and Kari, knowing this, had stocked her bar with a few bottles of wine. This particular one had been on the liquor store counter, on sale. "But thanks, I thought it was good too."

"Hey, wasn't Merit coming over?" asked Audrey.

"She said she was," said Faith. "Pass me that ashtray, will you?"

"How about her girls for the Cute Prize?" said Slip, and she took another cautious sip from her glass. "Kari, no offense, but what is this wine I'm drinking?"

"I don't know — Anne of Green Gables or something."

Audrey laughed. "Annie *Green Springs*. The preferred wine of underage drinkers."

Kari shrugged. "All I know is, it was on sale."

"I can see why," said Slip, but she took another game sip. "So what'd you think of your little acrobat?"

Faith smiled; she had been wondering when someone was going to mention her children. "He's good, isn't he?"

"Yeah. You don't mind if I take him on the road, do you? I've been thinking of getting a job outside the house."

"No kidding?" said Faith. "Me too. Well, first I need to go back to school. I'm thinking of getting an associate's degree in interior design and —"

A faint crash and a muffled scream stopped one sentence and started another.

"Did you hear that?"

"I did," said Slip.

"It's not the kids, is it?" asked Kari.

"Not ours," said Audrey. "Probably those bratty Lindgren kids from across the alley. I know Ray and Alice are out of town and those kids always throw a party when — hey, here comes Merit now."

They looked to see that Merit had stepped out in the rectangle of light that shone from her opened front door, but instead of answering their waves with one of her own, she was suddenly yanked back inside.

"What was *that?*" asked Slip.

"It's Eric," said Audrey, rising so quickly that the chains of the porch swing jangled. "It's that bastard Eric."

Without saying a word, Faith jumped off the porch steps and raced across the lawn.

"Where's she going?" asked Slip.

"Probably to get Wade and Jerry," said Audrey as she watched Faith run down the street. "But we can't wait for them. Come on."

She was off the porch and had run halfway across the dewy lawn before Kari and Slip caught up to her. They all crossed the street, Slip wincing as her bare feet made contact with a nugget of gravel or a sharp stone.

Racing up the wide stairs, Audrey banged on the door with one hand and turned the doorknob with the other. The door opened, and the women tumbled into a scene that would be relived at least once in all of their nightmares.

Stinking of liquor, Eric was standing under the living room archway, holding on to his wife by the hair. Blood surged from her lip, and one eye was closing in a swelling, purpling mass.

"Oh, look, honey," he said breezily, "we've got company." He pulled Merit's head up, and as she whimpered he turned to the women, smiled his bright white smile, and asked, "Now will you please get the fuck out of my house?"

"Eric, let go of her," said Audrey. "Let go of her right now."

"Who's gonna make me — you?" He laughed an unamused laugh and then, changing his voice so that it was smooth, almost solicitous, he said, "Merit, honey, your friend who dresses like a prostitute is here to rescue you. Please tell her you're not in need of rescue and to get some decent clothes on and *get out of my house!*"

As he yanked her hair again for emphasis, Slip said, "Let her go, Eric."

"Is this where you learn to be so disrespectful?" he asked Merit. "From these bossy so-called friends of yours?" His free hand smacked Merit across the face, and the act was so violent, so shocking that the women were frozen for a second.

But only for a second.

Kari could have sworn she heard someone scream "Aieeeeee," like the martial-arts expert she had seen on Johnny Carson, and suddenly all the Angry Housewives, at their angriest, flew at Eric, pulling at his arms, prying apart his fingers, trying to get him to let go of Merit.

Slip had never felt this element of fear with her brothers, but it reminded her of when she used to wrestle with them. She was always impressed how hard male muscles were, how *strong* a determined male could be.

"Let her go, you asshole."

They all looked up to see Faith standing just steps away, her arms outstretched and holding a gun.

"Oh, dear God," whispered Kari.

Eric laughed and in a poor approximation of a drawl said, "Why, look, it's the crazy cracker, here to blow us away with her son's toy gun."

"It's not my son's toy gun," said Faith, "it's Wade's. And it's real. Now let Merit go."

Like chorus girls wanting to showcase the principals, Slip, Kari, and Audrey stepped to the side. Eric still held on to Merit by the hair, and the look that he gave Faith was beyond contempt, emitting an evil Faith had a hard time staring back at.

"Merit, tell your southern cracker bitch friend that she's real funny — ha-ha — but we'd appreciate it if she took her stupid little toy gun and her stupid little friends out of our goddamn house!"

"Faith, you'd —"

Interrupting Merit, Faith cocked the pistol.

"Listen, you sorry son of a bitch, I've got witnesses, and if I shoot you, they'll make sure the law knows it was in self-defense."

"Oh, I'm scared," said Eric, but Faith could tell by the set of his jaw and by the question in his eyes that he was.

"I'm going to count to ten," said Faith, "and either you'll let go of Merit by then or I'll shoot you. One . . . two . . . three."

Eric let the count go to eight before he let go of Merit, pushing her to the floor.

"Satisfied?" asked Eric as Audrey, Slip, and Kari gathered her up. "Now get out of my house."

"Gladly," said Faith. "Let's go, girls." Walking backward toward the door, she held the gun on Eric until they were all safely outside.

Back at Kari's house, after locking the front and back doors, they hunkered around the kitchen table, sipping at the coffee (the brandy of Minnesota) Kari had brewed.

"I wished I still smoked," said Slip as Faith tried to light her and Merit's cigarettes with a trembling hand.

"Here," said Audrey, offering the flame from her lighter, which shook a little too.

"My stars, I have never been so scared in my life," said Kari.

"I know," said Slip, "and then when Annie Oakley bursts in with a gun — holy full bladder, I thought I was going to pee in my pants."

"I think I did a little," admitted Kari, and, scared as she was, a chuckle bubbled out of her.

They allowed themselves a laugh, but their fear was a wind that blew it out before it could ignite into something big.

"Well," said Kari, reaching for the phone mounted on her wall, "I think it's time we called the police."

"What?" said Merit, and the panic that had disappeared from her mashed face was back again. "No, no, Eric would *kill* me if I called the police." Her words were fuzzy through her swollen lips.

"Merit, he might kill you if you don't," said Faith.

"Yeah," said Slip, "and you won't always have Annie Oakley here to protect you."

Holding ice wrapped in a washrag to her eye, Merit tried to smile at Faith. "I owe you, Annie," she said, "and I'll pay you back someday, but I'm not going to call the police."

"Merit, listen —" began Slip.

"Actually, she may be right," said Kari. "I know this teacher whose husband beat her, and she said all the police ever did was give her husband a reprimand. No matter how many times they were called to the house, they never took him down to the station."

"Christ," said Audrey. "If Paul ever hit me, I'd knock his block off." She splayed her hands as if regarding her manicure. " 'Course, his method of hurting me was to have sex with the rest of the known universe." Sighing, she took a drag off her cigarette. "Has this . . . has this been going on for a long time, Merit?"

Merit nodded, and Slip asked what would set him off.

"Oh, the way I wore my hair or didn't wear my hair, the way I cooked a steak or didn't cook a steak, if I said something stupid or if I said something smart . . . really, it was anything and nothing at all. And when Jewel came along — well, he can't forgive me for not giving him his precious son." She fumbled at the pack on the table and placed a cigarette between her swollen lips.

Slip snorted a laugh. "No offense, Merit, but you look like you just went nine rounds with Muhammad Ali." Tears sprang up in her eyes. "I'm sorry. That wasn't very funny. I'm just so . . . shocked."

"Me too," said Kari. "I had no idea he was doing this to you, Merit. Why . . . what happened tonight? He seemed fine at the circus."

Merit shook her head. Tucking back a strand of hair that hung on her face, she winced and touched her sore scalp.

"He thought I was ignoring him at the circus," she said. "See, he thinks all things should come to a stop for me when he's around, but I guess I found the kids too entertaining, socialized too much, had too good a time."

"Is he always drinking when he goes after you?" asked Audrey.

Merit inhaled the cigarette and her lips formed a battered O as she exhaled. "I used to fool myself into thinking it was something he only did when he was drinking, because then I could make an excuse for it — 'oh, he's drunk, he doesn't know what he's doing' — but no, he hits just as hard when he's sober."

Kari asked him if he'd ever hurt the kids.

Tears welled in Merit's eyes — at least in the one that wasn't swollen shut.

"Not like he does me, but . . . they've heard him come after me. He would usually wait until they were sleeping or out of the house, but once he kicked me to the ground and as I was trying to crawl away I turned my head and saw Reni standing at the top of the stairs, watching. If you could have seen her face . . ." Merit took a napkin out of the little dispenser shaped like a cow and wiped her nose. "Well, she started to run down the stairs to help me as I was pulling myself up, but I motioned for her to get back to her room, hoping she'd leave before Eric saw her, but then he did see her."

The women around the table held their breaths, waiting to hear what Merit had to say, even though they knew she was going to tell them something awful.

"He smiled his big handsome smile — God, how I hate that smile! — and said, 'Oh, Irene, go back to bed, your mother is fine. She just did a very bad thing today and I have to teach her a lesson.' Reni asked in a tiny little voice, 'What bad thing?' and I saw the muscle in Eric's cheek bulge out and he said, 'I'm not going to tell you again, Irene: go back to bed. *Now.*' And she did, but not before she walked all the way down the steps to where I was leaning on the newel post. She put her arms around my neck and gave me a kiss, and as she turned around and started walking upstairs, I prayed hard for two things: one, that Eric wouldn't touch her, and two, that I would be worthy of my brave little girl's devotion."

"I'm so ashamed," said Kari, pressing her fingers to the corners of her eyes. "I live right across the street from you and I never suspected anything."

"What about you, Audrey?" asked Faith. "Didn't you ever, you know, see anything?"

Audrey kneaded her forehead; mascara was smudged under her eyes.

"Like I've told you before, Faith, I'm not frickin' Kreskin. It's not like I'm in charge of what I see." She wiped a drop of coffee off the table with her finger and looked at Merit. "Although I always did think he was kind of a control freak, but this . . . I never suspected any of this." Her eyes widened as something occurred to her. "Is that why you'd do those extravagant trips and falls, Merit? So in case we ever did see bruises you could blame them on your clumsiness?"

Merit nodded, her chin quivering.

"I should have seen something," said Audrey, disgust in her voice. "We all should have seen something."

"Well, I did a pretty good job of making sure you *wouldn't,*" said Merit. "*I* was so ashamed.

How could I let any of you — *anyone* — know what he was doing to me? I learned right away to scream real loud on the *inside,* because if I didn't make any noise, if nobody knew . . . well, then I could sometimes convince myself it wasn't really happening." She cocked her head and touched her swollen lip with her fingertips. "Tonight . . . tonight was the first time he ever hit my face — I mean with a closed fist. That's what really scared me — he was hitting me in a place where everyone could see. I don't know what excuse I would have come up with to explain — oh, dear God, I am so relieved I don't have to explain anything anymore!"

She couldn't hold it any longer — the floodgates broke and the tears crashed through. Audrey and Slip and Kari cried with her, and when everyone was spent from all the emotion, they made a nest of cushions and pillows in the living room and, like puppies, they fell asleep. All except Faith, who hadn't cried, who knew someone had to stay alert, had to keep her wits about her, because if she knew anything, it was that Eric might not be done, might decide to make a sneak attack. Dawn came and pinkened the room with light, and when the bright morning sun shone in Kari's eyes, waking her up, Faith was still wide-awake, sitting in the rocking chair, the pistol in her lap.

September 1976, 2:00 a.m.

Dear Mama,

Wade was *livid* that I'd taken his gun.

"What the hell, Faith?" he shouted. "What the hell? Why didn't you come get me? Me or Jerry? Why didn't you call the cops? What

310

were you trying to prove?"

"Wade, please, you're going to scare the twins," I said. The twins were trying to catch tadpoles down at the creek and couldn't hear us, but I felt I had to say something to calm him down. The vein in his forehead was bulging, and I was worried it was going to burst. "Let me fill up your glass."

I had made his favorite iced tea with enough sugar to bake a cake, but he wasn't interested in any of my diversionary tactics.

"Faith," he said, encircling my wrist with his hand. "Sit. Sit down and talk to me."

"Sure, honey," I said, "as long as you don't yell at me anymore."

"Okay." He sat there for a moment on the webbed lawn chair, looking down the sloped yard toward the creek. "Okay, I won't yell at you, but that doesn't mean I'm not still mad as hell at you." He finally took his tea off the patio table and took a long swig. "And you do know why I'm upset, right?"

I thought for a moment. "Because you didn't want me to get hurt?"

"That's right. I didn't want you — or anyone else — to get hurt. Now, why didn't you get me, Faith? Why don't you ever let me help you?" His voice sounded wounded, as if I had just called him a name.

"I let you help me all the —"

"No, you don't, Faith. You never talk to me about your mama or your daddy, even though I could help —"

"Wade, believe me, I've told you all you'd want to hear about my mama or daddy." I swallowed hard, my heart sounding in my ears.

"Fine," sighed Wade, meaning the exact opposite. "That's just fine."

"Wade, about the gun," I said, willing to let him yell at me about anything but my parents. "I was so scared I could hardly think . . . plus I didn't want any of the kids to wake up and get scared. I didn't want to ruin their camp-out."

Wade's jaw flexed its bunched-up little muscles, but he nodded, as if understanding the subject had changed and its return was non-negotiable.

"Why not the police then, Faith? Why didn't you girls call the police?"

"When we first heard Merit scream, I guess our instinct was to just go to her. I didn't even think of the police until it was all over, and then Merit told us she didn't want us to call them."

"And you listened to her?"

"Well, of course we listened to her! And why wouldn't we? She was the one who got beaten up, not us."

Wade swallowed down the rest of his tea and wiped his mouth with the back of his hand.

"If anything like that ever happens again — if Eric goes off on his wife, or somebody breaks into the house, or anything — before you do anything, I want you to get me first, okay, Faith?"

I just sat there, so he repeated, *Okay, Faith?*"

"What about when you're flying? Remember that first winter we were here and the lights went out and I didn't know what was going on? What if there's an intruder in the house and you're not home? What do I do then, Wade?"

"Then you can get my gun, Faith, but first I'm going to have to show you where I keep the bullets."

I heard him clearly, but I don't think my mind wanted to comprehend him. We sat there staring at each other, and I couldn't tell if Wade was ready to smile or yell at me some more.

"There were *no bullets* in that gun?"

Wade shook his head. "I've kept them in a separate place ever since the kids started walking around."

"So if there was an intruder, I would try to shoot him with an unloaded gun?"

"Faith, have we been broken into yet? And if we are, do what I've always told you: get the twins, lock yourselves in the bedroom and call the police."

"While he's breaking the door down." I was absolutely furious and scared, thinking of last night. "So there I was, threatening to shoot Eric Iverson with an empty gun?"

Wade nodded.

"Good grief," I said, feeling flushed. "What if he'd come after me and I fired?"

"Either way, Faith, there's no good ending. Either he would have beaten you up or you would have shot him. That's why you should have gotten me. There was no need for you to play the hero."

"I didn't want to play the hero," I said, feeling both a little sick and foolish. "I just wanted to help my friend. And I did, Wade. Slip and Audrey and Kari and I did help her,

313

as much as you think we're helpless females who can't do anything without our big, strong men."

"Oh, baby, you're not getting the point," said Wade, tipping forward on his chair to take my hands. "Do you realize what a strong possibility there was of you getting hurt? Do you think I could stand it if you got hurt, if some maniac hurt you while I was just down the block?" His voice caught a little; honest to God, Mama, I think he was ready to cry. *Man,* I thought, *he loves me.* I guess I always knew that, but still, sometimes it's a big surprise to me that *I* have a husband who *loves* me. That just blows my mind, as Audrey would say.

I don't think Wade would have worried so much if he knew how many times I pushed some drunken slob off you — I mean, I've had practice! At least I have to give you some credit — once they hit you, you always threw them out. Merit had been putting up with this crap for years.

Oh, before I forget, Mama, how's this for gall: somehow Mr. Iverson the wife beater found a florist that was open on Labor Day and sent all of us Angry Housewives a bouquet of roses. The note read (he sent the same one to all of us): *So sorry about the misunderstanding; it was a night I'm trying to forget, and I hope you will too.* Can you believe that? The florist tried to deliver to Audrey, but she took Merit and her girls somewhere — Kari thinks to a fancy hotel downtown. I don't even know if they'll be back for school tomorrow.

Well, Wade's upstairs waiting for me, Mama. I'm exhausted (and my hip aches from all that running), but there's nothing like knowing how much your man loves you to fire up the old libido, even though I'm still burned at him for not telling me about the bullets. Does he put me in the same must-be-protected-from-myself category as Beau and Bonnie? Oh, boy, the good old libido is fading fast, Mama — is he gonna hear it from me.

As always, I'm sorry, Mama,
Faith

August 1977

HOST: AUDREY

BOOK: *The Grass Is Always Greener Over the Septic Tank* by Erma Bombeck

REASON CHOSEN: "I figured we could all use a good laugh."

"Happy birthday, darling."

"Thanks, Mother."

"So, have you got big plans to celebrate?"

"I wouldn't exactly call them —"

"I hope you're seeing a nice man. A nice man should be taking you out for dinner and dancing."

"Uh, it's not in the cards tonight."

"Really, I don't know why you and Paul couldn't —"

"Mother, I've got to run. Thanks for the check."

"You're welcome. Buy yourself a dress — a *nice* dress; men don't care for all that skin, they like —"

Click.

My mother's phone call, with its implicit message — *you're a loser!* — didn't set the tone for my thirty-seventh birthday; I was already in a funk as deep as the Pacific. Paul had the boys for the weekend, which I thought might be a birthday present unto itself — two days of peace and quiet, imagine all the stuff I could get done — but all I managed to do was polish off a whole quart of orange sherbet on Friday night (I don't even like orange sherbet but bought it because I figure it's less fattening than ice cream. So what did I do? I doused it with about nine hundred calories of chocolate syrup to make it more palatable) and a whole pan of Rice Krispies bars (my birthday cake to myself) on Saturday. And that was just for appetizers.

I had turned down an invitation from a college friend of mine to go out — she had just gone through a divorce too, and her sense of desperation always made me feel more desperate. There weren't any invitations coming from the Angry Housewives, as Faith and her family were vacationing in Texas, Merit and her girls had driven down to Iowa for a family reunion, and Kari and Julia were up at Kari's brother's cabin.

I had been hoping for a nonprofessional phone call from my tax attorney — we had dinner last night and I thought a few sparks had flown, but maybe it had just been the wine.

No matter — I had all sorts of projects to start and books to read. But I couldn't seem to summon the energy to do anything but eat. Or smoke. Or sometimes both at the same time. I'm starting to get a little wheeze in my chest if I take a deep breath, which is very attractive if you happen to be attracted to emphysemics. And not only did I find a gray hair, I found a whole *patch* of gray right by my temple. At least my big beautiful breasts were still big and beautiful; they're like the Loyalist Party, always faithful to the queen.

I reminded myself that thirty-seven is *not* old . . . it just looks that way. No, I'm kidding; actually I look pretty good . . . next to my grandmother. Ba da dum.

By Saturday afternoon I realized that I was either going to overdose on sugar or my own bad humor, and I decided to treat myself to a movie. It's a therapy I highly recommend to anyone who's feeling a little melancholy — go see a movie by yourself. I'm not guaranteeing it'll cheer you up, but usually the people on the screen have bigger problems than you do, plus you have the popcorn all to yourself.

I saw *Stage Door* at a revival theater by the U, and even though I loved all those wisecracking actresses and looking at those narrow, clingy thirties dresses, even though Eve Arden's delivery always made me laugh, even though the popcorn guy honored my request for extra butter, by the end of the movie I was sobbing. The tears I wiped away were black from my mascara and I didn't need a mirror to know I probably looked a mess, which is why I didn't exactly appreciate hearing "Audrey!" when I went blinking into the lobby.

It was Stuart and Grant, the couple who lived next to me.

"Here," said Stuart, handing me a tissue. "We didn't use all ours."

"I personally was *unmoved* when that actress jumped out the window," said Grant. "It was just so obvious."

"So the kids are with Paul this weekend?" asked Grant, and when I nodded, he took my arm. "Good, then you can come have a drink with us."

"I could use a drink," I said, starting to feel weepy again. "It's my birthday."

"Your birthday!" said Stuart.

"Your birthday!" echoed Grant. "Then let's make it champagne."

We went to a bar in a hotel by the airport, and it was a pleasure getting drunk, especially with two men who found me fascinating. I didn't care that they were gay; they were men and they found me fascinating.

"God, you're a stitch," said Stuart.

"You're the stitch," I said. "Look at you. I have never seen a man wear a suit to the movies."

"Stuart is never *not* dressed up," said Grant, whose own style of dress gave a big nod to Bohemia (today he was wearing a flowing yellow shirt with a paisley scarf as a belt).

"Not even when he goes to bed?" I asked.

"Well," said Grant, opening one of the little paper umbrellas that came with our jumbo margaritas (we had decided that although champagne was a festive idea, we were all in a tropical-drinks sort of mood) and, fluttering his eyelashes behind it, "that's rather an impertinent question."

"So what's your impertinent answer?"

It turns out it was silk pajamas or nothing at all. I told them I wore flannel or one of Paul's old T-shirts.

"Even when you're entertaining?" asked Grant.

"Who's impertinent now?" I asked.

Grant shrugged. "A person would have to be blind not to notice the men that have paraded into your house."

"Maybe I'm holding auditions for a marching band," I shot back.

They laughed the way I used to make Paul laugh, and we ordered another round, or at least Grant and I did; Stuart was driving.

"So you're the responsible one, huh?" I asked.

"I guess I am," he said. "Not that Grant's not responsible, but I guess I am the one who always considers consequences."

"I'll consider the consequence of drinking this margarita," he volunteered, and took a long sip that emptied half his glass. "Ahh. Hey, after we're done talking about my irresponsible behavior, let's go watch the airplanes."

"Watch the airplanes what?" I asked.

Grant looked at me as if I were daft. "Why, take off and land, silly. You mean to tell me you've never sat in a parked car watching the airplanes?"

"I've always had better things to do in a parked car."

Grant whooped. "I'll bet. Now hurry up and finish your drink and we'll show you what you've been missing."

As far as the airplanes go, I don't think I was missing that much. As the mother of boys, I was not drawn to noise and motion as a means of escape or entertainment; I got too much of that at home.

We were parked, along with a half dozen or so cars, behind a chain-link fence that ran parallel to the runway. The first plane that thundered in did grab my attention, but like I said, there are many other ways I'd prefer my attention grabbed.

"Grant, Audrey's not enjoying this," said

320

Stuart as I sat between them in the front seat, my fingers plugging my ears.

Grant looked at me, as hurt as if I'd insulted him personally. "You're really not enjoying yourself?"

"A little," I admitted, "but not because of the planes. Because of you guys, because I like your company. Because I *needed* company."

"Stuart, how about if you just drive around — pick a scenic drive, maybe by the river — and Audrey here can tell us all her woes."

"How far do you want to drive?" I asked.

"As long as it takes," said Grant. "Right, Stuart?"

"Right," he answered, and started the car.

"Zo," said Grant in a thick Freudian accent. "Vhat seems to be troubling you, mein little veinerschnitzel?"

"Well, my biggest problem right now is that I'm thirty-seven years old and I'm afraid I'll be alone — without a man — for the rest of my life."

"That *would* be scary," said Grant, reaching over me to pat Stuart's thigh.

"Come on, Grant, let her talk," said Stuart, and talk I did.

The first time I knew Paul was having an affair — that night that started out so fun, with all the Angry Housewives getting stoned, and ended so scary, with Michael nearly strangling himself — I kept my suspicions from him . . . for about a day and a half. When I confronted him, it was a scene as overwrought as any in a high school production of *The Crucible*.

He of course accused me of being crazy, and

when I didn't back down, he, very lawyerly, demanded that I provide evidence for my charges.

"Well, if you're asking me if I've found lipstick on your collar or motel matchbooks in your pants pockets, no, I haven't. But I know, Paul, I know beyond the shadow of a doubt that you're sleeping with someone other than me."

Paul had had a serviceable if not distinguished career as a running back at the U and he could still get that arrogant jock look on his face, the exact same expression juvenile delinquents and loan officers have, the one that asked, *So? So even if you're right, what are you gonna do about it?*

We stood there staring at each other, pawing at the ground like two elks deciding whether to smash antlers or walk away. I myself could have gone in for a little antler smashing, but of course we had to be interrupted by a child — Bryan charging into the room, screaming that Davey had told him he was adopted and we weren't his real parents.

"Of course we're your real parents," I said, which gave him enough assurance to charge back out, screaming, "They are too my real parents, Davey!"

"But then again," I said, noticing a chip in my thumbnail, "I *was* awfully close to the fellow who installed our air-conditioning — wasn't that about nine months before Bryan was born?"

Paul shook his head. "Very funny, Audrey. *Very* funny."

"Maybe I'm not joking," I said, and even though I was, I was hoping he might, for a moment, feel a smidgin of the pain I was feeling.

Our marriage from that moment on was a

roller coaster, with us most often plunging downward.

I'm embarrassed to say that our sex life continued at its usual brisk pace — no sense in me missing out just because he wasn't. And I also — this is even more embarrassing — thought that was the one way I knew to hold him. Who was a more sexciting lover than me?

There was a time when the roller coaster seemed stalled at the top of a crest and I thought we were going to make it. It was right around when Nixon was resigning, so all of us were in a good mood. We hadn't been fighting, and I could tell that he wasn't doing anything on his lunch hour other than eating lunch. I was being reminded of everything I loved about him, his *masculinity* — his deep voice and oxlike shoulders, the way he could open a pickle jar and throw one of the boys up in the air (and catch him, too; thankfully he always remembered that part) as effortlessly as if he were throwing a beach ball. He made me feel safe. I remembered how he laughed at my jokes and how every now and then he would allow himself to get silly — doing a Bob Dylan impression while completely naked (there's a whole different subtext to "If I Had a Hammer" when it's performed in the nude) or playing crazy monster man for the kids and chasing them until they collapsed with giddy fright.

So Nixon was resigning (Slip went around singing, "Ding, dong, the crook is dead!") and Paul and I were treating each other with sort of a, I don't know, *tenderness,* and then we had to go to his stupid fraternity reunion. Believe me, cutting an old person's toenails (I used to cut my

323

grandfather's now and then, so I know whereof I speak — it was like trying to saw through an oak tree with a penknife) is more appealing to me than sitting around listening to a bunch of men reminisce about how many kegs they could go through in one night. I don't know why Paul wanted me there anyway, but at this point, any invitation he offered was a gift I wasn't about to refuse.

The reunion was held on a boat that cruised up and down the Mississippi, and I must admit, it started out to be fun; we were at a dinner table with people who did talk about how many kegs they could go through in one night, but then moved on to other topics. Paul, who hated to dance, even got out on the floor a few times and shuffle-footed his way to the music of a corny little combo whose lead singer occasionally brought out a kazoo. I was wearing a thin-strapped, low-cut (natch) black dress and had the gardenia corsage Paul bought me pinned to my hair, and I am being not immodest but factual when I tell you there weren't many men on that boat who *weren't* giving me the hairy eyeball.

"Paul, you're not going to keep this beautiful creature all to yourself, are you?" asked a fellow Delt, and at Paul's shrug, I was suddenly in the arms of an energetic banker who fortunately had more rhythm than personality.

I plastered on a smile as we moved effortlessly around the other dancing couples, enjoying my view of Paul, who wandered up to the bar and accepted a drink from the bartender. I saw the smile the blond, round-faced bartender gave him, saw that the smile went past the point of friendliness and into invitation, and I knew right away that this woman and my husband were going to know each other in the biblical sense.

About a year and a half later, when he was in a confessional mode and thought it was somehow therapeutic (for him, certainly not for me) to list every single woman he'd slept with, he referred to her as Betty, the bartender on the boat who was going for her master's in child psychology.

"Paul," I said, wondering why my heart still beat when it felt so dead, "I don't need a bio of your tramps."

I didn't need Slip to tell me that *tramp* was a sexist word — why wasn't the man who was cheating on his wife called the same thing? — but these women were tramps in that that's what they were doing to my marriage, tramping on it.

The confessional was the final straw. I had had my face rubbed in Paul's infidelity — I didn't have to *wallow* in it. I asked him for a divorce.

"But Aude," he said, truly shocked, "I love you."

I thought I'd call his bluff. "Well, then, would you agree to an open marriage? So I could fool around too?"

The shock only intensified on Paul's face. "Audrey, that's sick."

I had to laugh; laughter was the only glue that was going to hold me together.

"Did you know every time he had an affair?" asked Grant after I had told them more about my so-called psychic ability. We had crossed the bridge over to St. Paul and were driving along River Road.

"Well, I sort of knew it was a general pattern,

but that's not ESP — it's just sort of putting two and two together."

"Can you tell what'll happen to Stuart and me? Will we be together always?"

"Grant, please," said Stuart. "I don't want to know the future."

"And I can't tell it," I said. "God, Grant, you sound just like Faith. Except she always wants to know if I can see her past."

"Faith doesn't like me," said Grant. "If I'm out in the yard and she's walking by, she'll always pretend she doesn't see me."

"Is she a homophobe?" asked Stuart.

"No, I don't think so. Faith's just kind of a hard nut to crack."

"That still doesn't excuse the fact that she blatantly ignores me."

I'm sure it was fear that was driving Faith's unfriendliness. You didn't need any psychic abilities to know that Beau was gay; despite Faith's efforts to turn him into a macho little athlete, he was still a boy who was going to grow up uninterested in girls. I could guess that the less contact she had with men like Stuart and Grant, the easier it was to pretend they didn't exist or wouldn't influence her own son.

"So, tell us more," said Grant as we passed the stately homes overlooking the river. "Why, for instance, is a woman like you celebrating her birthday alone?"

"Grant!" scolded Stuart. To me he said, "Pay no attention to him, he has no internal censor."

"Well, look at her," said Grant. "She looks just like Cher — if Cher had any kind of appetite."

"Oh, not Cher," said Stuart. "Someone

earthier, more *Italian*, someone like Sophia."

"I love you, Stuart," I said.

Grant's elbow jabbed my side. "Well, he's taken. Now come on, it's your birthday. Why are you driving around St. Paul with a couple of gay guys?"

My split from my husband did hurt, but it was a lot more amicable than a lot of divorces (Merit and Eric's, for example, was *scary*). Paul quit the law firm, stepping out from under my father's shadow, which, even though long-distance, more and more began to oppress him. He joined a fellow Delt's firm and moved into an apartment downtown. Trying to get his college waistline back, he started walking to work and swimming every morning at the Y. He told me he wasn't seeing anyone "regularly" but was "dating" (translation: getting laid). He told me all this as if I were an interested pal, which I was, I guess.

My parents wanted me to move back to Chicago with the boys, which I found insulting: who did they think I was, Leslie Trottman, hotfooting it back to her parents' open arms and her parents' money?

I had enough of my parents' and grandparents' money right here in my own bank account (thank you, trust funds; thank you, inheritances) and I could be sure that their open arms would close soon enough in a stifling, inescapable choke hold. Besides, Minneapolis was my home. And what was I supposed to do without my book club?

"Kari had us over one night for supper," said Stuart, "and we ate leftovers from your meeting.

It was strange — all the food was red."

"She likes to color-coordinate the food to the book when she hosts," I said, laughing. "We were discussing the book *Carrie*. All the food had to be the color of blood."

"There was red bean chili, red cabbage salad," said Grant, shaking his head, "raspberry pie, and a fluffy pink Jell-O *thing*."

"I didn't think I'd be much of a fan of her color-coordinated meetings," I said, "but they are *interesting*. I remember when we read *Looking for Mr. Goodbar*. Everyone had to bring something chocolate."

"Oh, we liked those leftovers," said Grant.

"It's gotten to be sort of a tradition that we have supper with her the night after she hosts a meeting," explained Stuart.

I nodded. "I've heard her mention that, but it's Faith's meetings or mine where the really good themes and food come in."

"We're in the phone book," Grant hinted.

"Sorry, we're sort of a closed society."

So closed that I hadn't gone to the last two meetings . . . and not by choice, either. Oh, sure, Kari and Faith and Merit had all said I was being silly and to get over it and just *come*, but I knew that if I showed up, the Big Kahuna would freeze me out, if not leave altogether, and I didn't want to be the one who took the fun out of AHEB. The fun meant too much to me.

"What happened?" asked Grant as he lit a cigarette for me with the car lighter. "Who's the Big Kahuna?"

"Well, it's Slip, of course," said Stuart.

"*Slip?* That little tiny thing?"

"Grant, stop for a second and think," said Stuart. "She's physically tiny, but how would you describe her personality?"

Grant thought for a moment. "I guess the Big Kahuna is a good enough description." He exhaled smoke out the window vent. "I remember the first time she came over to the house to introduce herself. She brought along a petition — something about Indian rights, I think — for me to sign."

"That's Slip," I said grudgingly. Boy, did I miss her.

It started the way most fights do — over something small. Most fights, I'm convinced, start with something trivial; it's like you get a sliver in your toe and then try and try to work it out with a needle, then a tweezer, then a knife, then finally a backhoe, and by the time you're done you've got gangrene and they have to amputate your foot.

"Flannery told me Dave" — Slip, more than anyone, tried to abide by Davey's wishes not to be called Davey anymore — "has been . . . well, he's been getting in trouble in the lunchroom lately. Is he okay?"

She told me this last June, a few days before school was going to let out.

"Trouble? What kind of trouble?"

Slip pushed a red puff of hair behind her ear. She had given up trying to straighten her hair by herself and now had it done professionally. (It still frizzed up in humidity, but the volume of frizz was down by about 50 percent.)

"Well, she said he's been getting into fights, calling people names . . ."

I felt that rush of not-quite-nausea, not-quite-vertigo a mother always feels when she finds out her perfect child isn't so perfect.

"Hmmm," I said, "I'll ask him what's going on. That is, after I horsewhip him."

I'd thought Bryan would be hardest hit by the divorce. He was the most high-strung of my boys, the one who couldn't sleep well before a test. I practically had to sedate him the night before he was trying to win a president's physical fitness patch in the fifth grade — I think he thought he'd be failing his country as well as himself if he didn't win one. Of course, he did earn the patch, being a good strong athlete, even though he was running on about two minutes of sleep. He was the one who never teased his younger brother the way he himself had been teased. I think what might have helped him was that the parents of his best friend had just split up, so he had an ally who understood his situation exactly.

Michael is my easygoing, tumble-through-life kid, and while I know he was hurt, I also knew he had the sort of personality that would always work toward making him feel better.

But Davey — uh, Dave — well, he was sort of an enigma to me. He'd never seemed to need me like the other two. I'd always sensed that he tolerated rather than wanted my hugs and kisses. Of course, now that he was a teenager, I could no more hug or kiss him than I could an ape. He was almost fourteen, but I'd bet if he went to a bar, he wouldn't get carded. Paul and I are tall, but Dave is taller and has that kind of V-shaped build — big shoulders, narrow waist — that make it such a pleasure to watch the young Burt

Lancaster or Kirk Douglas on the late show. He has my dark coloring and Paul's clear blue eyes, and the girls are crazy about him; the brave ones call and ask to speak to him, the shy ones hang up as soon as I answer.

And yet there was something of a bully about him. I know kids are wired to torment their siblings (my brother Lewis loved to comment on my changing body at the dinner table: "not the drumstick — I'd like the *breast*"), but Davey always seemed to get more enjoyment out of Bryan's unhappiness than he should have.

"Davey . . . Dave," I said later that evening when he and I were the only ones in the TV room still conscious (*The Tonight Show* was a little too sophisticated for Michael and Bryan, who had fallen asleep before Johnny Carson finished his monologue), "I was talking to Slip today, and she mentioned that you've been having some trouble in the lunchroom."

"That stupid Flannery! She doesn't know what she's talking about! She is so stupid, Mom, you wouldn't believe it! She —"

"Shh," I said, seeing Bryan stir. "You'll wake up your brothers."

"Nobody likes her," he said in a hoarse whisper. "She's always sticking her ugly little face into everyone's business and —"

"Davey," I said, shocked at the vitriol in his voice. "Davey, calm down."

"How many times do I have to ask you not to call me Davey?" he said, getting off the couch. "Nobody ever listens to me around here!"

"Davey — Dave — where are you going? I'm not done talking to you yet. I want to know what happened."

"Why don't you ask Flannery? She seems to know everything anyway."

He hopped over an ottoman as easily as if it were a shoebox and was out the door before I could say anything, or before I could think of anything to say.

I didn't get around to talking to anyone at school before it let out for the summer, but I did run into Davey's homeroom teacher at the grocery store about a month later, and I pushed my cart alongside hers (noticing she was quite a fan of Salisbury steak TV dinners and rocky road ice cream) and asked her about my son.

"Oh, he's a very popular student," she said as she tried to cover one of the ice cream containers with a bag of celery. "But occasionally he thinks that his popularity should grant him special favors."

She set her purse on the pile of TV dinners. "For instance, he and his friends could hardly believe that we made them clean up after the food fight they started. They wanted to do the crime without serving the punishment."

"So you . . . so you're saying it wasn't that big a deal?"

"Mrs. Forrest, I've been volunteering as a lunchroom monitor for as long as I've been teaching, and you can see I'm no spring chicken!" Her laugh was as jarring as a jungle bird's. "Food fights have always been a part of an eighth-grader's life and always will be."

I raced out of my front door when I saw Slip the next morning.

"Slip! I just wanted to tell you —"

"That you're finally going to run with me? Thanks."

She stood there resting her hands on her knees, breathing deep. Her sweatshirt had a half moon of sweat ringing the neckline.

Slip had started running about three years ago, and what we'd been sure was a crazy phase had locked into a daily habit, seven days a week. She didn't miss an opportunity to invite us to join her, although none of us ever RSVPed with an acceptance.

"No, I just wanted to tell you that I spoke to one of Davey's teachers and she seemed to think that that lunchroom incident was no big deal. Just your average, out-of-control food fight."

"Food fight?" Slip looked puzzled for a moment. "Oh," she said, running two fingers under her sweatband. "I think Flannery was talking about more than just a food fight."

"Well, then, that's Flannery, isn't it?"

"What's that supposed to mean?"

The smart part of me said, *Watch it,* and the reckless part I give far more attention to said, *Let it rip.*

"It means that Flannery always has been prone to exaggeration, to tell a story in the most dramatic way possible."

"According to Flan, Davey has been —"

"And she's always been the neighborhood tattletale."

Slip stared at me, and even though her eyes were squinted, the anger still blazed through.

"Well, if she's always been the neighborhood tattletale, then Dave's always been the neighborhood bully."

"That is completely ridiculous."

"No, Audrey, it's not. Only you've always let those boys run wild, so you're not even aware of half the stuff they do."

"Oh, yes, I am," I said, feeling as if my lungs had shrunk in size. "Because Flannery Mc-Mahon, Little Miss Tattletale 1977, tells me so. Only maybe you can't see your own children's flaws because you're so busy with saving the world at large, running around like a maniac — literally and figuratively."

"Oh, literally and figuratively, huh? Speaking purely *figure*-atively" — she let her eyes slowly track my body — "yours could use some running, or some kind of exercise other than chasing after men."

"So I chase men, do I?"

"No, let me amend that — *hunt* them. My God, Audrey, a man can't walk by you without you pushing yourself up to him — I still can't believe how you came on to my brother Fred."

"I came on to *Fred?* Slip, I wasn't coming on to your brother, I was offering him a little sympathy. Your brother not only needed sympathy, he needed psychotherapy. And as far as pushing myself on men — maybe you should try to push yourself on your own husband, who probably only gets laid when you want to procreate!"

This was getting beyond low — we were hitting all the topics that were verboten to criticize: children, mothering style, weight, family craziness, sexuality. Slip looked at me as if I were a big huge load of dog shit she'd had the misfortune to stumble over, and I returned the look.

"Is that something you're seeing *psychically?* Something you're getting a *sense* of?" She wiggled her hands in front of her face. "Because you'd be dead wrong, Nosferatu. Just because you weren't enough for your man doesn't mean

I'm not enough for mine."

If she had slugged me in the stomach, I'm sure I could have breathed more easily. We stared at each other for a long moment, atoms and molecules of hate swirling in a furious cloud around us, before we both turned away. I don't know about Slip, but as soon as my back was to her, my face was wet with tears.

Sitting between Grant and Stuart, I was crying now.

"My God," said Grant. "That was no catfight, that was a brawl between two tigresses."

"Tigers," I corrected, bawling. "Slip says it diminishes women when you feminize nouns."

"Oh, Audrey," said Grant with a tenderness that made the tears pick up their pace. "You miss her, don't you?"

My head bobbled. "I'm not a part of her life anymore. I feel like my sister — and I don't even have a sister — told me she doesn't want me to be in the family anymore!"

"You know what she needs, Stuart?" asked Grant.

"What, Grant?"

"She needs to go to church with us tomorrow."

It was the last thing I thought he'd suggest, and the absolute last thing I thought I needed.

October 1977

HOST: **MERIT**
BOOK: *Tobacco Road* by Erskine Caldwell
FOOD SERVED: "Faith helped me with this one: greens and grits, and I laid out a pouch of tobacco for anyone who wanted a chew, but no one did."

Under no condition (except sick children) would Merit miss an Angry Housewives Eating Bon Bons meeting, but it wasn't as fun a group without Audrey.

Divorce had forged a deeper friendship between the two — they understood what the other was going through in a way those still married did not, in a way even Kari couldn't understand because she certainly would still be married had Bjorn not died.

Audrey was like the big sister Merit had never had, the funny, popular, been-around-the-block sister who had answers to questions that Merit hadn't even thought of yet.

Trying to bring about peace between the two warring parties, Merit had urged both Audrey and Slip to be the big one who apologized first, but now she was trying to put into practice the lessons she had learned from Eric the Brute. And one of those lessons was that she could only do so much. She could try to be a good friend to both Audrey and Slip, but she couldn't make them be good friends to each other. Her days of thinking that if she were perfect then the world might follow suit were over.

An attractive blond woman drove the girls home one afternoon after they'd spent the weekend with Eric, who was house-sitting his parents' grand Lake of the Isles house now that the senior Iversons spent most of their time in Florida.

"My God, Merit — you look *wonderful!* Younger somehow . . . but wiser."

"Joanie?" said Merit, flustered, as each of her daughters wrapped themselves around her. "What are you doing here?"

Her former sister-in-law laughed at the blunt question. "Soren and I are in the states for a couple of conferences," she said as the girls ran off to jump in the pile of leaves Merit had been raking. "I don't have to be anywhere for a while. Can I bother you for a cup of coffee?"

"Oh, yes, please, of course," said Merit, thinking her manners had run off with her poise. "Sure, come on in."

"My gosh, what a pretty kitchen!" said Joanie as they entered the sunny yellow room.

"Thanks," said Merit. "My friend Faith — she's gone back to school for interior design — helped me paint it. I'll take you on a tour of the rest of the house later. You won't believe the colors she talked me into."

"I love the curtains," said Joanie.

"Thanks. Faith picked out the fabric — she says sunflowers are always a good thing to look

337

at in the morning — and my friend Kari sewed them up."

"Sounds as if you have some good friends."

Merit nodded. "So when was the last time I saw you?" she asked as she poured coffee and served the brownies left over from last night's AHEB.

"At least three years ago," said Joanie, "when we were here for Christmas, remember? Soren tried to teach everyone to sing 'Jolly Old St. Nicholas' in Danish."

"Oh, yes," said Merit, smiling. She had only seen Joanie and Soren a few times during her marriage, and she had enjoyed every visit. "How is Soren?"

"Great, his practice is doing great. There're so many new things happening in heart surgery — that's what this conference at the university is for, and . . . oh, Merit, I'm so sorry about the way things turned out. I should have told you before you got married what you were in for."

Merit's mind swirled. "I beg your pardon?"

Joanie's smile was apologetic. "Well, of course, if you hadn't gotten married, you'd never have those beautiful girls — and my God, Merit, they're stunning and so *nice,* even though Eric treats them like second-class citizens. I chose not to have children myself; what if I were my parents all over again? I mean, I broke the pattern in marrying Soren — the dear man's never laid a hand on me. But who knows? A crying child, a whining child, and — there goes the back of my hand!"

The only indication Merit had that she was breathing was that she was still conscious. "What . . . ," she said finally, her voice a whisper, "what exactly are you talking about?"

"God, these brownies are good," said Joanie, helping herself to a second. "Danish pastries are world-famous, but to me, you can't beat American desserts like chocolate brownies and pecan and apple pie." She made fast work of the brownie, washing it down with the coffee Merit refilled her cup with.

"All right," she said, the business of satisfying her American cravings out of the way. "I know you know the story of the illustrious Iverson clan — our great tradition in medicine, blah, blah, blah — but what you probably didn't know is that Eric didn't become a wife-beater out of the blue. I mean, he had an excellent teacher in my father."

Merit's jaw dropped. "Dr. Iverson? Dr. Iverson . . . hit your mother?"

"Hit her, punched her, slapped her, and once sent her headfirst down the staircase."

"I had no idea."

Joanie's smile was grim. "That's because she's a good actress — just like you were, I'll bet. But unlike you, she wasn't brave enough to get out. She stayed, clinging to her pretty house and her status as if they could somehow keep her aloft. Of course they couldn't, which is why she's always half drunk."

"Your mother?" said Merit. Everything Joanie said was like a zap of electricity, shocking her even more. "I've never seen your mother anything but a gracious hostess, a —"

"Aha! That's the role she plays — gracious hostess! She'll make sure you have all you want to eat and drink, served of course on the finest china and best crystal — but did you ever have a heart-to-heart with her? Did she ever break out of being a gracious hostess to be a friend, a mother-in-law?"

Merit bit the middle of her upper lip.

"No," she said finally, "I can't say we ever had any sort of deep discussion."

"It's so sad," said Joanie, shaking her head, "and what's even sadder is she probably knew Eric was hitting you before anyone else. Knew and yet would never say a word."

"How can you — what makes you think —"

"Merit, my God, when I saw you that time at Christmas, *I* knew. It hurt me to watch you watch Eric. You hardly ever looked away from him. Really, you were just like a dog ready to jump and get him whatever he needed — exactly the way my mother is with my dad." She stared at her coffee cup. "I should have taken you aside right then and there and told you you didn't have to put up with that kind of shit, but it was Christmas and I hadn't been home for years and . . . oh, Merit, I'm so sorry."

Merit reached across the table and placed her hand over her sister-in-law's. A tear splashed on her knuckle and she said softly, "It's all right, Joanie. I don't know if I would have let you tell me those things then. I think I would have been too afraid to listen." She squeezed her hand. "But I'm glad you're here now, glad I *can* listen. It makes me . . . understand things more."

"Well," said Joanie, dabbing her nose with a napkin, "I don't know when I'll see you again, so I . . . well, I just feel so guilty. I feel I owe you something for all the trouble my family put you through."

"Your family didn't put me through any

trouble," said Merit softly. "Just Eric."

"I don't mean to excuse him, I really don't," said Joanie, pushing her blond bangs off her forehead. "But he got it as bad as my mother. Anytime any of us kids did something wrong, it was Eric who got punished. Oh, once in a while Douglas and I got walloped if we defended Eric a little too much, but mostly we became experts at cowering in our rooms while Eric got bounced around." She sighed, shaking her head. "Dad also had this particular nickname for Eric. He thought it was really funny to pronounce his name 'Earache.' 'You're a pain, did I ever tell you that, Earache?' " Joanie's eyes searched Merit's as if trying to find an answer there. "I felt so sorry for him, but more than feeling bad, I'd find myself resenting him because, just like my mother, he took it — took the abuse and never fought back."

A sadness settled in Merit's heart, thinking of Eric as a boy being slapped and hit and called "Earache" by the man who was supposed to hug him and call him names like "Sport" or "Tiger."

The coffee cup clattered as Joanie stirred cream into it.

"He . . . Eric's never hurt the girls, has he?"

"He's never hit them, but he hurts their feelings all the time."

Joanie bit her lip. "I know," she said finally. "I saw it this weekend — he runs hot and cold with them. I tried to talk to him about it, but my dear brother wasn't interested in what I had to say about his fathering."

"He wasn't interested in what I had to say either," said Merit. "About his fathering or anything."

"He's as insane as my parents," she said. She took a deep breath and expelled it. "So are you going to be all right financially?"

"Well, he's making the house payments, and with alimony and child support, I'm doing all right. I'm thinking of ways to bring in some more money — I don't want to go work until Jewel starts school — but for now I'm doing all right."

It was then that her girls decided to entertain their mother and aunt with a parade. They marched through the kitchen in their finest dress-up clothes, dripping with strings of pop beads and costume jewelry, asking if it was possible for princesses to have some of those brownies.

"Oh, yes, your highnesses," said Merit, standing up so she could formally curtsy. "And perhaps some milk to soothe your royal thirst?"

"Milk would be fine," said Jewel in her best haughty princess voice. She looked to her older sisters. "Wouldn't it, miladies?"

October 1977

Dear Mama,

Happy Halloween! Bonnie says this is her last year trick-or-treating — she says that next year, when she's twelve, she'll be "too mature for such kid stuff" (get her!), whereas Beau says he hopes to go trick-or-treating until he's at least in college.

I had a little scare at dinner that had nothing to do with Halloween — Bonnie announced that she was writing a story for school and she had to interview Wade (who, if I'm remembering his flight schedule correctly, should be in Philadelphia about now) and me about our families "as far back as you can remember."

"So, Mom," she said, "what do you remember most about your mom and dad?"

"Bonnie, put that away," I said about the notebook and pen she wielded. "We're eating."

"I'm done," said Bonnie, pushing aside her empty bowl. (Whenever I use one of Kari's recipes, the kids practically lick their plates clean.) "Now come on, Mom, tell me about Grandma and Grandpa."

I chewed a piece of meat extra long, giving myself some time.

"PawPaw was a doctor," said Beau. "And MawMaw was a housewife."

Bonnie put on her irritated face, an ever-popular look of hers.

"MawMaw and PawPaw," she said, shaking her head. "What are you, Beau, a hillbilly?"

"Well, that's what Mama calls them."

Bonnie rolled her eyes at her brother's idiocy. "Okay," she said, tapping her pen on the table. "Your mom's name was Primrose Reynolds and your dad's was James Reynolds. What were the names of your mom's mom and dad?"

"Um, Elmira Reynolds and um — he died before I was born — and Reed Reynolds."

Bonnie replaced her irritated look with her skeptical look.

"Wait a second, Mom — I thought Reynolds was your mom's married name. How come her parents have the same name?"

"Isn't that funny?" I said, my heart racing. "But actually, Reynolds is a very common name in the South."

"Really?" said Wade, pleased to have learned something new. "Like Olson or Anderson is here?"

I spooned some more beef stew into Bonnie's bowl. "You'd better eat a little more, Bonnie. You'll need your strength to tote around all that candy."

"So James Reynolds, your dad, was a doctor," continued Bonnie. "What kind of doctor was he?"

I felt as if someone had turned up the heat in the room around twenty degrees. "He was an . . . an obstetrician. That means he delivered babies."

"Yuck," said Beau, no doubt remembering the time he'd witnessed Merit giving birth, "I'd never want to be that kind of doctor."

"What did his dad do?"

"Uh, he was a lawyer," I said, the lie falling easily from my mouth.

"Jeannie Applebaum's great-grandpa was a furrier," said Bonnie. "So's her grandpa, and he says she gets a mink coat when she turns eighteen."

"A mink coat," I said. "My goodness."

"Hey, Bonnie, we'd better get ready," said Beau, looking at the clock above the sink.

"All right," said Bonnie, like a CEO with too many demands on her. "You're still going to paint my face, aren't you, Beau?"

My son looked at the clock again. "Mom, do you mind if we don't do the dishes right now? Or we could when we get back."

I smiled at my son, who's always so thoughtful about helping me. "I'll do them, honey."

"Okay, Mom," said Bonnie, dashing out of the kitchen, "we'll talk more when I get back home."

They were out until nine, Mama, and by the time they dumped their pillowcases full of Baby Ruths and Butterfingers on the newspaper I'd laid out in the living room, I had created a whole family tree that spanned five generations and included a captain in the rebel army as well as a celebrated pianist. And as I regaled Bonnie and Beau with stories of our illustrious ancestors, my pride almost, but not quite, overpowered my shame.

I'm sorry,
Faith

November 1977

HOST: **KARI**	
BOOK: *Terms of Endearment*	
by Larry McMurtry	
REASON CHOSEN: "I like how the	
man writes."	

"Listen," said Kari over the phone, "this dumb fight of yours — it's not fair to the rest of us. We want both you *and* Audrey at the meetings."

"I never said she couldn't go to any of the meetings," said Slip coolly.

"Come on, Slip, stop being so stubborn. Why don't you make up with her tonight?"

"Because I'm not coming to the meeting," said Slip. "You're right — it's not fair that Audrey misses all the meetings, so I'll sit this one out, okay?"

"Oh, honestly," said Kari, but Slip had hung up.

"I feel like the whole thing's going to unravel," Kari said that evening to Faith and Merit as they sat waiting for Audrey's arrival.

"It can't," said Merit. "I *need* my Angry Housewives."

"We've got to think of a way to get them back together," said Faith.

346

Kari shrugged. "I don't know what we can do when one person wants to reconcile and the other doesn't."

Faith finished the last quarter inch of wine in her glass. "What *is* her problem anyway? What's it been? Three months? Four months? Wouldn't you have thought they would have made up a long time ago?"

Flicka ambled over to Kari for a pat on the head. "Well," she said, obliging her, "I know they said some terrible things to each other."

"So what?" said Faith. "Everybody says terrible things once in a while. And when they do, it's up to them to apologize and make up."

"Mom, where's the Life game?" asked nine-year-old Julia, calling from the kitchen.

"In the basement cabinet," said Kari. "Right where it should be."

Faith had brought the twins and Merit her girls; book club night was as big a social gathering for the kids as it was for the adults. As the children grew, Jody Hammond and the fathers had been relieved of their baby-sitting duties, and now it was up to the older kids to look after the younger kids, a responsibility the older children *usually* didn't exploit.

"Is it time for snacks yet?" Julia's voice was hopeful.

"Not yet, but I'll let you know," Kari said. Then, standing, she asked, "Now, who can I interest in a drink?"

Faith was interested, but Merit, who really didn't care for the taste of alcohol and usually took a drink just to be polite, asked for a club soda.

"Yoo-hoo," said Audrey, stepping inside, followed by Bryan and Michael.

"You're kidding me," said Faith, watching them stomping off snow on the floor mat. "It wasn't snowing fifteen minutes ago."

"It is now," said Audrey. "We're supposed to get six inches."

"I didn't hear that," pouted Faith.

"The kids are in the basement," Kari told the boys, who quickly made their exit. She made Audrey a drink and, handing it to her, said, "I'm glad you're here."

Faith and Merit echoed the sentiment, and Audrey did what she had been doing a lot lately: she burst into tears.

"I have missed this so much," she said, reaffixing with her pinky a corner of her false eyelashes that had sprung loose. As if Carnaby Street still wielded fashion influence, Audrey still wore frosted lipstick and wouldn't leave the house without her false eyelashes. She liked the weight of them on her eyelids, liked how she could feel the tiniest bit of breeze from them if she blinked a lot. Plus she liked how she looked in them.

"I've read all the book selections — wasn't *Tobacco Road* a hoot? — but I wanted to talk to you guys about them! I felt deprived, incomplete — the way I do if I can't smoke a cigarette after sex! Oh, God, listen to me rant. I'm just so . . . I'm just so nervous!" Her wide mouth turned down at the corners and her eyes welled again with tears. "Imagine me being nervous about the Angry Housewives! Do you realize how lonely that makes me feel?"

Kari got the box of tissues and brought a plate of brownies to the table.

"Do you realize how *hard* it is having Slip mad at me?" she asked, shaking her head at the offered brownie (which showed Kari how upset she truly was). "It's made me wonder what kind of person I am. I always thought I knew what kind of person I was, always liked that person! It's like God pointing at you and deciding you're not worthy!"

"But you don't believe in God," Faith pointed out. She had been a little jazzed at the beginning of the feud, because it was exciting to have two good friends so mad at each other, exciting to hear both sides of the story. It made her feel at various times like a spy or a diplomat, or simply glad she wasn't the one fighting. But she had grown tired of it; they couldn't be Angry Housewives without Audrey, just as the Three Musketeers couldn't be themselves with Dartagnan or Aramis missing.

"If only the two of you weren't so blame alike," said Kari, who had done a lot of thinking on the subject.

"Alike?" said Merit. "Audrey and *Slip?*"

"*Audrey* and *Slip?*" repeated Faith. "I'd say they're a lot more different than they are alike."

Kari was surprised. "You really think so?"

"Well, sure," said Faith. "Just look at them, for God's sake. Could you ever see Slip wearing what Audrey's wearing now?"

Any time Audrey glanced down, which she did now, her first view was of her décolletage, which she displayed year-round, regardless of season. This evening she was wearing a snug V-neck lavender mohair sweater and tight jeans.

"It's true," said Audrey with a shrug. "I'd have to say I wouldn't be caught dead in the things

Slip wears — I mean, she thinks a crew neck is racy — but come on, girls, you can't judge a book by its cover."

"If you think that's true, Audrey, that you can't judge a book by its cover, then why do you choose to dress the way you do? Why even bother?"

Audrey inhaled her cigarette, thinking over the question, and then watched the smoke she exhaled. "Well, Faith," she said finally, "I just like to. I'm not trying to say I'm this or that by the way I dress. I'm just trying to say I like curves, I like my breasts, and here they are for whatever it may be worth to the rest of you."

"Well, see, Slip would say you're perpetuating our role as sex object and that you're subverting your real self by constantly showing your boobs."

Audrey nodded, more amused than irritated. "I seem to recall having conversations along those lines."

"And that didn't hurt your feelings?" asked Merit. "Eric . . ." She frowned, not liking to say his name. "The few times I wore something Eric hadn't picked out for me, he said things that made me feel so . . . bad."

Audrey shook her head. "Nobody — not the pope, not that guy who makes up those worst-dressed lists, and certainly not my husband, or ex-husband — could say anything about the way I dress and make me feel bad. Because I *like* it."

"See?" said Kari, raising her glass. "That's what I mean. Audrey has got a lot of confidence; Slip's got a lot of confidence."

"Yes," agreed Merit, "but I think Slip's confidence comes from what she does, and Audrey's confidence comes from who she is."

"Why, Merit," said Kari, "that's very astute of you."

"Very astute," agreed Faith, taking a cigarette from Audrey's pack.

Merit blushed like a schoolgirl whom the teacher had singled out for praise.

"So what else do you think?" asked Audrey softly.

"Well," said Merit, "now I see what Kari means. Everybody knows how much Slip cares about big things like injustice and women's rights and stuff. Everybody knows how hard she works to change things." She looked at the arrangement of glasses on the coffee table, trying to concentrate. "I think . . . I think you care as much, but you just haven't decided if your caring means very much."

Audrey exhaled a big puff of smoke. "So you're saying I'm more of a cynic?"

Merit made a moue, then smiled. "Am I?"

"I don't want to be a cynic," said Audrey, and Kari was surprised to see a glint of tears in her eyes. "I think cynicism is a fancy way of saying 'I give up' or 'I'm too lazy to try.' "

"I don't know," said Kari. "I think a lot of people use cynicism as an armor — they don't want people to know how much they do care, so they cover it up."

"What book are we discussing?" joked Faith. "*The Ego and the Id?*"

"What I think," said Kari, "is that Slip really wants to make up, just like you, Audrey, but she doesn't know how."

"Slip knows how to do everything," said Audrey.

This is Audrey talking? thought Faith. *Audrey, who loves nothing more than sparring with Slip?*

"So do you," said Merit. "You know how to do everything too."

"I know that has no basis in reality," said Audrey with a sad smile, "but thanks anyway. Now come on — if I'm going to hold it together at all, let's talk about the book." Suddenly energized, she reached for a brownie. "Who thought Aurora Greenway could have used a group like the Angry Housewives?"

The children knew the rules of the book club: they were not allowed to come into the meeting unless there was an absolute emergency. But what children consider an emergency, as opposed to what an adult does, meant at least one or two interruptions.

"Mom, Davey put Bryan in the clothes dryer" was an incident that happened several years ago and the only one that qualified as an emergency to both children and adults. It had the Angry Housewives breaking speed records as they ran down to Faith's basement.

As everyone charged into the laundry room, they were treated to the sight of Bryan, visible through the machine's porthole, holding on to the sides of the dryer drum the way someone does when they're in a funhouse barrel.

"Uffda," said Kari as Faith opened the dryer door and Bryan spilled out, dizzy but smiling.

"He wanted to go in there!" Davey had pleaded after Audrey yanked him by the arm, asking him what the hell he was trying to do.

"I did, Mommy," said Bryan. "It was fun!"

"We were all going to take a ride," said Davey.

Glaring at Flannery, he added, "Until someone tattled on us."

"I know a kid who died in a dryer," said Flannery quickly, trying to justify her tattling. "And if Bryan died, we probably wouldn't get to play at book club meetings anymore."

"You're right," said Audrey, her hand still clamped around her oldest son's arm. "If Bryan had died, you can bet you wouldn't get to play at book club meetings anymore."

Now Julia and Bonnie had trooped upstairs and were halfway into the living room before Kari asked, "No one's in the dryer, are they?"

"Oh, Mom," said Julia, "that was just that one time."

"Well, is there some other sort of emergency?"

The two girls held a whispered conference.

"We were just wondering," said Julia, "why Flannery's not here. Flannery always has the best ideas about what we should play."

"She's the oldest," reminded Bonnie, nodding her head.

"Flannery's not coming tonight, sweetie," said Kari, "but I know a game you can play."

"What?" they both asked, excited, as Kari threw a help-me look at her friends.

"Sorry! is fun, isn't it?" suggested Kari.

"We don't want to play a board game," said Bonnie. "The boys always cheat."

"Well, Beau and Michael don't," said Julia. "But Bryan does . . . sometimes. And Joe does too, but he's not here."

"I know what you can do," said Audrey, standing up and starting to gather some of the treats on an empty plate. "You guys can have your own book club meeting downstairs!"

353

"Oh, that's a good idea!" said Julia.

"But what about the boys?" said Bonnie, narrowing her eyes. "They can't be Angry Housewives."

"I guess you'll need to come up with your own name," said Faith.

"Angry Kids?" asked Bonnie.

"Um, I don't think that really describes who you are," said Kari.

"How 'bout —"

"Shh!" said Bonnie, pulling Julia's arm. "Don't tell them — it'll be our secret."

She accepted the plate of goodies with a polite thank-you, and the women listened to the girls' excited voices as they went into the kitchen and to the basement steps.

"What book will we talk about?"

"I don't know — how about *Black Beauty*?"

"Um, how about *Blubber*?"

"Oh, I love Judy Blume!"

Kari was wearing her light-up-her-face smile. "Good idea, Audrey," she said. "I think you might have started something."

"Oh, wouldn't that be cute?" said Merit. "No, wouldn't that be *great* if they did start their own book club?"

"Well, gee, Audrey," said Faith, who suffered little prickles of irritation whenever someone had a good idea she wished she'd thought of, "you've got such a creative mind, why don't you come up with an idea that'll make you and Slip friends again?"

Audrey inhaled deeply as she lit her cigarette and waved the match out. She and Faith were the holdouts; inspired by Slip, Merit (Merit! The human chimney!) had quit smoking *cold turkey* and hadn't cheated once. "I want to . . . every day," she had told the others, "but how can I when the girls tell me how much more they like to hug me because I smell so much nicer?"

Three of Audrey's expert smoke rings quivered toward the ceiling.

"Grant and Stuart said I should come up with some kind of extravagant gesture."

"Extravagant gesture?" said Faith. "What's that supposed to mean?"

"Well, you know," said Audrey, laughing at Faith's impatient tone, "something that will get her attention. Listen to me — I sound like some jilted sap trying to get his girlfriend back."

"So do you have any ideas?" asked Kari, checking cups to see who needed more coffee.

With a deep sigh, Audrey shook her head, her eyes staring ahead.

"Oh, my gosh, look at that snow," said Merit, following her gaze. "The girls are going to need their boots to walk home in that."

Faith stood up and went to the window. "They're not going to need boots, they're going to need *snowshoes*." She stood for a moment, a cigarette held to her lips, her other hand cupping her elbow. "Hey, I've got it! Why don't we have a snowball fight — just like we did when we decided to start AHEB? We can have it in Slip's yard so she'll just *have* to come outside."

"And then what?" asked Audrey.

"Well, then," said Faith, thinking, "you can hit her with a snowball and she can hit you and by the time you're done, all your aggressions will be out."

Kari shrugged. It might work.

"What about the kids?" asked Merit.

"We could leave a note," said Faith. "They might not even come upstairs, but if they do, they'll see the note."

"I'm in," said Audrey, stubbing out her cigarette.

Faith had become a devotee of the snowball fight, inviting her kids or Wade and once her in-laws, who'd come for Christmas, to wage snowy war. She had flung snowballs at Slip when she'd returned from a run, and at Kari and Julia when they were sliding down her hill to the creek basin. She had thrown a lot of snowballs since her induction, but the Angry Housewives had never had an all-out snowball fight like the one they had had all those years ago.

Until tonight. As the first snowball smashed against her shoulder, Faith was slaphappy, grabbing at the snow that seconds earlier had been falling from the sky. She was laughing maniacally — the only way possible to laugh during a snowball fight — and had just gotten Merit right on the butt when the front porch light of Slip's house came on.

Audrey looked up, hope inflating inside her, but instead of Slip coming out to play or to forgive, it was Jerry, in his robe, who stepped out onto the porch.

"Hi, Jerry," said Kari, and the others chorused their hellos. "We were hoping Slip might want to come out."

"I'm sorry," said Jerry, pulling on the lapels of his robe, "but Slip's asleep. Gil's a little sick and she fell asleep when she put him to bed." He looked around at the women standing in the falling snow. "I could wake her up."

"That's all right," said Audrey, knowing she wouldn't want to be roused out of a warm bed to dodge hard balls of snow. "I hope Gil feels better."

"Thanks," said Jerry. "Well, good night." He made a half turn toward the door and then stopped. "I sure hope things work out between you two, Audrey."

"Me too," said Audrey softly as Jerry went back into the house.

It wasn't that Kari was an insomniac; she just didn't need much sleep. Late at night, with the house making its graveyard-shift tickings and thrummings and creaks, she would work on sewing projects or organize all the scrapbooks she kept on Julia. Sometimes she just sat in the dark, looking out the sewing room window. It faced south and was perched high enough so that she could see Faith's and Slip's houses at the end of the block.

It was a time of prayer too, when she'd draw her chair close and thank God for all that she had to be grateful for. She sent up many prayers of gratitude as she looked out that sewing room window, watching the seasons strip the trees or fill them out, watching the path of the moon, the clouds roll in or tear apart, the quick darts of rabbits and birds and, once or twice, a deer.

She loved watching the seasons, which reminded her of people: spring with its softness and tender green buds was a baby, and as the flowers burst forth and the leaves unfurled, a toddler. Brash summer was a child, all blue lakes and blue water and yellow sunshine — full of possibility — until around mid-August it became a teenager, sulky and stormy, a little dangerous. Autumn, beautiful rusty gold and maroon autumn, was a matron in tweeds and sensible shoes who begged you to come outside and take a walk with her while listening to her recite Shakespeare and Byron and Shelley. In very late October, when the crispness of the air was turning cold and the billowing blue sky was now a gray canopy, Kari thought of her grandmother, who had lived with Kari's family after her stroke. The air and the earth at this time of fall was kind and wistful, just like her grandmother, who always seemed happy to see you, but you knew you wouldn't be together long.

And winter, of course, was the most ancient of white-haired, blue-veined relatives. But age didn't mean powerlessness, and this old crone always fooled you with how strong she really was. . . .

Seeing motion, Kari leaned forward. What or who was out in Slip's side yard at — she looked at the luminous face of the clock above her sewing table — 1:35 in the morning?

It didn't take her long to recognize Audrey; tall, statuesque Audrey was pretty easy to identify, even bundled up in winter, but who was the person next to her, helping her build the snowman? She squinted her eyes — it wasn't Paul, was it? No, Audrey and Paul were friendly enough; they hadn't had the acrimonious divorce Merit and Eric had, but still, they didn't go off together at 1:35 in the morning to build snowmen in a neighbor's yard — especially a neighbor with whom Audrey currently was not speaking.

No, that wasn't Paul, thought Kari, and with

the tip of her nose touching the pane, she squinted again.

Oh. It was Grant. Just last week, he and Stuart had accompanied Kari to the fabric store — she was making her brother Anders a sport jacket and wanted their sartorial advice (well, Stuart's; Grant's taste was better suited for help in outfitting a Vegas showgirl).

She watched several more minutes as they finished patting their snowman into place. Grant then took a flag of some sort that had been leaning against one of Slip's elms and stuck it in close to the snowman. Kari couldn't make out if there was any pattern on the fabric — from where she sat, it looked like a white banner.

Audrey took something out of a bag and pushed it into the snowman's head — a dark scarf of some kind. She then took out something Kari couldn't quite make out. It looked like a branch, maybe, or a hanger. They both gave the snowman a few more grooming pats and then raced off down the street.

"Good for you, Audrey," Kari whispered, smiling at whatever peace-making effort the snowman represented. And then she began sewing the pocket on the glen plaid jacket she was making for Anders.

December 1977

HOST: **SLIP**	
BOOK: *A Tree Grows in Brooklyn*	
by Betty Smith	
REASON CHOSEN: "Flannery's reading it in	
school and I remembered how much I loved	
it as a young girl."	

The edge of the sky was red that morning; it looked as if dawn had pulled an all-nighter and now had to face the world all cranky and blood-shot. Of course I know that dawn doesn't have a personality, but I do, and I sure felt all cranky. I didn't know about bloodshot because I didn't bother looking in the mirror when I splashed water on my face.

I was sure I was coming down with Gil's cold, and I hate coming down with anything; it makes me feel as if I'm not as in control of myself as I'd like to be. Plus it's no fun running when your si-nuses are all clogged up and your throat feels thick, but I knew not running made me feel even worse than running with a cold, so I ignored my husband's soft voice telling me to come back to bed, pulled on my long underwear and Jerry's old University of Minnesota sweatshirt, and pre-pared to meet the day.

Although what can prepare you for meeting a strange snowman in your front yard — especially a snowman you know you or your children did not make? A snowman ominously looming upward in a circle of trampled snow, wearing an awful black wig and holding a stick skewered with green olives (at least I think they started out being green; they had blackened in the freeze) and a white flag?

I blinked hard in that corny gesture of disbelief, but the snowman was still there. I pulled off the envelope taped to the olive stick.

The note inside read: *I surrender to this terrible war of ours. Please accept the olive branch I humbly offer with my sincerest apologies. Sincerely (I can't say that enough), another Angry (and lonely) Housewife.*

I jammed the note in my pocket. Taking giant steps in the snow to the plowed road, I began to run.

I was almost to Lake Nokomis when I started to smile. Halfway around the lake, I started to laugh. Hard. Hard laughter is good anytime, but on that cold morning in that gaudy sunrise it felt almost divine. When I had gone to bed last night with my sick and snuffling son, I had no idea that I'd wake up the next morning and something would make me forget about hating Audrey. I was so tired of hating Audrey, so tired of being the tight and unforgiving person I didn't think I was. It wasn't in my nature to be in fights with people; I had never been one of those nasty junior high girls who suddenly has a vendetta against her best friend, or the kind of girlfriend who liked to argue with her boyfriend for the sheer drama. I had always been a diplomat who brought people together (how many times had I served in that capacity when my brothers fought?), but I didn't know how to be a diplomat in my own battle. But I had accepted the olive branch from the snowman! I laughed again — it sounded like a phrase spies might use to check each other's authenticity. I had accepted the olive branch from the snowman! We were going to be friends again!

I knew she'd be up; in fact, I told her that when I saw her open the door as I ran up her walk.

"Oh, so now you've got ESP too?" she said, and quicker than you can say "I'm sorry," I was buried in her big hugging arms.

Jerry had heard me rant and rave about Audrey, but I'd never said anything to my kids, not wanting to start a whole neighborhood feud. Joe and Bryan played well together, and Gil and Mikey were the kind of best friends who couldn't walk together without draping their arms around each other's shoulders. Whenever Audrey's boys were over at our house, I made every effort to hide the fact that their mother, as far as I was concerned, was persona non grata. It was an easy enough task; boys at that age aren't sensitive to much other than their own needs and pleasures.

Flannery of course was a different creature; she knew exactly what was going on at all times. It was like having a tabloid reporter in the house.

"Do you think you and Mrs. Forrest will ever make up?" she asked me.

"Oh, I'm sure we will," I said, feeling as if I had just stepped onto the witness stand.

"What exactly are you fighting about anyway? Her creepy son, Davey?"

"Oh, there's a good one, Flannery," I said. "It's just the right size for Gil."

We were ambling through a pumpkin patch, picking out the pumpkins we thought would be transformed into the best jack-o'-lanterns. It was an annual fall ritual: spend the morning picking apples at an orchard a farmer opened up to the public and then pillaging his pumpkin patch. In between we had a picnic of summer sausage sandwiches and fresh apple cider. We'd been doing this since Flan was three and had only been rained out once. This particular visit had fallen on a day that Jerry said perfectly demonstrated "autumn's ability to stun the senses." Of course, my husband, Professor Meteorology, can wax rhapsodic about sleet storms and fog banks just as well, but in this case, he was correct: it was an absolutely gorgeous, sunny, burnished fall day.

Too bad my daughter thought she had to get the whole truth and nothing but the truth.

"Flan," I said, hefting a pumpkin, "why don't you try to find Dad and the boys?"

"Gee, Mom, why don't you try to change the subject in a more obvious way? Now come on, why don't you answer my question?"

I looked up at Flan. As much as I was used to looking up at practically everybody, it was disconcerting looking up at my own daughter, whose height had passed my own this summer. Even though it felt strange to be shorter than someone I'd given birth to, I was glad she wasn't going to be a shrimp like me. In all ways, evolution was on display; she was taller than me, certainly prettier than me (who wasn't?), and almost as smart as me (I wasn't ready to totally concede that one yet). Most importantly, there was not a red hair on her.

"Flan, what if I told you that some things are my business and not yours?"

"What kind of mother-daughter relationship is that? Don't you want us to be able to share everything?"

"Do *you* want us to share everything? If you do, why don't you tell me why you like Neil Norton so much?"

Flan's face reddened as if she'd come down with a sudden case of wind burn. "Who said I like Neil Norton?"

"Settle down," I said, chuckling at her outrage. "Nobody told me; it's just something I picked up."

"Because if Joe told you that, he's going to be in so much trouble —"

"Flannery, methinks you doth protest too much."

"Yeah? Well, methinks Joe is really going to get it."

We stepped aside to let a couple pass, the woman carrying a baby in her arms, the man three big pumpkins.

"So I'll bet you're fighting about Davey," Flan continued. "I'll bet you said something about him — something I'd told you — and she got all mad, right?"

I saw Jerry and the boys gathering up their things from the picnic table and wished they'd hurry up so I wouldn't have to answer Flannery's question. But I could feel her eyes on me like laser beams, and the words that I've spoken to my daughter throughout her life came back to haunt me: *Don't ever be afraid to ask me* anything.

A breeze fluttered by, carrying in it the scent of red apples.

"Well, Flan," I said, "I guess it started with something like that."

"So then it was my fault, right? I'm why you two are fighting."

Her voice caught me by surprise; she sounded as if she was on the verge of tears.

"Oh, Flan, no."

"Because I know I tattle sometimes — I mean, that's what people tell me — but I just feel like I'm telling the truth, you know? Reporting the facts. Last week this slam book was going around — you know what those are, Mom? Kids' names are at the top of each page, and then other kids write what they think about them, and on my page . . . on my page people wrote things like 'teacher's pet' and 'tattletale,' and one kid even wrote, 'I hate the little squealer!' "

"Oh, Flan!"

She sniffed, shaking off the hand I put on her shoulder. "Well, don't have a cow, Mom. Nobody had nice stuff written on their page, except for Sharon Emory, and that's because she's *perfect*. But it did make me think a little, that maybe it's better to protect someone than tell the truth."

For once I truly didn't have anything to say.

"But then I thought about it some more, and I thought, well, it depends on how much you like the person and what they need protection from. And it's not like I told the principal or anything on Davey Forrest; I just told you." She smiled slyly, her braces glinting in the sunlight. " 'Cause I knew you'd tell Mrs. Forrest, and then maybe if she yelled at him enough, he'd stop bugging people in the lunchroom."

"And has he?"

Flannery shrugged. "I don't really bother myself with what Davey Forrest does anymore. But you know what?" Again she had that sly smile.

"What?"

"I did leave an anonymous note on my homeroom teacher's desk, telling her about the slam book. And she confiscated it during first hour."

"Why'd you do that, Flan?" I was worried about her, worried about her getting caught, because seriously, nobody likes a tattletale.

"Because it was so mean! Because just because some jerk's bad opinion of me doesn't ruin my life doesn't mean it won't ruin Karen Yarborough's, who weighs about two hundred pounds, or Heather Lucchesi's, who's got the world's worst BO."

Well, if my daughter had to be a rat, then thank God she was a noble rat!

"Anyway," she said as Jerry and the boys waved to us from the other side of the pumpkin patch, "if something I said was the cause of your fight, I'm sorry, and I wish you'd tell Mrs. Forrest that. I don't like you two not being friends. It makes the whole neighborhood feel weird."

"Flan's a good kid," said Audrey after I'd told her all this as we had a quick cup of coffee before having to get our kids up for school.

"So's Davey," I said, and I did think so, on the whole. I mean, holy security shatterer, divorce puts kids through a lot. Knock on extremely hard wood that my children never have to cope with their parents' divorce.

"So when did you make the snowman?"

"Oh, it was after midnight sometime. Didn't Jerry tell you that after book club we came by to try to interest you in a snowball fight?"

I shook my head. "He was still in bed when I left for my run. He just muttered something about coming back to bed." I took a small sip of coffee; Audrey made it triple-strength, and it had an effect on me similar to that of putting rocket fuel into a VW Bug. "So then you guys decided to build a snowman?"

"No, then we all went home. I couldn't sleep, and then I happened to see Grant taking out the garbage — he says Stuart's in bed by ten-thirty, but he's a night owl — and so I invited him in for a nightcap and told him what I'd been up to, and after one or two martinis, we decided on the snowman . . . woman . . . uh, me."

"The olive branch was a nice touch."

"Oh, Slip, we had so much fun thinking of the whole thing. Grant's been pestering me all along to do something big — he's a fan of the grand gesture — to show you that I was sorry and wanted to make up."

I smiled, pushing aside my coffee before I went into cardiac arrest.

"Well, it worked. Peace reigns once more on Freesia Court. But now I've got to get my kids up."

Audrey looked at the clock. "Oh, yeah, me too," and without getting up from the table, she deepened her voice and hollered, "Davey! Bryan! Mikey! Time to get up!"

After whirling around in the mini-tornado of my own kids' morning routine, I got ready for work.

When I got my degree in history, I thought: *How will I use this?* Will *I ever use this?* The only teaching I could imagine myself doing was grandiose and not affordable in most school budgets — taking a classroom of high school freshmen on an overnight to the Colosseum, or sitting around telling ghost stories at Stonehenge. I didn't have the patience to map out the spice routes of Marco Polo on a dusty chalkboard while kids lobbed spitballs at my back. I did entertain working in a museum, preferably in a European capital, but when I met Jerry, cataloging artifacts in a musty basement office in Prague didn't seem as exciting as Jerry and then marriage and then kids.

I had been volunteering for years, of course, but when Mikey entered first grade, I decided it was time to get out in the real world and see what it felt like to collect a paycheck.

"Well, what exactly would you like to do?" Jerry asked, pen and notebook in hand.

"What are you going to do — interview me?"

"No," said Jerry, sitting on the couch. "I just thought it might be helpful if we write things down, make a list, see what jumps out at you."

"I'd like you to jump out at me," I said, kissing him. I found his interest in my burgeoning career exciting.

Jerry kissed me back a long luxurious moment but then pulled his face away. "I won't be that easily distracted, Ms. McMahon," he said, clicking the pen. "Now, come on. If you had the ideal job, what would it be?"

"I don't know . . . president?"

"Of what kind of company?"

"Jerry, give me some credit here. Of the United States!"

Jerry scribbled something on the pad. "All right, what are the first steps we should take toward reaching that goal?"

"Unfortunately, a sex change," I said. "The world's not ready for a woman president yet."

"Oh, it's ready," disagreed Jerry. "It just doesn't know it's ready."

God, I loved my husband.

"Maybe it'll really be ready when Flan grows up," I said. "She'd make a good president, don't you think?"

"So would you, Slip."

Did I say I *really* loved him?

We spent more than an hour writing all sorts of lists with headings like "Strengths" and "Goals" and "Ideals."

"Well, ma'am," said Jerry, tapping his pen on the paper, "from what we've been able to learn about you in this job interview, it would seem the perfect job for you is either liberating some oppressed country or starting a revolution right here."

"So where do I send my resume?" I said, feeling totally defeated. "Anarchy Inc.? The Corporation for Ending Tyranny?"

"Don't give up before you've begun," counseled my husband. "You might not find the perfect job your first time out, but for now, let's just get you out in the workforce and see if you even like it."

I did. Like it, I mean. I looked through I don't

know how many sections of classified ads, but it was only when I started to put the word out that I was looking for work that I began to hear interesting things.

Grant flagged me down one morning after my run.

"Hey, Audrey told me you're looking for work, and guess what?" he asked, wrapping his bathrobe around him as he raced down the front walk. "Stuart does some consulting work for this great little nonprofit company that gets housing for low-income people, and he was just in there yesterday and said it was chaos with a capital *C*. I mean, they're in *desperate* need of an office manager. I don't know if that's up your alley or not, but why not give them a call?" He looked around, as if only just aware of his surroundings. "What am I, nuts? It's *freezing* out here. Bye-bye, good luck."

I liked the name, Building Communities, and called them. Now I'll be starting the new year as an employed person. The hours are ten to three, which is *perfect* since the kids get off school at three-thirty, plus I don't have to dress up. That had been on my list — *Don't want to have to wear nylons* — and even though it ranked much lower than *Want to feel like I'm helping someone* and *Want to feel like I'm using my brain* it is my theory that panty hose, along with underwire bras and girdles, is part of a conspiracy to thwart women's circulation and thus their effectiveness. But I won't be wearing any of that . . . so watch out.

PART THREE

The Eighties

Dear Mama:

Well, break out the champagne and the rose
bouquets — it's official, I am now the proud
owner of a degree in interior design. To celebrate, Wade took me to a fancy restaurant
where a string quartet actually serenaded us at
our table! Wade made a toast — "May everyone's home be as beautiful as you've made
ours" — and as we started eating our meal, a
picture of you sitting on the back steps at
MawMaw's house popped into my head.

I remember it was a dusky summer's night;
the sky had purpled and was on its way to
darkness, and you were wearing a man's
sleeveless T-shirt and a pair of blue jeans
you'd cut into shorts, and I thought, gee, my
mama's so young and pretty. You weren't
drunk or even drinking, and I was so excited
to have you all to myself in this state that I was
standing in front of you, dancing around to get
your attention.

"Sit down, you little pest," you said, but it
wasn't in a harsh way, it was more like you
were amused by me.

"I can't sit down, Mama, I've got ants in my
pants."

"Then's all the more reason to sit down,"

you said. " 'Cause then you'll squish 'em."

I thought this was about the funniest thing ever, and I laughed and then you laughed, and I even allowed myself to plop into your lap. Lo and behold, you didn't toss me out like a hot potato.

"Do you know why I called you Faith?" you asked, pushing aside a hank of my hair to whisper in my ear.

" 'Cause you thought it was a pretty name?" I asked.

"Well, yes, it is a pretty name, but the reason I named you Faith is because as soon as I saw you I believed in you."

I remember wishing the earth would stop spinning right then and there because I wanted to be in that moment forever, in your arms that still smelled of the sun, with your words that you believed in me tucked away in my ear forever.

"What's the matter?" Wade asked, putting down his fork and steak knife.

"What do you mean?" I asked, feeling as groggy as someone waking up out of a trance.

"You look like you're about ready to cry."

I patted the corners of my eyes with my fingertips. "Oh, my. I was . . . oh, Wade, I just had the nicest memory of my mother."

"Did you, honey?" He reached across the table to take my hand. "Tell me it."

So I told him.

"Well, that's how I feel, Faith. I believe in you too."

I pressed my lips together; I didn't want salt water splashing all over my lobster thermidor.

"Thank you," I said finally. "But you've got

to understand, my mother didn't tell me things like that very often . . . ever . . . at all."

Wade shook his head, getting that disgusted look I hated to see.

"I'm glad she's not alive, Faith, because if she was, I'd —"

I squeezed Wade's hand. "Don't get all worked up, honey, it's nothing."

"Well, of course it is, Faith! I hate thinking of your mother — your own *mother* — being such a shit to you. Mothers are supposed —" But before he got a chance to finish telling me what mothers are supposed to do, the strolling violinists came over and we could pay attention to something other than the one nice thing my mother ever said to me.

But that was such a big thing, Mama! *The first time I saw you I believed in you.* Why had I forgotten such wonderful words?

We continued our celebration when we got home Mama, if you understand my drift, but after Wade went to sleep, I decided to get up and write you this. I was just so high!

Then on my way to the little room both Wade and I call our office, I passed Beau's room, and Mama, the noise I heard coming from behind his door stopped me cold. He was sobbing, Mama, sobbing as if his whole world had crashed down on him.

"Beau?" I said, knocking on his door. "Beau, honey?"

I didn't wait for him to answer, just went right on in there and sat on his bed. He must have stuffed his fist or his pillow or something in his mouth, because his sobs were as muffled as echoes. I put my hand on his back, and it bucked up like he'd been shocked.

"Beau, what is it?" I asked, and sat there for the longest time. My leg was falling asleep and I thought, okay, I'll leave, he doesn't want to talk, and then he said, "Mama, I feel like no one loves me."

Take a dagger to my heart and twist it as you plunge it in.

"Honey, how can you say that? I love you so much there aren't even words for it, and your dad loves you, and Bonnie, and your grand—"

"They all love Beau, but that's not really me."

"Who's the real you?" I said, rubbing his muscular back. "Superman?"

The reason I tried to make a little joke, Mama, is I was just so scared when he said that. What did he mean?

"Yeah," he said finally, "I'm afraid they think I'm Superman."

There was such resignation in his voice, Mama, but I didn't want to pay attention to it, didn't want to ask him what it meant, because I was scared. So instead I laughed like all was right with the world and the only thing he had to worry about was acne or getting his driver's permit.

Then I kissed him on the cheek and told him to get some sleep. As I closed the door to his room, I knew I had closed another door that he would never again open to me, and I felt terrible but in a way relieved.

I'm sorry,
Faith

TO: All Angry Housewives

FROM: Audrey

It has come to my attention that we have been meeting as a group for nearly twelve years and we have yet to leave Freesia Court for a meeting. That is why I am extending this invitation to join me at the beach home of my consenting parents for one action-packed,. memory-making, no-children-allowed weekend! Transportation and lodging provided. RSVP pronto.

When Merit got the invitation, she wondered on which beach Audrey's parents had a home. Was it a lake up north or maybe one in Wisconsin? And wouldn't it be better to go in the summer? Or maybe Audrey had a winter holiday in mind — should she bring her ice skates? Either way, the idea of getting away for the weekend with just the Angry Housewives was an exciting prospect as well as a scary one.

"Don't worry, we'll watch the girls," said her sister-in-law, Joanie, who was now living in Minneapolis while her husband, Soren, taught bypass procedure at the university.

"Oh, that'd be great," said Merit, who in Joanie had found a friend, a sister, and a trusted baby-sitter. "It's Eric's weekend to take them, but you know him. . . ."

With regard to Eric and his daughters, absence had not made the heart grow fonder; he canceled more of their scheduled weekend dates together than he kept, which suited the girls just fine.

"He never plays with us," said Jewel. "Whenever I ask him to play dolls, he always says, 'Not now.' "

"It's true," said Melody, nodding. "I used to think he wouldn't play with us because we played girl things, so I started asking if he wanted to go to the park and play catch or basketball, but he never wants to do that either."

"I'm glad he never wants us around," said Reni, "because I'd *much* rather be with you."

"Me too," echoed her sisters.

Merit was always touched by their loyalty but hurt by it too. Paul Forrest took an active role in his children's life, having them every weekend. Dave, Audrey's oldest boy, was even living with his father now for his last year of high school.

"I felt like a real failure when he told me he wanted to live with his dad," Audrey had admitted to Merit, "but it seems to be working out best for Davey *and* for Paul. He's finally seeing what it's like to be a parent twenty-four hours a day, although he does have his *Cynthia* to do the laundry, cook the meals, et cetera, et cetera."

Paul had married an associate's legal secretary, a five-foot-two twenty-five-year-old with poofy blond hair and a slight lisp.

My exact opposite, Audrey had thought the first time she saw her. But her boys told her how nice Cynthia was to them, and Audrey recognized that kindness toward them demonstrated a largesse of heart, and so she was nice back. Paul, grateful for the civility of both ex and present wife, matched it with his own, resulting in an easy relationship between all parties. While Audrey wasn't above joking about Cynthia to her friends, she couldn't imagine a better failed marriage, and she was well aware of how much the petite, sibilant speed typist had to do with it. She even had a positive effect on Davey, whose personality ran the gamut from angry to sullen.

"My parents divorced when I was eleven," Cynthia told Audrey over the phone, "and hoo boy, did I take it out on the rest of the world! So I talk to him — when he lets me talk to him — about my own experience, and I think it helps him."

"It does," said Audrey. "Thank you. Last time he was here he helped me with the dishes and we even sang along to the radio. We were actually enjoying being in each other's company! I can't tell you when that last happened."

"I'm glad, Audrey," said Cynthia, but the long pause after she spoke indicated to Audrey that something else was on her mind.

"Now, I'm only saying this because I'm concerned," she said finally. "But have you noticed how Dave is, well, sort of *mean* to his brothers?"

Air filled Audrey's chest, and she expelled it in a big sigh. "Yes, he's been that way all his life. Paul always says brothers are like that."

"That frustrates me about Paul too," said Cynthia conspiratorially. "But it's not true. Bryan and Michael get along wonderfully; sure, they fight now and then, but it's never meanspirited. Not like it is with Dave."

"What should I do, Cynthia?" It was funny; it seemed so natural that she solicit advice from her children's stepmother.

"Well, I like to point it out to him," she said. "Not in front of anyone, and as nicely as I can — usually I say something like, 'Dave, try to remember how your brothers look up to you and how much it hurts their feelings if you're mean to them.'"

Audrey swallowed, wanting to cry. If she had been a different mother — more vigilant, less laissez-faire, more like Cynthia — would Davey not be a bully?

"Audrey, he's basically a good kid," she said, sensing Audrey didn't want to speak or was incapable of it. "He's just got the most testosterone in the family."

"Don't tell Paul," said Audrey. "He thinks he owns that title."

"You're telling me," said Cynthia, starting up her hissing laugh again.

When Audrey and Merit compared single-mother stories, Merit always went away wishing Eric could find someone who was good for him, who could help him and thus help her and the girls (but then again, she would never wish Eric on any woman), whereas Audrey would think how much easier life would be if her boys were the all-for-one-and-one-for-all team Merit's girls were.

"But we're not going to talk about kids or ex-husbands at all on this weekend," Audrey told Merit when she came over to discuss the particulars of the invitation.

"We aren't? What'll we talk about?"

Audrey turned the burner on under the tea-kettle. "Besides the book? I don't know — geothermodynamics, the hostage situation,

Robert Redford's jawline . . ."

Excited, Merit clasped her hands together. "So where are we going to go? Where's your parents' beach house?"

"Malibu."

"Malibu," repeated Merit. "Is that the name of the lake or the town?"

Audrey studied her friend for a moment; she was never quite sure when Merit was being naive or trying to be funny.

"It's a town," said Audrey with a laugh.

Merit's eyes widened. "Malibu as in California?"

"That'd be the one."

The excitement drained out of Merit as if a plug had been pulled.

"Oh, Audrey, and I was so looking forward to this trip."

Audrey opened a cupboard. "Do you want any saltines? Or I've got some Oreos around here somewhere. And what do you mean, *was?*"

"Well." Looking flustered, Merit waved her hands. "How am I supposed to manage a trip to California? I barely make ends meet, Audrey."

Audrey closed the cupboard and, crossing her arms over her chest, looked at Merit. "You read the invitation, didn't you?"

Merit nodded.

"Then don't you remember what it said on the bottom? Transportation and lodging provided."

Merit's finger probed the dimple in her chin. "You mean to tell me you're going to pay my way to California?"

"Why not? I invited you, didn't I?"

"Audrey, I could never accept such a generous gift."

"Of course you can, Merit. Just like my grandfather — who loved to share — gave us the gift of all his invention royalties."

"Is that the grandfather who came to visit you after he died?"

Audrey nodded. "And the one who keeps reminding me of his generosity every time I get a check."

The five women clinked imaginary glasses.

"To Audrey, the hostess with the mostess." Faith covered her mouth. "I mean the host with the most."

"To sunshine in the middle of February," added Slip.

They clinked glasses again and then again after Faith's next toast.

"To luxury."

They waited for Kari, but when she didn't speak, Audrey said, "To Flicka."

It was the only thing that cast a shadow on their sun-splashed afternoon.

A half hour earlier, they had arrived at Audrey's parents' beach house, although "beach house" seemed something of an understatement for a five-bedroom hacienda attended by a housekeeping couple.

A flare of envy shot through Faith: *This is where Audrey gets to spend her vacations?*

"My goodness," whispered Kari.

"We owe it all to my grandfather," said Audrey, picking up Kari's whisper. "And the whirligigs he invented."

"Whirligigs," scoffed Slip. "Jerry says only Henry Ford did more to revolutionize factory assembly."

"Get her," said Audrey, elbowing Merit. "She sounds like a tour guide."

"This place needs one," said Slip, looking up at the vaulted ceilings and balcony overhanging the great room.

They debated what to do, and Audrey's suggestion (take a nap) was outvoted four to one in favor of Slip's (take a hike).

And so it was that they had just climbed a hilltop that smelled of sage and cypress, paying a spontaneous tribute to the dog that had been Kari's companion for years.

"She would have loved running around these hills," said Kari. "When she *could* run."

A week earlier Kari and Julia had taken Flicka to the veterinarian. She could no longer walk, so Kari and Julia had carried her to and from the car in a blanket.

"Do you want to be with her while she goes to sleep?" asked the vet, who had given Flicka her first shots as a puppy.

Kari, her vision blurred with tears, turned to Julia.

"Why don't we, Mom?" said Julia. "I think Flicka would like that."

The old dog managed to look up at her owner as Kari placed her hand on her head. Her tail thumped once on the steel table.

"Yes, Flicka," she said softly. "Remember how I got you? I had run into one of Bjorn's good friends — this was a couple years after Bjorn died — and he mentioned that his golden retriever just had puppies, and I said, 'Oh, Bjorn and I always talked about getting a retriever,' and a couple weeks later, the doorbell rang, and there he was, holding you. I always thought of you as a gift from Bjorn, because you always knew how —" Her voice broke.

"You knew how to take care of Mom," said Julia, who had heard this story many times. "You slept at the foot of Mom's bed, and whenever she was feeling really sad, you'd stop whatever you were doing and put your head in her lap." Julia placed her hand over her mother's, and the vet widened his eyes and clenched his jaw; he had found through years of practice that his tears only made everything worse.

"And then when I came along," said the poised twelve-year-old, "you weren't jealous or growly or anything — in fact, whenever I felt sad you always put your head in *my* lap."

A spasm punctuated by a sob surged through Kari's body. She saw the pain in her dog's milky eyes, and she knew that if she was going to make Flicka's last moments peaceful, she'd have to buck up.

"So you go to sleep, my dear, true friend," she said, scratching the retriever behind the ear (throughout the day she would hold her fingers to her nose and smell her old dog's smell, and in fact did not wash that hand all day so she could go to sleep with the scent of Flicka close). "We will never forget you."

"Kari?" asked Merit softly. "Are you all right?"

The older woman pushed her fingers under her sunglasses to wipe her eyes.

"Yes," she said, and her cheeks bulged as she blew out a lungful of air. "Although I was thinking, there ought to be a word for a person who loses their dog — you know, like *widow* or

384

widower — because really, you do feel widowed in a way." She sniffed. "As silly as that sounds."

"I don't think that sounds silly," said Slip. "Although I'd be lying if I said I'll feel anything but relieved when Pepe dies."

Pepe was a yappy little Chihuahua Gil had brought home one day. ("Mom, look — Kyle Price is moving to Wyoming and he said his mom said they couldn't keep their dog anymore and I said we've always wanted a dog and oh, Mom, can we keep him, please? *Please?*") Unlike Flicka, who had let the neighborhood kids dress her up for the annual circus, had fetched thousands of balls thrown by them, and had let them use her as a pillow when they were exhausted by their games, Pepe didn't like anyone but Gil touching him and would quiver and growl if anyone had the audacity to try.

Kari managed a laugh. "I'm not really sure he's a dog, Slip."

The mood brightened then as they exchanged stories about their favorite and least favorite dogs. Most grateful for it was Kari, the one who most needed the mood brightened. And as they began hiking back to the house, as a warm Californian breeze ruffled through her hair, as the Pacific turned somersaults on the sandy beach below, she thought that once again the Angry Housewives had done their jobs.

They wound up having their book discussion in a biker bar.

"Holy cow, look at all the motorcycles," said Faith as they pulled off the winding road and into a dirt parking lot.

"This is where we used to have hamburgers when we were kids," said Audrey, getting out of

the car. "You should have seen this place then."
She swept an arm out. "None of these houses
were here."

"I can't imagine it being more beautiful than it
is now," said Merit.

"And I return the compliment to you," said
Audrey, curtsying as she opened the screen door
for her friends. "Get a little California sun on
your face and you're absolutely dazzling."

"What about me?" said Slip, who smelled of
the Noxzema she had put on her sunburned
face. "Don't you think I look dazzling?"

"We told you to use sunblock, Slip," said
Faith. "But you said this time you could tell you
were going to tan."

"Yeah, yeah, yeah," said Slip, "can I help it
I'm a natural optimist?"

As they entered the bar, it took a moment for
their eyes to adjust to the dark interior.

"There's a booth," said Audrey, pointing to
the far corner, and as they walked toward it a
chorus of whistles from the patrons at the bar
followed them.

Giggling, they sat down and ordered a couple
pitchers of beer from a wiry waitress whose tattooed arm read *Tiny*.

"Oh, my gosh," said Merit. "Who do you suppose Tiny is?"

"Probably that guy," said Slip, nodding toward the bar. "That big fat guy in the sleeveless
T-shirt and the foot-long beard."

"Can you imagine that thing on top of you?"
asked Audrey.

None of them could, but the idea of it re-
started their giggles.

"You're a happy bunch," said the waitress,

plunking down two pitchers of beer.

"We're celebrating," said Audrey.

"Somebody's birthday?" said the waitress, and if she yawned she couldn't have sounded more bored.

"No, this one," said Audrey, nodding at Kari, "just got out of the slammer. First beer she's had in fifteen years."

"I'll bet," said the waitress, but a flicker of a smile appeared on her bored, tough face. "Fifteen years, huh? Must have been some crime."

"She ran an illegal Tupperware ring," said Slip. "In fact, she can get you some mixing bowls if you play your cards right."

A real smile grew on the waitress' face. "Can't say as I need any mixing bowls, but if you got one of them cake holders, I'll take it."

Shaking her head, Kari watched the waitress return to the bar.

"An illegal Tupperware ring," she said. "Couldn't you have given me a *real* crime?"

"Like any one of these guys around here has committed?" said Audrey. "I can't believe it. There always used to be a few motorcycles around, but man alive, I have never seen so much leather in all my life."

"Is it headquarters for the Hell's Angels or something?" asked Merit, with such seriousness that everyone burst out laughing.

"I don't know," said Slip, "but I think it would be in our best interest not to say anything derogatory about Harleys."

"Well," said Merit, "before a brawl breaks out, why don't we talk about the book?"

"What?" she said as her friends looked at her with a combination of bemusement and surprise.

"That didn't sound like you," said Audrey. "You sounded so decisive."

"So bossy," said Slip.

"Just like the rest of us," said Faith.

"They're right," said Kari, nodding.

Merit flushed. "It's just that I loved this book so much." She took the paperback out of her purse and held it to her chest. "My gosh, I don't know how many times I sobbed through it."

"Is that how you measure the success of a book?" asked Kari. "By how many times it makes you cry?"

"Well," said Merit, who long ago had realized that Kari liked to play devil's advocate in book discussions and that she shouldn't take anything she said personally, "if you care so much about the characters that you cry about them, something's working."

"But Merit," chimed in Slip, "you have to realize that some writers are good at manipulating emotions and will purposely kill off sympathetic characters so you'll cry. Remember *Love Story*?"

"Ugh, don't remind me," said Kari. "But I didn't find Judy — or Jenny, or whatever her name was — particularly sympathetic."

Faith set down her glass of beer. "But none of you can say this book was even in the same stratosphere as *Love Story*. The depth of this book, my Lord! Styron is such a good writer, and the questions he raises . . . ."

"Like what would have been your choice?" asked Slip, her voice soft.

"That," said Kari, no longer the devil's advocate, "was one of the hardest things I've ever had to read." She rubbed her arms. "I still get goose bumps."

Audrey tapped a cigarette out of her pack and halfheartedly offered one to Faith, the only other Angry Housewife who still smoked, although not with the regularity of Audrey.

"I guess a biker bar's as good a place as any to smoke in," said Faith, taking the cigarette.

"So what would be your choice?" Audrey asked, turning to Slip after she'd lit up. "If a Nazi was telling you that only one of your children was going to be allowed to live, which child would you pick?"

Slip's sunburned face blanched. "I couldn't pick."

"Neither could I," whispered Merit.

"Well, none of us could," said Audrey, "but admit it, didn't you think: if I *really* had to, which child would it be?"

"Thank God I only have one," said Kari, and goose bumps rose on her arms again.

"I tried to decide," said Merit, holding her beer glass with two hands and pressing it against her chin. "But I couldn't. Just thinking about it made me so scared . . . made me feel like I was going to throw up."

"Well, I was able to decide," said Faith, and even as the jukebox cranked out an old Johnny Cash song, as the line of leather-clad men up at the bar joked with one another, as someone in the back room shouted as the billiard ball fell into the pocket he had called, a hush fell over the corner table.

"Who?" asked Slip. "Who would it be?"

Faith's heart hammered. Why had she confessed this? The fact that she could pick and no one else could obviously showed what a terrible mother she was. Should she just make a quick joke? Tell them that she was only kidding?

"Bonnie," she said, and as soon as the name was out of her mouth, tears collected in her eyes. "I would have chosen Bonnie — and believe me, I thought about this from every angle — because if I chose Beau to live over Bonnie, he *wouldn't* have lived. I mean, maybe now, at the age the twins are now, but if they were little like Sophie's kids, then Beau would absolutely not have lived if he were taken away from me and put into a concentration camp." She blinked, feeling the wetness on her eyelashes. "Whereas Bonnie . . . well, Bonnie would not only live, she'd probably form a children's resistance unit and organize a massive breakout."

Faith's eyes searched her friends. "It doesn't mean that by choosing Bonnie to live that I love her more," she said, her voice catching, "I'd just want to make sure the one who got to live *would* live."

"Jesus Christ," said Audrey, signaling the waitress after she dabbed at her own tears. "We need another round."

The waitress, who was leaning over the bar, examining an earring a man with a thick silver braid was wearing, acknowledged the summons with a nod but took her time getting to the table.

"You girls are thirsty," she said, setting down the pitcher. Then, seeing the book on the table, said, "Oh, *Sophie's Choice* — I loved that book."

"You read it?" asked Faith, and the disbelief in her voice was so evident that Audrey kicked her under the table.

"You act surprised," said the waitress with a smirk.

"No, I —"

"How about that Nathan, huh?" asked the waitress, ignoring Faith. "Who was fooled by him?"

An informal poll was taken, and the waitress, one hand on a narrow hip, joined in on the discussion until a biker at another table yelled, "Hey, Shirley, get your skinny ass over here so I can order some food!"

"My public awaits," said the waitress, and after lifting her eyebrows in a look of bored resignation, she cocked her head toward the Angry Housewives. "You should check out *The Confessions of Nat Turner*, too. A whole different world, but Styron takes you right there."

An hour later the little roadhouse was packed with men and women and cigarette smoke hovered like cloud cover. The smell of hamburger grease and beer and perspiration was strong but not offensive; it smelled like a party.

The volume of the jukebox had been cranked up, and couples in leather and denim danced to a selection that hadn't been updated since the '50s: Elvis (lots of Elvis), Buddy Holly, Little Richard.

When Hank Williams started singing about how lonesome he was, the fat man at the bar the Angry Housewives had supposed was Tiny sauntered over to the table and asked, "Dance?" Faith assumed he was talking to Audrey, who in her tube top and short shorts looked most like a biker chick, but it was Merit for whom he held out his slabby hand. Merit's hand went to her chest and her eyes bugged out, and the word *apoplexy* popped into Kari's head.

But, surprising everyone, Merit took the

hammy paw of the 350-pound biker and let him lead her to the worn oak dance floor, where men and women were pressed together, barely moving.

"Oh, my Lord," said Faith as they all watched Tiny lift one of Merit's hands to his shoulder. "It's Beauty and the Beast."

The biker's other hand spanned the entirety of the small of Merit's back. Holding her as if he were an archaeologist and she were a prehistoric vase, he began to weave her through the crowd.

"He's actually *dancing*," said Slip. "He knows *steps*."

Once they began moving, Merit's stunned expression faded away and she smiled at her partner, seeing only her happy face in his reflector sunglasses. It was obvious Merit loved to dance; she moved so gracefully and assuredly in his arms that Tiny, with his bush of a beard and his too-tight sleeveless T-shirt, didn't look silly at all, but equally graceful and assured.

"Why, it's Fred and Ginger," said Audrey, and her opinion was shared by the couples out on the floor, who stopped their simple foot-shuffling to give the masters some room.

Another song came on, "Tutti Frutti," and Merit spun and twirled in a series of moves that her partner immediately picked up. Kari felt goose bumps on her arm again, but these were the kind that acknowledge an unexpected magic.

They danced to one more song — "Oh, Donna" — and when they were finished they earned explosive applause not only from the Angry Housewives, but from everyone else in the bar.

Tiny escorted Merit back to the table, executing a slight bow before kissing her hand.

"Thank you, milady."

"Thank *you*, Lionel," said Merit, flushed pink and as lovely as a child's idea of a princess.

"*Lionel?*" came the chorus of whispers as the hairy behemoth and his huge stomach made their way back to the bar.

"He said everyone calls him Lion," said Merit, pouring more beer into her glass. "But I reminded him of his mother, so I could call him what she calls him: Lionel."

"If that don't beat all," said Faith, and her accent came out, as it always did when she was truly flummoxed.

Everyone got out on the dance floor at least once (Kari with a biker whose bald pate was decorated with a tattoo of the marine slogan, "Semper Fi"), and when the bar closed they had numerous offers to continue the party elsewhere. Lionel even posed for a picture with them and reminded Merit that if she ever wanted to hit the road, she was welcome to hit it with him.

"And how 'bout you," said a guy named Deke, pulling Audrey toward a massive Harley. "You want to hit the road with me?"

"Sorry, Deke," said Audrey, finagling her way out of his grasp, "but after midnight we turn back into housewives."

"Angry housewives," growled Slip, assuming the pose of a gunfighter. The others, finding this hilarious, mimicked the pose, and the sight of five women aiming imaginary pistols at him did something to temper Deke's libido.

"You don't know what you're missing," he said, giving Audrey's behind a playful slap.

"Oh, now I think I do," said Audrey, watching as he listed toward his bike.

They sat in Audrey's parents' roomy Mercedes with the windows open, listening to the thundering power of dozens of motorcycles starting up, and watched as one by one they eased out into the black night like metal insects flying home after their nectar-gathering.

Shirley, the waitress, got on her own motorcycle and in low gear rumbled over to them.

"Going home to Tiny?" asked Faith.

Shirley laughed. "Nah, someone much more exciting — Sherwood Anderson."

Kari laughed. "Sherwood Anderson the writer?"

"I'm rereading *Winesburg, Ohio* and fuckin' crying all over again."

With that, she revved the throttle and was off.

HOST: **KARI**

BOOK: *My Home Is Far Away*

by Dawn Powell

REASON CHOSEN: "I think she's an

American treasure."

When Kari received the invitation to Mary Jo's wedding, her impulse was to send off a check with her best wishes.

She had good excuses not to attend. After all, the wedding was to be held in Washington, D.C., which involved a bit more of a commute than just going over the bridge to St. Paul; Kari didn't want to pull Julia out of school with Christmas break just two weeks away; she didn't have time to sew a semiformal dress . . . well, at least the long trip was a good excuse.

What held her back from responding yes was of course fear.

Mary Jo had made it easy for Kari. She had only seen Julia twice, at two family reunions, and while she had cooed over the child, she cooed just as much at her brother Randy's kids or her cousins'. Kari had been on pins and needles, certain someone would find out *something*, but on both occasions she had gone home nearly weak with relief: no one had found out or suspected anything.

Occasionally Kari got a postcard from a far-flung place whose exact location in the world she would have to look up on the huge globe she'd gotten for Julia (once a teacher, always a teacher). Kari was thrilled that Mary Jo had fulfilled her college wishes by studying abroad and after her graduation, traveling extensively. Glad for her niece, and glad for herself.

And so, realizing that her excuses weren't good after all, Kari found herself in a mauve silk dress sitting in a hotel ballroom, watching her daughter dance with her uncle Scott as a woman sang about how she would survive.

"Hello," said a bald man, pulling out a chair next to Kari's. "It's Mrs. Nelson, right?"

Kari peered into the man's face, and familiarity flickered in her brain until it ignited into an image.

"Larry," said Kari, "Larry the lawyer. I hardly recognized you without the love beads and the long hair." She looked down at his feet, clad in shiny dress shoes. "And where are your sandals?"

Larry smiled. "I was a man of my times."

"And times have obviously changed," said Kari, taking in his well-cut suit and plain red tie.

"So . . . how are things?"

"Things are well."

Larry followed her gaze to the dance floor. "She's a beautiful girl."

Kari's heart hammered. "Yes, she is. She's more than I could have ever imagined."

One of the groom's relatives (a builder who claimed to have developed most of Bethesda) sat down at the table with a refilled plate from the sumptuous buffet table.

"Tried the prime rib?" he asked.

"Yes," said Kari. "It's excellent." She turned back to Larry. Now that there was an audience, it wasn't safe to stay on the same subject. "So, are you still a lawyer?"

Larry shook his head. "Not anymore. Now I'm a judge."

"Oh," said Kari, fiddling with the neckline of her dress. "Bjorn . . . my husband was a judge."

Larry nodded. "I think Mary Jo told me that, way back when." He suddenly sat up straight, as if he'd gotten a mild shock. "Hey, would you like to dance?"

"I don't know how to dance to this kind of music."

Larry laughed as he stood up and took her hand. "Let's just waltz fast and call it disco."

Kari had expected to feel silly and out of touch; she certainly hadn't expected to feel such exultation. The music (this was the first wedding party she'd been to that didn't have a band, but a DJ spinning records) was loud and she couldn't understand any lyrics other than "stayin' alive," but she'd never had more fun on a dance floor. She and Larry had started off doing an up-tempo waltz, which, when coupled with a few do-si-dos, turned into a square dance which everyone seemed to pick up. Partners changed and swirled by, and Kari, whose deep laugh boomed across the dance floor, was swung and flung until she was dizzy.

"Aunt Kari," said Mary Jo, passing by her in a swirl of ivory satin, "I see you met Larry!"

"I almost didn't recognize him!" she shouted back, gasping as her partner nearly hurled her off the dance floor and into one of the tables.

"Hi, Mom!" said Julia, whizzling by, tendrils of hair springing out like curly ribbons around her forehead.

"Hi, honey!" said Kari, finding herself in the arms of Mark, the groom.

"Mary Jo told me you were a woman of many talents, but I didn't know you could dance, too."

"Is that what I'm doing? I thought I was just trying to stay on my feet."

"You have a beautiful daughter," said Mark. "Although, considering her mother, how could she not be?"

The music suddenly dimmed for Kari, and the colors of the party dresses and the sprays of flowers faded. He knew what Kari didn't want known.

"Excuse me," she said, and sidestepped her way through the dancers back to her table and the prime rib eater.

"You tried the shrimp?" he asked.

She shook her head, grabbed her purse off the table, and looked for someplace that might offer her a little air.

I'm being silly, she scolded herself as she race-walked toward a French door. *Of course Mary Jo's going to tell her husband about the baby she had long ago; a good marriage is based on trust.*

Cold air smacked her in the face as she pushed through the door and onto a patio occupied by a couple (one of Mary Jo's bridesmaids and, if memory served her correctly, a Spanish diplomat) for whom Kari's presence was obviously unwelcome. Kari ignored their put-upon looks (hadn't that Spanish diplomat come with his wife?) and walked to the other side of the patio, wishing she had brought her coat, even though her shivering had just as much to do with her fear as with the cold.

She knew everyone was going to find out. What would her dear brother Anders think, her letting him believe that Julia was his niece instead of his granddaughter? And Sally? And Mary Jo's brothers? And, most importantly, what would Julia think? She hated to think of the deep hurt they were all about to be pushed into.

Realizing this intruder wasn't going anywhere, the couple slipped out, but Kari, so agitated by fear and worry, didn't even notice their departure. Nor did she notice Mary Jo until her niece put her hand on her shoulder.

"Oh!" said Kari, startled.

Mary Jo smiled, but her blue eyes (so like her aunt's) were crinkled with concern.

"Aunt Kari, what's the matter? Mark's worried sick — he said one minute you're laughing like Santa Claus and the next minute you're running off the dance floor as if he'd done something to offend you."

"You told him, didn't you?" Kari said, her voice both angry and plaintive. "You told him about Julia!"

Suddenly Mary Jo was the opposite of a blushing bride; all color leached from her face.

"No," she said quietly. "I didn't tell him. I've never told anyone."

Kari opened her mouth to speak but it took a few moments for any words to gather.

"You never told Mark? But . . . a wife tells her husband everything."

Mary Jo shook her head. "Not this wife."

"But he said something about Julia being

beautiful and taking after her mother!"

"Geez, Aunt Kari, can't you take a compliment?"

Again Kari opened her mouth and had to wait for the words to catch up. Finally she said, "Don't you think by not telling him you're deceiving him?"

"First you're yelling at me for telling, and now you're yelling at me for not telling. Which way do you want it?"

Taking her niece's hand, Kari managed a weak smile. "Mary Jo, I'm . . . glad you didn't tell. And relieved. But surprised. I just assumed you wouldn't want any secrets between you."

"There are worse things a couple could have between them. I'm thirty-two and Mark'll be forty — it's not like we both haven't lived lives before we found each other." Letting go of her aunt's hand, Mary Jo watched as a hotel employee swept snow off the courtyard. "Look, Aunt Kari, the fact that I had a baby when I was young is not the least bit relevant to the person I am today. I had sex, I got pregnant, I gave birth . . . end of story. It was the beginning of your story, but really — and I don't mean to sound cold — it was the end of mine as far as the baby went. I didn't regret having her, but I didn't miss her, I didn't long for her, I only felt relief. Relief that I got to go back to being who I wanted to be." Mary Jo folded her arms across her chest. "So you think I'm deceiving Mark by not telling him? I thought I was protecting you and Julia. I thought that's what you wanted."

"It was," said Kari, feeling the sting of tears in her eyes. "It is."

"I don't know what you've told Julia —"

"Only the story I told everybody else. So far she seems happy with that."

"Good," said Mary Jo. "But if and when she wants to know more, it's up to you what you tell her. You're the mother. You get to decide what's best for your child. I'm ready to cross any bridge I need to, or you need to; I just don't see the need to build a bridge to cross when we're perfectly fine where we are."

"We are," Kari whispered. "We're perfectly fine where we are."

"Then let's get back to the party," said Mary Jo, taking her aunt's arm, "and get some of that prime rib I've been hearing so much about."

As she recounted the wedding and reception in their hotel room that night, Julia was giddy.

"Mom, did you see that guy I danced with at the end?" she asked, crawling into the bed Kari was already settled into. "The guy with the longish hair and the red plaid sash thing —"

"Cummerbund," said Kari.

"Yeah, that thing. Anyway, wasn't he *cute?* He's a sophomore at this private school here, the Friends School. I said, 'You mean everyone gets along really good?' and he laughed and said, 'No, it's run by Quakers,' and I said, 'What do you have for breakfast?' and he said, 'Huh?' and I repeated the question and he said, 'I don't know — eggs, bacon, pancakes, the usual stuff; why?' and I said, 'I just thought you'd be eating Quaker Oats all the time,' and I know it was a dumb joke but we both laughed like a bunch of lame-os and then he said he thought I was one of the prettiest girls he'd ever seen!"

As she drew in a load of air, Kari smiled.

"You're not one of the prettiest girls I've ever seen," she said, pushing a tendril of hair off Julia's forehead. "You're *the* prettiest."

The fourteen-year-old girl tucked her hands behind her head and stared at the ceiling.

"Do you think my biological mother was pretty?"

Kari's heart seized up to the size of a walnut.

"I'll bet she was," continued Julia. "Not that I'm bragging or anything . . . but it's fun to have people think you're pretty, isn't it?"

"I . . . I wouldn't know."

Julia turned to her. "Oh, don't be so modest, Mom. You're the most beautiful mom I know."

Okay, Kari thought, *it may look like a hotel room, but I've actually died and gone to heaven.*

"Thank you, darling." Kari bent down and brushed her nose against her daughter's. Her heart pounded as she sorted out the words she wanted to say. "Julia . . . would you like to know who your real mother is?"

"*Biological* mother, Mom," said Julia. "You're my real mother."

"Well, I know you're curious and must have a lot of —"

"Mom? No offense, but do we have to talk about this right now? Because I'd really like to talk about Jeremy — that's his name; doesn't it go good with Julia? Julia and Jeremy? I mean, I know I'll probably never see him again, but right now I'd just like to talk about him. Or if you're tired, I'd be just as happy to lie here and think about him."

"Go ahead," said Kari, kissing her daughter's cheek. "Go ahead and talk about him. I'd love to listen."

As Julia babbled on about Jeremy's favorite sports — "He plays rugby, Mom! I told him that's not even a sport up in Minnesota!" — Kari leaned back on the plump hotel pillows and thanked God for the day, and especially the respite.

September 1983

HOST: **MERIT**
BOOK: *In The Spirit of Crazy Horse*
by Peter Matthiessen
REASON CHOSEN: "Someone I respect at
work said I should read it."

Merit was back to typing, and although her speed (107 words a minute) was a source of pride for her, it was a small source, especially now that there were word processors and one little key could erase a mistake as if it never happened.

All of the Angry Housewives were now working outside their homes. Faith was a decorator; Slip helped people get jobs and housing; Kari had gone back to substitute teaching when Julia was in the second grade; and Audrey, who didn't have to work, hostessed ("They won't let me call myself a host, Slip!") at a restaurant downtown, patronized by lots of businessmen, including occasionally her ex-husband.

"It's not as if it fulfills me on an intellectual level," she explained, "but it's fun. I get to dress up, flirt with a lot of guys, and eat free. Can't knock those benefits."

Merit wasn't fulfilled on an intellectual level at her job either, nor did she find the typing of endless reports on city planning *fun,* but the money supplemented what the court forced Eric to pay her every month. He had included snide notes with every check until Audrey dictated a letter Merit sent to him, informing him she'd sue him for harassment if he persisted in such mean-spirited, childish behavior.

Merit solicited Audrey's advice on many subjects, including household management (Audrey had taken her through a tour of her basement, showing her how the fuse box worked, where the gas and water lines were, and how to relight the furnace), but the advice Audrey gave to her about men and dating went in one ear and out the other, with no absorption by the brain whatsoever.

After her divorce, Audrey had slept with any man who was willing to spring for dinner or a movie (she never told them those bargaining chips were superfluous and that she would have slept with them anyway), but she felt she had grown up and the sex-without-love stage now bored her.

Her bedroom was on the first floor and the boys' were upstairs; still, she didn't like sneaking men in at night and pushing them out before her sons woke up. And she didn't like waking up smelling of liquor and different brands of cologne and aftershave. She still subscribed to her basic rule — *I'll date anyone who asks me, as long as there's not drool on his chin while he asks* — but she realized there was no harm in getting to know someone before she invited them to bed.

"And that's what you should do, Merit; get out there and see what's happening in Man Country!"

"I'm not really interested," Merit said with a shrug. Closer to the truth was that she had *NO DESIRE IN THE WORLD!* to visit "Man Country" let alone browse inside its borders. What if she wound up with another Eric? A man whom she'd thought was the answer to her prayers, and *was,* if she'd been praying to the devil. No thanks — if it was her fate to not be with a man, that was a far better fate than being with a man like Eric.

It was a given that whenever Merit was out and about, men were interested. Men in her church asked her out (at the annual picnic, waiting for their children to get out of Sunday school, and once in the communion line); men at work asked her out (fortunately, her boss was married and one of the few men to whom this served as a deterrent); men in the grocery store, the butcher shop, the bookstore asked her out. Remnants of her high school self remained in that it pained her to hurt anyone's feelings, but at least she was able to say no, and underneath that no was *I'm as happy as I've ever been with my girls and my girlfriends — I don't need you right now.*

If only I had a better job, she thought, finishing a report on the feasibility of restructuring the infrastructure according to budgetary guidelines or some such blather (Merit had no retention of what she typed; after the fourth or fifth "in accordance with" or "recent studies show," her mind flew out the drafty office window and didn't come back to its host until the last piece of paper was out of the printer.)

At least relief was only ten minutes away: lunch.

"You want to go down to the cafeteria?" asked Bree, the only interesting person in the whole office.

"I was going to the library to see if I could play the piano," said Merit, more an apology than a statement.

"That's cool," said Bree, taking a mirror out of her desk drawer to check on her kohl-lined eyes. "I wish I could play an instrument. But I seem to have some sort of tonal deficiency that has doomed me to live my musical life as only a fan."

Bree had recently vacationed in London and had returned talking about how something called punk rock was already passé there, "and it's too bad, because it was going to change the world." She was the one who passed books on to Merit with urgent orders: "You *have* to read this."

She was trying to figure out what to do with her master's degree in anthropology, and until she did, she typed at the desk behind Merit's.

"You want anything?" she asked, lifting the strap of her huge shoulder bag over her head. "A bag of chips? Some yogurt?"

Merit held up a brown paper bag. "I'm all set, thanks."

"Well," said Bree, leaving the office even though it was eight minutes away from being officially noon, "I hope you get in."

This referred to the library's first-come, first-serve policy to use the pianos.

"Me too," said Merit. "I could really use it."

Among many of the bastardly things Eric had done, taking the piano (originally a gift from his parents) ranked right up there with a fist in the face.

"But what about the girls' piano lessons?" Merit had asked.

"Tell them if their mother hadn't divorced their father, this never would have happened."

Upon hearing that the music had stopped at the Iverson house, Audrey had promptly bought Merit a piano.

Merit was overwhelmed by her friend's generosity, which Audrey shrugged off.

"Consider me a patron of the arts, Merit."

"I swear I'll pay you back."

"Don't you dare," said Audrey, miffed. "This is a gift."

She couldn't afford lessons with Mrs. Klanski, so Merit taught the girls herself. Fortunately the girls liked to practice, and thirteen-year-old Melody in particular (*I guess I named you right,* Merit often thought as she listened to her daughter play) showed a real talent. Which was all well and good, except that it was hard getting in her own time at the piano. Which is why, when she wasn't spending her lunch hour reading, she was spending it trying to play the library piano.

Luck was with her that afternoon; one room was occupied by a young man hunched over the piano so that his hair nearly brushed the keys, but the other room was open and there were no names on the sign-up sheet.

Sitting down on the bench, Merit attacked the keys, playing rousing versions of "Battle Hymn of the Republic" and the marine hymn and nearly every song written to inspire men to go to war.

When she emerged from the room, it was as if she'd spent time in a gym; she was hot and sweaty and somehow cleansed.

"Bravo," said a man sitting in a plastic chair against the wall. "Bravo."

Merit turned toward the escalator, not hearing him.

"Bravo," insisted the man, following her. "Bravo."

"I beg your pardon?"

"I was commenting on your performance," said the man and Merit caught a glimmer of two gold teeth just at the corners of his smile.

Merit said later that that was why she'd stopped to talk to the man, fascinated as she was by a particular symmetry he presented not only in his teeth, but in his long curving sideburns, which looked like two hairy parentheses ("Does that mean his face is parenthetical?" asked Audrey), by the way the lapels of his pale blue leisure suit ("Oh, no," said Slip, "he's still wearing one of those?") were perfect angles.

"I was playing that loud?" asked Merit. The rooms were not soundproof, but unless someone was playing fairly energetically, people outside couldn't hear.

"It's my ears," explained the man. "It seems I have exceptional hearing — especially when it comes to music. Especially when it comes to beautifully played music."

Merit's initial fascination was fading fast. Another guy trying to pick her up.

"Hmmm," she said. "Well, I've got to be going. Nice to meet you, Mr. . . ."

"Paradise," said the man, extending his hand. "As in you've found yours!"

"I beg your pardon?"

"That's my name!" he said gleefully. "Frank Paradise!"

"Is that right?" said Merit, giving him an almost civil smile before turning on her heel.

"Wait, miss — please," said Mr. Paradise. "Let me give you my card."

"No, thanks," said Merit with a wave of her hand. As she walked toward the escalator, she thought how proud the Angry Housewives would be of her assertiveness. She had turned a guy down without apologizing once.

Paradise was there the next time Merit played on the library piano, and the next time and the next.

Seeing him, she'd joke, "My Paradise," which brought on a smile and a flash of those gold teeth. But she said nothing more, and he didn't pursue her after she stopped playing, though he did offer his bravos.

After the fourth or fifth one-man ovation, Merit finally changed her tactic of heading directly to the escalator and instead sat next to him in one of the plastic chairs lined up against the wall.

"Mr. Paradise," she began.

"*My* Paradise," he corrected. "I like it when you say 'my Paradise.' "

Dear God, thought Merit. *Maybe he's a little soft in the head.*

"Mr. Paradise," she said, raising her voice as if volume might increase his comprehension. "While I'm flattered you like my playing, I really am getting a little uncomfortable with your presence here."

"Then have a cup of coffee with me."

"I will not," she said, leaning away from him. "What on earth makes you think I'd have a cup of coffee with you?"

Mr. Paradise shrugged, and the stiff polyester of his leisure suit (this one was brown with wide white topstitching) took its time falling back on his shoulders. "Nothing makes me *think* you will, but everything makes me *hope* you will."

"Oh, for . . . oh, for . . . ," sputtered Merit, rising. "Can't you just leave me alone?"

Mr. Paradise's face fell like a hound hearing "Bad dog!" from its beloved master. In a lifetime of facing disappointed male faces, this was by far the most disappointed.

"I'm truly sorry if I offended you in some way," said Mr. Paradise, being careful not to look her in the eyes. He stood up. "That was not my intention, believe me."

"Oh, all right," said Merit impatiently. "I'll have coffee with you. *One cup.*"

The sun broke on Mr. Paradise's face. "One cup," he said, as if those words were the winning answer to a question he'd been asking all his life.

It got to be a regular Thursday engagement: a cup of coffee in the basement cafeteria of Woolworth's. On the other days of the week, Merit played the library piano, or if she didn't get in, she took out whatever book she happened to be carrying in her bag and found a window to read by. Mr. Paradise, thankfully, never trailed after her, never found a book of his own and planted himself next to her, but would simply wish her a good day and depart. Merit was sure that if he had a hat, he would have doffed it.

But on Thursdays, she spent her entire lunch hour sitting on a stool in front of a flecked Formica counter, drinking coffee with Mr. Paradise.

"Sorry I'm late," he said one day as he raced

in, sliding onto the stool so that it swiveled violently and his knee smacked against hers. He quickly swiveled back. "A fellow at my bus stop had a heart attack."

"Oh, my," said Merit. "Is he all right?"

Mr. Paradise shrugged. "Time will tell. He was breathing on his own by the time the ambulance got there."

The waitress brought them their standard order: cherry pie à la mode for Merit and wheat toast with extra jelly for Mr. Paradise.

"So, Miss Mayes" (in some conversation he had learned her maiden name and had called her by it ever since; she called him by his surname as well), "have you given any more thought to my proposal?"

With a scratchy paper napkin, Merit blotted a glutinous blob of cherry filling off her lip.

"I have, Mr. Paradise, and my answer's still the same. I don't think I'm ready yet."

"Oh, go on," said an old woman sitting next to Merit at the counter. "Nobody's getting any younger, and good husband material is hard to find."

Mr. Paradise laughed at the look of horror that swept across Merit's face.

"I'm not asking her to marry me, madam. I'm merely asking her to sing in public."

"Well," said the old woman, looking Merit up and down, "you *should* marry her. When's a guy like you ever going to find as good-looking a woman as this one?"

"I quite agree with you, madam. However, at this moment in time, we're discussing music. But thank you for your interest in our affairs."

Dismissed, the old woman swiveled her stool

around, turning her back to them.

"But one day you might be ready?" asked Mr. Paradise, picking up the conversational thread that had been yanked out.

"I might," said Merit, and then the two of them, in a delayed reaction to the old lady's comments, burst out laughing.

"Hey," said Merit later that evening, "they're talking about Mr. Paradise."

"Who?" said Reni, who, for her civics class, made a point of watching the news with her mother.

"Shh," said Merit, listening to the news reporter who was describing how Harry Swann, waiting for the bus that would take him to the art museum ("I really wanted to see that Monet exhibition," he said from his hospital bed), suffered a heart attack and was revived by a man with whom he'd earlier been chatting ("We were mostly talking about the weather — isn't that what people at bus stops talk about?").

A paramedic who'd been on the scene was interviewed, saying that everyone should learn CPR so that they could save a life like the Samaritan who'd worked on Mr. Swann: "All we did was continue what this guy had started. It's not a hard procedure, and all you have to do is call the Red Cross to set up a class."

The television reporter thanked the paramedic for the unsolicited Red Cross commercial and, looking earnestly into the camera, said, "And we here at Channel Eight, along with Mr. Harry Swann, whose heart, while battered, is still beating, thank the gentleman who stopped to help a felled citizen and then, seeking no glory of

413

his own, strode off into the noonday sun."

"You know the guy?" asked Reni, staring at her mother, who stared at the TV, her mouth unhinged.

"Yes . . . yes, Mr. Paradise. The man I have coffee with on Thursday afternoons. I've told you about him."

"Mother," scolded Reni, "I'd remember you telling me about having coffee with some guy on Thursday afternoons — especially some guy named *Mr. Paradise.*"

"Mom, when's dinner?" asked Melody, running into the room with her younger sister.

"Yeah, we're hungry," declared Jewel.

Merit turned off the TV.

"Why don't you girls set the table?" she said. "And Reni — how about you make the salad?"

"Mother," said Reni in the way only a fifteen-year-old girl can say it. "You aren't going anywhere until you tell me about this Paradise guy."

"But there's nothing to tell," said Merit, hating that she could feel a blush heat up her face. "Mr. Paradise is a friend of mine — believe me, he's only a friend — and he and I get together on my lunch hour every Thursday to have a cup of coffee and talk."

"Talk," said Reni. "What do you talk about?"

Merit played with her collar. "I don't know. Probably the same things you talk about with your friends."

"Sex?"

Looking at the sly, bet-you-didn't-expect-that look on her daughter's face, Merit smiled.

"Well, usually we talk about things we know something about."

★ ★ ★

The talk was what had made her agree to a second coffee date with Mr. Paradise; she hadn't had such a relaxed conversation with anyone outside the Angry Housewives in years. He was an odd fellow — he had the courtly manners of a 1930s leading man but the scrappy looks of a character actor from '70s B-movies. Sometimes his speech resembled his manners ("I'm half a century young," he said when Merit asked his age); other times he spoke, if not like a gangster, then like a gangster's friend ("I'd like to bust that ex of yours right in the snoot"). He was thin, and even in his polyester flares, Merit could see that he was bowlegged. He wore boots with heels that pushed him close to six feet yet he didn't have a tall man's presence. But the funniest thing about him was the attention he paid to Merit. He listened to her as if she were the ruler of the free world and he a reporter getting an exclusive interview.

"He forgets his own children's birthdays?" he asked during the second coffee date.

Merit nodded solemnly, staring at the girls' school photographs she had laid out for him to see.

"The girls are used to it. That's the problem; they're so used to his bad behavior that they're not even bothered by it anymore. His one great lesson to his daughters is that they shouldn't count on him for anything because he won't deliver."

Mr. Paradise twisted his mouth as he scratched one of his sideburns.

"That, Miss Mayes, is a crying shame."

Merit nodded. "The good news is, he's

moving to Florida — hallelujah — so he won't be around here anymore."

"Good riddance," said Mr. Paradise.

"Exactly. I'm hoping that when he leaves I won't feel so . . . unsafe. I feel at any time he might break into my house and beat me up again . . . or worse."

"Oh, Miss Mayes," said Mr. Paradise, concern pushing down his dark, bristly eyebrows. "We must hustle you girls out of that house posthaste and find a secret location."

Merit laughed. "Oh, I don't really think he's going to do anything crazy — he hasn't yet. It's just that, I don't know, I guess when someone's really hurt you, there always seems to be a possibility for more."

"Have you got an alarm system? If not, let's install one today. I know a —"

Merit laughed. "I don't think you need to worry about it. Really, I'm fine. The girls and I are fine."

Mr. Paradise dipped the tip of his knife in the little plastic jelly packet and spread the orange marmalade on a triangle of toast.

"I can't say as I like your former husband," he said, "and you sure did the right thing by getting out of that . . . mess. Still, I have to feel sorry for a man who hasn't figured out how to love his own family."

"Do you . . . do you have a family?"

Mr. Paradise squinted and a burst of wrinkles fanned out toward his sideburns. "Well, my mother's still alive and I have a sister in Anchorage, of all places, but no, I have never been lucky enough to find the woman who would become my wife and the mother of our children."

His smile was rueful. "I always wanted a little girl. I've had a name picked out for years: Portia. Portia Paradise — can you imagine how a girl could take on the world with a name like that?"

Merit smiled but felt a little sad, missing the girl, Portia Paradise, who was never to be.

"Oops," said Mr. Paradise, looking at his Timex watch. "You'd better be on your way, Miss Mayes, if you don't want to be late for work."

Merit got off the stool as if she were arthritic. "Maybe I'll see you at the library tomorrow?"

Mr. Paradise tucked a dollar bill under his plate. "There aren't any maybes about it."

HOST: **AUDREY**

BOOK: *A Confederacy of Dunces*

by John Kennedy Toole

REASON CHOSEN: "I could relate to

the title."

At one-thirty in the morning, I heard Bryan yell, *"Mom!"* in my ear and scrambled up on the bed, ready to rip into him for waking me out of a dead sleep like that. Only he wasn't there. A gust of wind blew raindrops in through the open window, and I was filled with a cold that had nothing to do with the temperature.

I saw my son lying on the sidewalk in an eerie light so blue that the blood that trickled from the gash above his eye was black. Someone in a dress lay by him, her limbs bent at such odd, horrible angles that she looked like a human swastika. A van, the van that Bryan had gotten into that evening, lay on its side, its front as wrinkled and broken as the cars we saw in the demolition derby the boys had begged me to take them to a few years ago. Someone was walking around the van — it was so hard to see things clearly in that eerie blue light. Someone was walking around moaning, holding his head, and finally I could see it was Jeff, the boy who'd been driving. He was holding his head and his moans got louder and louder and became screams, became wailing, keening screams, and I did not know the screams were mine until Michael burst into my room, swatting the light on and yelling, just as Bryan had yelled, *"Mom!"*

It wasn't long after my terrible vision that I got the call from the hospital.

"Run and get Grant," I said, throwing off my pajamas (superstition had kept me in them; if I didn't get dressed for a trip to the hospital or, God forbid, the morgue, then maybe I wouldn't have to go after all; maybe it was all a terrible dream).

Grant was an insomniac, especially since Stuart, his longtime love, had left him (Grant was truly angry at me for not warning him, but I, like everyone else, had had no prescience of this totally surprising and incomprehensible event), and even if he had been asleep, he was the type of friend who would gladly wake up in the wee hours to help a pal. So were the Angry Housewives, but it was easier waking up one person than a whole household.

Grant had the Lincoln warmed up and purring by the time I finished dressing (a task harder than I'd ever imagine — for the life of me I couldn't figure out how to put on my pants or where my socks went).

"Mom, hurry!" Michael kept saying, which made me get all the more confused and agitated, and as I raced across the lawn to Grant's driveway, unbuttoned clothes trailed after me.

"Oh, God, Grant!" I screamed as I fell into his front seat. "Oh, God, Bryan is —"

"Hennepin County?" he asked, referring to the hospital, and as I was incapable of answering, Michael said yes.

The streets were slick with rain, and I realized that though I had always liked the sound of water splashing off car tires, I could never like it again, because maybe the rainy streets had caused the accident.

In that horribly lit emergency room that made everyone look lost and spooky, like survivors of a nuclear holocaust, we were told that Bryan was now in surgery, that there were multiple injuries. I watched the nurse's mouth move and had the odd sensation that I was falling into it, falling into those awful words.

"You better sit down," said Grant, holding on to me as I swooned. "Michael, can you get your mother some water?"

"Do you need to lie down?" asked the nurse.

I shook my head. Lying down would somehow be a surrender, and that was the last thing I was willing to do.

Paul got to the hospital about a half hour after we did. He and Cynthia and their two-year-old son had moved out to a suburb so new that their backyard faced a cornfield.

"I always thought it would be Davey," I said dully as we took a walk to the coffee machines. "I always thought it would be Davey who'd have the car wreck."

"Oh, Audrey," said Paul sadly.

"Well, didn't you? I mean, he's the reckless one, the one who always gets into trouble —"

"Past tense, Audrey. He hasn't gotten into any trouble lately."

"That we *know* of."

It soothed me, talking about the familiar topic of Davey and his problems while who knows what was happening to his brother. But it was true — after several years of rebellion that veered into criminality (vandalism, driving while under the influence, and a petty theft that got him a month in the workhouse), Davey seemed to be settling down (knock knock *knock* on wood). He was living with his girlfriend and working with a company that customized kitchens. Then again, maybe we weren't hearing from the cops because he was twenty-one now.

"Ouch," I said, coffee splashing on my hand as I took the paper cup out of the little window of the vending machine.

"He should be here soon."

"Davey?" I asked. "You called him?"

"Well, of course I called him, Audrey. Bryan's his brother."

Of course he was; I was ashamed that I hadn't thought to call him myself. But since Davey had graduated from high school (at least he'd managed that), he hadn't been much of a force in his brothers' lives. Bryan and Michael only saw him at holidays, and only the holidays when Davey stood to gain something (Thanksgiving, for dinner, and Christmas, for dinner and gifts).

"Mr. and Mrs. Forrest?" asked a doctor, coming toward us. My insides took a dive. Honestly, I was surprised I could still walk toward her with all my vital organs so displaced.

"He's out of danger," were the first words she spoke, the words that made me want to kiss her face, hug her, lift her up to the ceiling. Instead, I burst into tears.

"He's got a rough road ahead of him," she continued, as if more solemn news would turn off my waterworks. "He's broken his pelvis and his right leg. He'll be in a wheelchair and then on crutches for quite a while, and he'll need a lot of physical therapy."

"Oh, God," I said, both in horror at the severity of injuries and in thanks that I wasn't hearing worse things.

"He punctured a lung, tore his right rotator cuff, and broke a thumb," she said, "but all in all, he's a lucky young man."

"Can we see him?" I asked, and I could feel the wall of tears pushing against the rickety dam of calm I struggled to keep upright.

"He's not quite ready. We have to set his broken bones and put his leg in traction." The doctor looked away; I don't think she could stand the look on my face. "But soon. Soon. We'll let you see him as soon as possible."

Davey had arrived, disheveled and wild-eyed, by the time we got the go-ahead to see Bryan, and he held my hand so tight I almost yelped, but I was not about to tell him to loosen his grip.

I stood there in the hospital room flanked by Paul and Davey and Michael, looking at my middle son, whose first word after *Mama* and *Dada* had been *kiss*.

A pulley held up his leg, which was in an ankle-to-hip cast. He looked almost comic, like the ski-accident victim in movies who's nearly mummified in bandages. Tubes from machines making various noises were threaded into him.

"Bry?" said Davey, his voice cracking.

"I don't think he can hear, honey," I said. "He's sedated."

"Bry, we're here for you, buddy. I know you must be scared, but it's gonna be fine, you're gonna be just fine; we'll be throwing the football around in no time."

My sons had played a lot of football as boys, but Davey hadn't thrown a ball to his brothers in years. Still, I think we all appreciated his words.

Michael, who was truly Bryan's best friend, stood by, mute, his hand cupped around Bryan's right foot, about the only area that wasn't bandaged. And the world kept spinning.

When Bryan woke up, he looked at me and said, as if he were claiming ownership, "My mom."

"Oh, my darling," I said, leaning down to kiss his forehead (next to the bandage), his cheek, his lips.

"I remember calling you," he said.

"I know. I heard. Scared me half to death."

"Am I okay?"

After I gave him the running list of his injuries, he whispered, "Jenny?"

I assured him she was all right; in fact her only injury was a cut along her hairline that required fourteen stitches. Jeff, the boy who'd been driving, the one I'd seen in my dream, had a head injury whose effects would not be more fully known until some time had passed.

"What about Amber?"

Either I paused too long or the look on my face told him everything. The girl I'd seen bent like a swastika was dead.

"Mom, what happened to Amber?"

"Listen, Bryan, why don't you just get a little rest now?"

"Mom, did Amber *die?*"

Not wanting to, I nevertheless nodded, and Bryan's face scrunched up like a baby's the moment before he lets out a wail.

"Amber *died?*" he asked, his voice begging me to recant.

I nodded again as Bryan shook his head.

"She can't. She can't have died. She's the one who said she had to get home or her parents were going to kill her. Guess the car crash beat them to it!" He barked out a terrible, one-syllable laugh that slunk into a low moan.

He dissolved into tears then, and I held him as best I could, considering the casts and pulleys, held my dear, dear boy.

"I knew I'd find you in here," said Grant one evening, sliding onto the polished oak pew.

"Just saying my daily thanks."

I would have choked on the words a couple of years ago, but I had taken Grant up on the invitation he offered on my depressing thirty-seventh birthday and gone to church with him and Stuart the next day.

"So how long have you been going here?" I'd asked as we climbed the narrow stairs to the small church.

"Oh, this is our first time," said Grant.

"We don't have a home church," said Stuart, smiling at the confusion on my face. "We pick out a different church each week to go to."

"So you're not Methodists?" I asked, reading the sign on the lawn.

"As much as we are anything," said Grant. "Wherever we go, we participate in whatever they do. We kneel at the churches that have kneelers, we take communion at the churches that offer it, and we clap hands in the churches that have rowdy choirs."

That this particular minister was young and awfully good-looking made it easier for me to pay attention to him. Unfortunately, his oratorical skills were not much above those of a high school debater who'd gotten knocked out of the semifinals. But the soloist — a woman with gray hair who wore saddle shoes, of all things, under her choir robe — had a beautiful, stirring voice, and afterward the three of us went out for pancakes. So when they invited me the next week, I agreed, and that Sunday morning I listened to a Unitarian minister ruminate about his favorite red sweater. He had a nice way of telling a story (too bad he didn't have the Methodist minister's looks), and afterward we went out for eggs Benedict. The third Sunday we listened to a member of the congregation give a homily about her missionary upbringing and afterward had brunch at a restaurant that served complimentary mimosas. All and all, it wasn't a bad way to spend a Sunday.

I kept going, and as the months passed, something began working on me. Doors were opening, shades were lifted, and lo and behold, a little light began sneaking in. I started feeling for the first time in my life that someone or something — hell, I might as well call it God — cared about me. It wasn't a sudden vision that had me flailing at the preacher's knees (as congregants at one church we visited did) or speaking in tongues (we had yet to find a church where they did that). Rather, it was as if a warm spring day had moved into the spot in my heart that for so long had been held hostage by winter. All bloom seemed possible.

In the chapel, I took Grant's hand and squeezed it.

"Thanks," I whispered. The chapel was empty but still inspired quiet.

"You're welcome," he whispered back. "For what?"

"I was just sitting here thinking how being able to pray helps me, and then I thought how I wouldn't be able to pray if it wasn't for you and Stuart taking me to church all those Sundays ago."

"We just invited you to go," said Grant. "You did all the work." He smiled, but there was a flicker of anxiousness in his eyes.

"What's the matter?"

"Stuart called me today."

"He did?"

Biting his top lip, Grant nodded.

"And?"

"And he wants to meet me for a drink. He says he's sorry about a lot of things."

I studied my friend's face for a moment.

"And what do you think?"

Tears shimmered in his eyes. "Oh, Audrey, I'm on cloud nine, to tell you the truth. But I'm also scared that I'm getting excited about a possible reconciliation when he only wants to tell me he's sorry he took my blue cashmere sweater or my Pierre Cardin cologne."

"And what if he does?" I asked. I was not willing to put anything past Stuart (a man I had liked very much until he ditched Grant).

"I guess I'd just have to deal with it."

"Nothing much else you can do."

"Thanks for the advice," he said with a smirk. "Now I don't have to write Ann Landers."

"Are you sure you want to do this?" asked Slip, the first to arrive for book club.

"Like I said, it'll be a good distraction." I took her plate full of little quiches. "Oh, good, I don't have any hors d'oeuvres. I just had time to run to the bakery and get some cookies."

When I set the quiches down on my woefully bare dining room table, Slip gave me a hug. (When you're five foot ten it's awkward being hugged by someone nearly a foot shorter, but the awkwardness was short-lived, giving way to the general warmth and appreciation one feels for, and in, a hug.)

The Angry Housewives had pulled out the stops in helping me in the three weeks since Bryan's accident. Dinner every night had been provided by one or the other — Kari's hamburger and potato dish earned five stars from the Forrests, as did Merit's lasagna (Reni was doing most of the cooking in the family, and she was *good*). Faith brought over a whole roast turkey with all the trimmings, and Slip brought over crockpots of the barbequed meatballs she brought to neighborhood potlucks, remembering how much the boys liked them. She and Grant also brought practical household things that I had no energy or wherewithal to restock (we'd be wiping ourselves on newspaper and brushing our teeth with dry toothbrushes if it weren't for them) as well as more frivolous items, magazines and bubble bath and chocolate bars, along with advice to "get some time by yourself."

I was able to get plenty. Davey — *Dave* (I vowed I was going to finally honor his request to be called what he wants to be called) came by every day. As soon as he got off work, he drove over and spent the evening with his brother, watching TV (they hooted and hollered at the over-the-top actors on *Dynasty*, and Dave could render Bryan and Michael helpless with laughter as he tried to match steps with the dancers on *Soul Train*), or playing Crazy Eights or poker (penny limit) or Monopoly or Sorry!

"How's Bryan doing with school?" asked Slip.

"The teachers make up a packet for him every week and send it home with Michael. They tell me he's all caught up, and guess what?"

Slip started smiling, probably in response to the big smile that had broken out on my face. "What?"

"He got accepted into USC!"

When the other Angry Housewives arrived, Slip and I were holding on to each other, doing the same excited, clasp-arms-and-hop-up-and-down dance we'd done when she told me two years ago that Flannery had gotten accepted into Yale.

"So where is the college boy?" asked Kari. "I want to congratulate him."

"He's at his dad's. Michael too. They'll be there a couple days; Paul thought I needed a break."

"That was nice of him," said Merit.

I nodded. "Cynthia's made a new man out of him."

Our meeting turned out to be a cry-fest.

"What gets me," said Kari, the first of us to

lose it, "is that it's such a story of a mother's love. She would not let her son's words die with him."

We were talking about how the author had killed himself and how his mother pushed and prodded and finally got someone interested in the manuscript — Walker Percy, no less.

"I just think," said Kari, and this is where the tears started spilling, "that mother love can do just about anything." She took a deep breath. "I am just so honored to be a mother — and so privileged!"

"Here," I said, passing her a Kleenex box. (Since Bryan's accident they were as regular a fixture on every end table as ashtrays.)

"Was he upset because he couldn't get published?" asked Merit. "Is that why he killed himself?"

"It might have been a contributing factor," said Slip. "But I'm sure there are a few writers out there who can't get published and still manage not to kill themselves." She stared at her hand, wrapped around the stem of a wineglass. "Flan read this book, and after she heard what happened to the writer, she asked me if I'd do the same thing for her Great American Novel — which, you'll be happy to hear, she's written thirteen pages of."

"Really?" said Merit. "Oh, that's so exciting. What's it about?"

"Flan's only willing to tell me the page count, nothing else. And I said to her, 'I would if I believed in your work, which naturally I'm going to do, because I believe in you.' " Now Slip was tearing up. "Then I said, 'But don't you *ever* put me in the position Mr. Toole's mother found herself in.' "

Kari passed the Kleenex box to Slip.

"She laughed and said, 'Mom, I am the most mentally healthy person I or my twelve other personalities have ever met.' "

We laughed then: some relief from this scary talk of children's suicides.

Slip blew her nose. "The thing is, she's right. Flan's always been Flan and perfectly happy to be so. I felt the day she was born that this little baby knew exactly who she was and what she wanted from the world."

"That's a gift," said Merit.

"Bonnie read the book too," said Faith. "I think it's great that even though Flan's away at school, they're still keeping up their version of Angry Housewives."

It *is* wonderful, when you think about it — the book club that Bonnie and Julia plotted in Kari's basement when they were little is still going all these years later. A shift in the power structure occurred after the second or third meeting, with Flannery stepping in as co-leader along with Bonnie.

"It's not exactly a democratic group," Kari had told me long ago. "Julia says nobody gets to pick the books or lead the meetings but Flannery and Bonnie."

Lesson: bossy girls might be a pain, but they get what they want.

"Wouldn't that be something if she really becomes a writer?" asked Merit.

"It's what she's wanted to be ever since she was little," said Slip.

"Imagine discussing her book at book club!" said Kari. Her blue eyes misted over again. "Can you believe this? Yesterday our kids were babies getting rocked during our meetings, and now they're grown-up, or close to it. Julia's going to be sweet sixteen!"

Faith nodded. "The twins are graduating from high school next year."

"And Joe and Bryan this year," said Slip, and then she started as if she'd been tapped on the shoulder. "Hey, Audrey, I just realized: you haven't lit up once tonight."

"I quit," I said, feeling shy. "I finally decided to get aboard the non-smoking train. Although right now I am *dying* for a cigarette."

"So what finally did it for you?" asked Slip. "The hacking cough? The stinky clothes? The wheeze whenever you took a deep breath?"

I smiled, but words were having a hard time gathering themselves in my throat, seeing as a huge lump had lodged itself there.

"It was Bryan," I said finally. "He told me that Jeff — that's his friend who was driving — was lighting his and his girlfriend's cigarette when he lost control of the car. And I thought, *I can't smoke anymore. I can't do something that's responsible for my son's accident.*" I looked at my hands; they seemed big and awkward without a cigarette jammed between my fingers. "The boys are thrilled." I felt a tear dribble down my cheek.

"I'll bet," said Faith. "Although doesn't Dave smoke?"

I nodded, weary. "I'm hoping he'll grow out of it."

"I see him at your house practically every evening," said Kari. "That must be a big comfort to you."

"It is." A tear decided to keep the one on the other cheek company. "He's like a changed boy

. . . uh, man. Although I was dumb enough to ask him why he was being so attentive to Bryan."

"And?" asked Slip.

"And he got mad at me, like he always does. But after he'd huffed and puffed and muttered about asking stupid questions, he came into the kitchen — I've been spending a lot of time in the kitchen if you haven't noticed; I think I've put on ten pounds since Bryan's accident — and said, looking me right in the eye, which is very unusual for Dave, 'Mom, I'm only doing for Bryan what he'd do for me in the same situation.' Then he grabbed a doughnut from the box I had in front of me and left. And I realized he's not a lost cause after all."

"Oh, Audrey," said Kari. "You never really thought that."

Miserable, I nodded. "I hate to admit it, but I did. I mean, I was happy that he was at least gainfully employed and had a girlfriend who didn't have track marks running up her arm, but I thought as far as his being a loving, caring part of my family . . . well, that *was* a lost cause."

No one spoke for a moment.

"It's just such a crapshoot," I said. "I don't think I'd ever win a mother-of-the-year award — I admit I let my boys run a little wild — but still, how can one son get into trouble over and over and another one get accepted into USC with an academic scholarship? These kids are like vessels you pour your love into. And some of those vessels are big and strong and happy to hold all the love you want to pour in, and others have cracks in them and the love isn't worth much because it all leaks out. I used to think love could save anything, but it can't if the vessel's cracked."

Everything seemed to tumble down on top of me: Bryan's accident, Dave's return to the fold, the poor Toole guy who could create such a big, funny world and still take himself out of the one he lived in. I put my head in my hands and sobbed, cried, and wailed. My friends didn't try to stop me. Instead, to the accompaniment of soothing voices, my back was patted, my shoulders rubbed. When I was all cried out, I took my hands away from my face and smiled a weak smile.

"Thanks. I needed that."

Slip refilled the wineglasses. "You know what you were saying about kids being like vessels? Well, cracked ones can be repaired, Audrey. I think that's what's happening to Dave."

"Oh, God, I hope so."

"I think Kari's right about mother love," said Merit softly. "About it being so strong. But when you think of it . . . we haven't been using it to our best advantage."

"What do you mean?" asked Faith.

Merit dabbed at her eyes with her ring finger and then prodded the dimple in her chin. "I mean," she began, then thought for a moment. "I mean we should figure out a way to marshal it somehow. What mother can stand to see her son go to war?"

"Oh, God," said Slip, "When I think of my own boys going to war like my brother did — God, I almost get sick."

Goose bumps rose on my arm. "Can you imagine if Vietnam were still going on?"

Merit nodded. "So why haven't mothers gotten together — mothers from all over the world — to stop wars? Why do we put up with it?"

None of us had an answer for that.

"I just get so frustrated," Merit went on, and her little dimpled chin started quivering. "I'm terrified for my girls because of all the murderers and rapists out there in the world, yet I haven't done a single thing to get them off the streets. Why don't I? Why don't *we* stop rapists and murderers? There're plenty of mothers — we could be bigger than the FBI, the CIA, all the police forces in the world. Why aren't we organized?"

"Why don't you get on that?" said Faith. "Why don't you let that be your pet project?"

"You don't have to be so snide, Faith," I said. "I think what Merit's saying is right on. Mothers united would be a powerful force."

"As if it could ever happen," said Faith.

"Have you got any better ideas?" asked Slip.

"Better ideas with regard to what?" Faith's cheeks were flushed, her eyes bright. "Of course murderers and rapists should be stopped, but I sure don't think they're going to be stopped by a bunch of mothers."

"I know it sounds kind of silly," said Merit. "It was just something I'd been thinking about."

"Hey, don't apologize," said Slip, glaring at Faith. "You're not the one in the wrong."

"What're you picking on me for?"

"I guess I'm just a little fed up with your negativity."

"My negativity?" said Faith. "So I happen to think a union of mothers is —"

"It's not just that," said Slip. "You find all sorts of things to be negative about lately."

Faith's mouth opened, and after a few seconds it shut again. She got up and walked to the closet to get her raincoat.

"Faith," said Slip with apology in her voice, but Faith was deaf to it.

"Good night," she said to the rest of us and then before she opened the door to leave, she burst into tears.

That made it unanimous.

June 1985

Dear Mama,

Even though I have lived over half my life as the new Faith, it's always been a battle keeping the old Faith pushed down and out of sight. Lately I feel like a kettle that's ready to blow its top, feel like I'm the stuff in a witch's cauldron, boiling, bubbling, churning, steaming.

Tonight my babies graduated from high school, Mama! My babies who just yesterday learned all the words to "I'm a Little Teapot" and wouldn't stop singing it; my babies who just yesterday held my hands as I walked them to kindergarten!

I cried as soon as the procession started — I'll bet the composer of "Pomp and Circumstance" was a sadist whose intention in writing that piece was to make people cry. I think Wade was tearing up too, although since he got that permanent (men getting permanents — what's the world coming to?) I can barely stand to look at him to see what he's doing.

Bonnie marched around the football field like she was the queen of the Nile entertaining her subjects, but Beau searched the stands until he found us and then waved like he'd just gotten back from war.

I tried to listen to the commencement

speaker, but I was screaming inside, *They don't care about your advice — they're young! Tell me something that'll help me cope with my babies growing up and leaving me!*

Mama, I was so proud when I found out they were twins. I had pulled off something really special. In the doctor's waiting room I used to look at all the other pregnant women and think, "I'm not just having one, ladies, I'm having *two*." And then when they were born and they turned out to be a boy and a girl, that really sent me to the moon. I mean, any old egg can split and make identical twins; *two* of my eggs had been fertilized.

And, Mama, I raised them right. I poured all my energy into being not like you (no offense). I was there to sing to them and read them stories and help bury their goldfish at sea (flush) and make them pancakes shaped like bears (Bonnie's choice) and ducks (Beau's). I was there to make dozens of snowmen with them and color in dozens of coloring books, and too many times to count, I pretended I was the customer when they played store or school or airplane.

When they got a little older, I bought them the same kind of clothes all the other kids were wearing, sat with them while they did their homework (well, sat with Beau; Bonnie liked to do hers alone in her room), and made hot chocolate and toast for them when they wanted to talk.

How I loved those times at the kitchen counter, Mama, when Bonnie would tell me why she liked a certain boy and, even though she knew he had a girlfriend, "he'll like me because I'm so much more interesting than Molly Dodge!" and Beau would tell me what it felt like when he was on the high bars whirling around — "Like a cat, Mama. Not like someone's pet, but like a big cat — a lion or a tiger or a cougar when they're running really fast and all of a sudden they make a jump through the air and all their muscles are straining and pulling and they feel so powerful."

Mama, I was there to make them dinner every night and make sure they had clean sheets and that they wore their retainers.

I did a good job, Mama. Beau even wrote in this year's Mother's Day card, "I couldn't imagine a better mother." Can you believe it? I spent my entire childhood imagining a better mother!

A memory jumps into my head — I was twelve years old, and after hearing snotty Tayla Gordon brag at school how she and her mother were going out for tea at the Fordham Hotel on Mother's Day, I thought, *I'm gonna take my mama to tea too!* I labored for hours making a fancy invitation, and when I gave it to you you laughed and said, "My land, I've never been to a tea before. I feel just like Queen Elizabeth!"

I bought all the ingredients I needed with money I'd made from cashing in bottles and baby-sitting and spent all morning baking a spice cake and making fancy little sandwiches whose recipe I found in the Betty Crocker cookbook I checked out of the library. I picked a bunch of lilacs and set the table with place mats I'd made out of construction paper in the shape of daisies. I was so excited sitting at that table waiting for you, but then three o'clock rolled around, and then three-thirty, and then four o'clock, and by the time it was five, I was resigned that you weren't going to show up, and I ate my cucumber and tomato sandwiches and sliced myself a piece of cake. By the time you stumbled in after midnight, crying, "Oh, baby, I forgot all about our little date," I had hardened my heart to a little stone.

"Faithy, please forgive me," you said, flopping down on my bed, your breath a stink of beer and smoke. "See, I remembered, but then I got —"

"Don't even bother," I said, holding my hand up. "I don't need to hear your excuses. Happy Mother's Day."

The scorn in my voice made the words sound as if I were wishing you anything but, and your face fell, and I liked that it did.

Any tea party my kids invited me to, any athletic meet, any spelling bee, you can bet I showed up.

And today Beau and Bonnie marched past me in their blue gowns on the way to somewhere I won't be going to. What'll I do, Mama? I have spent eighteen years perfecting the role of mother, and now the whole play's changed and I've gone from the lead actor to making the occasional cameo. So who am I supposed to be now?

I'm sorry,
Faith

HOST: **SLIP**

BOOK: *Out on a Limb* by Shirley MacLaine

REASON CHOSEN: "I got it for a dollar at

a garage sale."

"Slip," my brother Fred said over the phone, "I've decided I'm going on a peace march."

"Good for you," I said. I had heard any number of plans and schemes (most of them lame-brained and cockamamie) from my brother in the collect calls he made to me every month or so, and I had often toyed with the idea of telling the operator, "No, I don't accept the charges," because inevitably the phone calls would exhaust or depress me.

Fred had stayed in Detroit, working whatever job he could hang on to between his drinking jags. But Lady Luck had the grace to pay a visit to my brother, in the guise of another veteran who happened to be working in the same restaurant at which Fred bused tables. This man led him into an AA group composed almost entirely of veterans, and for Fred, it was a lifeline he could finally grab on to. The phone calls began to be more hopeful; I began to hear the old Fred more and more, and I began to think: *Maybe my brother* did *survive Vietnam.*

"What kind of peace march is it?" I asked.

"It's for global nuclear disarmament."

"I'm all for that. Where is it?"

"Well, it starts in L.A. and it ends in Washington, D.C."

The phone receiver slipped from its perch under my chin.

"Come again?"

Fred laughed, a dear laugh with no traces of hysteria. "From L.A. to Washington, D.C. They think it'll take about nine months."

"Nine months?" I said, envisioning the pull-down map in my seventh-grade geography class and its multicolored span of states. "You're going to walk from L.A. to Washington, D.C., in nine months?"

Fred laughed again. "Yup. I'm going to follow the example my sister has set for me lo these many years and become, and I quote, 'an active participant for change.'"

We kept track of his route on a map pinned to the kitchen bulletin board, and when the red line cut into Iowa, I called Jerry, who was in Seattle for a week teaching a seminar.

"Jerry, I'm thinking of putting a couple days' mileage in on that peace march."

"Sounds good," said my husband, who'd support me if I told him I was joining the Hare Krishnas. "Don't forget the mosquito repellent."

The look on my brother Fred's face when he saw me walking through a field of tents was the same one he'd worn when he'd won the city spelling bee in the seventh grade, and I told him so.

He laughed, his arms still around me in a hug. "That was such a fluke victory — I got all the easy words. I didn't know how to spell *any* of the words my opponents got." He hugged me again. "So how long are you here for?"

"Just a couple days. Jerry's away at a seminar, and Gil's in the Boundary Waters for a month."

Fred hugged me a third time. "God, I am so happy to see you, Slip. Let me show you around."

In less than a half hour I'd been introduced to at least twenty people and toured the day care and school buses, the mail truck, the food prep truck, and the porta-potties.

I was impressed. "It's a movable city."

"*Peace* City," said Fred. "We've even got a mayor."

After being served dinner (watery chili and a salad) by a sunburned crew from the food truck, Fred and I sat on a hill by his tent in the velvety summer night air, listening to two guitarists play dueling Dylan. The country sky was throwing the kind of party it can't in the city; stars from all over showed up, and not one a wallflower.

"I could get used to this," I said.

"It's not a bad life," said Fred. "Except for the damn chiggers." He scratched his leg. "And it beats a picket line around City Hall."

"So how do you think it's doing? It's not getting much press."

"You know how it goes, Slip — things move inch by inch, step by step. You just hope you're heading in the right direction."

At dawn, a group of singers strolled around the camp, imploring everyone to wake up.

"Oof, I'm stiff," I said, sitting up and rubbing my lower back. "Thanks for giving me the side of the tent that was on top of *granite*, Fred."

"Quit your bitchin' and get dressed. You roll

up the sleeping bags and I'll take the tent down. Then we'll load everything up on the gear truck."

"When's room service?" I whined.

"After the hour massage and facial," said Fred. "Now move your butt, private."

It was a fine sunny day with cows ambling over to watch the parade that was happening beyond their fences, and I exchanged greetings with teenagers Fred introduced me to as Serenity and Zeus.

"Don't you wish Ma and the old man had used a little more imagination when it came to our names?" Fred asked after they'd passed. "Although Slip's pretty imaginative, as far as nicknames go."

"And don't forget our Indian names," I said. "We were the only kids I knew who had Indian names."

"Except for Indians," said Fred.

"Yeah, but we didn't know any, Laughing Spaniel."

Fred had shaved his red cloud of a beard off, allowing his smile to be fully seen. It was the kind of smile that made you want to smile back at it, and I did. A middle-aged woman said hello, her head bobbing to music from her headphones. Fred explained the march would group together when entering into big cities but often was stretched out so far that you could walk with a distance of a city block or two between you and the next marcher.

"I was so scared I was never going to see Laughing Spaniel again."

"Me too," said Fred. "But he's back. Sometimes he doesn't stay very long, but I don't worry that I'll never see him again."

"Keep it moving, Fred," said a white-haired man as he sidled up next to us. "If we all moved like you, we'd never get anywhere."

"Aw, shut up, old man," said Fred, and for a second I was ready to jump in and apologize for my horribly rude brother, but then Fred's smile broke out. "Slip, meet Stan. Stan, this is my sister, Slip."

"Pleased to meet you," said Stan, tapping the brim of his visor. "Any sister of Fred's is a friend of mine."

"You want to walk with us a ways?" asked Fred.

"Let me take a rain check," said Stan. "I'm trying to catch up to that cute gal from New Zealand."

He power-walked ahead of us, as bowlegged as a cowboy.

"What's he do in real life?" I asked, "ride the range?"

"He broke both his legs in World War II," said Fred. "He was a POW on Bataan."

"Good heavens," I whispered.

"I love to walk with him and I hate to walk with him," said Fred. "Because when you walk all day with someone, they tell you their stories, and believe me, his stories are as bad as mine." He shook his head. "And his was supposed to be the *good* war."

The sun was high in the Iowa sky, but I felt as though a cloud had passed over.

"Then why do you love to walk with him?" I asked.

"The same reason I love doing the work I do," said Fred, taking my hand. "Because I know how much I can help someone by listening to him, just like I know how much being listened to has helped me."

"Will you go back to counseling when you're done with the march?"

"Yeah. It's really saved my life, Slip. Isn't that funny? Only by trying to help someone else save their life could I save my own. I'm just so grateful I figured it out. I know a lot of people who didn't."

A pickup truck sped by and a shirtless man in the back cab yelled, "Get a job!"

Fred gave him the peace sign.

"Fuck you!"

Fred laughed. "There's something about the peace sign that seems to bring out aggression in certain people."

"Yeah," said a marcher who was passing us. "Like macho jerks and world leaders."

She put down her book to add, "One and the same."

"How can she read while she walks?" I asked. "Look at all the scenery she's missing."

"True," said Fred, scanning the tasseled greenery that rose from each side of the road. "But it's not like this is the first cornfield we've walked by, Slip. Remember, we already walked through the whole state of Nebraska." He squinted, watching the woman ahead of us. "Speaking of books, Slip, how're the Angry Housewives doing?"

"Great," I said. "We just read *Out on a Limb* by Shirley MacLaine, and after we took a vote as to whether or not we believed in reincarnation — the vote was four to one, by the way, with only Faith dissenting — Audrey told me I probably had a past life as a robber baron, screwing the people blind, which would explain why I was such a guilt-ridden proletarian now. Then I told her she was probably Caligula . . . or maybe Machiavelli."

Fred laughed. "So what do you guys say to insult one another?"

"That's the beauty of our friendship, I guess. We *can* insult one another. Although Faith got pretty mad when I said she could have been Houdini, the master of illusion."

"What did you mean by that?"

"Well, according to Faith, more than I had intended. Really, I thought I was flattering her. I mean, you should see her house — it's gorgeous. She thinks of colors and fabrics no one else would ever use and it looks great, and she whips together these book club meetings with inspired themes. Anyway, she got all huffy and asked if I was calling her a big phony, and I said of course not, and then all of a sudden she's out the door."

"Guess you touched some kind of nerve."

"I know, but I can't imagine what. There *is* an element of reserve about Faith, but I don't know . . . maybe you don't talk about your problems when you don't really have any."

"Maybe," said Fred. "Or maybe she *is* hiding something. Maybe she's a nymphomaniac with a raging mescaline habit."

I laughed. "Nymphomania's *Audrey's* thing. But mescaline? Hmmm. Could be. I did see her digging up a bunch of mushrooms last spring. . . ."

We had already eaten the packed lunch (peanut butter sandwiches on brown bread as dense as insulation, and a vegetable called a jicama that tasted like a cross between an apple and a potato), but when we reached town, we decided to stop in the café for a little dessert.

"Fuckin' peacenik."

The words were like a semaphore, stopping me in my tracks.

"What'd you say?" I asked the two men who stood leaning against the wall of an establishment whose sign read Fast and Lu's Tavern.

"Leave it alone, Slip," advised Fred out of the side of his mouth.

"No, I don't think I will." I regarded the skinny, balding man closest to me. "Did you just call me a 'fuckin' peacenik'?"

"No, man, he did." He jerked his head toward his friend, who had about fifty pounds on him and twice the hair.

I gave him a pleasant smile. "Why would you say such a thing?"

"Slip, let's go get that pie." Fred nodded at the men. "Good day, gentlemen."

"No, really," I persisted. "Do you think you're insulting me by calling me a peacenik?"

The burly guy sneered. "Hell, yeah."

"So you don't believe in peace?"

"He don't give a shit about peace," said the skinny guy, "unless it's a piece of ass."

"That's *funny*," I said.

The burly guy sneered again. Maybe it was his only expression.

"I don't believe in peace, and I don't believe in hippies and draft dodgers like you."

Fred stepped forward. "Did you serve in 'Nam?"

"Sure did and I got a fuckin' Purple Heart to prove it."

"Me too, man," said Fred and suddenly the burly guy was all over my brother, patting his shoulder and asking if he could buy him a drink.

"Slip?" asked Fred, but I shook my head. "I'll just go get some coffee at the café. I'll meet you in — say an hour?"

Exactly an hour later, after I had enjoyed my coffee and a piece of the best banana cream pie I'd ever eaten and was sitting on a bench outside the café, Fred sat next to me.

"How'd it go?" I asked.

"Well, the first thing he said was, 'Is that tiny little spitfire always so ready to pick a fight?' "

"Tiny little spitfire," I muttered.

"And I said, 'Yeah, she pretty much always is.' " Fred smiled, but it was the kind of smile that had more sadness than joy in it. "Guy had *two* tours there. He's pretty messed up."

"You mean you didn't recruit him to join the march? Fred, what's happened to your powers of persuasion?"

A couple marchers approached, asking if the food in the café was good.

"Try the pie," I said. "The pie's out of this world."

I turned back to my brother.

"Fred! What's the matter?"

He was sitting with his arms crossed, chin tucked into his chest in the I'm-ready-to-cry pose he'd had since he was a child.

"Steve — that's his name," he said, his head shaking back and forth. "Man, the guy's been through the wringer. Can't hold a job, been married and divorced twice, and says that every day when he wakes up he wonders if this is the day he's gonna lose it and go completely nuts.

" 'How've *you* held it together?' he asked me, and I told him it was only recently that I had.

" 'And you know what's really helping me?' I said, and he looked at me all eager like I was about to give him the secret answer to all his problems.

" 'What? What is it?' he said, and I said, 'Well, war didn't work for me, so now — just like the Beatles song — I'm trying to give peace a chance. Maybe it'd help you too.' "

Fred impatiently wiped a tear that leaked out of the corner of his eye.

"You should have seen the look that swept across his face, Slip. Saddest look I've ever seen.

" 'I couldn't do that,' he said. 'It would make everything else I did seem . . . pointless.' "

Fred expelled a blast of air.

"Isn't that sad, Slip? I mean, I know it's not so simple, but wouldn't you think that if you were in a trap, rather than gnawing off your foot, you just might reach for *any* key?"

I looked up at my little brother, and all I could think of to say was "I love you, Fred."

"Right back at you, sis."

For a long time we sat shoulder to shoulder on that bench, letting that summer sun warm our freckled faces as we watched those around us going about their business — townspeople mailing their letters and buying their groceries and making their bank deposits, and peace marchers saving the world.

July 1986

Dear Mama,

I am coming apart at the seams. Really, it's as if my sanity's been basted up in a lumpy

448

package and now it's pressing against those wide stitches, ready to pop out.

Slip came back after visiting her brother on a peace march, and I asked her what good was possibly going to come from a bunch of old hippies walking across the country.

"Faith," she said, "what's really bothering you?"

"What do you mean?" I asked, feeling all panicky.

"Well, you act like everything's so pointless lately. I was really excited to see Fred — I'm so proud of him — and the first thing I hear out of your mouth is something snide."

"I was just kidding," I said, my words all blustery.

"Ohhh," said Slip. "In that case — ha ha ha."

And now Wade's asking me all the time, "What's wrong, Faith?" but how can I ever tell him? How can I tell him that I've told so many lies that I don't know what's truth and what's not anymore? That I feel as unreal as a mannequin, as fake as brass pretending to be gold? And the more fake I feel, the meaner I get, Mama — I can't stand all these real people who feel safe enough to be themselves!

My insides are always churning, and the only reassurance that I'm not going to blow up is that they've churned plenty and I haven't exploded yet. But I'm getting worse and worse at pretending I'm fine, worse and worse at keeping this TNT inside me unlit.

I'm sorry,
Faith

HOST: MERIT

BOOK: *The Accidental Tourist* by Anne Tyler

REASON CHOSEN: "I like the title — it

---

seems we're all accidental tourists at some

---

point in our lives."

"I don't think I can go on, Frank," she said as she sat in the tiny room that served as both a dressing room and a storage closet for cleaning supplies.

"It's just a bit of stage fright," counseled Mr. Paradise, who sat in a folding chair next to a mop and bucket. "All the big stars have it."

Merit looked into the streaky mirror, trying to steady her hand so that her lipstick might reach somewhere in the vicinity of its target.

"You're going to be wonderful," said Frank.

"Thank you," said Merit, squeezing the fine-boned hand that rested on her shoulder. She wasn't convinced she believed him, but she appreciated his absolute sincerity.

In fact, she was convinced that he was about the most sincere man she had ever met, as well as the kindest, and their friendship had turned into courtship, which had turned into love. Liking the name, the Angry Housewives and Merit's children still called him Mr. Paradise, and Frank's friends called her Miss Mayes, and even the couple, although they most often called each other by their first names (or "darling" or "sweetheart" or "precious") hadn't shed their formal mode of address entirely.

Merit's girls loved him. The man played endless games of Frisbee with Jewel and practiced the waltz and two-step with Melody before she went to her first formal dance. Reni, who had pretty much relieved Merit of the burden of cooking, loved inviting him for dinner because his pleasure at eating the food she cooked was so unabashed.

"Not only does he talk to us," the girls told their mother, "he actually listens!"

He even went so far as to take their sartorial advice, investing in a few sport coats and a pair of loafers, although he couldn't completely be weaned away from his leisure suits and white patent leather shoes.

Ears are the true erogenous zones, Merit thought; nothing made her feel more loved and cherished than the full attention Frank gave to what she had to say. She listened to him as well, although now, as she powdered her nose for the third time, she wished she had tuned him out when he first brought up the idea of her playing for an audience.

"I'm not the piano bar type!" she had told Frank when he broached the subject of playing at Claudio's, one of several lounges in town he had a financial stake in.

"There is no piano bar *type*," said Frank. "There's Claudio himself, Mr. Love Song, who plays even though his arthritis is killing him because he can't bear to be away from the ladies, and there's Madge, who's happiest when she can sing something sad. Then there's Lulu, the jokester down at Jake's, and Meyer at the Tiki Room, who thinks he has to give people the history of every song they request, and —"

"Okay, okay," said Merit. "What I meant is that all of them aren't terrified of sitting in front of people and singing and playing!"

Frank shrugged. "And by the time you play your first chord, you won't be either. You'll be making music and making people happy all at the same time. Yikes, Merit, do you realize how many people wish they could have that experience?"

So Merit had let Frank take her down to Claudio's, had let herself play a few pieces for the man whose swoop of silver hair was like a wave frozen in full crest (in the dressing room, industrial-size cans of hair spray shared shelf space with cans of Comet) and whose black silk shirt was half unbuttoned, better to display several gold chains resting on a mat of crinkly silver chest hair.

But Claudio Renatti's ostentatiousness was limited to his dress. His personality was as open and enthusiastic as a child's, and upon meeting Merit, he grasped her hands with his stiff, knobby ones and said, "My Thursday night pianist just gave notice, and if that's not a sign that you should be playing here, I don't know what is!"

Thinking she needed a gimmick, she'd practiced songs that had something celestial in the title: "Moon River," "Fly Me to the Moon," "Stars and Stripes Forever," "Sunrise, Sunset."

452

"Girls," she'd call from the piano, "help me out — what other songs have moon or sun or stars in them?"

"Mom, make it easy on yourself," Reni counseled. "Play songs you like."

"They probably just want you to play requests anyway," said Melody.

"Requests," said Merit, looking stricken. "I forgot all about requests."

"Mr. Paradise says that's mostly what they play in piano bars," said Jewel, nodding.

"What if I don't know how to play them?"

"Mom, you know how to play by ear just as well as I do," said Melody.

The look Merit gave Melody told her what they both knew: Melody was the superior piano player, whether reading music or playing it by ear.

"We'll help you," said Reni, sitting next to her mother on the piano bench. "Come on, you guys, let's request songs for Mom."

"Okay! How about 'Happy Birthday'?"

"Jewel," scolded Reni as Merit launched into the song, "we're supposed to be testing her."

"I'll bet a lot of people request 'Happy Birthday,' " said Jewel, sitting on the other side of her mother.

"That's not the point," said Melody. "Okay, let's see . . . how about 'Alison' by Elvis Costello?"

Merit sat frozen at the keyboard. " 'Alison'? I've never heard of it."

"Then you ask the person who's requesting the song to sing it," advised Melody. "And then you just chord along with it."

"Good idea," said Reni.

Standing behind her mother, Melody started

singing the song, and after a moment, Merit began to play chords.

"That's it, Mom," encouraged Jewel. "That sounds *great*."

Merit knew that "great" was beyond overstatement and asked, "Give me another one."

"Um, 'Time After Time,' by Cyndi Lauper," said Jewel, and was rewarded by a nod from her sisters.

"I'm sorry," said Merit. "I don't know that song, but if you sing it, I'll try to chord along."

"Very good, Mother," said Reni. "Only say it as a fact, not an apology."

Merit smiled — what would she do without the advice of her girls? She raised her hands to the keyboard, but when the girls started singing, she was reluctant to start playing, so lovely were their voices and the automatic harmony Melody took whenever singing with anyone.

"Mom, come on," said Jewel, giving her mother a nudge, and Merit began to play, thinking there were many delights to this world, and accompanying her singing daughters, who were pressed against her on the piano bench, was one of them.

Now, having finally put her lipstick on in its proper place and patted her huge waterfall of hair (her girls had fixed it and somehow with the blow dryer and curler iron had gotten it to about four times its normal volume) Merit looked in the mirror at Frank standing behind her and said, "Well, I guess it's show time."

"It's times like this I could really use a cigarette," said Audrey, dipping a piece of breaded shrimp in cocktail sauce.

She and Slip and Kari sat in a booth upholstered in a slippery gold vinyl, nursing gaudy drinks whose swizzle sticks were kabobs of pineapple and maraschino cherries.

"I know," said Kari. "I haven't felt this nervous since I watched Julia's debate team in the city finals."

"At least the crowd looks friendly," said Slip, looking at the people seated around the piano.

"Friendly but *old*," said Audrey. "I can imagine the requests she's going to get — 'Tea for Two,' 'Sweet Adeline.' "

" 'Good Night, Irene,' " said Slip.

" 'By the Light of the Silvery Moon,' " said Kari. "Well, at least that would fit in with her celestial theme. Say, look — that woman over there looks like an older version of Faith."

"She does," agreed Slip. "Although Faith would never wear her hair like that, even when she's eighty."

Faith had been invited to attend Merit's debut, but lately she always seemed to have other plans whenever the Angry Housewives got together outside of book club.

"Here comes Mr. Paradise!" said Audrey.

When they had first met the new man in Merit's life, they were not particularly overwhelmed.

"He dresses like the kind of guy who takes a business meeting in an RV park," Audrey told Slip.

"He looks like the kind of bad guys they have on *Starsky and Hutch*," Slip told Kari.

"He reminds me of a farmhand we once had," Kari told Faith, "and every Saturday night before he'd go to town, he'd dress up in a plaid shirt and comb his hair with rosewater."

"You said the pickings out there were slim," Faith said to Audrey, "but I didn't know they were that slim!"

But now, as the three women watched the rangy man in the pale blue leisure suit lope toward the piano, they all thought how lucky Merit was to find such a kind and gentle man who so obviously thought the world of her.

Flashing his gold-highlighted smile, Mr. Paradise waved his crossed fingers at them before sitting in the seat saved for him by Claudio, who had come to support his new employee.

The piano bar owner now stood, resplendent in his gold chains and silver hair, and addressed the crowd, the older women looking at him with the same longing teenage girls direct at the school hunks.

"Ladies and germs — and you are, ya big mugs — it is my great pleasure to bring to the piano a beautiful young lady who'll tickle all of you as she tickles the ivories. Let's have a hand for . . . Miss Merit Mayes!"

"Hey, she's using her maiden name," said Slip as the Angry Housewives clapped heartily and Audrey stuck her long-nailed pinkies into her mouth and whistled.

From the back of the room, Merit approached the piano, the skirt of her long gown swishing, and people sat up straighter, their drinks held midway between the table and their mouths, surprised and somehow honored by her beauty.

"God, look at her," said Audrey, finishing off the last of the breaded shrimp. "She looks like she's about twenty-five."

All of the Angry Housewives were now in their

forties except for Kari, whose forties were getting to be an ever-distant memory.

"I love her hair," said Slip, unconsciously patting down her own wild red mane.

"Reni and Melody did it," said Kari. "They told Julia they wanted her to look like Miss America."

"Hello," said Merit, arranging her skirt as she sat at the piano. "As Mr. Renatti said, I'm Merit, and I'm absolutely thrilled to be here. Absolutely terrified too."

The crowd laughed, and a few people offered words of encouragement, including Audrey, who yelled out, "We're in your hands, Merit."

Merit smiled. "Then how will I be able to play?"

The crowd laughed again.

"I knew she knew how to sing and play the piano," said Slip, "but I didn't know she knew how to *banter*."

"This song," said Merit, playing a few chords, "is for all of you."

She proceeded to sing "You Are My Sunshine," followed by "You Are the Sunshine of My Life," followed by "Starry Starry Night." Each song earned a burst of applause.

"See, I thought I needed a gimmick," said Merit. "My daughters told me it was hokey, but I thought, there's nothing wrong with songs about the skies."

"Especially when an angel's singing them," offered an old gentleman, holding up his martini glass.

"Then, sir, this one's for you," said Merit, launching into "I Only Have Eyes for You." (Merit didn't care if the title didn't have any ce-

457

lestial words in it, as long as the lyrics did.)

Sitting on that tufted vinyl piano bench, Merit found that the rapid heartbeat, the clammy hands, and the slight nausea all but disappeared, and she was beyond happy. She was herself — thoroughly and fully Merit Mayes, the girl she had been before her band teacher lunged at her, before her looks got in the way of how people perceived her, before she married Eric, the man whose goal was to take away as much of her as he could.

As she breathed in the potpourri of fried appetizers, perfumes and colognes, cigarette smoke, and liquor and heard herself singing about the stars being out, she winked at Frank, whose face lived up to his name. If ever there was a man who could offer her paradise, it was he.

September 1986

Dear Mama,

I just got off the phone with Wade — he's on a layover in Hawaii, and I needed to tell him about his mama. Dex called me tonight. For a long time they've been trying to believe that Patsy's forgetfulness was only that, that her little blank-outs were just the result of being overtired, but after seeing the doctor, they got a different diagnosis: my mother-in-law has Alzheimer's disease, which is what they call senility nowadays. Poor Wade; he broke down and cried.

"How can that be? My mama's one of the sharpest women I've ever met!"

Thinking about Patsy sure doesn't help my already bluer-than-blue mood. I'm so lonely, Mama, lonely as a mother can be in a house where there aren't any more children. Why didn't I have more? Why didn't I just keep having children so I'd never be in a house with just myself?

It was the first day of school — I watched out the window as Gil pulled up to Audrey's house in the old station wagon all the McMahon kids have driven, watched as Mike came bounding out the door and jumped in. The youngest boys in the neighborhood are now seniors in high school! Then they picked up Melody and Jewel (I can imagine the boys that'll be hanging around Merit's house, because her girls are absolute knockouts). Jewel's in eighth grade and Melody's a junior, and time feels like it's wearing running shoes.

I had an appointment with this couple who live in a seven-thousand-square-foot house (we could have put MawMaw's little shotgun house inside theirs about ten times), but I canceled it — I just didn't have the energy to do anything but drive to Beau and Bonnie's old elementary school and sit under the big elm tree and sob my eyes out. It seems like yesterday I was packing lunches in their Partridge Family lunchboxes, and now I have no idea what they eat for lunch, let alone breakfast and dinner.

After I dried my eyes I went home and cried some more. When it seemed I'd cried myself out, I called Beau, telling him how much of the day I'd spent blowing my nose and dabbing my eyes with a tissue. (If I had told Bonnie, she would have scolded me for being a sentimental old fool, but Beau never makes me feel stupid no matter what I tell him.)

"I know this is the beginning of your sophomore year," I said, "but at three-thirty I still looked out the window, hoping to see you coming up the sidewalk with your arms full of books."

"I worry about you, Mama," he said. "Why don't you come down and visit me?"

As soon as he said it, the heaviness in my heart lifted and I thought, Yes, that's what I'll do; I'll go visit Beau at Tulane and then I'll go visit Bonnie at Oberlin. I felt as happy as a robin on the first day of spring.

"What if I did, Beau?" I said. "What if I did come and visit you? Would you regret offering the invitation?"

"Of course not, Mama. I'd love to see you. You think Daddy would like to come too?"

Bonnie's a Yankee through and through — we're Mom and Dad to her — but like any good southern boy, Beau still calls us Mama and Daddy.

"He probably would," I said, "but I think I'd like you all to myself."

"Sounds good to me, Mama. And I want you to meet someone."

"Oh," I said, my happy little heart beating a little faster. "You've met someone special?"

"I think so," said Beau.

"What's her name?"

"Shelby, but Mama —"

"How's Roxanne going to feel about that?"

Roxanne is Beau's high school girlfriend, who pledged her undying love to him, even though she's going to school in Illinois and Beau's in Louisiana.

"I don't know, Mama. So when do you want to come out?"

"You tell me."

"How about in a month or so, Mama? School's just starting, and I'd like to get settled into my classes first."

"Of course," I said. Beau doesn't make the dean's list by not managing his time properly.

By the time I got done talking, I was cheered up enough to call Bonnie. She was full of news, and I submerged myself in her chatter about roommates and professors and cafeteria food like it was a cool blue balm.

Then Dex called me with the news about Patsy. Why did I have to answer the phone? Would it have been too much to ask for a good mood that lasted more than an hour?

I'm sorry,
Faith

461

December 1986

HOST: SLIP

BOOK: *West with the Night*

by Beryl Markham

REASON CHOSEN: "For the vicarious thrill."

Kari always resisted offers to turn her annual Christmas party into a potluck affair; this was one party that she liked to host by herself. She spent weeks making and then freezing elaborate cookies — spritz, pfeffernuss, chocolate-cherry pinwheels, almond crescents, meringue snowballs, and of course her always requested brownies. Julia had been helping her in the Christmas party preparations since she was a little girl, and this year she had asked, shyly, if Kari might allow her and Reni to make all the food.

Julia's enthusiasm was such that Kari hated to turn her down, even as she hated to relinquish her duties. She did relinquish them, though; it was her daughter's last year at home (Julia was waiting to hear from several colleges, particularly Northwestern, which was her first choice), and Kari was willing to give Julia practically everything she wanted. Fortunately, Julia hadn't caught on to that yet.

The day before the party they shopped, and that evening and the next afternoon the two girls sliced and diced, whisked and folded, baked and fried while listening to Christmas carols. An hour before the first guests were to arrive, they called Kari down from her banishment in her upstairs sewing room.

"Oh, my," said Kari as they shyly took her to the dining room table, which had been set with her Christmas table linens and dishes and trays of hors d'oeuvres and Christmas cookies.

"Plus we've got cheese and shrimp puffs that we'll put in the oven right when the guests arrive," said Julia proudly.

"It's absolutely lovely," said Kari, admiring an arrangement of tiny quiches. "Where did you get all these recipes?"

"Mostly from *The Joy of Cooking*," said Reni, "and some are just things that I thought up."

"She was the head chef," said Julia, "I just did what she told me to."

"Well, it looks absolutely wonderful, girls, and I can't wait to try everything." Now it was her turn to be shy. "Of course, you don't have to wear these, but while you were cooking up a storm, I was sewing up one, and . . . well, I just thought it might be fun for you to have something to wear that matched."

"Wow," said Reni when Kari presented the vests to them. "You made these while we were cooking? They're beautiful!"

"That's my mom," said Julia proudly. "Come on, let's try them on."

They were fitted, lined vests, made out of a soft Santa-suit-red wool, with an appliqué of a Christmas tree on one of the pockets.

After fastening the gold buttons, the girls gave Kari an impromptu fashion show, complete with sucked-in cheekbones and I-can-barely-stand-to-be-bothered looks.

"Thanks, Mom!" said Julia, enveloping the sewing wizard in a hug.

"Yeah, thanks, Kari!" said Reni, joining in.

"You're welcome," said Kari, not wanting to smell anything but their clean hair, not wanting to hold anything but their slender teenage bodies, not wanting to let go.

Sniffling, Kari told me all of this when I went over to her house to help her before the guests arrived. (She might not accept food contributions, but she will accept manual labor.)

"I wasn't prepared for how fast she'd grow up," said Kari as we checked the glasses and silverware for any spots.

"I know. They tell you that when your baby's got colic and you're sleep-deprived and you think, 'I *wish* the time would fly' and then boom — the next thing you know they're asking for car keys or informing you they're on the pill."

"Flannery's on birth control pills?"

I had to laugh; Kari looked as if she'd just been bitten by a scorpion.

"Kari, I told you that. She's been on the pill since she was a senior in high school."

Muttering some Norwegian epithet, Kari sat down heavily on the dining room chair.

"That's not to say she *needed* them," I said. "In fact, she didn't lose her virginity until she went away to college, but she wanted to be prepared, and I certainly supported that." I looked at my friend, who was still muttering. "And I distinctly remember you telling me you'd support Julia whenever she asked for birth control."

"Good gravy," said Kari, "I must have completely blocked that conversation from my mind." She tucked a sheaf of white hair behind her ears. "I guess it's easy to say you'd support your daughter's birth control choices when it's a hypothetical situation, but now that Julia's a senior . . . oh, my gosh, what if she's already had sex? What if she's pregnant this very minute?"

"Calm down, Kari. Julia doesn't even have a boyfriend, does she?"

"Not that I know of."

"Well, I'm sure you'd know it if she did. But either way, I'd talk to her, let her know what her options are."

"But I don't want her to have any options about sex!"

I had to laugh. "Of course you do, Kari. You want her to have options about everything — especially sex."

All of the children who were away at college (except for Beau, who chose to go skiing with a group of friends) were home and came to the party, and they were grown-up enough so that they could enjoy themselves among us adults — at least for a little while — before they retreated to the basement and their superior music and better conversation.

Audrey's handsome boys filled the room with their tall, muscular bodies, and Dave, whose personality finally seemed to have caught up with his looks, joked and flirted with everyone, even his old nemesis, Flannery, who, surprise surprise, looked anything but bothered by his attention.

Bryan, who went to USC, and my son Joe,

465

who went to the University of Wisconsin, re-united with yelps and punches on the arms. Michael and Gil followed them around like trainees, awed by these college boys.

Bonnie and Flan (when she wasn't laughing at Dave's jokes) sat together on the couch, talking to Merit and Helen Hammond about how they still kept up their book club by phone and mail.

"She's the only one whose taste I respect as much as mine," said Flannery, "although I *cannot* understand her infatuation with Anaïs Nin." She smiled as Bonnie made a face at her. "So, Mrs. Hammond, why didn't you ever join the Angry Housewives?"

"Oh, I'm not much of a reader," said Helen with a shrug, not aware of the look of surprise and pity that passed among Flannery and Bonnie and Merit.

Reni and Julia, in their matching vests, patrolled the crowd, offering trays of cheese puffs and mini shish kebabs. Reni's younger sisters, like Michael and Gil, were occupied trying to appear older (and cooler) than they were.

I was making the rounds with a tray of the girls' cheese puffs when I saw Faith. She was wearing the fancy green crocheted gloves (obviously Kari's work) her Secret Santa had given her, and she was dipping into the punch bowl once again as Grant walked over to her.

"Hi, Faith," said Grant. "It's so nice to see Bonnie again. Hearing her talk about midnight pizza parties makes me want to live in a dorm again." After a long, uncomfortable pause, he asked, "Is Beau back too?"

"No," said Faith, and instead of meeting his eyes, she looked at his bright red bow tie patterned with snowflakes. "He took a ski trip with some of his friends."

"Oh, that sounds like fun," said Grant but seeing Faith's expression harden, he added, "but not so fun for you, I'll bet."

"What do you know about what's fun for me?"

"I . . . I was just thinking —"

"Well, don't think. Especially about things you know nothing about."

Relief flooded Grant's face when he saw Kari carrying a tray of glasses, and he excused himself, practically running toward her, asking her if she needed help.

"Cheese puff?" I asked Faith, sticking the tray in Faith's face, "or will you be sticking to liquids this evening?"

A smirk puckered Faith's mouth. "Who are you, the drinks police?"

"If I were, I think I'd have to give you a citation, ma'am."

"Very funny. Ha ha ha."

"Really, Faith, maybe you should cool it a little. This is a Christmas party — you're supposed to be feeling jolly and full of goodwill toward men."

"Goodwill toward men — isn't that Grant's job?"

Sometimes a cutting remark is just that — you feel you've been nicked, pricked, hurt by meanness.

"I don't know what your problem is, Faith, but whatever's making you feel bad enough to be so mean, you'd better get over it."

She dipped the big ladle into the spiked punch and filled her glass again. "I'm sure there are people just dying for some of those cheese

467

puffs," she said, dismissing me, and like a kid facing my least-liked teacher, I was happy to be dismissed.

Wade was on his way up from the basement after losing a game of pool to Dave when I met him on the staircase.

"Hi, Rudolph," he said, looking at the felt antlers I wore.

"My Secret Santa gift," I explained. "I always expect something like Chanel Number Five and I always wind up with something like this."

"Well, antlers suit you," said Wade, smiling.

"Thanks," I said dryly.

Wade took my arm. "Actually," he said, "you're just the person I wanted to see. Got a minute?"

"Not for pool," I said. "I don't play."

"Neither do I, judging from my last game." He looked over at Dave, who was racking the balls up to play against his next victim. "No, I just wanted to talk to you . . . just for a minute."

"Sure," I said. "I was going to hide out down here anyway — Melody and Jewel are trying to organize a sing-along, and I figure if they can't find me, I can't wreck it."

"Thanks for warning me," said Wade. "Choir's the only class I ever got a D in."

We sat down on a couch on the other side of the rec room.

"So what's up?" I asked. "You want some advice on what to get Faith for Christmas?"

Over the years, I had changed my opinion of Wade, who with his crew cut and military posture had struck me as something of a hardass. As time passed, he grew out his hair a bit (even

468

perming it once, which gave him the sort of frizz I've spent my whole life trying to get rid of) and didn't think it always necessary to tuck his shirt in, relaxing enough in the mid-seventies to actually wear a pukka-shell necklace and flared pants. More importantly, he didn't automatically dismiss my politics the way Eric and occasionally Paul had; he asked me questions but didn't seem to patronize me. I thought Faith was lucky to have him and didn't like seeing the sad smile on his face.

"Wade," I said, "what's wrong?"

Sitting forward, Wade wrung his hands and blew air out of his lips so that they vibrated.

"It's just . . . I . . ." His hands made a papery sound as he wrung them, and he sat for a moment staring at them. Finally he looked up at me and asked, "Does Faith seem unhappy to you?"

I didn't need much time to answer yes.

"Well, more mad than unhappy — she and I just had a little altercation at the punch bowl."

"She's not drunk, is she?"

"You know Faith, Wade. She doesn't get drunk . . . she just gets mean."

Wade wrung his hands again as if they were sopping wet, and I wouldn't have been surprised to see water drip.

"I don't think she means to be mean, but . . . well, you know how disappointed she was when Beau asked her to postpone her visit until after the new year, and then when he didn't come home for Christmas . . ."

I nodded. "Still, Wade, you have to admit she's not the most pleasant person to be around when she drinks."

"It's not only when she drinks," he said,

looking pained. "Hasn't she seemed, in general, sort of sad, or mad, or both?"

Again, it was a question I didn't need to mull over.

"Yes, Wade. She has. She seems to have less patience for things lately — even us Angry Housewives. We hardly see her anymore outside of book club."

"She's so wound up. I ask her to tell me what's wrong and she acts like I'm making an accusation."

Across the room, there was a muted crack and then Dave whooped as he made a shot.

"She does seem to be extra-sensitive lately."

"Lately?" said Wade. "It's been going on for months."

I thought of Faith getting all bent out of shape when I had said she might have been Houdini in a past life; thought of how snotty her response had been to my visit to the peace march.

"You're right. She hasn't been herself for a while."

"Is it . . . is she going through the *change* or something?"

I laughed at Wade's pronunciation.

"You make menopause sound like leprosy," I said. "And no, I don't think she is — but she'd tell you if she was, wouldn't she?" I reached for a handful of mixed nuts set on the coffee table before us. "What does she say to you?" I cupped my hand to my mouth and dropped the nuts in.

"That's just it — she won't tell me anything. Faith likes to keep a close counsel. Not that that's bad, that's just how she is. But, knowing how you girls — uh, women — talk, I thought maybe she told you what's been —"

"Well, there you are!" said Faith, waving to us as she careened down the staircase. "I've been looking all over for you, Wade. We're all singing upstairs, and it's just like a Hallmark card come to life!"

"Hi, Faith," I said, brushing a peanut skin off my skirt. "Wade and I were holing up down here so we wouldn't have to sing."

"Well, I'll tell you what," said Faith, taking Wade's hand. "You can stay down here and be a Scrooge, but I'm taking my husband upstairs for a little Christmas spirit!" Her voice was as bright as a siren, with just as much of an edge to it.

"Faith," said Wade, standing up, "really, I'd rather —"

"Come on, they were singing 'Little Drummer Boy,' your favorite."

As Faith pulled him along, Wade turned back to shrug at me. I shrugged back.

I picked through the nut bowl, trying to find those elusive cashews. I knew the way to shake this sudden disquiet was to go upstairs and listen to "Little Drummer Boy" and the rest of the sing-along's repertoire, but finding three cashews *and* a pecan, I settled back on the couch to watch Dave congratulate Don Hammond on a good shot and to think about what might be the matter with Faith. *Was* she going through menopause? If so, someone would have to take her aside and tell her that the change of life didn't have to mean a change of personality too.

HOST: **AUDREY**

BOOK: *The Fountain Overflows*

by Rebecca West

MEETING HIGHLIGHT: "Audrey insisted we all speak in English accents (Faith sounded just like Glenda Jackson) and served us tea and these hard biscuits called scones."

It's not often you get to *really* surprise someone, but I *really* surprised Faith.

"Oh, my God," she said, one hand splayed on her chest, the other clutching at the wing of one of the damask chairs that decorated the small, antique-filled lobby. "What are *you* doing here?"

"I was in the mood for some strong coffee and a beignet."

I didn't expect Faith to burst out laughing, but I was hoping the mortification on her face would ease up a bit. Really, if faces could break, the concierge would have been picking up pieces of Faith's nose and forehead off the thin Persian rug.

"Could you at least pretend to be somewhat *pleasantly* surprised?"

"I . . . I just would have liked to have been warned."

Feeling like a virus Faith wished she'd been in-oculated against, I decided to go for bright and cheery. "So, what shall we do tonight?"

"Actually, I'm expecting Beau."

"Oh," I said, finally deciding to take the hint she was so desperately shoving in my face. "Maybe we could get together afterward; I'm in room —"

"Beau!" Faith shouted.

"Beau!" I said as a tall, lanky, and absolutely gorgeous man walked into the lobby.

As Slip would say, holy Adonis. Now, I remember Beau being a cute kid, in sort of a dorky way, but I had no idea he was harboring this *hunk* inside himself.

"My goodness!" he said in a real live drawl, "it's an Angry Housewife! Mama, you didn't tell me Mrs. Forrest was coming!"

"I . . . I didn't know," said Faith, clinging to him as if he had the word *lifesaver* printed on his sleeve. The arrival of her son had loosened the tension in her face, and she offered a genuine smile. "She just showed up, minutes ago."

"The temperature last night was twenty-eight below," I said. "So my question to myself was: who needs this? Why don't I just fly on down to New Orleans and surprise Faith?"

I failed to mention that I had had a feeling — a deep feeling — that Faith was in trouble.

"She scared the livin' daylights out of me," said Faith, matching her son's new drawl with her old one. "First I thought something had hap-pened at home —" She looked at me, a flash of fear falling over her face. "Nothing bad *has* hap-pened, has it?"

I shook my head. "Oh, no. Like I said, I just

needed a change of temperature."

"It's too bad you're not more spontaneous," said Beau with a laugh before he gave me the once-over. "My gosh, y'all haven't changed at all."

"I know you're lying, but keep it up," I said with a wave of my hand.

Age hadn't been cruel to me, but it wasn't bending over backward for me, either. I had packed on more than a few pounds (and with menopause looming near, I was sure there were more to come), and I was hoping, but not quite believing, that with my height I could somehow carry it off. And I don't know that I could still have described myself as brunette, seeing as how the gray had well-established squatter's rights.

Beau's eyebrows raised then, as if boosted by the force of a good idea. "Hey, you're gonna join Mama and me for dinner, aren't you?"

"You don't have to ask me twice," I said, ignoring the look on Faith's face that begged me to decline the invitation.

The maître d' at Arnaud's showed us to our table as if we were visiting royalty and he was a page honored to be in our company.

"Man, I could get used to this southern hospitality," I said, putting my napkin onto my lap.

"I am so excited to be here," said Faith, her cheeks flushed, her eyes dancing. It was odd — as reluctant as she'd been to have me join them, she was as excited as a girl at her first dance, whereas Beau, who had been Mr. Convivial, was now decidedly gloomy.

"Beau hasn't told me a thing about her," she said after we'd ordered our drinks. "Every time I press him for details, he says, 'You'll see,

474

Mama.' " Faith touched Beau's sleeve, smiling. "Why, she's probably a big old tub with rotten teeth and body odor."

"Mama," said Beau, his fine handsome face flushing. *"Please."*

"I'm telling you — Roxanne, the girl he left behind? She writes *me* from college. I think she figures if she stays on my good side, Beau won't forget her so easily."

Beau was looking a little green around the gills, and I wasn't surprised when he excused himself to the men's room.

"Faith," I said as we (along with every other female customer) watched him stride across the restaurant, "when did he grow up and become such a movie star?"

Faith made a moue. "Like mother, like son, I guess."

"I think I should powder my nose too," I said, standing up. "If the waiter comes, order me a big exotic drink."

I stood by the men's room, waiting for Beau to come out, and when he did, he still wore that look somewhere between nausea and terror.

"Mrs. Forrest!" he said, a little yelp of surprise in his voice.

"Please, call me Audrey. What's the matter, Beau?"

"How did you . . . oh, yeah, Mama told me you've got the sixth sense."

"Beau, I wouldn't need any sense but sight to know something's bothering you. Now, do you want to tell me about it? Maybe I could help."

"I think I'll save your offer for when I really need it." He looked at his watch. "Which should be in about five minutes."

"When you tell your mother about your boyfriend?" The thought was out of my mouth before my internal censor showed up for duty.

Beau's mouth dropped open like a trapdoor.

"I'm sorry, Beau, I had no right to say that."

After the stunned look faded from his face, Beau raked his hand through his curls and offered a crooked smile.

"Congratulations, ma'am, you win the Kenmore washer and dryer." He shook his head. "I don't know why I didn't tell Mama before — but she was just so thrilled when I went out with Roxanne, and she automatically assumed Shelby was a she. Oh, Lord, what could I be thinking, springing it on her like this?"

"Are you sure you'll be springing it on her?"

Beau narrowed his eyes. "You don't miss much, do you, Audrey? But no, Mama's spent too much energy making me straight to think I could be anything but." He sighed and looked at his watch again. "Shelby's supposed to meet us at the hotel after dinner — he's at a lecture right now — but after I tell Mama about him, I have a feeling the meeting will be canceled."

"Would you like me to leave?" I asked. "I can fake a headache or something."

"Oh, Mrs. For— Audrey, *please stay*. I could use the moral support."

Back at the table, Faith was drinking one of three mint juleps.

"When in Rome," she said, holding up her glass. We all toasted Rome, and Beau and I seemed in a race as to who could finish our drink faster.

"Beau," scolded Faith, "I hope you don't drink like that all the time."

"Only when I'm conscious," he said, à la Groucho Marx.

He caught my eye and we laughed, the kind of laugh that's just a screen door holding back fear.

"So, tell me all about your life here," I said. "What kind of classes are you taking?"

"Oh, Audrey," said Faith, "I don't want to talk about school. I want to talk about Shelby."

"Let's order first," said Beau, hiding behind the big, tasseled menu. "I'm starving."

We ate the way I like to eat — as if we didn't know where our next meal was coming from. Conversation was not at a premium as we made our way through gumbo and jambalaya and various incarnations of shrimp and seafood.

"Oh, my," said Faith, pushing her plate aside and patting her mouth with her napkin.

"Let's get some coffee," I suggested, for now I wanted nothing more than to curl up on the banquette and take a nap.

"Good idea," said Faith, looking at her reflection in a spoon as she reapplied her lipstick. "I need to perk up for when I meet Shelby."

I saw Beau go pale. Then a look of resolve — the look my son Bryan got on his face the first time we put him on water skis — changed the features of his face.

"Mama," he said, "Shelby is not my girl-friend."

Faith looked like she'd been asked how many stars there are in the Milky Way.

"What? What do you mean? Did you break up?"

Beau gave a nervous little laugh, and raked his hand through his hair.

"Actually, Mama, no. No, we didn't break up.

What I mean is . . . well, Shelby's not a she, he's a he."

"He's a he?" said Faith like an English student learning a phrase she doesn't understand.

Pressing his lips together until they disappeared, Beau nodded.

"He's a he and he's my boyfriend."

Faith's circumflex eyebrows, which could look both mean and exotic, knit together, and she offered a jagged little smile before lurching up.

"Excuse me," she said, and then she was out of the booth and racing through the restaurant as if someone had just cried, "Fire!"

Beau and I stared at each other.

"I'll go after her," he said.

"No, I will," I said. I took a couple hundred dollars out of my purse and gave them to Beau. "You take care of the bill and meet us back at the hotel bar."

When I was pregnant with Michael, Davey had woken Bryan out of a sound sleep, told him that I had had the baby, and asked if Bryan wanted to see it.

Oh boy, did he; Bryan had been so excited about becoming a big brother.

Davey had held Bryan's hand, and they'd crept down the hallway to the newly decorated nursery.

"There she is," Davey had said softly as they entered the moonlit room. "Your new baby sister." Leaning over the bassinet, he'd carefully pulled back the corner of the satin baby blanket to reveal the baby. Bryan, expecting to see a sweet little pink face, hadn't been prepared for the furry, scary one that stared back at him. Not only did his screams wake up Paul and me, they practically brought on my labor.

"I was just playing a joke!" Davey had laughed as Bryan wailed in my arms. "It's just dumb old Doogie!"

Doogie was Davey's long-discarded, one-eyed teddy bear.

Bryan had lain on his tummy on his bed and cried for what seemed like hours, and that's the way Faith was crying now: on the bed, on her tummy, absolutely bereft.

I had chased after her out of the restaurant, through the French Quarter, into the hotel, and into her room, and had been rubbing her back for what seemed like a quarter century, my hand ready to fall off at the wrist.

"Faith," I said for the thousandth time, "Faith, it's all right, honey."

I guess saying a thing for the thousandth time is the charm, because she pushed herself up on her arms, gasping mightily as if she'd just broken the surface of a slough she'd been under for too long. She sat on the bed, facing me.

"No," she said, her voice ragged, her face battered with tears, "no, it is not all right, and you know it!" She paused and stared at me. "What are you doing?" she asked as I picked up the telephone receiver.

"I'm calling the hotel bar," I said. "I'm going to tell Beau to come on up here."

"No, you're not!"

I set the receiver down. "Faith, you need to talk to your son. He's been waiting downstairs" — I looked at my watch — "for over half an hour, and you *need* to talk to him. I'd be happy to stay with you, or I'll leave if you want."

"No," said Faith, panicky. "Don't leave."

I dialed the bar. After speaking briefly to Beau, I cupped my hand over the bottom half of the receiver and asked, "Can Shelby come up too?"

Faith rolled her eyes like the prelude to a swoon.

"Good God, *no*. That little bastard *cannot* come up."

I relayed Faith's message, in somewhat softer terms, to Beau. Minutes later, there was a soft knock on the door.

Faith scrunched up against the tufted headboard, hugging a pillow to her chest as I opened the door for Beau, who looked like he'd shed a few tears himself.

"Mama," he said softly, but as he came toward her, Faith held up her hand.

"Don't come any closer, Beau. You can sit on that chair by the table. Just don't come any closer."

Poor Beau; his whole body sort of collapsed under those words.

I am not proud of the fact that in my career as a mother I have said some hurtful things to my children (once I called Davey a "fucking juvenile delinquent"), but I can't ever remember a child of mine crumpling in utter dejection the way Beau did now (in fact, I had gotten the distinct impression that Davey had *liked* being called a "fucking juvenile delinquent").

I poured water from a carafe on the nightstand and gave both Faith and Beau a glass. Me, I could use a cigarette.

"Beau," I asked, "you don't happen to smoke, do you?"

Looking sad, as if he had disappointed me too,

Beau shook his head.

"That's good," I said. "I don't either — I mean, I quit a long time ago, but I just thought how a cigarette might be a good thing to have about now."

I bit my upper lip to stop myself from babbling.

"I'm surprised," said Faith, looking coldly at her son. "You do *everything* else."

I could see the emotional shift on Beau's face; the hurt and fear stepped aside, replaced by anger.

"What exactly is that supposed to mean, Mama?"

"Not smoking probably leaves you more room for all your other vices."

"All my other *vices?* Is that what you think Shelby is — a *vice?*"

"Well, he's not the girlfriend you led me to believe he was, that's for sure."

"Mama, you're the one who made that assumption, I . . . well, I should have set you straight right away, but I guess I wanted to postpone" — he waved his hand in the air — "all of this as long as possible."

Faith stared at him for a moment, her expression unreadable, and then looked at me. "I could use a cigarette too."

"You want me to run downstairs?" I asked. "There's a cigarette machine in the bar."

Faith studied me for a moment. "Should we?"

I shrugged. "It's been a long time — we'd probably get pretty light-headed."

"I know. And what if it took just one cigarette to make us start up the habit all over again?"

"That would be a drag," I agreed.

481

"Excuse me," Beau said, standing up.

"Where are you going?" asked Faith.

"I'll be right back."

In less than a minute he was, bearing a pack of Kents.

"Hey," said Faith. "My old brand. Where'd you get them so fast?"

"There was a guy ready to get on the elevator," Beau said. "I asked him if he had any cigarettes I could buy."

"Well, that's nearly a full pack," said Faith. "Why didn't you just ask for a couple?"

"Mama, you wanted cigarettes, I got cigarettes. I didn't know you had a particular number in mind."

"Well, we might be tempted to smoke the whole thing. If you'd just gotten one or two, the temptation wouldn't have been there. In fact, I think you should throw out the whole thing."

"What?" said Beau, looking at his mother as if she had just recited the Twenty-third Psalm in pig Latin, and then turned to me, as if I could somehow translate.

"I . . . I . . ." So much for my translation skills. I looked at the pack of cigarettes Beau held in the palm of his hand, and knew that if I pulled one out, I might keep pulling and pulling. "It was so kind of you to get these, but I guess I'll have to pass too."

He looked at me and then back to his mother the way a wary orderly might look at two unpredictable inmates in a psych ward.

"But I paid five dollars for the pack," he said.

"Five dollars?" said Faith. "That's ridiculous, Beau! It's not even a full pack."

Beau opened his mouth to say something but,

thinking better of it, clamped it shut until it was a thin, lipless line. He looked up at the ceiling briefly and then did a neat about-face and walked to the window. He pushed it open, flung the pack of cigarettes out, closed it, and turned back toward us, brushing his hands together.

"Litterbug," said Faith, which struck all the nuts in the nuthouse — and, after a moment, the orderly too — as hilarious, and we laughed our heads off.

"I don't want you to be gay!" Faith said at one point that long night.

"Believe me, Mama, I didn't want to be either. And I tried hard not to be — you know how hard I tried." His gymnast shoulders rose in a shrug. "But there comes a time when you just sort of give up. Give up the charade and realize: this is who I am."

I nodded. "That's what Grant said. He said that it was like being forced to do everything awkwardly right-handed when you could do everything easily left-handed."

"Exactly," said Beau.

"And finally he realized all the problems he'd face being gay were less than the problems he faced not being himself."

"This isn't about Grant," said Faith tightly.

"Audrey's just trying to help, Mama," said Beau, whose patience with his mother, while exemplary, occasionally had to crack.

"How can she help? None of her sons is gay."

"That I know of," I said, and both Beau and I laughed.

"I'm glad you two think this is so funny." Her eyes glittered like paste jewels. "I'm the one who has to worry about my son, that he's not catching that AIDS virus or getting turned down for a job or an apartment . . . worrying that a group of football players is calling him a fag before they beat him to a pulp!"

"You're right, Faith," I said, humbled. "That is a lot to worry about."

Beau looked at her steadily and said, "I thought what you'd worry most about was what to tell your friends, or Grandma and Grandpa."

Earlier I had seen what Faith's words did to Beau; now I saw the effect his had on her.

"Oh, Beau," she whispered, her face white.

We sat there under the shade of those words for a while, Beau fiddling with a pen on the nightstand, Faith on the bed staring at the toes of her crossed feet, and me wondering if I should race downstairs and search the street for that pack of cigarettes.

"Hey," I said finally. "We ran out of the restaurant before we got any dessert."

"Well, let's go get some," said Beau. "Come on, let's go get Shelby and get us some pie."

We wound up at a little all-night diner off Bourbon Street, waited on by a sharp-featured woman whose Cajun accent was so thick I could understand about every fifth word she spoke. She was the chatty type of waitress too, handing us menus with a greeting that sounded like, "Y'allwaleconaPapa'swaydefoohissogooy'allgonethankayoudyedayngonewaytaven."

"Uh, thank you," Faith said.

The diner smelled of strong coffee and a day's worth of food cooked in a deep-fat fryer.

"I like this place," I said, looking at the sign that announced *THE SECRET'S IN OUR SPICES* and the autographed black-and-white photographs of musicians like Louis Armstrong and Pearl Bailey and Count Basie that hung on the white plaster walls.

"Shelby introduced me to it," said Beau, smiling at the young man seated next to him. He had straight black hair and the angular features of a Native American, and he probably turned as many heads as Beau did.

Although someone at the next booth might glance at Faith and think she looked perfectly normal, I had felt her shaking next to me since we'd been seated; it was as if a tiny motor was idling inside her, unable to shut off. I watched Faith's throat rise and fall as she swallowed her Coke.

"Where are you from . . . Shelby?" she asked, saying his name as if she'd been forced to.

"Shreveport."

"His people have been here since the eighteenth century," said Beau.

Faith allowed herself a smile. "You said 'people' instead of 'relatives.' You're getting to be a real southerner, Beau."

"Just like my mama."

"Heyaallgoweeyourfoodnawwashaplaesthey'shot."

The waitress set down our food, and I proceeded to bite into the best pie I'd ever tasted in my life.

"Oh, my God," I said. "We've got to get this recipe for book club."

Beau laughed. "Praline pie — isn't it great? Shelby knows all the best places in New Orleans — all the places the tourists don't know about."

"He really is . . . you two really are . . . *boy-*

485

friends, aren't you?" said Faith. "It's not a stage or anything, is it?"

Sadness flooded Beau's beautiful blue-green eyes even as he smiled at Shelby. "You've always known it's not a stage, Mama. You just didn't want to admit it. Almost as much as I didn't want to admit it."

"But you . . . you and Roxanne seemed to really like each other."

"It was a lot easier to go to the prom with Roxanne instead of Denny Auerbach."

Faith's eyes grew wide. *"Denny Auerbach?* Denny Auerbach the quarterback, who Wade said had the best arm in high school football, is *gay?"*

Beau nodded, and we laughed — at how he'd widened his own eyes to mimic his mother's, I guess, and at how much it was we didn't know.

"Oh, Beau," said Faith finally. "What am I going to tell your daddy?"

"I'll tell him," said Beau. "Although he's probably known all along too."

"And Bonnie?"

Beau rolled his eyes. "Of course Bonnie knows, Mama. She's my twin sister." He scraped the plate with his fork, collecting the last morsel of pie. "Remember those teen magazines she used to subscribe to? She never read them; she just passed them on to me so I could cut out pictures of John Travolta and the Bay City Rollers."

"Oh, Beau," said Faith.

"Howyeealldowhenwoujalikes'morepieh?"

We stayed in the café until dawn, sipping at our rich, chicory-flavored coffee.

"You can't believe how relieved I am not

486

having to lie to you anymore," said Beau. He sprawled in his seat the way a boxer sits between rounds, totally exhausted.

"I told him," said Shelby, who had gone from hardly speaking to an active participant in the conversation. "I said once you tell your parents, you'll feel you've been set free."

"Do your parents know?" asked Faith.

Shelby nodded. "I told them when I was a junior in high school."

"You did? What did they say?"

"Well, after they calmed down — and it took them a while — they said they were glad to have an end to the lies."

"I don't know what it would be like not to lie," said Faith wistfully.

"What do you mean, Mama?" asked Beau, leaning forward. "What do you have to lie about?"

Batting back tears, Faith looked at her son and then at me. "Oh, only about little things — like who I really am."

"I think we all wonder about that sometimes," I said, wanting to get Faith off whatever self-imposed hook she'd been hanging herself on. She looked miserable and it had been too long a night of her looking miserable.

"That's right," said Beau, taking her hand and holding it between his as if to warm it. "But if you've done something terrible — if you're a kleptomaniac or stepping out on Dad — well, you can always tell me. Except maybe not the stepping out on Dad — that'd be too weird."

"I'm not stepping out on your dad," said Faith. "You must think we're terrible," she said, smiling at Shelby.

"Not at all," said Shelby, smiling back.

"You do know, Mama," said Beau, "that there's nothing you can do that would ever make me stop loving you."

For a long time, Faith looked at her son's hands holding hers. When she finally spoke, her voice was soft. "I feel the same about you, Beau."

The soft and heavy air nudged inside the café every time someone opened the door, and when a gnarled old man shuffled from table to table selling roses, I bought one, thinking that life was like a flower — showy and colorful and indescribably delicate, and even if aphids or worms or mildew destroyed it, it still couldn't change the fact that it had been a *flower*. I don't know what showed on my face, but something must have, because Faith looked at me as if she saw something she hadn't seen before. Then she suddenly took charge, saying we were all tired, and didn't Beau have a big calculus test he had to study for, and it was time to go back to the hotel.

As we stood at the cash register arguing with Shelby, who insisted on paying the bill, a huge black man dressed in white carried in a tray of freshly powdered beignets, and I bought four, even though everyone insisted they could not possibly eat another bite.

"Turn right at that church," Faith said.

"That's a church?" asked Audrey. "I thought it was a shack."

Faith smiled, but it was the smile of someone out on a day pass. She was dazed; it baffled her how she had wound up on a field trip with

Audrey, driving into her hometown of Trilby, Mississippi.

She had slept fitfully after they returned from the diner (the *Times Picayune* had already been delivered to her door) and had plans to spend the day doing nothing more energetic than rolling over in bed.

But a little past noon, hunger had gotten the best of her, and she'd thrown on some clothes and run a comb through her hair, deciding to sit on the hotel's patio drinking strong coffee.

In the lobby, Audrey's bright face had been like a strong dose of sunshine, and Faith had squinted, feeling a flare of a headache.

"The queen's awake!" Audrey had said cheerfully, rising from her chair. "Good morning . . . uh, afternoon, Faith!"

" 'Morning," Faith had mumbled.

"Guess what? I rented a car, and we're going to go exploring! I want to go see some bayous and alligators and hear some zydeco played by some old-timers on a rickety old houseboat."

"I . . . um . . . I'm expecting Beau."

"Why, Faith, you little liar. He's going to be studying all day for that calculus exam, remember?" Audrey had taken her friend by the arm. "You'll be back in plenty of time to have dinner with him, but for now, you're coming with me."

They were almost over the Lake Pontchartrain causeway when Faith snapped out of her daze enough to say, "If you're looking for bayous or alligators, you're going the wrong way."

"What do you mean?" asked Audrey, who was the type of navigator who was always convinced she was going the right way, despite all evidence to the contrary.

"Bayou country's to the south. You're heading north."

"North?" pouted Audrey. "Oh, well, so we'll take a little detour . . . what's up this way, Faith?"

"Not much, although you could always hook up to Route Fifty-nine and see Trilby, the little town I grew up in."

The horror Faith felt was immediate: what on earth had she been thinking?

"Great idea! I don't think I really wanted to go out in a swamp anyway."

"At least swamps can be exciting," said Faith, trying to keep her voice light. "There's not much of that in Trilby. In fact, there's *nothing* in Trilby. Let's turn around and find those alligators."

"Too late, we're on our way to Trilby." Audrey paused for a moment. "Where *is* Trilby, anyway?"

"It's in Mississippi, by Hattiesburg," said Faith, and then she burst into tears.

"Aw, Faith," said Audrey, "I know you've had a pretty emotional twenty-four hours. But for what it's worth, I've never seen Beau happier."

Holding up her hand, Faith shook her head. When she had control of her voice, she said, "I'm not crying about Beau. Well, I guess I am . . . partly." She wiped the heel of her hand against her nose. "But like he said, I guess deep down, I always knew he was gay. In a way it's a relief to have him admit it and to realize that I still do love him as much as I ever did."

"Of course you do."

"But another thing he said is true too. He said what he thought I'd worry about most was what to tell my friends. So I'm crying about that too — that I'm so shallow and my own son knows it!"

Audrey laughed.

"I'm sorry," she said as Faith wailed. "I'm not laughing at you, I'm laughing *with* you. Everyone worries about what their friends think . . . it's human nature."

"Everyone might worry," said Faith, a big sob shuddering through her. "But not as much as I do. And Beau doesn't know — no one does — how *much* I've worried . . . how my whole life has been a *lie* because of that worry."

Another sob, this one an aftershock of the more potent one, rippled through Faith. "So what I'm also crying about is if we go to Trilby, I'll be found out, and I don't know if you're still going to love me after that."

A few miles outside town, the fear inside Faith was as cold as a Minnesota January. She hadn't been back in how many years? Twenty-five, twenty-six? Progress had visited though; they passed a Wal-Mart where farmland used to spread its green and brown quilts, and farther up, a truck stop with enough gas and diesel pumps to fuel an advancing *and* retreating army.

The car windows were open and the air smelled of dirt and grass and thistle, the essential smell of Trilby that the years and progress hadn't erased. As they turned by the old run-down church — the church where DellaRose had gone — Faith felt the poised and confident woman she struggled to be shrivel up the way MawMaw's camellia bush (her one flowering

491

plant) would during hot spells, felt her real self rise up like a wild weed.

"Where to now, Faith?" asked Audrey.

I don't have to really show her. I could take her by the mayor's house, or by the Stevensons' . . .

"Take the first right after the railroad tracks. On Pullman Road."

In silence, Audrey drove the car over the patched tar streets, past houses whose paint was peeled and blistered and on whose sagging porches saggy couches or chairs were propped.

They drove a few blocks after the turn and then Faith said, "That's it, Audrey, right there."

Audrey pulled over, parking next to a tree whose roots bulged up in knobs above the ground.

"Which one, Faith?"

Oh, that swanky one with the jasmine climbing the veranda.

Audrey looked at the house she pointed to. It was a reminder that no one had won the war on poverty; in fact, it looked as if poverty was throwing a victory party. A tipped-over wagon, a deflated rubber ball bleached by the sun, and a plastic pop bottle littered the cracked sidewalk that led to the house, which was almost as narrow as it was small.

Rust bled onto the concrete step from an iron handrail, and the shutter of one window was missing half its slats. Age had worn the house down as much as neglect, and its very frame, under roof shingles that were split and curled, seemed hunched.

"So you can see," said Faith, "that Daddy didn't have much of a medical practice. In fact, Daddy didn't have much of anything. The daddy that I told you was a big important doctor? Well, that daddy does not exist."

Faith closed her eyes, not wanting to see her friend's face, but she opened them shortly after, not wanting to see MawMaw standing at the mailbox, shaking her head as she got another bill she couldn't pay; not wanting to see her drunk mother picking herself up off the sidewalk, cursing, then laughing as she realized she hadn't spilled any whiskey, her skirt caught up in its waistband so that she revealed the backs of her thighs and a crescent of shiny underwear fabric.

Her chest heaving as if she'd chased the car rather than ridden in it, Faith stared straight ahead. In her confession, she neither felt a gush of relief or shame; she only felt numb, as if she had gotten a full-body shot of novocaine.

"So you never knew your dad?" asked Audrey.

What'd I just say? thought Faith, but she said, "Well, I was only two weeks old when he left. He was seventeen years old when I was born."

"Michael and Gil's age." Audrey clicked her long nails on the steering wheel. "You want to go anywhere else, Faith?"

"Yes. I want to show you where I killed my mother."

The words screamed in Faith's head, so it took her a moment to realize she had spoken them out loud.

January 1987

Dear Mama,

Well, guess what: the people I love most in the world now know everything I've been hiding all these years.

I can't believe it — this is the first time in

my life I have not had any secrets, and I feel like I've lost half my body weight. I'm forty-six years old and I feel as new as a baby, Mama!

Audrey left New Orleans a couple days ago, and the twins went back to school yesterday. Wade and I are flying home today, and so are his parents.

Yup, this turned into a whole family reunion, and all because of you, Mama.

Audrey doesn't shock very easily, but sitting in that rental car in Trilby, she looked as stunned as a victim of a lightning strike.

"Let me drive," I said, and without saying a word, Audrey and I switched places.

I don't know if an electrocardiogram could have recorded the rhythms of my heart, Mama; it was banging against my chest like it was Houdini trying to get out of a trunk he was really locked in. And yet even though I was on the verge of cardiac arrest, I felt an eerie sort of calm, the way a fugitive must when he's finally walking toward the circle of squad cars and the guy with the bullhorn. The running was over. Who knew what horrible things lay in store, but at least the running was over.

I turned onto Hopper Avenue (remember how the streets in this crappy neighborhood were named after train cars, as if its residents needed more reminders that they lived by the railroad?). A man walking a pit bull nodded at us and said, "Nice car." The houses weren't as neglected as those on my old street; in fact, it looked as if some people understood the concept of home maintenance. I drove past Kiki Krebs' house — remember, Mama? She's the girl whose stepfather shot her mother in the

494

leg because he didn't like the way she fried his eggs.

I drove on, my heart still galloping, my jaw clenched so tight it was a wonder my teeth didn't crumble.

When we reached the city limits, the tarred surface of Hopper Avenue gave way to dirt and I followed it, the silence in the car punctured by the car thumping over potholes. Progress hadn't reached this side of town; fields were still being farmed and we passed an old red barn whose roof still sported the painted sign that had been there when I was a kid: Home Pantry Grits.

When I saw the roadhouse, my heart lurched, seeing as beating wasn't getting it free. Instantly I was as weak as Melanie Wilkes after childbirth, but I managed to pull over to the side of the road. I don't think I knew my head was resting against the steering wheel until I felt a hand on my back, and I jumped, making the horn beep.

"Faith," said Audrey. "Faith, tell me what happened."

Well, that had been my plan, Mama, but there was a roadblock in my throat that my words couldn't get past.

"Faith, do you want to get out of the car?"

I nodded and opened the door, practically falling out. A strong breeze whipped past us, and Audrey held down her skirt with her hand against her thigh.

"Should we walk a ways?"

When I nodded, we began walking toward the roadhouse.

"The Beehive," said Audrey when we got

close enough to read the plastic sign perched in the dirt parking lot. "Closed for renovations."

"It wasn't the Beehive back then," I said, my throat roadblock lifting. "It was Red's, and open twenty-four hours a day. It was the hot spot for all the county's alcoholics."

I felt like a tour guide giving chirpy commentary on the building that had figured in so many of my nightmares.

"It was windy that night too," I said, watching as the leaves of a big weeping willow swept a corner of the parking lot. "But it wasn't cold like this — it was the middle of the summer and so hot that my hair was as wet as if I'd just washed it.

"I had come home the summer before my senior year at the University of Texas," I said, my voice without inflection, like someone in a trance. "I don't know why I'd come back — I guess a part of me must have missed my mama, even though the far bigger part was thrilled to be away from her. Wade and I had just started going out, and he had no idea what I was coming home to — I'd sort of made up this fantasy childhood where my daddy was the town doctor and my mama hosted dinner parties and spent her days doing good works. I couldn't even think what I was going to do when Wade asked to meet them."

Audrey had her arm around me, her eyes squinted against the dust the wind blew up. Even though she was so close I could feel the heat from her body, I had the strange feeling that I was alone, or as alone as a person can be among ghosts.

I stared past them, seeing your big blue Chevy with the sharp fins parked among the rusty pickups and old Fords.

"Mama had promised me that we were going to go to Hattiesburg and spend the day shopping for clothes for me to take back to school — she said her new boyfriend was flush with cash and loved to give her spending money — and I was so excited; I couldn't re-member ever taking a shopping trip with my mama.

"Well, the day we were supposed to go, I woke up to find a note. It said she had to run a few errands but would be back in a jiffy and then we'd be on our way. At lunchtime she called, full of apologies — a friend of hers needed her to baby-sit for a little while, but it shouldn't take long and then we'd go.

"I sat in that ugly little house and waited all afternoon for my mama to show up. She fi-nally called at six, full of apologies, and I could hear in her voice that she'd been drinking. Of course she'd been drinking! Why would I have thought any differently? I really lit into her then, calling her every name in the book and some that were too terrible to make it into any book. I said I never wanted to see her and her stinking lying face again, and slammed down the receiver and bolted out of the house. I was crying and so mad at myself that I still cared enough to cry."

There was an old picnic table bench shoved up against the wall, and we sat down on it, Audrey staring at me like a scared parishioner listening to a preacher who had gone off the deep end.

"I was so mad at my mama and myself for expecting her to change that I couldn't see straight. I tore down Pullman Road — you had the privilege of seeing that beautiful residential street, Audrey — when who should pull up in his big old convertible but Lyle Dube, the biggest troublemaker my high school had ever seen. I jumped in without a thought, and when he asked me what I wanted to do, I said, 'Anything you want, Lyle.'

"One of the many things I've neglected to tell you all these years," I said, emotion like a tugboat engine chugging through me, "is that in my youth I was a bit of a . . . well, the word used by my fellow classmates was slut. Remember at book club when everyone was telling about when they first had sex and I said it was with Wade?" I shook my head. "Wade was about the . . . well, let's just say he wasn't the first. The first was when I was fifteen."

The sun had begun its descent beyond a copse of trees by the horizon, and I remembered something you once said about sunset, Mama. I had come upon you standing in the threshold of the back door, holding the lip of a beer bottle with one finger, and I felt like crying because you looked so sad.

"How can things be so golden and beautiful when you feel like such shit?"

Of course, I didn't have an answer for you then, Mama, and I didn't have one for myself, sitting there on that bench feeling the same exact way.

"Faith," Audrey said, "you don't really think we'd think less of you because you lost your virginity at fifteen?"

I nodded, tasting snot in my throat.

"And everything else there is to know about me. Like what I did with Lyle." I think if I had more in my stomach, I would have thrown up, Mama. But I was there to tell my whole story and so I forged on.

"See, Lyle had already quit school before I settled down. He didn't know how I'd stayed out of trouble my senior year, didn't know I had become a completely different person in Austin; all he knew was the old Faith Reynolds. And when he said, 'Well, let's go down to the pond,' I said sure, and when we got there and he jumped all over me, I jumped right back. When we were all done we did it again, and when I was buttoning up my blouse, I wondered if there was ever a person in the history of the world who felt as low and little as I did right then.

" 'Aw, Christ,' he said, looking at his watch. 'I gotta go, Faith.' He put his belt on, and the buckle clicked against the stick shift, and the sound of that made me want to howl in shame.

" 'Doreen gets off work at eight-thirty,' he said, 'so, uh, you mind if I drop you off downtown?'

"I shrugged — what did I care? I'd just fucked — excuse my French, but that's what it was — someone I didn't even like in a car next to a stagnant slough that wasn't even close to being a pond.

"So he very unceremoniously dropped me off in our bustling 'downtown' — he could have slowed the car down and pushed me out the door, for all I cared — and I wandered Main Street, all three blocks of it, thinking,

What did I just do?

"Then I remembered my mother and I started thinking, It's all her fault that this happened, and I decided to go find her at Red's and tell her I never wanted to see her again."

Oh, Mama, how was I to know that wish would come true?

"I walked all the way to Red's," I went on. "At least five miles away, but my anger was like a big wind just pushing me along.

"The place was packed when I got there, and I got squeezed and felt up and pinched as I walked to the bar, which didn't do anything for my anger, I can tell you that. When I got to the bar, I tapped my mother on the shoulder, and when she turned around she smiled this big sloppy grin and said, 'Hey, everybody, it's my baby, Faith!'

"I pulled her off that bar stool like I'd pull a sack of flour off the grocery shelf.

" 'Hey,' she said, 'what are you doing?'

" 'I'm taking you home, Mama.'

" 'Well, I don't think she wants to go home,' said some guy who'd exceeded his limit long ago.

" 'Tough shit,' I said, and Mama laughed.

" 'You tell 'em, Faithy,' she said.

"She was plowed, my mother was, and I had a hard time steering her out of the bar. She was giggling like crazy, waving to people and saying, 'Look at my daughter, Faithy — isn't she pretty? She's come to take me home.'

"It was hot and damp when we got outside, and I was so mad — just incensed. I was ready to beat up my own drunk mother right there in the parking lot.

" 'What we gonna do, Faithy — throw our own little party?' Mama asked, and I said, 'I don't think so!' and she laughed and said, 'I got ears, you don't have to yell, honey.'

" 'I do have to yell,' I said, 'because I want you to hear how much I hate you!'

"You've got to understand — up to this point Mama was having a good time — I think she thought it was cute that her daughter came and dragged her out of a bar. But when I said that, her face sort of caved in.

" 'I know you don't mean that, Faithy,' she said finally, and smiled like she was having a hard time remembering how to.

" 'I do, Mama,' I said. 'I just came by to tell you I'm leaving. I'm going back to Dallas, and if I'm lucky, I'm never coming back here, and if I'm even luckier, I'm never going to see you again.' "

Talk about kicking a dog when it's down, huh, Mama? Remember how you looked at me? Confused as if you hadn't heard right, but behind that was a deep pain because you knew you had.

"A couple bumped into us. They were on their way to a hangover too, and the woman said to you, 'What's the matter, honey? You look like you just lost your best friend.' And you said, 'No, but my daughter just told me she doesn't want to see me anymore.'

" 'Well, hello to you, Miss Ungrateful Little Bitch,' said the man, and I said, 'Shut up and mind your own business, you old drunk,' and I'm sure fists would have flown if somebody hadn't popped their head out of the screen door and yelled at the couple to come on inside because Booney Cunningham was buying everyone drinks.

"My mama staggered to her old Chevy; she was wearing high heels and trying to walk like she had every right to wear them, but her ankles kept turning.

" 'Where do you think you're going?' I asked, and she said, 'Out of your life — that's what you want, isn't it?'

" 'You can't drive,' I said as she got in the car. 'You're plastered.'

"She laughed. 'If you don't think I can drive like this, you don't know a thing about me.'

"She backed out and the car made a wide arc, and I grabbed the door handle and jumped in. Then instead of pulling out of the parking lot, Mama rested her head on the steering wheel and started crying hard.

" 'Oh, God, Mama, I do not need this right now.'

" 'I know that,' " she wailed, " 'I know you've never needed anything I had to give you.' "

I felt a hot gush of anger again remembering that night, but, Mama, it was nothing like the inferno that was in me at the time. I don't think I could have hated you more at that moment, and that hate was like lava pouring through my body. I got up from the bench; Audrey's body heat was making me feel choked. The sun had set by now, and dusk was unfolding its purple blanket.

" 'Anything you had to give me?' I said, my voice high-pitched with rage. 'And what might that be? Nights alone when you stayed out with some lowlife like that — that guy in the bar? Whole days when I wasn't allowed to make any noise at all — not even talk — because you had such a bad hangover? Or maybe you're referring to today, when what you gave me was another one of your promises that I should know by now don't come any way but broken.'

"Mama lifted her head, wiped her eyes with the palms of her hands, and said, 'I'm sorry I'm such a disappointment to you,' and then she stepped on the gas and tore out of the parking lot.

" 'Mama, pull over and let me drive!' I said as she barreled out onto the potholed road.

" 'Why should I? I drive home every night, and most of the time I'm a lot drunker than I am now,' she said, stepping on the gas, and I could see she was trying to hold on to whatever power she still might have over me.

" 'Mama, please,' I said, scared as the car plowed through the dark night.

"She turned onto the county road, driving fast but not weaving.

" 'Please what, Faith? Please apologize for being such a godawful mother? Don't you think I apologize for that every day of my life?'

" 'What?' I asked. It was not something I'd expected to hear.

" 'Christ, Faith,' my mother said, her voice bitter. 'Don't you think I apologize every day for everything?'

" 'Who do you apologize to?'

" 'Why, you, baby.'

"Hearing the total defeat in my mama's voice, I was suddenly ready to forgive everything, to start over, to try to understand her more, but then she started laughing, laughing like crazy, and I don't know if it was a release from an awkward moment or just my mama being mean.

"The car swerved then, and I shouted at her to pay attention, which must have tickled her rancid funny bone all the more, because she swerved the car again and then again, like the road was some slalom course.

"By this time my fury was enormous. If I'd been older, I'd probably have had a stroke. First she'd toyed with me and now she was making fun of me. Then I saw the headlights.

" 'Mama, there's a car coming!'

" 'I see it,' Mama said, still chuckling away. 'I got eyes.'

" 'Well, then, move!' I screamed.

" 'I am,' she said, still doing that infernal swerving.

" 'Mama!'

" 'You used to think this was fun when you were younger.'

" 'I don't think it's fun now!'

"The headlights were getting closer and I could hear the blare of a horn and Mama's laughter, and then we were in the right lane and I thought we were okay, but then she swerved again into the oncoming lane and I lunged over and grabbed the wheel, turning it to the right. I guess I turned too hard because a second later we were off the road and a second after that I heard this big explosion. Then there was dead silence except for the tinkling of glass, which sounded like chimes in a light breeze."

I looked at Audrey, whose false eyelashes

fringed wide-open eyes.

"And that's how I killed my own mama."

Well, Mama, of course I was taken up in my friend's arms and told how I certainly did not kill you and how awful it must have been for me keeping that inside all those years, etc., etc., etc., and then when we got back to New Orleans, Beau heard the whole story, and he called Wade and Bonnie and they flew down here, and we even visited your tiny little grave next to MawMaw's. Wade and Bonnie seem pretty shell-shocked, so I'm a little scared as to what the repercussions might be. Still, while I don't know if it's peace I feel, I feel better than I have in a long time.

> I'm sorry, but I'll bet you are too,
> Faith

HOST: **SLIP**
BOOK: *The Awakening* by Kate Chopin
REASON CHOSEN: "It's one of the books that should be on everyone's must-read list."

"Holy burden to bear," I said after we heard Faith's story. "Is that how you hurt your hip?"

Faith nodded. "I was thrown out of the car, but that was the only thing that broke. It healed fast, although I probably shouldn't have gone back to cheerleading that fall."

"Geez, Faith, what a lot to keep to yourself."

"It dragged me down for years." She looked around at the group. It was the day after Faith came back, and she had summoned us to her house. She had brewed a pot of coffee, but there were no accompanying treats — a sure sign of the seriousness of the meeting.

"So why didn't you tell us?" I asked. "Don't you know we would have helped you? Why didn't you trust us?"

"Slip," said Kari, "don't yell at her."

"I wasn't yelling," I said with a little pout. "Or if I was, it's just because I'm . . . well, I'm hurt, Faith. I don't like you shutting us out."

"That's the same thing Wade and Bonnie said," said Faith. "In fact, Wade left for a trip today, but he said that when he gets back, he might need some time away from me, just to sort things out." She let out a little sob. "And Bonnie's feelings are really hurt. She brought up this family tree story she had to do for school when she was about eleven, and she just screamed at me, 'Not only did you lie — you made up this whole ridiculous fantasy! You made me a liar!' " Faith dropped her chin and her shoulders shook. "But Beau — Beau just sent me those flowers." She nodded to a huge spray of yellow roses. "The card read . . ." But her crying made her unable to finish.

I took it upon myself to take the card out of its little plastic holder.

" 'I'm too far away to hold your hand in person,' " I read, " 'so I'm holding it in my heart.' "

Holy misplaced vengeance. I'd been so ready to punish Faith for not trusting me with her secrets — isn't that what friends are for, hearing about the things that don't make you perfect and loving you anyway? — that I'd failed to see how long she'd been punishing herself.

"I'm not too far away to hold your hand," I said, sitting back on the couch and taking her hand.

"Me neither," said Merit, taking her other hand, and we all sat there sniffling, thinking our own thoughts.

"I'm sure glad you were there with Faith," said Kari finally to Audrey.

"I was honored," said Audrey in a surprisingly humble voice.

"Why'd you go down there anyway?" I asked.

When Audrey didn't answer right away, Merit asked, "Did you . . . know something was going to happen?"

Audrey nodded, and I saw there were tears in her eyes.

"Audrey," said Kari, "are you all right?"

"I . . . well, something happened to me in New Orleans too."

"You mean other than saving my life?"

Audrey laughed and brushed away her tears with her two middle fingers, being careful not to poke herself in the eye with her long nails.

"You're being a little dramatic, Faith. All I did was listen."

"And I think that's all a person needs some-times to . . . well, to stay alive. Someone who'll listen." Faith widened her eyes and took a deep breath. "From now on, I'm never going to keep anything secret."

"Now, don't go crazy," I said. "Speaking for myself, I don't want to know *everything*. I just don't like to be frozen out."

"In that case," said Merit, "maybe I should tell you my secret."

"Oh, no," I said, "this isn't going to turn into a group confessional, is it? Because I don't really want to know who picked their nose as a kid or who slept with Todd Trottman while Leslie was soliciting for the Heart Fund."

"Todd Trottman," said Audrey with a laugh. "Eww, not even *I* would sleep with that fascist."

"It's only a secret," said Merit, ignoring our conversation about our old neighbors, "because I haven't told anyone yet. Get this: I think I'm going through menopause."

"Menopause," said Kari. "But you're only, what — forty-three?"

Merit nodded. "But I haven't had my period for two months."

There was a knowing exchange of looks.

"Merit," said Audrey, "maybe you're pregnant."

Merit did a spit take worthy of a Marx Brothers movie.

"Pregnant?" she said after wiping her mouth. "I can't be pregnant. Frank told me he's sterile."

"Maybe," I said, "he meant in the extra-clean sense."

That night I lay awake, staring at Jerry. He was always such a sound sleeper. Certainly that was the mark of a man with no secrets . . . or was it? I moved closer to him, trying to discern whether the peacefulness on his face was earned or whether he was trying to hide something.

"Jerry," I said, shaking his shoulder.

He was awake instantly, with that wild-eyed what's-wrong? look.

"Whuh?"

"Jerry, do you have any secrets you want to get off your chest?"

The man stared at me for a moment.

"Go to sleep, Slip," he said, rolling over.

I was comforted by Jerry's failure to humor me. Any other reaction would have convinced me that he might have secrets after all, although what kind, I could hardly imagine. If there's one thing I know, it's my husband. Then again, I had thought I knew Faith too.

I swatted my pillow a couple of times, as if recontouring it were going to help me go to sleep faster. Faith's confession had unsettled me — it wasn't what she told us now, but what she hadn't told us for so long. I don't like what I know to be true *not to be true,* because if it isn't, then what do I know?

I lay there in the dark, trying to think of any secret I might have kept from the Angry Housewives, and honestly, I couldn't. They knew that I had cheated on my twelfth-grade English exam ("That's one of your great shames?" Audrey had asked, practically hooting. "For crying out loud, I copied all my math homework from seventh grade on!"), knew that I felt inadequate for not nursing my first two kids, knew that in an effort to become taller I had tried all sorts of strange remedies, including tying my ankles to the bed frame and stretching to reach the headboard every single night of my thirteenth year.

That's not to say I didn't keep some things private — I didn't tell anyone about my sex life because I don't believe a sex life is anybody's business but that of the participants — but I had never misrepresented myself with a secret.

My head was buzzing (why did I drink coffee past five p.m.?), so, conceding defeat to insomnia, I got out of bed.

Some people opt for a glass of milk. My method of nudging myself back toward sleep is to get a little physical activity. I don't mean I whip on my running shoes and take a jaunt through greater Minneapolis. Usually all it takes to calm down my central nervous system enough to accept sleep is a little yoga and some upside-down pacing. Yes, I've found that my particular skill, coveted by all kids and most adults — walking on my hands — can be soporific when used at the right time.

Once when she was about seven, Flan had woken up from a nightmare and was not responding to any of my or Jerry's efforts to console her. Finally, out of desperation (she *wailed* when she was scared), Jerry had suggested that we try to amuse her.

"Why don't you walk on your hands?"

"Are you nuts?" I'd asked, but, willing to try anything, I flipped forward onto my hands and began walking around her small bedroom, greeting everything I saw at my upside-down eye level.

"Hello, dolls," I'd said, passing Flan's dollhouse. "Hello, Lincoln Logs. Hello, fuzzy bunny slippers."

The wailing hadn't stopped but definitely ebbed.

"Do you see Mommy, Flan?" Jerry had asked. "Isn't Mommy funny?"

"Hello, game of jacks, hello, *Heidi* book."

By the time I had taken my topsy-turvy inventory of what was on Flan's floor, my daughter was soothed to the point of laughing, and Joe, who had been awakened by all the hubbub, was standing in the doorway, requesting that I do his room next.

That night I'd gone back to bed and fallen asleep so fast and thoroughly that the next time I couldn't sleep, I stole downstairs and did a room-by-room tour on my hands. Even if it didn't make me sleepy, I thought, it would entertain me, but I'd slept soundly again afterward and had been using the technique ever since.

The living room was filled with a soft gray light as I hoisted myself up onto my hands and began walking around the couch and toward the archway that separated the living room from the dining room. Not to brag, but I'm a pretty skilled hand-walker; I can turn tight corners and go up stairs (not too many, though; more than five scared me). I always felt a sense of accomplishment when I navigated through a particular angle or narrow space.

"Geez, Mom!"

Startled, I scrambled to my feet.

"You scared me!"

"Sorry, Gil," I said, rubbing my temples. My head always pounded if I got up too quickly. "What time is it? Did you just get home?"

Gil looked at his watch. "Twelve-forty, and yes, I did."

The youngest and the only one still at home, Gil enjoyed a much looser curfew than his siblings had, yet rarely abused it.

"Are you hungry?"

Gil smiled. "If you made me something, I'd eat it."

At the kitchen table, enjoying the macaroni and cheese I warmed up for him, Gil, familiar with my alternative-to-sleeping-pills method, asked, "So why couldn't you sleep?"

"Well, I was with the Angry Housewives tonight and drank a lot of coffee." I helped myself to a forkful of the macaroni and cheese. "And Faith told us all about her trip to New Orleans and . . . and a lot of secret stuff."

Gil perked up. "What kind of secret stuff?"

"Oh, about finding out that Beau was gay and —"

"She just found out that Beau was gay? Mom, that wasn't exactly a secret."

"Well, it was to her." I proceeded to tell him the story Faith told us and was able, for once, to shock my seventeen-year-old son.

"Wow," he said, shaking his head. "Poor Mrs.

Owens. Trying to keep all that a secret all that time."

"Well, not only that, but creating a whole different reality: making her father a doctor and all that. My God."

Gil laughed.

"What?"

"You sound so offended. Like those stories she made up were a personal assault."

"They were in a way, I guess. I mean, don't you feel betrayed when somebody lies to you?"

"Depends on the lie, I guess. I don't think Mrs. Owens said anything to hurt you personally, Ma. She was just trying to protect herself — and trying to protect you from the person she thought you couldn't handle."

I sat for a moment considering this. "I . . . I just don't like people keeping things from me, no matter what their motive is. I don't like to be lied to."

Gil got up and, opening the refrigerator door, took the milk carton and proceeded to down its contents.

"Use a glass!" I said, which had to be up there on the top ten list of things most said by a mother.

"What you fail to realize," he said, reaching into the cupboard for a glass, "is that most people haven't had the kind of life you have, Ma. You had a stable home, were raised by parents who loved you, found a husband who loved you, and had children" — he lowered his voice in a tease — "who *worship* you. So why do you need to make anything up? You've got the perfect life."

He filled his glass with milk and returned the

carton to the refrigerator. I stared at him.

"How'd you get so smart?"

Gil tapped his forehead with his finger. "I'm taking psychology this year, remember?"

"Oh, yeah. And what kind of grade did you get last semester?"

My son, who has a grades-are-a-pointless-reward-system-that-encourages-rote-learning philosophy (one he actually wrote a paper on), smiled. "A C-minus," he said.

Because I still believe we have to have some kind of system by which to measure a student's progress, and most of all because I'm his mom, I smiled back and said, "Imagine how you could analyze me if you got an A."

PART FOUR

The Nineties

HOST: **MERIT**

BOOK: *Handling Sin* by Michael Malone

REASON CHOSEN: "Someone at the piano
bar recommended it — she said she had
laughed herself into convulsions."

The day after Audrey suggested Merit might not be going through menopause at all, Merit bought a kit and holed up in the bathroom long enough to read a copy of *Woman's Day* from cover to cover. Finally she was able to give in to the call of nature, peeing a steady stream and at the last moment aiming onto the strip of paper she held under her.

When the results confirmed Audrey's suspicion, shock, like a big bully, pushed her back onto the toilet.

This can't be happening, she thought. *I'm forty-three years old.*

Frank's bewilderment was bigger than Merit's.

"But I was told long ago I had an extremely low sperm count."

"I thought you said you were sterile!" said Merit.

"And I thought 'extremely low sperm count' and 'sterile' were sort of interchangeable." A moment passed before a big, gold-glinted smile

517

cracked though the bewilderment on his face.

"Aw, gee, Miss Mayes," he said finally, when his muscles tired from smiling, "I'm as tickled as a human being has a right to be. In fact, I'm surprised I'm still sitting here — I feel light enough to be floating up among the stars." He took Merit's hands and kissed them. "Now, of course I have some questions I must ask you. Number one: are you as thrilled as I am?"

Merit had to smile; he was practically bouncing with excitement.

"Number two," he continued, "do you believe in miracles? And number three: will you marry me?"

Frank's enthusiasm was catching. Merit's children were the joy of her life, and to have a baby with the man she had found true love with would certainly be a gift. Yet she found herself saying, "You don't have to marry me, you know."

Glee surged through Frank's body, making him writhe as if he were electrically charged. Finally, to ground it, he slapped his knee. "Oh, that's very noble of you, Merit. It's not as if we haven't been talking about it."

It was true, they had been.

"All right, then," said Merit, suddenly shy. "In answer to your questions: I don't know, yes, and the sooner the better!"

They hugged then, Merit catching a nail on the fibers of Frank's leisure suit jacket, and when they finally let each other go, Frank asked, "Did you keep it?"

"Keep what?"

"The strip thing. The tester." He shook his head, trying to come up with the right word. "The test thing that told you you were with child."

"Oh, *that* strip thing," said Merit. "Well, no, I didn't . . . but it still should be in the bathroom wastebasket."

"Let's get it now," said Frank, pulling her off the couch. "We've got to frame it or gild it or *something*."

Merit felt sheepish as she gathered her girls around the dining room table. If ever there was a case of "do as I say, not as I do," this was it.

After much beating around the bush, she finally smashed the bush to smithereens.

"You're what?" said Reni, while her younger sisters engaged in a contest to see whose jaw could drop further.

"You heard me," whispered Merit, drawing dashes in the tablecloth with her thumbnail, color blooming on her face.

"You mean you and Mr. Paradise had *sex?*" asked Jewel. After a moment of silence, everyone burst out laughing.

"Mr. Paradise and I love each other very much," she said, trying to bring some decorum into the discussion, "and we've talked of getting married, and in answer to your question" — a picture flashed in her head of Mr. Paradise and her in the dressing room at Claudio's piano bar, a room that was used more for undressing than dressing — "well, yes, I guess we did."

This caused another wave of laughter from the girls, and when it had ebbed, the girls had a store of questions and comments.

"So are you gonna marry him, Mom?"

"When's the baby due?"

"Did you think about having an abortion?"

"What am I supposed to tell my friends?"

"I don't know *one person* whose mom is having a baby."

"Weren't you using birth control?"

"I won't be the youngest anymore! In fact, I'll be — wow — fourteen years older than her . . . or him."

"What do you think you're going to have?"

"How are you feeling, Mom?"

It was the last question that brought Merit to tears.

"I feel all sorts of things," she said, her voice catching. "Scared, surprised, a little embarrassed . . . but most of all, excited."

"If you marry Mr. Paradise," said Melody, "he'll be our stepdad, won't he?"

Merit nodded.

"Then I'm excited too," she said, and her sisters nodded their assent.

The night before their wedding at the downtown courthouse (the important thing for them was the marriage, not the ceremony), Merit drove over to Frank's house (he had sold it and all its furniture to a young couple recently emigrated from Ukraine who would be moving in at the end of the week).

"I've got something to show you," she said, clutching a shoebox to her chest.

"What is it, honey?" he asked, curious and a little frightened.

Merit didn't say anything until she was seated on a plaid recliner in the small, narrow living room. Mr. Paradise sat across from her on the plaid davenport, his hands clasped around his knees. He didn't like that his bride-to-be looked so serious the night before their wedding, and found himself tensing his wiry body until he felt his bones might spring out of their sockets.

"Frank," began Merit, "I'm going to show you something I've never shown anyone." She lifted the cover. "Promise me you won't think I'm a mental case."

Frank's mind reeled, unable to understand even a smidgin of what Merit was talking about.

Slowly and deliberately, as if she were displaying pre-Columbian artifacts to a group of archaeologists, Merit took each item out of the box and set it on the pine coffee table that along with the plaid furniture had been sold as a set.

Frank's mind continued its uncomprehending spiral. Why wouldn't his beloved be able to throw away scraps of paper, crumpled tissues, a half-eaten baby biscuit, and a Q-tip that looked used, for heaven's sake?

Merit stared at the coffee table, her expression serious bordering on angry, but when she looked up at Frank she laughed.

"Oh, my gosh, Mr. Paradise — you should see your face! You have no idea what this is, do you?"

Pulling down his jaw, Frank scratched his sideburns.

"No, I can't say as I do."

Merit scrambled off the recliner and rushed to Frank's side, telling him the whole story of how she had put these things in her hair as a protest against her ex-husband's cruelty.

"And that helped you?" asked Frank when she was finished.

Merit nodded solemnly. "I think it kept me sane. Knowing this" — she unfurled a slip of paper that read *Dr. Eric Iverson is a quack* — "or this" — she held up a tissue — "having this stuff in my hair was my secret way of dishonoring Eric, of sticking out my tongue or giving him the finger all day long. And he had no idea."

"My brave Merit," said Frank, and he held her lovely face in his hands and kissed her.

After the courthouse ceremony and a bridal luncheon at Dayton's Oak Room, Reni drove her sisters back to school (Melody didn't want to miss choir and Jewel had a biology test), and the new Mr. and Mrs. Paradise walked hand in hand to the library, where Frank sat on his old vinyl chair and watched Merit through the glass as she played "Ode to Joy" and "The Man I Love" and "Maybe This Time."

At one point, Merit looked up to see Mr. Paradise wearing a peaceful smile on his face and sitting ramrod straight (the same posture he always had while listening to her play), and she thought, *That man is the father of my baby and my new husband.* The thought was as soothing as a psalm.

That night Claudio threw them a reception at the piano bar, and the Angry Housewives showed up in mismatched bridesmaids' dresses (although they all did share an overabundance of flounces and ruffles) Slip had scrounged up at Goodwill.

In the hotel room they had booked for their weekend honeymoon, Merit changed into the sheer black negligee the Angry Housewives had given her and arranged herself like a pinup girl on the bed. But pinup-girl positions aren't necessarily comfortable ones, and she rearranged herself again, wondering what was taking her groom so long. Finally she decided to investigate.

Frank was in front of the mirror, fiddling with his hair.

"Don't worry about your hair, handsome," she said, standing behind him and putting her arms around his waist, "I'm just going to mess it up in bed anyhow."

He smiled sheepishly, and immediately Merit knew something was up.

"What's going on?" She scrutinized him in the mirror, noticing that one hand was closed in a fist. "What have you got in your hand?"

"Nothing," he said unconvincingly, and then, noticing what she was wearing, he said with much greater conviction, "My God, Merit, you look beautiful."

"Don't change the subject. Now come on, Frank, open up."

Reluctantly Frank relaxed his hand, displaying a small tuft of hair with a candy heart attached to it.

"What *is* that?" said Merit.

Frank's laugh was tinged with embarrassment. "Well, it was supposed to be my secret way of honoring you, of saying that I'm the luckiest guy in the world."

Merit gingerly lifted the hairy heart off his palm and read, " 'Be mine.' "

"I glued it to my hair," he said as he bent his head to show her. "There's another one in there, but it's a bear to get out."

Frank's great oiled pompadour was as capable of subterfuge as her French roll had been. Pushing a section of it aside, Merit saw another candy heart hidden inside it.

"You didn't glue this to your scalp, did you?" she asked as she began to pry it out.

"No, I didn't glue it to my scalp. I'm not a sadist."

Merit twisted the candy heart.

"Ow!"

Several hairs clung to this heart too, but she held it between her fingers, inspecting it as if it were the Hope Diamond.

" 'I luv you,' " she read as a lump grew in her throat.

"I do," he said, and his hands slid over and up the sheer fabric of her negligee until they found skin.

As much as Merit's girls joked about their mother's condition to each other, the girls were thrilled that their mother had found someone like Mr. Paradise with whom to fall in love and have a baby. It made them believe in happy endings.

They rarely saw their own father, who was remarried to a very tan, very blond jewelry sales rep in Boca Raton. The favorite part of their visits was the part when they boarded the plane back to Minneapolis.

"I don't even feel like he's my dad," Melody had said on their last flight home, to which Reni replied, "I don't think he feels like our dad either."

But Frank Paradise, as soon as he met the girls, had asked them more questions than their father had asked in a lifetime. He took such an interest in what they did and thought that when Merit asked them what they thought of him, Jewel said, "He's like a teacher who thinks you're the smartest kid he's ever taught."

They had hunkered around the coffee table

playing Monopoly or Risk, Parcheesi or Scrabble; they had taken walks along the creek and Minnehaha Falls; they had, one rainy Saturday afternoon, watched an Abbott and Costello festival on TV, ordering pizza and entertaining themselves with endless versions of "Who's on First?"

High school friends of Melody's and Jewel's were always surprised to hear what the girls had done the night or weekend before, that the sisters had willingly, *happily* spent time with their mother and her new husband.

"You couldn't pay me to go to a movie with my family," said Chloe, Jewel's best friend. "I don't care if it had Tom Cruise *and* Matt Dillon in it."

Reni came home from school as often as she could; fortunately, Carleton College was less than an hour away. She loved school, but she loved her family and missed not only her mother and sisters but Mr. Paradise, with whom she liked to talk about astronomy, a shared interest.

"I'm not a churchgoing man," said Frank one night, sitting outside with Reni on lawn chairs, looking up at the stars. "But how can a person think there's not a higher power when they look up at this? Or when they look at this?" he added when Merit came out to sit with them.

Mr. Paradise was bowlegged and scrawny and wore dated clothes and a hairstyle that should have been retired into the Greasers Hall of Fame, but he was their mother's prince and therefore royalty to the girls.

"So what do you hope it'll be?" Jewel asked one evening, helping him and her mother plant impatiens in the shady wedge of earth under the backyard maple.

Mr. Paradise patted the soil for a moment before saying, "Well, a healthy baby would be wonderful. A healthy baby *girl* would be divine." He looked worriedly at Merit. "Don't get me wrong, I'd be perfectly happy if it was a boy."

"I know you would, Frank," said Merit, aware it was the truth. She divided a clot of pink and peach flowers. "I know that whatever we have, we'll be thrilled."

When Merit gave birth to a healthy six-pound-two-ounce girl, she was thrilled. Frank, on the other hand, was way past thrilled.

"It's Portia," he said in the reverent tone newscasters used when Neil Armstrong first stepped on the moon. "It's our Portia."

She wasn't a beautiful baby in the classic round, plump way Merit's other daughters had been; Portia had bandy legs and wrists the circumference of a pencil and a head that, until she got hair, was decidedly pointed. She was a colicky baby, and Frank, insisting that Merit try to sleep, walked the floor with her, patting her tiny back and feeling just as bad as she did when she bunched up in pain. She often woke up Jewel and Melody with her cries, but it was hard to bear any resentment toward someone who brought such happiness into the house. It didn't hurt that the baby loved to be sung to by the sisters, pursing her tiny mouth into an O of astonishment and kicking her feet in rhythm and pleasure. When she got older, Melody would put her in a little backpack when she played the piano, and the baby would jump up and down with excitement, singing along in baby syllables, kicking Melody's kidneys. Portia was pampered and petted and never in want of

526

arms to hold her or lips to kiss her.

Now, as a three-year-old, the little girl was being groomed by her two older sisters in preparation for Reni's college graduation ceremony.

"Hold still, you little monkey," said Jewel, trying to brush the small girl's hair.

"Don't wanna hold still," said Portia. "Wanna play with Dolly."

"Don't you want to look nice for Reni's graduation?"

"Alweady look nice. Look at my pwetty dress."

"Your dress is very pretty," agreed Melody. "Now your hair needs to match it."

"My hair's alweady pwetty," said Portia of her yellow hair.

"But it also needs to be brushed," said Jewel, "so you don't look like a wild animal."

"I *like* wild aminals — wild aminals like lions." She curled her fingers into claws and let out a leonine roar.

"Good heavens, is there a lion in the house?" asked Mr. Paradise, appearing in the doorway.

Portia bared her teeth again and roared, sending Frank down the hallway calling, "Help!"

Delighted, the little girl giggled, holding her fists to her mouth.

"What a naughty little lion you are," said Jewel, fastening a barrette in the yellow fluff of her sister's hair. "Scaring your daddy like that."

"He's not weally scared," said the three-year-old wisely. "He's just foolin'."

"I don't know," said Melody. "He looked pretty scared to me."

A cloud of concern passed over Portia's pixie features.

"Daddy?" she cried, and was out of the room in a shot.

After the family had settled itself in their seats and before the ceremony started, Merit excused herself. Emotion welled up inside her — Reni graduating from college! — and she wanted to be alone for a moment to compose herself. She found a drinking fountain and ducked her head toward the spigot, slurping up the cool water.

Standing up, she wiped her mouth with a ridge of knuckles and found she couldn't move her hand off her face.

She had known Eric was coming, but that didn't temper her reaction toward seeing him. A person might be warned of a tornado, but there's a vast difference between hearing a siren and seeing an airborne car or an uprooted pine tree whirl past you.

It was cruelty more than age that had trampled on the handsome face of Eric Iverson. To Merit his was the face of a hardened criminal sneering out at the world from a post office Wanted poster.

Merit turned, pretending she didn't see him but she had only taken a few steps before she felt his hand touch her arm. She flinched as if snakebitten.

"Merit," he said, and she forced herself not to scream, not to shield her face.

"Eric." Her mouth was so dry that her upper lip caught on her teeth.

"How many years has it been? My God, you're still absolutely ravishing." He looked her up and down. "I'm glad I didn't bring Pam — she would not appreciate seeing what a beauty my ex-wife still is."

"Excuse me, Eric, I have to get back to the ceremony."

"Come on, Mere, it hasn't started yet. Don't tell me you can't give the father of your children a couple minutes." He grinned, but Merit could see the tension in his jaw.

A group passed them in the hallway, including a small boy holding the hand of a solid-looking patriarch, and Merit wanted nothing more than to take the other hand and be led away from Eric to safety. But anger flared up amid the pile of fear and intimidation she had raked up around herself, and that flare was strong enough to ignite.

"Look, Eric," she said, wondering how long she could stand there without her heart beating, "you're not the father of *all* my children, and —"

"It's pretty obvious with your youngest." Eric chuckled, looking at his fingernails.

Merit was torn between two desires: the rational desire to walk away and the irrational one that wanted to know what he was laughing at. Irrationality won.

"What's so funny?"

Eric looked up from the fascinating scenic vista his fingernails offered him. "Well, come on Mere, you've got to admit that one's not going to win any beauty contests."

All sorts of thoughts imploded in Merit's head — *Don't lower yourself to his level! Don't defile yourself! Just walk away!* — but her brain was listening to no command other than the one that bellowed, *Smack him!*

Her arm drew back, and a second later her palm, in a deep resounding crack, slapped against his cheek.

Shielding the wounded side of his face with his hand, he gaped at Merit, but it didn't take long for his surprise to turn to rage. Merit stepped back, frightened and sickened by the fury in his eyes, the same fury she had seen dozens of times in their marriage.

"Why, you —" he began, but his threat was cut off when two elderly women, fanning themselves with the commencement programs, turned in the hallway toward them.

"Good evening, ladies," said Eric, as cordially as a cruise director. "Big night tonight, isn't it?"

"Oh, yes," said one of the women. "My grandniece's graduation!"

"My grand*daughter's,*" said the other.

Eric's smile twisted into a sneer as soon as the women passed them.

"Don't you ever do that again," he said, and the menace in his voice turned Merit's knees to jelly. Nevertheless, there was no way her words could be stopped.

"And don't *you* ever say anything that reminds me how truly mean and stupid you are," she said, "because if you do, I won't just slap you; I'll do what you did to me all those years and beat you silly."

"Come on, you know I never beat —" he began, but Merit held up her hand and shushed him.

More than anything she wanted to get away from him, away from the toxic cloud that was his aura, but she wanted to let him know one more thing.

"Life with you was hell, Eric, but I guess I had to live through hell to get to paradise." A zip of pleasure made her eyes round and her mouth purse — my gosh, she had said a line worthy of the Angry Housewives!

I can't wait to tell them, she thought as she hustled toward the commencement stands, where she'd watch the eldest of her four spectacular daughters graduate magna cum laude.

HOST: **AUDREY**
BOOK: *The Stand* by Stephen King
REASON CHOSEN: "I like to read fun and scary horror stories because our own horror stories are scary enough but never fun."

It was in counseling Faith that I finally came to realize how strong my own faith was.

"I think I might want to be some kind of minister," I said to Grant a couple days after I had returned from New Orleans.

We were sipping peach brandy in Grant's cozy little den, whose walls he had painted deep scarlet and whose sofa and chair were upholstered in a deep green velvet. It made you feel Christmassy in a no-pressure, don't-have-to-buy-any-gifts sort of way.

Grant's eyes widened and he coughed discreetly, as if he wasn't shocked by what I'd said but had only swallowed wrong.

"Some kind of minister," he said, "as in a minister of culture or a minister of finance or a minister minister?"

"A minister minister," I said, feeling like I wanted to burst out laughing and crying at the same time.

"Audrey," said Grant, taking my hand and

holding it in his like it was some sort of treasure. "How did this all come about?"

"It all started when you and Stuart invited me to go to church — I've told you that. For a long time I just tagged along for the brunch afterward, but . . ." I stopped for a moment, my feelings too big for words. "Well, more and more God has grown to be a presence in my life."

"Audrey, you're crying."

"I am?" I swiped at my cheeks, and sure enough, they were wet. "Well, I just . . . I just . . . oh, Grant, in the hotel room in New Orleans, I saw God."

"Was he there for Mardi Gras?" Grant let go of my hand to get to his brandy. "I'm sorry, Audrey, I shouldn't joke about seeing God." He took another liberal sip. "So what'd He look like?"

"He didn't look like anything. I mean, there was no white beard or long robes or anything. He was . . . it was . . . more of an aura."

"Well, maybe you left a light on." Grant drew his mouth together in a thin line. "Sorry. No more jokes. It's just that . . . well, I don't know that I've ever met anyone who's seen God before, Audrey. And because it's you — because I know you can see things other people can't — well, it makes me believe you, and that makes me scared."

"But you believe in God, Grant."

He nodded. "That doesn't mean I want to see Him. Or have my friends see Him. That just seems too . . . I don't know, too *weird*."

I sat for a moment, remembering everything, and even though I felt calm on the inside, I could feel the tears oozing out of my eyes.

"That night I was in my hotel room after Faith and I got back from visiting her hometown, trying to go to sleep, when all of a sudden — well, this light filled the space around my bed. I froze — really, I was scared stiff — but then all the fear just evaporated like teakettle steam when you turn off the burner. Instead I felt . . . I felt like a baby, Grant, a baby being rocked in loving arms that I knew would never drop me."

"It sounds like a hymn."

Nodding, I wiped again at the tears that were leaking out of me without my consent. "And then He said, 'Help me, Audrey. I need your help.' "

"God asked you to *help* Him? Help Him do what?" Sitting on his legs, Grant leaned toward me on the couch until I could feel the heat of his breath and smell the peaches in it.

"Help Him in His work is what I think He meant."

"Well, what did His voice sound like? Was it like Charlton Heston's or more urbane, like John Gielgud's?"

"You don't believe me."

"I don't want to believe you," said Grant. "I don't want to believe that God would come into your New Orleans hotel room and tell you to help Him with His work. It's too scary." Two diamonds glistened in the corners of his own eyes. "But I do believe you." The tremble that was in his voice zigzagged into his hand as he reached for the decanter on the coffee table.

He refilled our glasses and we sat there quietly, or as quietly as two people can be when their breathing sounds as if they've just raced each other around the block.

"So what *did* His voice sound like?"

"I don't think I really heard His voice with my ears. I think it was just in my head, the way you hear your thoughts. And you know how your own thoughts sound like the voice you think you have?"

"What do you mean?"

I took a big sip of my brandy and the syrupy taste of peaches spilled down my throat. "Well, have you ever heard a recording of your voice and you think, 'ugh, that doesn't sound like me'?"

Grant nodded. "I hate hearing my voice. I sound so whiny."

"And what does your thinking voice sound like?"

"Like Charlton Heston. Or John Gielgud."

I smiled. "Well, I can't say who my thinking voice sounds like, but I heard God in it."

"So God's a woman?"

"I . . . I don't think so. No, I don't think God's a man or a woman. All I know is I heard God's voice in my thinking voice."

"So maybe it's true what they say in Sunday school?" asked Grant, his voice as light as a boy's. "That God's inside all of us?"

The simple logic of that first surprised me, then made me happy.

"Maybe so. Maybe He — or She or It — is."

Grant raised his glass. "Then let's drink to that. To God inside all of us — or is that sacrilegious?"

I shrugged and took a drink. "God probably appreciates being toasted."

Grant clinked my glass with his own. "You're gonna be a wonderful minister, Audrey."

★ ★ ★

I believe in luck and I believe in God. In my case, it seemed they joined forces like tag-team wrestlers, knocking away obstacles and putting the opposition in full nelsons and sleeper holds.

Doubt shadowed me as I began my pastoral training (taking classes with earnest men young enough to be my sons), but just as I was ready to admit I wasn't up to the challenge, Kari might drop by with a plate of divinity ("Can you think of anything more appropriate?" she asked), or Slip might show me an article she clipped out of *Time* about sexism in the church and tell me how much the world needed strong leaders like myself, or Faith would give me a gift certificate for a full-body massage from a client whose spa waiting room she'd just redecorated. Merit, knowing how much I enjoyed Portia's company, would send the little girl over and we'd spend a blissful afternoon playing or coloring, or Portia would quietly page through one of the many picture books I had saved from my boys' childhoods as I grappled with subjects like forgiveness or eternity.

"Mama says you're going to be a pastor," Portia said one day as we were building a castle.

"Ouch," I said as the sharp edge of a Lego met the soft edge of my butt. With my hands, I swept the area clear of all hard plastic and repositioned myself.

"I hope so," I said, snapping a window into place. "Although sometimes it seems I've bit off more than I can chew."

"You bit off more than your shoe?"

I chuckled and explained the saying.

"I don't think I'll be a pastor when I grow up,"

said Portia, and I looked at the five-year-old wistfully, knowing how fast that time would come. I missed the screaming, laughing children who'd grown up and left the neighborhood, missed my own houseful of screaming, laughing boys. "Mommy says my grandpa was a pastor too, but he died." She added another row to the tower. "I don't think being a pastor would be much fun."

"How come?"

Portia shrugged her narrow shoulders. There was not an ounce of fat on her anywhere and she was all sharp angles, but I couldn't imagine a more huggable kid. "I don't think it would be very much fun having to love God all the time."

I bit my lip, not wanting Portia to think I didn't take her seriously.

"What do you mean, honey?"

The little girl looked at me with the bright blue eyes she'd inherited from Mr. Paradise. "I mean sometimes it's fun to be naughty."

I nodded. She had a point.

"You can still be naughty and be a pastor."

The little girl's eyes grew round. "You can?"

"Sure. I want to be a pastor but sometimes I want to do naughty things. Or say naughty things like *poopy* or *potty-head*."

Portia looked at me for a moment as if I had lost my marbles. "Auntie Audrey!"

"Poopy, potty-head!"

It took only a second for Portia's look of surprised outrage to change into a look of sheer glee.

"Poopy, potty-head," and then besting me, she added, "Pee-pee, bottom, *vagina!*"

We stared at each other for a moment, our

537

mouths O's of shock, reveling in our naughtiness before bursting into laughter.

"Oh, Auntie Audrey," she said after our laughter had sapped all energy out of our bodies and we sagged against each another, limp as noodles. "That was really naughty and that was really *fun!*"

"Yes, it was," I agreed. "It was more fun than naughty, though."

"But those were such bad words!"

"They weren't said out of meanness."

"*Potty-head* is mean."

"Yes, but you knew I wasn't calling you a potty-head. I was just saying the words because I knew they'd make you laugh."

Portia sat for a moment, staring at the castle we'd taken a break from building. "So you can say some words to make someone laugh and that's okay, but if you say the same words to make someone feel bad, then it's naughty?"

"Something like that. But you wouldn't want to say *potty-head* to very many people, even if you meant it just in fun."

"I'm going to be in first grade next year."

"I know you are, Portia," I said, following her conversational left turn. "You're getting to be a big girl."

She picked up a Lego half person — a head on top of an open-ended half circle — and placed it inside the tower.

"That's the princess who wants to be rescued."

I found another person and placed it on the drawbridge.

"Here's the prince who's coming to save her."

Holding the princess to the window, she

shouted, "Poopy potty-head!" Then she looked at me, wary and mischievous at the same time.

"She's saying that out of meanness," she said. "And that's why the prince won't rescue her."

"Maybe he will anyway," I said, and the Lego prince in my hand took a giant leap so that he hovered by the tower window. "It doesn't matter what you call me, my darling princess, I still love you!"

I've seen clouds pass over people's faces, but what passed across Portia's sharp little features was the sun.

"Oh my darling prince," she said, her Lego princess jumping up and down, "I love you too!"

I really enjoyed the classroom mock counseling sessions. That morning, with a fellow seminarian from Pierre, South Dakota (whose dimples, I couldn't help noticing, were deep enough to hold water), I had been counseled as to how to handle my excessive gambling, and I counseled him about his rampant alcoholism. I went home feeling like I was Dr. Joyce Brothers and C. S. Lewis rolled into one. *Parishioners, bring on your problems, your fears and phobias: I can handle them.* My hubris lasted until the early evening, when Grant came over, asking if I'd like to take a walk.

This put me on immediate alert. Whatever Grant and I do together always involves some kind of chair; our sedentary friendship does not involve exercise. But I grabbed my jacket and off we went, down the block toward the creek.

The second clue I was given that something was wrong was that Grant wasn't saying anything. (I sometimes wonder if naturally quiet people get boisterous and noisy when they're upset.)

"Maybe I should just shut up," I said after failing to get any kind of response after what I thought was my very funny recounting of the counseling session ("And then I said, 'Money's the least valuable commodity you lose when you gamble' ").

"Earthling, earthling — do you read me?" I said as he walked with a haze over his face, seemingly oblivious to me or his surroundings. "This is Uranus."

No response.

"Grant, look — there's an albino squirrel!"

He looked to where I pointed, startled.

"Aha, you *are* conscious."

When his eyes met mine, a section of my heart caved in. I had seen sadness and I had seen terror, but I couldn't think of the last time I'd seen them together.

"Audrey, Stuart's HIV-positive."

This is the picture postcard that was frozen in my memory: an impossibly blue October sky, red and gold leaves lying on the grass like discarded pompoms of Team Nature. Minnehaha Creek was meandering its way down to the river, its water brown and foamy as root beer. It was the kind of day that deserved a big bow around it, the kind of day that made you happy to be in the human race because this was a gift too big for just one person . . . and yet if it was so beautiful, why was I suddenly wishing for yesterday?

"Grant," I said, and it sounded as if I had swallowed the desert. "Grant."

His arms were around mine and mine were around his, and we stood until our brains were able to send messages that jump-started our legs. We staggered to a park bench as if we'd both been punched in the stomach.

"He called me this morning," said Grant.

My reflex was immediate: I whispered, "Bastard."

He had been coming in and going out of Grant's life, claiming first that he couldn't live without Grant and then that he couldn't live with him. When I first met Stuart, I'd had him pegged as the stable one in the relationship; he was so calm and self-assured, while Grant seemed flighty and insincere. Stuart wore the beautifully cut suits, the grown-up clothes, while Grant belted his pants with scarves and wore shirts the color of poster paint. But Grant's flamboyance only accessorized his deeper qualities, which were kindness and generosity and a heart as loyal and true as I had ever known. Grant never strayed from Stuart, even when he tried to convince me that "this time I'm absolutely through with him."

"I can get along without sex," he'd told me more than once. "I mean, come on; there's always chocolate."

"He called me from Miami," Grant continued now, a little jag in his voice. "Not to alert me, but to accuse me. He said that he wanted to thank me for giving him AIDS."

"That *bastard*," I said, but it was way too small a word for my rage.

"I started crying — as much as I didn't want to, I couldn't help it, Audrey — and I told him that was impossible. He knew he was my only lover."

"Ever?" I asked, taken aback.

"Ever since our first date way back when."

541

Grant shrugged. "What can I say? I'm one of the last old-fashioned girls."

"I wonder how many men Stuart had," I said bitterly. "I'm sure every time he ran out on you he found someone else and —"

Holding up one hand, Grant shook his head. "It'll drive me crazy if I think like that, Audrey."

"When are you getting tested?"

"Tomorrow. Will you go with me?"

"Of course I will. What else can I do?"

"Well," said Grant, who's not afraid of seizing a moment, "how about letting me join the Angry Housewives."

"You still want to be a member? You haven't mentioned it for years."

"I've never stopped wanting to be a member; I just quit asking because I got tired of always being shot down."

Our vote for his inclusion was unanimous.

"Let me be the one to tell him he's in," said Faith, "since I was the one who kept him out for so long."

"He'd like that," I said, sending up a balloon of thanks to God for another sign of grace.

Miracle of miracles, Grant tested negative.

"Although I am going to get another test in a couple of months," he told the Angry Housewives at his first official meeting, "just to make doubly sure."

"So how could Stuart have it and not you?" asked Slip.

Good old Slip, I thought; *can't talk about her own sex life but doesn't mind asking someone else about theirs.*

Grant helped himself to a bowl of grapes. (I had racked my brain trying to figure out what scary food to serve along with our Stephen King discussion and had come up with nothing more unusual than grape "eyeballs," cupcakes with gumdrop tombstones, and a cold pasta salad I had tried to mold into a brain. It was not my finest effort.)

"Well," he said finally, "we haven't been together for —"

"Never mind," said Slip. "It isn't any of my business. I'm just glad you're okay."

"Me too." He took in a deep breath. "Wow. To be given a clean bill of health and be invited into the Angry Housewives . . . well, let me toast my good fortune."

"Here, here," said Merit, picking up her glass.

After we had all toasted, Faith said, "I'm sorry I voted against you for so long, Grant. I was just . . . scared."

"That's why your vote now means so much to me," he said.

"I was so scared," repeated Faith, the tip of her nose growing pink. "You know, I was in denial about Beau being gay and . . . well, I'm sorry I was mean to you."

"You weren't mean," said Grant. "Just a little cold. But now you're warm, and I can't tell you how much I appreciate the rise in temperature."

"I just think of people being mean or cold to Beau because of what he is and I can't stand it. I can't stand to think that I was one of those people."

"Don't worry about it, Faith," said Grant, and I could tell he was eager to get the focus off himself and onto the meeting. "Now, when am I

543

going to learn the secret handshake?"

"Secret handshake?" said Merit. "We don't have a secret handshake."

"You don't have a secret handshake?" said Grant, his voice dripping with disbelief. "What kind of two-bit book club is this?" He tsked, shaking his head. "All right, then, teach me the secret pledge."

"Secret pledge?" began Merit. "We —"

"Ah yes, the secret pledge," said Slip. "Can we trust him with it?"

A log popped and the fire threw up new flames.

Slip's smile would have made a fox's look benign. "Okay. How does it start again, Faith?"

Faith's shoulders bounced once in a quick laugh. "Actually, it's so secret, I'm a little unsure how it starts. Audrey?"

All eyes were on me, and most of them were twinkling.

Standing up, I struck a classic assembly reciter's pose, elbows out, each hand around the opposite wrist. I stood for a moment, screaming internally for inspiration to come. Suddenly Henry Fonda's black-and-white face came into my head (I'd just seen *The Grapes of Wrath* on the classics channel) as well as his stirring, you-can't-beat-me-down speech.

"Wherever there's a book to read," I said, my voice gravelly, "I'll be there."

I ignored the hoots and hollers.

"Wherever there's a friend in need —"

"Hey, you rhymed," noted Grant.

I glared at him for interrupting the flow. *"I'll be there."*

"Wherever there're potluck lovers to feed . . ."

544

Merit and Kari stood up like soldiers and joined in on the chorus, and I don't know who made the alteration but we all said it: "*We'll* be there."

"We were all going to have the pledge tattooed on our bodies," Slip said to Grant as she too stood up. "But it's a little long."

"Wherever there's . . ." My mind scrambled, trying to think of more rhyming words.

"Wherever there's a woman with a mean husband from whom she needs to be freed . . . ," offered Merit, speeding up the words so they'd fit the meter of the rhyme.

"We'll be there." Now everyone was standing and lending their voices to the chorus.

Kari took a tiny step forward and her words came out faster than Merit's. "Wherever there's a baby who needs to have its diaper changed because it peed . . ."

"We'll be there."

"Wherever anyone has questions about their creed . . . ," I said.

"We'll be there."

"Wherever anyone needs to spill their guts," said Faith, "without judgment or . . ." She looked wildly at the rest of us and then (talk about grasping at straws) added, "Or feels like quoting Margaret Mead . . ."

Irreverent laughs interrupted the chorus, and then an adjustment was made to it — I think it was by Kari — "Angry Housewives will be there."

"Wherever," began Slip when we'd composed ourselves, "people are given lousy diagnoses, or need advice about their kids, or want to learn about blow jobs, or get tired and need someone

545

to take the lead . . ."

"Angry Housewives will be there."

I wondered when I had dropped my pose to hold Merit's and Slip's hands, but I had. We were all standing there, holding hands like a prayer circle, an encounter group, or a team before the big game, and I thought, *Okay, I'm gonna lose it,* but then Slip asked Grant if he'd mind reciting the whole thing back to us.

"Actually, I was thinking this might be a good time to dig into the dessert I brought. I didn't bring anything to fit the theme of the book — horror doesn't exactly inspire a lot of recipes — but some people have said it's the best dessert they've ever tasted."

"Ooh," said Faith. "What is it?"

"Well, it's called I Must Be Dreaming Cheesecake. It's chocolate drizzled with caramel and —"

But we didn't let him finish. Really, I'm surprised someone wasn't bloodied in our mad scramble to beat one another into the kitchen.

HOST: KARI

BOOK: *My Antonia* by Willa Cather

REASON CHOSEN: "I needed my Cather fix."

When Anders' wife Sally died, his will to live followed suit. Kari went over to her brother's house as much as possible, cooking up meat loaf dinners (you'd never know it was his favorite, the way he picked at it), playing card games (inevitably, he'd lay his hand down after a few plays and stare off), and trying not to get *too* annoyed at the television set, which as far as she could see was never turned off.

Her brother, so interested in life, now hadn't the strength or interest to open up a newspaper, turn on the radio, or ask Kari about herself and Julia. His wide interests narrowed to one single subject: how much he missed his wife.

"I'm worried about him," said Randy, the one child of his who didn't live states away. "He won't even come to our house for dinner."

"That's right," said Beth, Randy's wife. "He says he doesn't have an appetite."

"I know," said Kari. "It looks as if he's lost at least ten pounds."

"When Nichol brought over her new baby," said Randy, "he cried and cried, saying how it wasn't fair that he got to see their first great-grandchild and Sally didn't. Nichol felt terrible."

"Uffda," said Kari. "That's not like him at all."

"Libby's his only great-grandchild," reminded Beth, shaking her head.

Kari knew from her own bout with grief (and *bout*, she thought, was an apt word; dealing with a spouse's death was like being in a boxing match and knowing you were going to get battered) that Anders might hear whatever advice or solace she had to offer, but that didn't mean he'd listen to it. When Bjorn died, Kari had at least had youth and its resilience on her side; Anders was seventy-seven, and if he thought his life was over, it was likely that his body was going to be in agreement.

And so while it saddened Kari when one morning Anders failed to wake up, it didn't surprise her. In his eulogy, Kari paid tribute to what she thought was most important about her brother: the great love Anders had been blessed with.

"He was a good man made excellent by loving so deeply," she told the mourners at the funeral.

The Angry Housewives, who sat together in the scarred pew of the Lutheran church, each had their own thoughts regarding the eulogy.

Blessed is right, thought Audrey. *Finding true love is as much of a gift as being able to paint or sing or understand nuclear fission.* (In college, her youngest son Michael had finally been able to focus on academics rather than his fervid social life and had nearly completed his master's degree in physics.)

Audrey wasn't bitter that she hadn't yet found true love; instead, knowing others had found it, she was hopeful that she might. And hope itself, she was finding, was enough of a gift.

Finding her talents and sense of irreverence better suited to guiding and counseling teenagers, Audrey was now a youth minister at a Unitarian church. She also volunteered Tuesday mornings at an AIDS hospice, giving whatever comfort she could to people whose need for it was like a mountain she knew she'd never be able to climb. Still, hope was her rope, her ice axe, her Sherpa guide.

Slip stifled a yawn, which was a reaction not to Kari's words but to a fatigue that made her suspect lead had replaced all the blood in her veins.

Having never experienced this sort of weariness before, Slip thought she could will it away, and weeks later was astonished that the fatigue was stronger than her mind. As much as she tried to hide it — her high energy defined her more than her freckles or her size — Jerry couldn't help but notice.

"I'm taking you to the doctor," he said one evening as he watched her trudge up the stairs, holding on to the banister as if it were a tow rope.

And he had, the day before, and now they were waiting for blood tests that would show what Slip was almost convinced was a potent case of anemia. It was the *almost* that bothered her. When Slip was certain of something, she was *certain,* but now a tiny moth of doubt flitted around in her head and she was unable to swat it away with assurances.

Pay attention, Slip scolded herself, but seconds later she was trying to talk herself into believing that maybe it was mononucleosis. *I could have picked it up from a client at work or one of the kids' friends.* The moth thrummed its wings inside her head.

Slip forced herself to listen to Kari's words. She had met Anders and Sally at the big events in Julia's life, from christening to graduation parties, and it was true, the two of them had obviously still been in love. But true love doesn't seem so miraculous when one has it oneself, and Slip couldn't imagine anyone on the whole planet better suited for her than Jerry. She had no doubt that Jerry felt the same way. Her daughter Flannery, who had broken up with the second boyfriend she'd assumed was going to make the transition into being her husband, complained about it to Slip over the phone.

"If you and Dad hadn't had such a perfect marriage, my standards wouldn't be so high."

"I'm sorry," said Slip with a chuckle. "Not about my so-called perfect marriage, but about Loren. I know you thought he might be the one."

"Oh, Mother," said Flan impatiently, " 'the *one*.' Does 'the *one*' choose you or do you choose him? Does 'the *one*' even exist?" She exhaled a long sigh. "At least I've got more time to work on my novel."

Slip felt her eyelids, also weighted with lead, begin to drop. Jerking her head back, she opened her eyes as wide as she could, so that Faith tilted her head toward her and asked, "Slip, are you all right?"

"Fine," snapped Slip.

Well, what's up her hind end? Faith wondered. But whereas the old Faith would have pouted about being wrongfully scolded (and then assumed that maybe she *had* done something

550

worth scolding), the new Faith simply brushed off Slip's bad mood.

Daily there were instances in which she recognized how different the new Faith was from the old Faith — when Audrey announced yesterday that Dave and his wife were having another baby, Faith didn't feel that old pinch in her heart, didn't immediately start to count up the good fortunes of someone else, finding her own came up short in comparison.

Bonnie, for instance, had been living for years with her boyfriend and seemed to have given marriage and children no more thought than she gave to what the weather was going to be like the next week. While Faith sometimes fantasized about now nice it would be to hold a grandchild in her lap, she no longer stood over the pot of what is, stirring in little poison dollops of "but it should be like this."

"Not only was Anders a husband," Kari continued, "he was a father, and his arms were a wide net for his children, always open and ready to catch them."

Faith thought of Wade and how hard it had been for him when he found out his son was gay. Of course, at the same time he had learned his wife had been lying to him for years; Faith didn't blame him a bit when he moved into a hotel, telling her he needed to think things through by himself.

Two weeks later he returned, telling her — yelling at her — that what hurt him most was that she thought he couldn't handle the truth about her. Hell, he loved her, and if she'd been an ex-con with a tattoo, he'd still love her, didn't she know that?

"I'm so sorry, Wade," she said. "I thought I was keeping secrets to protect you, not to betray you."

He agreed to see a counselor with Faith, although for the first few sessions he was mute, feeling as shy and stupid as a boy dating a foreign exchange student. Gradually he began to talk, and what he talked about was not Faith's betrayal, which he was beginning to understand, but what it felt like to have his only son be gay.

"I can't stand to think of him having sex," he said, shaking his head.

"Do you think of your daughter having sex?" asked the counselor, and Wade felt an impulse to slug her in the mouth.

"Jesus, no!"

"Then give Beau the same courtesy you give your daughter," said the counselor.

Wade wondered how much he had played a part in his son's gayness — "Was it something I did or didn't do? Something I said or didn't say?" — and when the counselor told him it was all right to feel hurt ("after all, you have lost the son you thought you had, but remember, you still have a son"), he had bowed his head and cried in a way he couldn't remember crying.

Faith's heart had opened like a sunflower on a summer morning, and she touched his back, her hand moving slightly as his shoulders shook, filled with love for her husband.

She wrote to her mother that night, describing how they had left the counselor's office exhausted and puffy-eyed but holding hands. Her letters to her mother were too much of a habit to break, but they had lost all accusation and resentment, and most of all, they had lost their sorrow.

Grant and Merit flanked the other Angry Housewives, and Grant felt it a sign of his mental health that when Kari was talking of true love, he wasn't blubbering about Stuart.

He had flown out to Baltimore when Stuart called from a hospital. He had said his goodbyes, proud that he hadn't broken down (he had cried, but there was a big difference in Grant's mind between breaking down and crying). Stuart hadn't apologized for anything — not for his infidelity or his lying, or for the unsafe sex from which he had gotten AIDS and with which he could have passed the virus along to Grant; in fact, he accused Grant of deserting him in his time of need, "because you always were a selfish bastard."

"Really?" Grant had said, his knuckles white pebbles under his clenched fists. "And I always thought you liked me because I was good for a laugh."

A smile had stretched itself across the emaciated planes of Stuart's face. "You're right, you were."

That was as good as it was going to get for Grant during that bedside visit, but it had been good enough, and when he kissed the dry, hot forehead of the man he had loved more than anyone else, he knew that, for at least a little while, Stuart had loved him too.

It was only Merit, who usually listened to people with the avidness of a show dog awaiting commands, who was not moved by Kari's words to ponder love; in fact she had no idea what Kari was talking about, having tuned out her voice.

Her mind was on her daughter Reni, who had come into the piano bar last night with another medical student and after listening to at least a half dozen requests, politely made her own. "Will you play 'The Wedding March'?"

As soon as the words had been released into the air, Merit knew what was being said.

"Reni!" she said, touching each patron on the shoulder as she rushed around the piano to hug her daughter.

"Who's the lucky man?" one of the regulars asked.

"Why, Dale, of course," said Reni, breaking the hug. She leaned back slightly and looked at the young man who sat next to her, beaming like a lighthouse beacon.

"Dale!" said Merit. "I thought you two were just study partners!"

"We were," said Dale, looking beatific and uncomfortable at the same time. "But I was studying her all along."

"It took me a while to realize that," said Reni. "But when I did, I thought, *Hmmm, he's almost as interesting as viral pathogens.*"

"Gee, you're a romantic," said a regular who only requested songs by the Gershwins or Irving Berlin.

"Yeah, Merit," said another. "Don't you have any songs about viral pathogens you can play?"

Reni blushed. "That's just what we were studying when . . . when I noticed how long his eyelashes were."

Merit leaned toward Dale and peered into his eyes. "Oh, my, you're right, Reni. They *are* long."

It had been a festive night at the piano bar, with toasts made and a free plate of Claudio's chicken wings (the house special) delivered to the newly engaged couple. Merit honored request after request, glad that there were so many love songs that there was no danger of running out.

After the funeral luncheon, Kari and Julia and Mary Jo, who had flown in from London, helped put away the chairs and tables in the church basement.

"Kari, please. You don't have to do this," said one of the older men of the congregation.

"I want to, Norman. I thought Anders might appreciate it."

A twinkle found its way through Norman's milky blue eyes. He and Anders, in their capacity as church volunteers, had put away thousands of tables and chairs, and Anders, lounging now on some celestial surface (Norman doubted it was a cloud but didn't doubt that it was soft and comfortable), was probably getting a kick out of watching his sister and old buddy doing manual labor.

"Well, now," said the old Swede, "just don't hurt yourself."

When they were done, the three women sat down on the stage, admiring the clean empty space before them.

"Say, would you gals like some coffee before I dump out the last pot?" asked one of the church circle women, coming out of the kitchen.

"No, thanks, Agnes," said Kari. If Jesus had appeared at their banquet and offered to turn water into wine, the parishioners of Lake Hiawatha Lutheran would have thanked him but politely requested coffee instead.

"Do you need anything else?"

Kari shook her head. "We're fine."

"All right, then, but you just give a holler if you need *anything*."

"I will," said Kari.

The remaining members of the kitchen and cleanup crews said their goodbyes, reminding Kari to call if she needed anything and double-checking whether all the kitchen lights and burners were turned off.

In the silence the volunteers left behind, the three women sat with their hands tucked under their thighs, their legs dangling over the edge of the stage.

"What are you thinking, Mom?" Julia asked, seeing the slight smile on her mother's face.

Kari leaned into her daughter. "How happy I am to see you, even if it's under these circumstances." Julia had recently been transferred to her ad agency's West Coast offices. "And you too, Mary Jo. You're both so cosmopolitan. San Francisco and London. My goodness."

The smile returned to her face as she sat quietly for a moment. "And I was also thinking of how many things happen in church basements. I mean, all the fancy stuff — the sermons, the baptisms, the weddings, the funerals — go on upstairs, but it seems I have more memories of what's happened in church basements."

"Like your mother's book club?" asked Julia.

Kari's smile widened as she nodded. "Yes, I was thinking about all those women getting together at that little country church and riling up old Mr. Moe, and I was also thinking about Norman — one of the men putting the tables and chairs away, the tall, good-looking one."

Julia nodded, even though she would never

have described the old, stooped man as good-looking.

"Anyway, after Bjorn's funeral, when everyone was gathered down here for the luncheon, Norman offered to get me a plate of food. I said I wasn't hungry, but he said I had to eat something. He walked away, and the next thing I knew, he set a plate of chow mein in front of me — I'm not kidding, it was piled this high!" Kari gestured with her hands. "I was absolutely numb with grief, but something about that plate piled up a mile high with chow mein made me laugh. It was a tiny little laugh — I doubt if anyone could even hear it — but I was so grateful to Norman for it, because it seemed some kind of proof that God was still at work."

"I remember what good friends Dad and Norman were," said Mary Jo. "Remember how they used to do that dumb little clog dance every year at the church social?"

Kari smiled. "Sven and Ole, the world's worst dancers." She looked over her shoulder at the stage. "I'll bet the floor's all dented from the way they used to pound on it." Kari sat for a moment, remembering the twin looks of glee that both men wore as they clomped around in their Bermuda shorts and curly blond wigs. She felt a stirring of sadness in her chest and pressed her lips together. "Norman's wife, Lois, told me how hard Anders' death hit him. He said there's hardly anyone left he can talk to about the war or Benny Goodman or what good cars Packards were."

"I loved those church socials," said Mary Jo. "Once I saw Miss Schaeffer, the choir director, kissing Mr. Byers behind the fish pond game."

"Quentin Byers?" asked Kari. "Quentin Byers who was married to Winnie Byers?"

Mary Jo nodded. "And it was a pretty passionate kiss."

"And Nelva Schaeffer quit right around the time the Byerses left the church," said Kari, remembering. "Oh, my."

"Well, I kissed Nate Wheelock down here after confirmation class," said Julia. "Lydia Schaumberg saw us and threatened to tattle to Pastor Kittleson unless we each gave her a dollar."

"Why, the little extortionist," said Mary Jo. "Did you pay her?"

Julia nodded. "I think we even gave her an extra quarter, for insurance."

Kari laughed. "That's what I mean about church basements. Upstairs people behave, but it's down here that you really get to know them."

She looked at her watch, thinking they'd better move along, when suddenly she was floored by the situation she was so comfortably in: sitting on the lip of a stage with her daughter and her daughter's biological mother! And she hadn't been scared or nervous at all! A thought occurred to her, and its power was enough so that Julia and Mary Jo noticed Kari sitting frozen, her mouth hanging open, her eyes fixed in a stare.

"Aunt Kari?" said Mary Jo, whose immediate thought was of a stroke. "Are you all right?"

"Mom?" said Julia, draping her arm around her mother and shaking her a bit.

Kari blinked and took a deep breath, deciding to go ahead. She looked evenly at Julia.

"I was just thinking," she said, taking her daughter's hands in her own, "that I have something to tell you, but I've always been waiting for the right time and the right place. Well, I think I've found both." She turned to her niece. "Do you think I've found both, Mary Jo?"

Confusion wrinkled the younger woman's features, and then fear paled them. She sat for a moment biting her lip before, almost imperceptibly, she nodded.

Kari had the odd thought that if she could look inside her mind right now, it would look like the Scrambler, a ride she'd once taken with Julia at the state fair. Like the cages the riders sat in, emotions were thrusting back and forth, nearly colliding with one another: Fear! Exhilaration! Doubt! Calm! Terror!

"Julia," she said, and her voice, scratchy and screechy, startled her. She cleared her throat. "Julia, you know how you've always said that you don't want to know about your real mother until I'm ready to tell you?"

Julia nodded, the nostrils of her fine nose flaring.

"Well," said Kari, and she paused for a moment as she swallowed hard. "I think I'm ready to tell you — that is, if you want to know."

If Kari's voice had sounded like a cat's in heat, Julia's high little moan sounded like a kitten's.

Mary Jo stared down at her folded hands.

A minute ago it had seemed so right, but now Kari felt on the verge of not just tears but hysterical tears.

"So . . . do you want to know?"

Julia looked as if she'd been slapped. "I don't know. Yes, I guess. Yes. Hold your foot out, Mary Jo."

"What?"

"Hold out your foot!" said Julia, her voice sharp.

Mary Jo straightened her leg so that it was parallel to the floor. Julia did the same.

"You see?" she said. "The whole time we've been sitting there, I've been noticing your feet, how long and narrow they are, just like mine. I wear a ten extra narrow. What do you wear, Mary Jo?"

"About the same," mumbled Mary Jo.

Julia turned toward her mother, her eyes furious. "So tell me the story you've always told me."

"I'm not sure I —"

"The one about how you got me!"

Kari visibly cringed; she wasn't used to her daughter yelling at her.

"Well," she said carefully, hoping this was the answer Julia wanted to hear, "a long time ago, when she was at college, your mother became pregnant with you, and because she couldn't keep you, she decided to give you to me."

Julia blinked so rapidly she looked as if she had gone into a seizure, but Kari couldn't seem to lift her arms out to shake her, couldn't seem to move at all.

When the blinking stopped, two strands of tears, like liquid jewels, coursed down the lovely planes of Julia's face. "And that college girl," she said softly, looking at Mary Jo, "was you."

As Mary Jo nodded, Kari's prayer was a silent shout: *Dear God, please make this be all right!*

Julia dipped backward as if she'd been pushed, then plunged forward, boosting herself off the stage. "I . . . I . . . I need to be alone."

Kari and Mary Jo watched as Julia raced

across the shiny linoleum floor toward the door that led to the hallway and bathrooms.

"What have I done?" whispered Kari.

"What have *we* done?" whispered Mary Jo.

"It just seemed like the right time," said Kari, her voice plaintive.

"I know. My first thought when I heard Dad died was *Oh, no,* and my second thought was *Now maybe Kari will tell Julia about me.*"

"I'd better go after her," said Kari, easing herself off the stage.

"She said she wanted to be alone."

Kari looked at the woman with whom she had shared her most profound secret for over twenty-five years. "Sometimes when people say that, it's the last thing they want."

HOST: GRANT

BOOK: *A Farewell to Arms*

by Ernest Hemingway

REASON CHOSEN: "No offense, ladies, but sometimes we just need to read a real man's book."

My dad was a World War II veteran and therefore a member of "a brotherhood you could never understand."

I can't count the times he told me this, and each time he did, regret would thicken his voice, making him sound as if he had a cold.

When I told him Uncle Sam had deemed me 4-F (bless my flat, flat feet), he looked as bereft as a new widower.

He didn't know I was gay yet, but then neither did I. I was the kind of kid who thought his main purpose in life was to please his parents, and so I honestly thought I was as dejected as he was that I wasn't packing up my kit bag and heading to Da Nang or Phnom Penh or any of those other two-name places that sounded like train stations in hell.

So there I was in school, at the University of Arizona in Tucson, sitting in back of long-haired kids (whose sex was unknown until they turned around) with my own precisely cut hair, which I parted as carefully as a surveyor dividing up property lines. I wore a sport coat and tie and carried my books in a briefcase, if you can think of anything more pathetic for a college student during the late sixties. I had the admiration of all my parents' friends, who wished their own damn hippie kids would take a lesson from Ed and Verna's clean-cut son and straighten up and fly right!

I strode briskly across the campus in my high-water black pants and polished wing tips, behind kids whose bell-bottom hems were ripped and crusted from dragging on the ground, who reeked of patchouli oil while I smelled, just faintly, of the aftershave my mother ordered through Avon.

I still listened to my Connie Francis and Bobby Vee 45's, neatly filed in a blue plaid carrying case, while Bob Dylan and Joan Baez blasted from behind one dorm door and Jimi Hendrix and Janis Joplin blasted from behind another.

It makes me sad to think how clueless I was back then; how, not wanting to get my polished wing tips (with the arch supports) wet, I completely sidestepped that whole big wave of youth culture.

After graduation, as the war raged on, I was working in a bank as a loan officer, trying to banish the mind-numbing boredom I felt by extending my cocktail hour from before dinner to before bed. I was twenty-two years old and felt like an old man, yet my parents were proud of me. My parents' pride; that's what motivated me. Somehow I thought it was a worthy enough payoff.

What few friends I had were as straitlaced and out of touch as I was: with department store suits and clean-shaven faces, we banded together to disparage hippies and the Rolling Stones and free love.

One afternoon as I sat at my desk gnawing on the Tums that had become a regular part of my diet, a man came through the glass door of the bank. Through meeting him, another door opened, and that one led to my new life.

The man's name was Perry, and he was the biggest queen I'd ever seen in my life. Of course, I didn't know what a queen was back then — I just thought, *What is this fag doing sitting on the other side of my desk? How dare he?*

I wanted to tell him to kindly take his pansy little self out of my place of business but the bank manager who kept a plaque on her desk that read CUSTOMER SATISFACTION IS OUR #1 PRIORITY was keeping her beady little eyes on me.

"So what does a guy do to get a loan in a place like this?" he asked, flashing me a white and shiny smile. I use the word *flashing* in the what-perverts-do sense; his smile was licentious.

"First of all," I said, feeling the muscles in my forehead contract as my eyebrows edged down over my eyes, "what kind of loan are you applying for?"

"Well," he said, turning the turquoise bracelet around on his wrist, "I want to renovate the old Vista Theater on East Fifth Street. Do you know it?"

He flashed his smile again as I shook my head.

"Oh, it's an absolutely fabulous Art Deco building — well, it will be once it's renovated. And once it is renovated, it's not back to second-run movies, which is what was showing there up until two years ago. No, once the renovation is complete, I'm moving in my company, the Sexual Freedom Theater. Do you know it?"

"The Sexual Freedom Theater," I said, coating each word with equal parts condescension and distaste.

"Why shouldn't a woman play Hamlet? Why shouldn't a gay man play Stanley Kowalski? Not that we're relying on old standards, of course; our aim is to present works by playwrights and actors who live on the cutting edge of today's society."

A headache, like a summer storm, blew into my head. This guy talked so fast, so breathlessly, and about things I could barely comprehend. I shuffled around in my desk and gave him some papers.

"Fill these out," I said, as brusque as a Soviet customs agent.

The potential loanee stared at me for a moment and then with a little salute said, "Yes, sir."

That meeting with Perry was the tremor that started the avalanche. I went out that night with some of the automatons from work, regaling them with impersonations of the flaming queer who wanted to start a sexually free theater. Slamming down drinks, I slammed this guy relentlessly, viciously, until Brenda from investments said, "Gee, you really hate the guy, don't you?"

Did I? I asked myself as I lay in bed that night,

my head pounding as if my heart had relocated underneath my forehead. Did I hate him or just hate the way he was so gay? And why was his gayness such a personal affront to me?

The next day, I was compelled to take a walk during lunch that would lead me past the Vista Theater. I convinced myself that I just wanted a little on-site inspection of the theater this Perry wanted to renovate.

A small group was corralled under the marquee, pointing at some architectural detail.

"Why it's my loan officer!" said Perry, and before I could cross the street unnoticed, and without my permission, he took my arm, introducing me as "our potential savior."

"I'm nothing of the kind," I said, shaking his hand off. Little did I know how much more, and in how many ways, he would touch me.

Perry helped excavate the real me buried under all the bullshit. I had always liked girls, always preferred their company, but never *liked* them, never lusted after them. My celibacy didn't seem odd to me; I thought I was a late bloomer and it was only a matter of time before I would meet that perfect person and fall in love. The biggest surprise — that the perfect person happened to be a theater director with a hairy chest — was that it wasn't, after all, that much of a surprise.

Under Perry's sponsorship, I joined two new groups: my own generation and the gay culture.

I celebrated my new memberships with sex, drugs, and rock and roll. The old Grant shrank and shriveled away like the Wicked Witch of the West (leaving, I imagined, the smoking puddle of a Robert Hall suit and some charred wing tips), and a new Grant emerged, as flamboyant as the other was conservative, as loud as the other was quiet, as free as the other was not.

Stuart couldn't believe it when I told him my coming-out story — he said it sounded too implausible, too sudden. How could I have gone from the straight life to the gay one so suddenly?

"Ah, but see," I said, "it was a celibate life. I just *assumed* it was a straight life, because I didn't know any better."

My poor parents didn't know what to think. My dad never wanted to see me again, and my mom had to abide by her husband's wishes, at least when he was home. When she had some privacy, she'd call me on the phone, and occasionally we'd meet for breakfast in a run-down little diner in South Tucson, where our anonymity was pretty much guaranteed. She always brought me a bag of her famous homemade cinnamon rolls (God, they just *dripped* with icing) — to me it's not the idea of Mom and apple pie that makes me teary-eyed, but Mom and cinnamon rolls.

I knew I was a disappointment to her, but I also knew that her love was stronger than her disappointment, and that's some knowledge.

My dad . . . well, dear old immovable Dad died in his sleep several years later without ever having reconciled with his queer son. There will always be a bruise in my heart because of that; it's always sore, even though Mom has tried to speak for him, tried to convince me that he really did care.

Once, she said, she came home from bridge club to find him sitting on the bed, holding a picture of the two of us on a family vacation to

Hoover Dam, sobbing like a baby.

"Yeah, that was a pretty lousy vacation," I joked.

"He loved you, Grant," said my mother. "But he just didn't know what to do with it."

A snort ripped out of my nose. "Uh, how about showing it? Isn't that what you're supposed to do with love?"

I don't know why so many men have such a problem showing their feelings, hiding them away like they're a deformity too ugly for public viewing. And then the irony, of course, is that the very act of hiding is what's deforming. My dad was deformed by his inability to love me, his completely lovable son.

I see mothers on TV whose sons are on death row and they'll look into the camera and say, "He may be a murderer, but he's my son and I love him." And I always cry, wondering why a gay man's father found it harder to love his child than a serial killer's mother loved hers.

All right, enough already. I really don't know too many people who have parents who haven't harmed them in some way, but as Audrey says, it works both ways — think of how many kids have hurt their parents. It's nothing but goddamned human nature.

Audrey, being of the cloth now, didn't say "goddamned," although she still said things like "*sin*sational" and "*sex*citing." I think I might love Audrey more than anyone in the world.

I told her that once, and she said she felt as if I'd just handed her a warm, sweet-smelling baby to hold.

I love all the Angry Housewives. Just as I could never understand the brotherhood my dad was always going on about, he sure as shit wouldn't understand the sorority I'm a part of. Proudly a part of. I haven't been in the trenches of war with these women, but I've been in the trenches of daily life with them, and if you ask me, that forges the stronger friendship. And if you're turning in your grave, Dad, sorry, but maybe it's time you found a new position anyway.

December 1995

Dear Mama,

Wade and I flew down to Texas to visit his folks. Of course poor Patsy didn't know who we were — she kept asking Wade over and over again, "Do you like to wear hats, little buddy?"

It breaks Wade's heart to see her, and it doesn't do mine much good either — Patsy was never anything but nice to me. How many times had she made gentle overtures to me, letting me know that I could trust her with anything I might want to tell her? There she was all those years, waiting for me to unburden myself, and by the time I got brave enough to, she wasn't Patsy anymore.

Dex feels betrayed by her disease; he only visits her when we come down, and he gets mad when she says things like "Do you like licorice, young man?" He'll yell at her, "I'm not a young man, Patsy, I'm your goddamned husband who hates licorice!"

Dex is eighty-two years old, but a young eighty-two. He spends his time out at the country club, golfing on the days when his knees don't bother him. I think I would have thought of him as cavalier if I hadn't learned from my own self that how a person acts isn't necessarily a true depiction of how that person feels.

It's the first year we've missed Kari's Christmas party. I'm Slip's Secret Santa — I got her a lacy black thong and would love to see her blushing freckled face when she unwraps it.

Someone put garlands up in the nursing home, but the smell of urine, the cries of pain and scared shouts, and the rows of white-haired people slumped in the stalled wheelchairs that line the hallway (talk about gridlock) somehow diminish the festive factor.

With my voice, I don't know what I was thinking, but I somehow managed to corral a group of residents into the common room, and as this four-hundred-pound aide played the piano, I conducted a Christmas singalong.

There were a few game participants, raising their barely audible voices in "We Wish You a Merry Christmas" and "The First Noel," but most people sat hunched and silent as gargoyles.

"That sure was nice of you, Faith," Wade said afterward. He sat with Patsy, holding her hand. "Wasn't all that singing nice, Mama?"

"Barbara Stanwyck knew how to wear a hat," said Patsy. "And so did I."

"Yes, you did, Mama," said Wade, kissing her on top of the head.

"Did I tell you Mel Mathius left Carol?"

asked Wade on the plane ride back to Minneapolis.

"He did?" I said, feeling sad for the woman I'd known for years through the Pilots' Wives Association.

Wade nodded. "For a flight attendant who's younger than their daughter Maureen."

"Don't ever leave me for a flight attendant," I said, trying to make my voice threatening. Mel Mathius wasn't the first of Wade's pilot friends to do that exact thing.

"I won't leave you for anyone, Faith." He squeezed my hand. "I love you more than I ever have."

Oh, Mama, nothing Wade could say could mean more to me than that — after all we've been through, he loves me more than he ever did. Of course, he's not stupid like all those Mel Mathiuses; he sees that even with my wrinkles and sags and graying hair, I'm a deeper, richer person than I was when I was young and cute. Young and cute and, oh yeah, wrapped up in so much fear and jealousy that I was afraid to be the real me.

I'm still busy with lots of clients but also manage to volunteer with Slip on her Habitat for Humanity projects. I still remember the first house I worked on; the homeowner's absolute joy got me involved in my latest venture, helping people with the *interiors* of their houses. Paying in sweat equity, these homeowners help me (and usually one or two Angry Housewives) paint their rooms, slipcover their furniture, and sew curtains. I've done almost a dozen homes, and, Mama, not to brag, but these people are left with homes that wouldn't be out of place in *Architectural Digest.* Okay, *Family Circle.*

The gratitude of these people, Mama! If it were translated into dollars, I'd make Donald Trump look like a pauper.

Why didn't I know this years ago, Mama, that by helping people, the person who would be helped the most was me? Ha! It figures, my own selflessness is actually selfishness. Oh, well, it works for me.

Love,
Faith

HOST: **SLIP**

BOOK: *The Beginning and the End*

by Naguib Mahfouz

WHAT I FELT UPON FINISHING THE BOOK:

"Unsettled."

"I felt like I was in a world I didn't understand when I read this book," said Merit.

"I thought everybody was *way* too much in each other's business," said Grant. "I mean, there's such a thing as family loyalty, but their loyalty, their interdependence, brought down the whole family."

"I didn't want the sister to die at the end," said Faith. "It was so unfair."

"Life for women in that culture is pretty unfair," I said. "Strike that. In *all* cultures."

Audrey made a little funnel with her hand and announced into it: "And she's off and running."

"Well, as long as she is," said Grant, settling back on the couch, "pass me that hummus."

And so I ranted and raved about what an unjust world it is for so many people, but most of all for women. I wondered what it was that men feared so much about us that made them want to oppress us, to silence us, to make us invisible. Holy when's-the-ERA-gonna-pass, it was nothing they hadn't heard from me before, until I said, "I think we need to organize an action. Remember, Merit, when you wanted to unite all the mothers to stop rape and war and murder? Well, this would be a worldwide action where *all* the women of the world go on strike — and let's see how long it takes for the world to stop."

" 'A worldwide action where all the women of the world go on strike,' " said Grant. "That might take a bit of organizing."

"I just get so fed up," I said. "I get fed up by the term 'women and minorities' — as if we're some weird caste of people, as if we're not half the friggin' population. I get fed up with the rapists who say, 'She asked for it,' when they try to explain their despicable crime. I get —"

"Could men go on strike too?" asked Merit. "Because Frank would. He told me the other night how he'd like to be a woman for one day, just to see what it felt like to be the superior sex."

"Good old Mr. Paradise," said Audrey. "I'd let him go on strike with us. Or would men screw up the dynamic, Slip?"

"Maybe our male supporters could stand on the sidelines," I said. "In high heels. Applauding us and fetching us coffee."

"Ooh, I look great in heels," said Grant.

"All right," said Faith, "what's our first step? Getting hold of all the women in the world? Who wants to be the contact person?"

"I'm serious," I said, even as I laughed. "Something has to be done for our daughters. For the world's daughters."

"I'm all for that, Slip," said Kari quietly. "The world *has* to get better for our daughters."

A pall fell over the room then as all of us con-
templated, I suppose, the odds of ever achieving
that. And more than one of us, I'm sure, was
thinking of Kari wanting to make the world
better for a daughter who wouldn't have anything to do with her.

Jerry accuses me of being judgmental, but it's
hard not to be when you can see things so
clearly. If there were a motherhood contest and I
was a judge, I'd give Kari a score of ten. Yet
Julia hadn't spoken to her in over six months.

"What am I?" Kari had asked me. "What am I
if Julia doesn't want me to be her mother anymore?"

It had taken all of us by surprise when Kari
told us who Julia's mother was. My gosh, it was
right out of one of the soap operas Mr. Klanski
used to tell me about while I waited for Flan to
finish her piano lesson.

And speaking of Flan, I did not think she was
a font of understanding in the matter of Julia and
Kari. We had spoken on the phone yesterday.

"My God," she said. "Poor Julia, she must feel
so betrayed."

"I'm sure she does," I agreed, but I had relaxed my own policy on secrets, realizing they
were most often defensive and not offensive
weapons. "But to not speak to Kari all these
months? Not to return her phone calls? Kari's
practically out of her mind."

"Well, she really should have told Julia long
ago," said Flannery. "I mean, it *is* a pretty big
lie." I heard her sigh. "Geez, you and your
friends. First Faith creates a whole fantasy life
and expects her kids to believe it, and now Kari.
Are you harboring any big secrets, Mom?"

"Yes, I'm a visiting alien from Uranus," I snapped. "Flannery, how many times do I have to tell you this? Julia didn't want to know! It wasn't a lie — not even a lie of omission. And it's not just Kari's doing — both Kari and Mary Jo agreed to this. They thought they were doing the best thing."

"Hey, don't yell at me. I didn't do anything."

There was a long silence as I played with the phone cord.

"Now can we get back to the reason I called?" Flannery finally said.

I felt a little zip of excitement. Had she met someone?

"Sure."

"I finished my novel. I'm sending it to you by overnight mail."

I drew in my breath. "Oh, Flan. Congratulations."

My daughter had begun and ended a half dozen novels since college, but for the past few years she'd been working on one, sharing its progress with me as if it were her firstborn.

"I can't wait to read it."

"I can't wait to have you read it. But you have to promise that even if you hate it, you'll say you love it."

There was a rare shyness in my daughter's voice.

"That's an easy promise," I said, "because I know I'll love it."

A few days after Kari introduced Julia to her birth mother in the church basement, I got the news from the doctor: I had Hodgkin's disease.

"Hodgkin's?" I cried to Jerry as we drove

home. "Who the hell is Hodgkin? What makes him think I want his disease?"

"We're going to beat this, Slip," he said, clutching the steering wheel so that his knuckles formed little white peaks under his skin. "We *are* going to beat this."

Jerry's a scientist; he believes in facts. If he says something, it must be true.

I've completed my course of chemo and my blood counts are what they should be. My doctor says if I'm not in remission, it looks as if I'm headed there. The past couple months have been rough; if I never throw up again, it will be too soon for me. But besides my regained health, there's been an incredible silver lining to this big black cloud: all my hair fell out. My awful frizzball red hair. I actually preferred being bald; I didn't have to wake up every morning wondering how I was going to batten down my hair. But then — oh joy, I can hardly stand it — my hair's started to grow back in, and *it's not frizzy*. It's still red, but no matter — the frizz is gone. The hair that used to evoke pictures of electrocution or a permanent gone terribly, terribly wrong is as unkinky as Prince Valiant's. Straight and smooth. I can't believe it. Only about an inch and a half has come in, but I pay more attention to my hair now than a Miss Minnesota contestant. Jerry teases me about my new vanity, but I think anyone who's lived under a mushroom cloud of hair all her life has a right to spend a little extra time in front of a mirror.

Grant stayed afterward to help me clean up. We've always gotten along, but one weekend when I was sick from chemo, he earned extra brownie points by reading aloud our book club selection, all 342 pages of it, pausing only during my trips to the bathroom to throw up.

"Slip, don't you think it's about time we plan a road trip?" asked Grant, twirling the last triangle of pita bread in the hummus. "Let's read a book set in Italy or the Greek isles — I'm getting so sick of winter. And then — Slip, what's wrong?"

"Oh, my gosh," I said, and with an armful of dirty dishes, I raced to the kitchen.

"Slip," said Grant, chasing after me, "you're not feeling sick, are you?"

I threw the dishes (as much as I could throw them without breaking them) into the sink and wiped my hands on the gingham dish towel that hung on the oven handle.

"Slip," said Grant, begging for some sort of explanation.

"Oh, Grant," I said, pulling the brown-paper-wrapped package off the baker's rack where I'd put it earlier that day and hugging it to my chest. "It's Flan's manuscript. It came when I was making the tabouli, and I forgot all about it."

"Flan's manuscript? Oh, Slip, how exciting. Open it up so we can start reading it right now."

Jerry has often said I'm just like a toddler in showing my feelings on my face, and Grant obviously saw that I did not regard his suggestion as a good idea.

He laughed. "For God's sake, Slip, you look like I just asked you to strip."

"Well, I . . . I think I'd like to open it up and read it with Jerry."

"Of course you would," said Grant, and within minutes he was out the door.

I called Jerry down from his exile in the den (all the husbands beat a hasty retreat when the Angry Housewives meet), asking him to join me in front of the fire for a glass of wine.

There is nothing quite so cozy as an old married couple on a worn corduroy couch, snuggled in front of the fireplace.

"How are you feeling, honey?" asked Jerry, his nose snuffling around in my short, deliciously straight hair.

"Not so good," I began.

"Slip?" said Jerry, worried.

"Not so good," I continued, "but *great*." I lifted up a pillow under which I'd hidden the package. "Jerry, it's Flan's manuscript."

Jerry sat for a moment, silent. "Flan's manuscript? Right there in your lap?"

I nodded, sure that my smile was touching my ears.

We exchanged that glorious aren't-our-kids-something look that parents are sometimes privileged enough to share, and then Jerry nudged me. Hard.

"Well, open it up, for God's sake, and let's start reading."

The fire snapped its fingers, demanding our attention, but we had none to give. Our concentration was totally on the opening of the package.

"Do you want to start or should I?" asked Jerry.

"Maybe you should," I said, passing him the stack of pages. "I'm too nervous."

Jerry accepted the manuscript as solemnly as a tribal chief accepting a peace offering and began to read.

"Wow," I said after he'd read a few lines, "it's fantastic!"

Jerry chuckled. "I haven't even finished the first paragraph."

"You can tell a lot by the first paragraph."

I snuggled closer to him, and as he began reading again, I closed my eyes, enjoying beyond measure the singular experience of my husband giving voice to our daughter's.

HOST: **KARI**

BOOK: *Kristin Lavransdatter*

by Sigrid Undset

REASON CHOSEN: "How am I ever going to

turn you into honorary Norwegians if you

haven't read this book?"

"This is the lefsa," said Kari, handing Slip a tray of Norwegian tortillas. "That's the krumkakka over there, and I've got the smorebrod and cheeses in the fridge."

"And how are we supposed to drink this aquavit?" asked Slip.

"Straight," said Kari. "But *sparingly*."

She had even planned to wear her Norwegian national costume (she had gotten it when she was seventeen and it still fit) and teach the Angry Housewives a Norwegian drinking song, but the lessons in Norse culture would have to wait: Kari had a more important meeting to attend.

"Kiss Julia for us all," Slip said as Kari got on her coat.

"I will," said Kari, "if I can stop kissing her myself."

On the plane, Kari thought of the hastily arranged trip she had made all those years ago to pick up the infant her niece had somehow "found" for her. It pleased her that again she was going to San Francisco, only now her baby was twenty-eight years old. Twenty-eight years old. Tears blurred Kari's eyes as she stared out at the gray wintry sky around her. Because of their estrangement, she had missed out entirely on her daughter's twenty-eighth year.

She had sent a birthday card, of course, and a dusky rose blazer she had sewn out of a soft wool and lined with cranberry silk. Julia was so easy to sew for — almost a perfect size eight, except that Kari always had to make adjustments for her wide shoulders. She received no acknowledgment of the card or gift, but neither had she received an acknowledgment of any of the dozens of letters she had sent. Until now.

Julia had finally called, finally said the word that Kari had waited nearly a year and a half to hear: "Mom?" She had added bonus words: "I'm so sorry. I love you. Can you come out here?"

If Kari had had a gauge to measure her feelings, it wouldn't have worked; her happiness and gratitude were off the charts. They had spoken for two hours, laughing and crying as they caught up, and finally Kari had felt brave enough to ask, "What happened? What finally made you call me?"

"Oh, Mommy," she said, a hitch in her voice. "I kept every letter — I just never opened them. I knew if I did, I'd want you back in my life again, and I just wasn't ready for that. I was so mad at you and Mary Jo."

"I am so sorry," said Kari, and she was; her

sorrow was ocean deep, sky high. "How many times have I played that day back in my mind, wishing I hadn't said anything, wishing that —"

"It's okay, Mom. I mean, it wasn't at first, but it is now."

Kari heard a faint whooshing noise.

"Can you hold on for a sec, Mom? I'm making myself a cappuccino, and if I don't open the valve now, I won't get any steam."

Kari waited as the whooshing grew louder, and a moment later Julia was back on the phone.

"So anyway, Jared, Jared Lipinsky — I've been seeing him for a couple months, Mom, and well . . . I . . ."

Kari laughed. "My goodness, Julia, are you in love?"

"Yes! Yes, I think so. No, I *know* so. Oh, Mom, he's so great; he's funny and kind. I met him at work; he's the vice president of creative affairs. He just seems to understand me so well. To the rest of the world I seem pretty together, but he could tell right away that something wasn't right with me, and when I told him about you he said, 'I don't think you can really be happy until you reconcile with her,' and even though I knew what he was saying was true, I needed a little more time."

Julia paused and sipped her cappuccino. "Anyway, last night I made the time. Jared was out with some clients and I was all alone in the apartment, so I dragged out the big box I keep in the closet. It's full of your letters — and that jacket, Mom; thank you, it's beautiful. Anyway, last night I started opening all the letters up and reading them. By the third I wanted to call you, but it was past eleven here and I didn't want to wake you up in the middle of the night."

"You can wake me up anytime you like," said Kari.

"I've got the letters right here, Mom. Let me read you one." She took another sip of her coffee and Kari heard a slight clink when she set the cup down.

My dear Julia,

I know the chances of you throwing this letter away before you even open it are high, but I will keep sending you these letters in the hopes that you might mistake one for a bill and open it.

It is what keeps me going, Julia: hope. It makes me get up in the morning and turn on the coffee and read the paper and decide that yes, I'll get on with my day.

Missing you is like having had an arm or leg amputated; I am constantly aware of my loss, but hope makes me think that someday the arm or leg will be reattached.

Three quick breaths rose out of Julia's throat. "That's just how I felt, Mom — like a part of me was missing." Then she continued.

Life goes on, but it is a different life, a life with a hole in it. At book club I listen to Faith tell stories about the museum in Atlanta that hired Beau and the kind of cases Bonnie deals with as a social worker. Merit passes around Reni's wedding pictures. It was a beautiful wedding, Julia — imagine Merit's lovely girls as bride and bridesmaids, and when Melody and Jewel and Portia sang, "True Love," I think we all felt like cavemen (or cave people, as Slip would say) coming across a flowering rosebush. Reni had told me that she asked you to come but you'd said it would be too awkward. "Do you talk to her much?" I asked, so hungry for news of you, even if it was news that you wouldn't be coming to your old friend's wedding because you didn't want to see your mother.

That mark right there is a big teardrop that just splashed on the paper. You'd think I'd learn by now to type these letters so they wouldn't be so waterlogged.

So when all my friends talk about their children at book club (Audrey brought her new grandson, who's the biggest baby I'd ever seen — eleven pounds at birth! And guess what — Flannery finished her book and has an agent sending it around!) I listen with happiness and sadness, wishing I could add to the conversation.

But I will one day, Julia. Someday, some way, I will.

Your loving mother,
Kari

There was a long pause, and Kari heard her daughter sipping her cappuccino. It made her wish she had her own cup of coffee.

"I'm really sorry I wasted all this time being mad," said Julia finally. "It was just so hard to get out of. It was like I was inside this . . . this *box* of anger without a key. Jared's helped me a lot, Mom. His own mother died when he was only thirteen, and he told me he could understand my hurt, but he thought I was compounding the hurt by pushing you out of my life. 'Bring her back in,' he kept saying. 'I promise you you'll feel better if you bring her back in.' "

"I like this Jared," Kari said, her throat full.

"Good, because he's going to be your son-in-law. Now when's the soonest you can get out here?"

Kari had gotten on a plane the next day. Staring out the little oval window, she replayed the conversation over and over in her head. When the flight attendant asked her if she wanted chicken or beef, Kari shook her head.

"My daughter and her fiancé are taking me out for dinner!" and from the odd look both her seatmate and the flight attendant gave her, she gathered there may have been a wee bit more enthusiasm in her voice than it would seem the statement called for.

HOST: **MERIT**
BOOK: *Ladder of Years* by Anne Tyler
REASON CHOSEN: "She's one of my favorite writers — I feel like her characters could live on my block."

It was one of Merit's great pleasures to have introduced to Frank the joys of reading. Unlike Eric, who resented Merit's attention being taken away by books, Mr. Paradise was made happy by anything that made Merit happy.

When she was pregnant with Portia and reading *The Great Gatsby* for book club, he asked her to tell him about it, and displayed enough interest that Merit suggested he read the book himself.

His face fell (Merit was struck by how thin angular faces seem to fall farther than round ones) and he said, "I . . . I . . ."

"What is it, Frank?"

"Well," said Frank, stroking his sideburns with his thumbs, his particular nervous tic, "the thing of it is . . . I don't read too well. I always jumble up the letters or something."

"Oh, Frank," said Merit. They were sitting next to each other on the couch, and to be any closer to him, she would have to climb on his lap, which she did. "You mean you have dys-lexia?"

Frank shrugged. "If that's when you jumble up the letters, that's what I've got."

"Well, we can get you help for that," said Merit. "Jewel's best friend has dyslexia, but she's been getting special help, and Jewel says she reads like crazy now."

"Really? I'd sure like to learn to read better." He stroked Merit's pregnant belly. "I want to be able to read to the baby."

And so he met weekly with an earnest young man from the University of Minnesota who never made Mr. Paradise feel ashamed of his in-ability to distinguish a *z* from an *s* or laughed when, for the fourth time in a session, the older man read *am* as *ma*. For homework, he pre-scribed a lot of reading out loud, which Frank chose to do in Merit's company.

Sometimes he'd get through a chapter without his eyes and head hurting from the effort of descrambling words, and when he couldn't, he'd hand the book to Merit and say, "Finish it up, will you, honey? I want to find out what hap-pens."

When Portia was three weeks old, Merit came home from running errands to find Frank holding the baby in one arm and a copy of *The Three Little Pigs* in the other.

" 'Then I'll huff and I'll puff and I'll blow your house in,' " read Frank.

Setting her purse on the table, Merit laughed. "How's she liking it?"

"Next to 'Little Red Riding Hood,' " said Frank, "I think it's her favorite."

Although Frank could (and did, albeit slowly)

read his own books, they'd gotten used to the ritual of reading aloud, first to Portia and then, after she fell asleep, to themselves, cozying up in the big plush armchair. Frank started off reading, but after one or two pages, he'd hand the book over to Merit, claiming that hearing her read was almost as good as hearing her sing. They usually read whatever book was going to be discussed at AHEB, and when Merit returned from a meeting, Frank would grill her on what the Angry Housewives had thought of the book's theme or this character's weakness or that character's strength.

"Can you believe that next year our book club will have its *thirty*-year anniversary?" Merit asked Frank as he helped her clean up after a meeting she had hosted.

"Thirty years," said Frank, helping himself to a piece of Faith's peanut brittle. "Think how many books that is."

"We're trying to figure out a big splashy way to celebrate," said Merit. "Any ideas?"

Frank unlodged a chunk of peanut from between a gold tooth and a regular one. "Hmmm. Maybe something to do with a T-shirt?"

"What?"

"Well, you know how the girls gave us those T-shirts for our fifth anniversary with a picture of us printed inside a heart? Something like that."

Merit brushed the couch cushions. It was easy to know where Audrey sat during a meeting; she always left behind a telltale trail of crumbs.

"That's a good idea — I'm sure one of us could dig up a picture taken at a book club."

"Or what about your books?"

"What do you mean? A picture of the books we've read?"

"No, you wouldn't have space for that. How about a list — you've kept track of all your books, haven't you, Merit? So how about making T-shirts with a list of all the books your club has read?"

"Oh, Frank," said Merit, setting down a pile of dishes so she could hug her husband. "That's a great idea."

"I've got another one," said Frank.

"Can't it wait till we finish cleaning up?"

"It could, but why should it?"

"You're right," said Merit, taking him by the hand and pulling him down on the couch. "Why should it?"

HOST: **AUDREY**

BOOK: *Eastward Ha!* by S. J. Perelman

HOW MANY TIMES I LAUGHED OUT LOUD

WHILE READING THIS: 107

My ex-husband, Paul, died today. When I called my son Bryan in California to tell him the news, he asked me, "Did you feel it?"

"No," I said. "No, I didn't have a clue."

"Wasn't he important enough to you?" said Bryan, sounding like an accusatory little boy. He drew in a breath of air. "Sorry, Mom. It's just that you always know the important stuff before it happens. Remember my accident?"

I shuddered at the mention of that awful night.

"I just thought you would have seen Dad in a vision or something."

"Oh, Bryan, I hardly ever see visions any-more." (Actually, I was surprised and somewhat disappointed that I hadn't an inkling of Paul's death.) "I think the last time I absolutely knew something before it happened was when I guessed my Secret Santa present was going to be a five-pound box of chocolates and it was."

Bryan allowed himself a little laugh before the gears shifted and he let out a gasp.

"How did it happen, Mom? How did my dad die?" The years dropped away; by the sound of his voice, my son was no longer thirty-three, but eight.

"His heart," I said. "On the golf course this morning. Cynthia said he'd just bogeyed the second hole when he sank to his knees as if he'd decided to pray."

"Aw, Ma," said Bryan, his voice choked.

That's when I lost it too. I had been stunned when Cynthia called to tell me the news, and remained stunned when I called my other sons, but now the novocaine was wearing off and the nerve was exposed. There was something so lost in Bryan's voice that I felt lost too, and I always cry when I'm lost.

I managed to compose myself enough to give him the funeral details, and after hanging up the phone, I immediately went to my place of comfort and refuge: the kitchen, and in particular, the refrigerator.

I'm not proud of my reliance on food during times of crisis. I'm a minister, for Christ's sake (that pun *is* intended) — why does ice cream always come before prayer?

Sitting at the kitchen table excavating rocky road with a wooden spoon, I allowed myself the luxury of pouting over my eating. Why could my spiritual hunger (surely the hardest hunger to assuage) be abated, and yet my physical hunger was rarely satisfied? I was way beyond voluptuous now; my hips looked as if I was wearing a hoop skirt (an especially attractive look in jeans), and my butt — why, it was my own private subcontinent. It could have its own flag and constitution.

I try to avoid rear views of my body at all costs. The last time I looked I was especially saddened that even my *shoulders* had gotten fat. They were padded and puffy, and my bra straps cut little ravines through them.

I could have gone on and on (like my thighs, ha-ha), but then my mind flashed on Paul and the smile he'd worn as I did a little strip tease for him on our wedding night.

"All mine," he had said, his grin as crooked as his bow tie. "I can't believe you're all mine."

He actually rubbed his palms together the way my grandfather would when dinner was set on the table.

Paul. He was so big and strong, so *manly.* My mind swirled with memories: of him yanking up his swim trunks after he climbed atop the dock we'd been diving off and then, making sure no one was looking, pulling them down and back up in one fast, furious move, flashing me. I pulled up my bikini top then, but I was caught by another swimmer, a teenage boy whose eyes were as big and buggy as fried eggs, and Paul laughed so hard he fell off the dock. I remembered the first time I cut his hair and how I liked to run my hand up the back of his slightly flat head, his short (Paul always kept his hair short, even in the shaggy sixties) thick hair standing up between my fingers like dark brown grass. I recalled ironing a white dress shirt for Paul and watching him shrug it over his shoulders, and how delicious the smell of starch and aftershave was to me. I thought about how one time I'd looked out the back window to watch him having a sword fight with Dave, using the plastic swords they'd gotten at the Renaissance Fair. And the sex . . . I'd thought the sex was the foundation of our marriage, but obviously that was destined to crumble, seeing as Paul was building foundations all over the place.

It took a while, but after the divorce we'd become friends. We weren't *great* friends; he was sort of a second-tier friend, like an old high school pal you'd occasionally skipped class with or copied homework from, the kind who always brought back pleasant memories.

Poor Paul. Poor Cynthia — I think her love made him a better man than he had been. Poor Dave and Bryan and Michael; they are, as Michael said, half orphans now.

I dressed — I had an appointment with a pregnant teenager in a half hour at the church — and went outside looking for a shoulder I could have a quick cry on, feeling comforted that there were so many shoulders, all within walking distance, that I *could* cry on.

Grant's were the first I saw. He was standing in his front yard watering his rhododendron bush.

His back was to me, and I stood on my steps for a while, watching him. He wore shorts imprinted with smiley faces and a broad-brimmed straw hat, and he was drawing figure eights in the air with the water from the hose.

I don't recall moving, but Grant sensed my presence and turned around.

"Audrey!" he shouted, and I realized I was crying.

"Paul died," I said as we both ran toward the short hedge that divided our property. "He had a heart attack this morning."

Grant jumped over the hedge, and the shoulder that I had so badly needed was mine for the taking.

"Poor Paul — he was only fifty-eight," I said, my cheek pressed against the ridge that was Grant's clavicle. "He used to tell me he was going to live to be a hundred, and I always believed him — he was so big and strong."

I stood there in the shelter of Grant's thin arms, crying for my ex-husband who, like so many men, wasn't so big and strong after all. Their hearts couldn't keep up with all that was asked of them and were crushed by all that gristle and muscle and testosterone and type-A blood pressure.

"Come on inside, sweetheart," said Grant, "and I'll make you a cocktail."

"I can't," I said. "I've got to go to work." I inhaled a deep breath and took a half step backward. "How do I look?"

"Thank heaven for waterproof mascara," said Grant, pressing a thumb under my eye. "There. Nothing less than stunning."

"That's my motto," I said gamely, and after accepting one more quick hug, I got in my car to see what help I could offer a teenager who was with child and desperately wished she wasn't.

"I would have had an abortion, but I didn't even know I was pregnant until I was almost six months," said the fifteen-year-old, who swiveled back and forth in the suede chair, her arms crossed over the basketball-shaped mound her sleeveless Mickey Mouse T-shirt stretched across.

Dumb kid, I thought, very unpastorly, but you'd be surprised at the unpastorly thoughts that found purchase inside a pastor's head — at least this pastor's head.

"So how far along are you now?" I asked with what I hoped was a concerned yet gentle smile.

Her head tilted, Cara looked up at me, contempt and pity hardening her pretty, country-girl features. You could tell she didn't believe that there are no stupid questions, and that I had just asked one.

"Far enough to know I still don't want it."

I knew Cara's aunt Diane; she was a regular parishioner and the reason Cara was seeing me. The girl had been sent from her home in Wisconsin to live with Diane, who asked (or, more than likely, forced) Cara to come to me for counseling. This was our first meeting.

"So your aunt tells me you're giving it to a couple to adopt?"

"No, I'm going to sell her to the circus."

I leveled my gaze at this little smart-ass. "To whom? The acrobats? Tightrope walkers? The elephant trainers?"

She picked up the pace of her swiveling, irritated that I had horned in on her little joke. "Whatever."

The word *whatever* is like fingernails on a chalkboard to me. It's not witty, it's not clever, it's smug and lazy, and this morning I had no patience for it. I turned in my own swivel chair and stared at the window for a few moments, my back toward the surly young girl.

I had opened it earlier but kept the blinds drawn, and they shuddered as a breeze rippled through. I knew it was totally unprofessional, totally noncompassionate to turn away from her like that, but I just needed to look at something other than a teenager's sneer (the worst kind, I think).

Cara was wily; when I turned around, I was surprised to see she was out of her chair and heading toward the door.

"Hey, wait a second," I said. "Where are you going?"

"What do you care?" she asked.

"I do care," I said, ashamed of myself and my childish behavior. "I care a lot, but I certainly understand why you would think I don't. That was very rude of me to turn away from you like that. I'm sorry." The girl was at the door, her hand reaching for the doorknob. "Please!" I said, nearly shouting. "I've had a rough morning. I shouldn't take it out on you."

The girl hesitated for a moment. With her back turned toward me, you couldn't see her pregnancy at all, and she looked like a teenager whose biggest worry was passing her driver's permit test. Then she slowly turned around, her big belly preceding the rest of her by nearly a foot.

Walking toward me, she kept her eyes on the toes of her heavy Doc Marten boots, as if they were headlights and the journey from the door to the chair was a long, dark one.

She sat down on the chair, her eyes still downcast, and asked, "Did you ever think maybe I had a rough morning, too? Did you ever think that lately every single fucking morning is a rough one?"

"I didn't," I said, sincere apology in my voice. "I didn't and I'm sorry."

A piece of blond hair had slipped out of its little bow barrette, and Cara tucked it behind her ears. "Aren't you going to yell at me for swearing?"

I shook my head. "There are a lot of things I yell at people for, but swearing's not one of them."

"What is?"

I inspected the ceiling tile for a moment as I thought. "Well, when my sons were home, I used to yell at them all the time for finishing the ice cream. I used to hide the ice cream, and when they found it and ate it, I yelled."

"I don't like ice cream," said Cara.

"You don't like *ice cream?* Is there something the matter with you?"

A tiny smile played on the young girl's face, and a little dimple puckered her cheek.

"I don't like chocolate either. Anytime I got any — like in my Easter basket or in my Christmas stocking — I gave it to my little brother."

"That must have made you pretty popular with him."

The girl nodded, and for the first time I saw a glint of tears in her eyes.

"How old is your brother?"

"Fourteen. He's only eleven months younger than I am. His name is Sam. He's a skateboarder. And really into hip hop. He's like the coolest kid in Eau Claire."

"Sounds like you think a lot of him."

Cara nodded. "I do. I miss him a lot, even though he's mad at me now. Almost as mad as my parents for, you know, getting p.g."

I shifted my weight in my chair and folded my hands. I could tell that she wanted to talk now, and I wasn't about to get in the way of that by opening up my own big yap.

"Like I wanted to get pregnant! Like that was

my goal or something! Get a job at the Dairy Queen, try out for cheerleading, and oh yeah, get pregnant the first time you have sex!"

"It was your first time?" I asked, ignoring my own advice to keep quiet.

"First and only time," said Cara. Her chin quivered, and I could see the determined effort she made to stop a chain reaction. "I had liked him, like, all year, and finally he notices that I actually do exist and we went out a few times — he drives — and then one night his parents weren't home and he invited me over and made me dinner! It was like pizza and a salad, but still, he had candles and everything and I felt so cool, so grown-up, you know? And then we started making out and he was telling me how much he loved me and how beautiful I was, and the next thing I know, he's got his thing in me."

Her voice shuddered. Her eyes were full of a betrayal and pain a fifteen-year-old shouldn't have to feel.

"I was so scared, but I pretended I liked it, you know? I didn't want him not to like me, stupid idiot that I am. So now I'm going to have a baby and *he's* going to Michigan State."

"He's not taking any responsibility for the baby? Because you can force him, you know. You can take him to court."

Bitterness colored her laugh until it really wasn't a laugh anymore. "I don't want to have anything to do with him. I *hate* him. I hate this baby because it's part of him, even though I know it's not the baby's fault."

"Your parents, did they —"

"My parents didn't do anything but throw me out of the house when I started to show — when

I started to be an embarrassment to them! I mean, my dad's like Mr. Big Shot Businessman — Mr. I Own the Hardware Hank *and* the Ben Franklin Store. He couldn't have his pregnant, slutty daughter scaring away customers!"

The dam broke then and she leaned forward, cupping her face in her hands with the bitten nails and crying the way a scared and pregnant teenager has every right to cry. I went to put my arms around her, and the way she welcomed them made me sorry I hadn't offered a hug a long time ago. She was starving for contact, for consolation, for her back to be patted and her hair smoothed.

"You didn't say anything about God," she said after she had depleted my Kleenex box. She rubbed her swollen eyes with her fingers. "I didn't want to come here because I thought all you'd talk about was God and how I had sinned."

"I'm kind of a funny minister," I said. "I don't talk a lot about sin. I think it's more important to talk about what comes after — how we can make things better. And you already are making things better — you're giving a baby to a couple who can't have one of their own! That's such a huge gift, Cara. That's more than making lemonade from lemons — that's making a lemon meringue pie, or even a *bakery* full of lemon meringue pies!"

The girl laughed. It was a wan little laugh, but still, I was glad to have given her at least a few seconds of cheer.

"As far as the God part comes in, I want you to know that I'm here for you whenever you need to talk, and if you feel God in these talks, that's great. My main goal is to help you, Cara."

"I could use help," she said, her voice trembling.

"Good," I said, smiling at this lovely, brave girl with the little-girl barrettes in her hair. "Could you use some lunch too? I'm starving."

The smile that broke out on her tearstained face was quickly extinguished when she looked at her watch. "I'd love to," she said, "only my aunt's picking me up at noon. We're going to a Lamaze class."

"We'll do it another time, then," I promised. "I'm *always* up for lunch."

Cara stood, locking her fingers together and stretching her arms out in front of her in a classic pose of bashfulness. "Thanks a lot . . ."

"Audrey. Call me Audrey."

"I've never called a pastor by their first name before."

"Whenever anyone calls me Pastor Forrest I never know who they're talking to."

Cara smiled. She had beautiful white teeth — homecoming queen teeth and I wondered if that title had been forever forfeited.

"Well . . . should I come here next week, then?"

"Please do," I said. "I look forward to seeing you again."

The girl flushed. "Thanks . . . me too." With sort of a shrug, she turned toward the door, then back toward me again.

"Pastor — um, Audrey, when I first came in here, remember we were talking about rough mornings? And you said you had one? What happened?"

My heart suddenly doubled its weight. "Oh.

601

Well . . . my ex-husband died. The father of my children."

Cara bit her lip. "I'm sorry to hear that."

And then she reached out and hugged me, and I hugged her back, feeling how, except for that basketball pressing against me, she was so small and delicate. But I knew inside that small and delicate frame there was a strong, willful girl who had the grace to ask about my rough morning in the midst of all of hers, and I thanked God silently for being in the room, and I thanked him again for following me home, for when I drove the car up the driveway, all the Angry Housewives, probably alerted by Grant, were there to offer their condolences, their hugs, and a pitcher of margaritas that Grant had whipped up.

January 1998

Dear Mama,

Wade just passed by my office on his way to the bathroom (he goes to the bathroom *a lot* lately) and asked, "Are you coming to bed soon?" I said, "As soon as I write to Mama," and he stood there in his underwear and then, nodding, said softly, "Tell her hey from me." So hey from Wade, who understands my need to write to a woman he's never met, a woman who's been dead for over thirty-five years.

Snow is falling fast and furious. It's like the angels have gotten restless and are throwing a wild pillow fight. I'm up here writing by cozy lamplight, the old cashmere afghan Wade gave me eons ago spread over my lap.

Beau said that he thinks I'm more a northerner now than a southerner, and I think he's right. When I say "home" now, I think of here, this place of windchill factors and rowdy angel pillow fights.

I'm blathering on and on about the weather and such because I'm afraid to tell you the big news. I'm afraid because whatever I write down makes it more real, and . . . oh, Mama, I've got a sister! Well, a half sister, of course, but there's someone on earth who has the same daddy I do! Or did! (Excuse me, I thought I was cried out, but here come the waterworks again.)

Okay, here's one of the biggest stories of my life.

Back in New Orleans, when I finally came clean to him about my past, particularly my past with you, Mama, Beau got the idea to go looking for my father.

"I didn't tell you, Mama," he said, "because I didn't want you to say no, and even if you didn't say no, I didn't want you to be disappointed."

He knew only what I knew of my father: that his name was James O'Brien.

"There's a lot of James O'Briens out there," Beau told me. "I narrowed them down by age and location, but no one I contacted had fathered a little girl in Arkansas in 1942.

"It got pretty frustrating, and I sort of dropped the whole search when Shelby and I were living in Europe." (That's your big-shot grandson, the art historian, working in places like Stockholm and Milan!)

Anyway, when they came back to the States last year he decided to pick up the search, but again he had no luck in finding *the* James O'Brien. Then a week or so ago he was browsing one of those Internet sites (you wouldn't believe the world we live in today, Mama) where adopted children are looking for their birth families or vice versa, and he comes across a message: Looking for Faith, older daughter of my father, James "Jimmy" O'Brien; not married to mother at time of birth (1942) but mother's name was Priscilla (?) Reynolds. Any information, please contact Vivien Pearson.

Beau couldn't believe it and e-mailed (don't ask me to explain it, Mama) the woman right away and asked if it was a possibility that the mother of the woman she was looking for was named Primrose and not Priscilla. She answered him right back and said, "My father only gave me this information on his deathbed and I could barely hear him so yes, it's possible the name was Primrose. Anyway, I have a letter for her."

It came today, Mama, and I've read it at least fifty times. It's from my father — in his very own handwriting! — and this is what it says:

Dear Faith,

The only excuse for doing what I did to you and your mama was that I was seventeen years old when you were born and couldn't handle being a daddy. I ran out on your two-week birthday — I don't know, everyone seemed to be hollering at each other that day: me, your mama, her mama. Even you were hollering, lying in that little drawer, smelling of wet diapers . . . it was just way too much for me. In my whole life, I've never been more ashamed of anything than running out on you. (Your mama I'm not so ashamed of running out on, ha-ha.

Whew! She was a pistol!)

I was lost and aimless for the next couple months. I worked on an oil rig, in a meatpacking plant, and in the stockroom of a store that sold Confederate souvenirs. (Flags, Jefferson Davis hats, copies of deeds to slaves, and the like — you wouldn't believe the market for crap like that.) Then Uncle Sam caught up to me and I was shipped overseas — even fought in the Battle of Anzio, but I don't really want to get into that. Suffice it to say I'm glad I have two daughters who won't have to know what war is like.

When I got back to the States, I followed a buddy of mine to Tampa, Florida, which seemed just as good a place as any to settle down. I met the girl who became my wife — Phyllis was her name, and she had a little dance school called On Your Toes. She was a real good teacher — even taught me how to dance, and we spent many happy weekend nights at nightclubs doing the waltz, the rhumba, the tango — you name it, we danced it.

I went to school on the GI bill, but I didn't last a year. I guess I'd seen too much to sit at a desk all day. Phyllis asked me what I had wanted to be when I was a little boy, and I said I'd always thought being a fireman would be a good job. She said, "Well, Jimmy, what's holding you back?" Nothing was, and I retired two years ago after thirty-eight years of firefighting.

The reason I'm writing this letter is I've got emphysema so bad, I figure I'm just a couple good coughs away from meeting my

Maker. I'm hooked up to oxygen and everything, so I'm at the phase where I want to settle my scores, you know?

I know it's hard to believe, Faith, but you've been in my thoughts during all the important times of my life. Not in the big, light-up-the-sky way Phyllis and Vivien have; more like a little candle.

I never told anyone about you, Faith, and in one way I feel real bad and cowardly, but when you don't tell your wife a big secret right off the bat, you know there'll be hell to pay when you do tell her. So you avoid the hell altogether.

I will tell you this, Faith: just as Vivien's face was always in my mind whenever I knew there were children in a burning house that had to get out, yours was too. Your little tiny baby face. My little candle.

So I'm writing this to tell you a little bit about me. Sorry that I didn't dare do it until I'm ready to leave this world.

Is this any comfort to you at all? More than anything, I hope so, Faith. I know I was worse than a terrible father to you; I was no father at all. Some might say I've been a good man, and God knows I tried to be, but I also know that a deserter is the worst coward there is, and that's what I am. It's my dream that life's been good to you.

Love,
Your dad, Jim

Mama,

Isn't that something? A letter from *my dad.* Saying I was his *little candle!* But this joy — oh, my gosh, this bliss — is tempered by the fact that his other daughter, *my sister,* doesn't want to see me. She attached a note to the letter saying as much, but I'm not about to let the only blood relative I have reject me, so I called information in Tampa and got her number.

I got an answering machine and launched into my self-promotion sales drive, and when I got a call the next day I thought, *Yippee, it worked!* but it wasn't Vivien, it was her daughter Lauren, my niece.

"I hate to be the one to tell you this, but my mother asked me to deliver a message to you, and the message is that she doesn't want to hear from you again."

"What?" I said, her words taking my breath away worse than a kick to the stomach.

The young woman sighed. "I know that's a pretty harsh thing to hear. I'm sorry Mom's being so rigid — I personally would love to meet you — but right now she feels it's her job to support my grandma, who wants nothing to do with you or the thought that Grandpa had a relationship with somebody else. Grandma's a wonderful person, but she does have this jealous nature, and my mom's inherited it too. See, for so long she was her father's one and only precious daughter, and I don't think she's ready to be knocked from that position, you know? I mean, it's all come as quite a shock to both of them." She took a deep breath. "Whew. Have I made any sense at all?"

I finally managed to push some words past my kicked-in stomach.

"But we're *sisters!* She'd like me! I'm a fun person, and as far as our dad goes, she had

607

him her whole life!" I heard the tears in my voice. "I only had him for the first two weeks of mine!"

"I know," said Lauren, "and I sympathize with you totally. I mean, if I couldn't see my dad — he and my mom got divorced when I was fourteen, but we're real close — why, I'd just be so depressed!"

She stopped talking for a moment.

"Uh, Faith, are you crying? Listen, I'll work on her. All this is just so new for her; it's going to take time, okay? It'll really be okay . . . Aunt Faith."

"Thank you," I said, my voice strangulated in my throat. "Thank you for calling me that."

"You're welcome, and like I said, I'll work on her. But if I were you, I wouldn't try to contact her — any reconciliation is gonna have to come from her." There was a slight pause. "She's awfully stubborn, but I'm sure everything will work out."

"I hope so," I said, and boy, Mama, if that isn't an understatement. Can you imagine what that would be like — to have a sister I could go visit and talk to on the phone and buy Christmas presents for? A sister who could tell me all about that seventeen-year-old who was my dad and grew into hers? Oh, Mama, the fact that she's in this world makes my heart so full, and the fact that she doesn't care that I'm in this world too makes it empty right out. What if she never wants to see me?

I know what your uncensored advice would be, Mama: well, then, fuck her.

Oh, boy, as much as I don't want to, I think I'm going to have to start crying again. How

can a person feel so excited/happy/surprised/
delighted/awed/sad/ miserable/hurt/rejected all
at the same time? The thing I'm gonna hold
on to, though, is this: I was my daddy's little
candle.

Faith

HOST: **GRANT**

BOOK: *Love in the Ruins* by Walker Percy

REASON CHOSEN: "I loved *The Moviegoer*, plus the title spoke to me."

One night last fall, thinking about Stuart and whether or not I was ever going to find someone I might love as much as I had loved him, I called Audrey over to keep me company.

"I was just going to call *you*," she said. "I was sitting here feeling so sad about Paul."

I hurried over, bringing a pineapple upside-down cake (from *The Joy of Cooking* — it's the best ever) I'd made earlier that evening. After taking one bite, Audrey put her fork down and said, "Grant, why don't you move in here with me?"

"Cake's that good, huh?"

"I'm serious," said Audrey, and I could tell by her voice that yes, she was. "Come on, think about it. Why should two good friends who happen to be single live in two big houses?"

"Because we *are* good friends. And we want to stay that way. We'd probably drive each other nuts living in the same house."

"Oh, I don't know about that. Think of it — you'd get the benefit of my company, not to mention my wise pastorly counsel, and I —" She speared another forkful of cake. "I'd get the benefit of your baking and your excellent housekeeping."

"Why don't you just get a maid?"

"You know I'm teasing," said Audrey. "I'd get the benefit of having one of my best friends share a house with me."

"Well," I asked, coughing away the lump that sprouted in my throat, "what about my cat?"

"Lillian?" said Audrey, as if she hadn't thought of her. "Well, we could always put her to sleep." Seeing my face, she added, "Grant, I'm kidding."

"What if I meet someone? What if you meet someone?"

"Grant, look around this house. It was big enough to raise three boys in. It's big enough to hold three adults if one of us should get so lucky — four if we're both so fortunate." With the side of her fork, she cut another piece of cake. "The house is getting too big for me alone. I've honestly been thinking of moving to a condominium, but I can't bear the idea of leaving Freesia Court. So really, if you'd move in, you'd be doing me a big favor."

"You'd want me to sell my *house?*"

Audrey shrugged. "Mine is all paid off. If you lived here, you'd live mortgage-free."

"Well, let me think about it," I said in a voice that sounded as if I wasn't sure I'd think about it at all.

I did, though. And the more I thought, the more sense it made to me.

"But Audrey," I said in one of the dozen or more conversations we had about the topic, "what if we found we didn't get along as room-

611

mates? What if we couldn't stand one another?"

Audrey laughed. "Then I suppose you'd move out — or I'd move out. Whatever comes up, Grant, I have faith that we'd figure things out."

I sold my house in November to the Wahlbergs, a young couple with a baby, and I moved in in December. I happened to be Audrey's Secret Santa that year and gave her an atomizer of perfume. Over the logo, I pasted a piece of paper with these words on it:

ROOMMATE RIDDER
Whenever you're troubled by pesky
roommates, one shot of the Roommate Ridder
will send the pesky roommate out of the house
until he's cordially invited back.

Audrey hefted the bottle in her hand as if she were trying to determine its weight.

"Gee, I wonder if my Secret Santa could get this for me in a ten-gallon size?"

It's only been three weeks, but so far we're a great match. In fact, as soon as Kari came over for book club and smelled what I had in the oven (a toffee bar pie), she asked if we wanted a third roommate.

"Or at least let me come over on the nights Grant cooks."

"Kari," said Audrey, "Grant cooks every night."

Kari shook her head. "Some people have all the luck."

"Yeah, and I'm just grateful mine seems to be *good* right now," I said. "Bad luck's a pain in the ass."

"Amen," said the youth minister.

The others arrived and agreed that the pie smelled so good that we should forgo tradition and eat before the discussion.

"How about we make our thirtieth-anniversary plans?" said Audrey, taking the first piece of pie that was cut. "We said we were going to do that at the last meeting."

"I can imagine you thirty years ago," I said. "I bet you all reeked of hairspray and Charlie cologne."

"More like cigarettes and liquor," said Kari. "Uffda, the air used to be blue with smoke."

"Thirty years," said Merit, shaking her head.

"Is it going to be a year-round celebration?" I asked, directing the question at Slip, who'd been uncharacteristically quiet. "Or are we just going to have some sort of blowout party?"

Slip shrugged.

"A blowout party sounds good," said Audrey. "Food, liquor, and a recounting of some of the stories we told the night we discussed *Everything You Wanted to Know About Sex*."

Kari licked her fork (my toffee bar pie tended to make the best manners fly the coop). "You know, I like that recounting idea. Not necessarily those stories we told *that* night —"

"Hey," said Audrey, "you never did tell us what you think about blow jobs."

"I know," said Merit, sitting forward. "How about if we each choose our favorite book to re-read and discuss?"

"I like that idea," said Faith. "Kind of a greatest-hits thing."

"Well, I for one, ladies, have the memory of a sieve," said Audrey. "How am I supposed to remember all the books we've read, let alone choose my favorite?"

"I've kept a list," said Merit, raising her hand like a kid in school.

"You've kept a *list?*" asked Audrey.

Merit nodded. "Every night after book club, I'd go home and write about the meeting. I'd do it in the bathroom, where Eric wouldn't see me — you remember how weird he was about me being in book club."

"I can't believe you were married to that psychopath," said Faith.

"I kept track of who hosted the night, why they chose the book, what food was served — stuff like that."

"You didn't!" said Kari, delight in her voice.

"I did."

"That's a historical document you've got on your hands, sister," said Audrey, taking her second piece of pie. "You've *got* to type it all up for the rest of us."

"Maybe Mr. Paradise and I are already planning something," said Merit, her voice teasing.

"Well," said Slip softly, "I don't know about this greatest-hits idea. What if I want to celebrate our anniversary by reading a new book?"

"We read new books all the time," said Faith impatiently. "I just thought it might be fun to take a look back."

"It also might be fun to take a look forward," said Slip, reaching for the big leather bag that slouched next to her chair. She set the bag on her lap and sat regarding us for a moment, her tiny little teeth bared in the shit-eatingest grin I'd ever seen in my life.

"For example," she said, reaching into the bag, "I don't know about the rest of you, but I think this book would make for a *great* discussion."

She held the book out to us, her hands cupping the lower part, her chin resting on the top.

"*Winter Gardens*," said Faith. "I never heard of it."

Slip's grin, which couldn't get any bigger, somehow did as she opened her hands, uncovering the author's name at the bottom of the book.

"Flannery McMahon!" said Faith.

"Flannery McMahon!" echoed Merit.

"Oh, my God," said Audrey, "it's Flan's book!"

"Flan's book!" said Kari, and I reiterated, "Flan's book!"

"That's my daughter," said Slip, and I thought then that if every single kid could hear their mother speak of them with such love and reverence, the world would change in an instant.

We inspected the book like monkeys checking for fleas, commenting on the typeface and the cover art.

"This is just a bound galley," Slip explained. "The real book won't be out for a couple months."

"Is this the cover they're going to use, though?" said Merit. "It's like a picture of a dream."

"Flan doesn't like it," said Slip. "She thinks it looks like a young-adult title."

"She looks so sophisticated," said Audrey, seeing Flan's stamp-sized picture on the back. "What did I always tell her? 'Flan, you've got to wear a little more makeup.' "

It was only when Faith opened it to the dedication page that we shut up.

" 'To my dad,' " she read, " 'who taught me about weather, and my mom who taught me about books. I'll never run out of things to talk about.' "

In my innocence, I thought the night was ending when Audrey and I got everyone their coats. Standing in the foyer, watching them dig their gloves out of their pockets and prop their hats on their heads, I stifled the full, happy yawn of a host who knows what a good time everyone had at his house (and it *did* feel like my house), and who also knows how good it's going to feel to crawl into bed. So when Slip said something, I hardly paid any attention, thinking it was the same let's-bolster-one-another chatter everyone makes before they go out into a cold winter night.

But I saw Kari's head jerk in a funny way, like a dog hearing a far-off whistle, and Faith's hands seemed to be stuck to the scarf around her neck.

"What did you say?" I asked, even though I knew immediately I did not want to hear her answer.

"The cancer came back," said Slip, and even though her voice was just above a whisper, it roared in my head.

"Where?" I asked.

"I didn't want to say anything earlier," said Slip, buttoning her top coat button. "I wanted Flan's book — the good news — to get all the attention."

"Where did it come back, Slip?" It seemed desperately important that I know the cancer's location.

"In my back," said Slip. "In my hip."

"Your back *and* your hip?" I could hear the hysteria in my voice, and I knew Audrey did too, because she said, "Get your coat on, Grant, and let's all take a walk."

Our boots sounded like squeegees against glass as we plowed new tracks through the white-and-blue snow. It was the only sound we made as we trudged down the block, the moon small and dim in the sky, like a nightlight that needed to be recharged.

"Jerry's in Canada," said Slip as we passed her house. "At a conference on glacial ice. I haven't even told him yet."

What could we say to that? There weren't words, although I saw Kari, whose arm was looped through Slip's, pull her a little closer.

We sidestepped our way down the hill that led down to the creek, and when we reached the basin, we stood there for a bit, a mute herd of middle-agers in winter wear, needing a wrangler to tell us what to do.

"Remember our first-ever snowball fight?" asked Faith.

There are times in life when exactly the right thing is spoken. For instance, there is no more perfect answer than "I do" when asked if you'll love, honor, and cherish the person wearing a veil (or, in my case, a tuxedo) next to you. When you're delivering foodstuffs and medical supplies to a starved, war-torn country, "Don't shoot! Red Cross!" is a pretty good password. And when you're huddled in sadness with your dearest friends, a reminder about how you all began can have amazing restorative powers.

At least it did for us.

"Of course, I wasn't here on that night, but if I had been," I said, squatting down to pack some snow, "I could have taken everyone on with one hand tied behind my back."

"He just challenged us, girls," said Faith, and within seconds snowballs were flying through the frosty January night.

Merit knocked off my ratty Russian fur hat (it was politically incorrect — the fur, not the Russian part — but it was a remnant from the costume department of the Sexual Freedom Theater, and I figured the beaver or whatever animal it was who gave its pelt would have been long dead anyway) with a well-aimed fastball, and Slip threw one that cannonballed on my right shoulder.

When I had heard the story of that first snowball fight (it was part of the lore and I had heard it several times), I was always told of the laughter, the cackling, but now I got to hear it, contribute to it. I'll have to discuss this theosophical theory with Audrey: hysterical laughter might not be *the* rapture, but it's at least *a* rapture.

Splat! Speaking of the pastor, I got her good.

We threw and laughed, our breaths blasts of vapor in the air, and threw some more. When a snowball Kari threw clipped me on the jaw, I pretended the force knocked me back into the snow. I was tired, and it was a good dramatic effect.

"Women win in a knockout," said Audrey, standing over me.

"It wasn't a fair fight," I complained.

"It never is."

"Hey," said Merit, watching as I moved my

hands up and down and my feet back and forth, "he's making a snow angel."

Everyone followed her over to a fresh patch of snow that hadn't been trampled in our snow fight and lay down in a wide circle, giving the person next to us room to make wings and a skirt.

"What a beautiful night," said Faith, "except there aren't any stars out."

"Cloud cover," said Slip. "It'll probably snow again tonight."

"Well, let's not lie around here till it does," said Audrey. "I'm freezing."

We got up to admire our circle of angels, and then Merit took Slip's arm.

"Those are yours, Slip," she said. "Your angels, who are going to watch over you and keep you safe."

I thought it was a wonderful sentiment, but apparently Slip did not agree.

"They're just going to get covered up by snow," she said.

"Yes," said Audrey, taking her other arm. "But they'll still be there. *We'll* still be there, whenever you need us."

"Do you think I'm stupid?" asked Slip. We were all taken aback for a moment until she added, her voice ten times softer, "Don't you think I already know that? Holy what-do-you-think-I-count-on — *it's our pledge.*"

I hung back a little with Slip; we held hands as we trudged up the hill.

"I hate that your cancer's back," I told her.

"Me too. Although I knew it had come back, even before the doctor's report. I've just been feeling sort of punk."

"Are you going to have chemo again?"

Slip nodded.

"Well, look on the bright side," I said. "Last time after your hair fell out it came back straight. Maybe this time it won't come back red."

"God," said Slip with a laugh. "That would almost make all of this worth it."

Epilogue

September 1998

FAITH

In the hospital, we had learned that the busier our hands were, the less often we used them to grab at tissues to wipe our eyes or blow our noses. And Slip was still adamant: no crying.

Audrey was a veritable knitting factory, churning out enough baby paraphernalia to keep her grandchildren in sweaters and booties until far past the time they'd be able to fit into such stuff. Grant, her knitting pupil, worked on a muffler that was lopsided and knobby with mistakes. Kari solicited from us all our mending projects, and she patched and darned and let out the hems of Portia's dresses (she was a rare breed, a tomboy who loved dresses). Merit read, or at least she always had a book on her lap, and I worked on my scrapbook.

Of course, Flan agreed to be the visiting author at our book club, and we pulled out all the stops. Slip's dining room table looked like a bakery outlet, loaded with bars and cookies and pies.

"Wow," said Flan, "I remember you guys eating a lot, but I don't remember *this* much food."

Audrey added a brownie to her plate. "I'd probably be a size six if it weren't for these meetings."

"You've never been a size six in your life," said Grant.

"Shut up and pass me a lemon bar."

It was our best meeting ever; how could it not be? Bonnie (she and Flan still keep their little book club going in a fashion, e-mailing their comments on books) came, and while we thought of swinging open our usually locked gate and inviting all family members, we decided no, we wanted our first real live author all to ourselves. Besides, a big publishing party/reunion picnic (we were so excited — practically everyone's kids were coming home) had been planned for the next day, so it wasn't as if we were completely selfish.

We all wore the T-shirts Merit and Mr. Paradise had made for us, and every time we looked at the columns that scrolled down our bustlines, we were swept away by a memory.

"Oh, *The Martian Chronicles*!" said Audrey, pointing at my chest. "Remember how we discussed that the day after Nixon resigned?"

"A bad year for America, a good year for books," said Kari. "Look, that was the year we read *The Age of Innocence* and *The Heart Is a Lonely Hunter*."

"Oh, my gosh — look at what's under 1984! *The Drifters*! You all complained that it was too long, but when Bryan had his accident it consoled me because it *was* so long. That same year

I plowed through three other Michener books."

"And look under 1969," said Merit. "*A Good Man Is Hard to Find* by Flannery O'Connor — and now we've got our own writer Flannery right here!"

"And speaking of Ms. McMahon, how about we get started with the discussion?" said Slip from her chair. "We don't want to keep the esteemed author waiting."

"So where do you get your inspiration?" Merit asked once we had finally settled in the living room.

"From everything," said Flan. "From real things — an old man's face, the sky, the smell of Dentyne gum. From imagination. And from memory — what started my first chapter was the memory of my mother pushing my stroller with one hand and carrying a picket sign in the other."

Slip dabbed at her eyes with a tissue, her hand a small bony claw. "And at the time I thought I was only trying to stop a war or get the Equal Rights Amendment passed. Little did I know you were going to make a *novel* out of it."

As Flan talked about her book and answered our questions, Slip's face was flushed, her cinnamon-colored eyes glittering with excitement. She looked positively feverish, but I chose to think it was due to maternal pride and not to her illness. I clung to denial the way Beau had clung to his baby blanket — until it was a patch, and then a rag, and then a shred.

It was pretty hard not to see that the possibility of her rebounding this time was remote; there was hardly any of *her* to see. She sat on

Jerry's recliner, buried up to her neck under a quilt. (The rest of us were sweating in our shorts and commemorative T-shirts.) Slip had always been tiny, but she had been huge in her tininess; now I was afraid that if I pulled away the quilt, I'd find nothing there at all.

As sick as she was, though, she was in her glory, whether listening to Flan tell the story of how she got her agent or to Bonnie telling us she'd been worried about not liking the book and then having to fake liking it.

"But I *really* liked it, Flan. I started highlighting the parts I thought were really well written, and look." She flipped through some pages. "It's *full* of highlight."

The smile on Slip's tiny, flushed face was beatific. "Damn right it's full of highlight."

At the backyard picnic the next day, Slip oohed and ahhed at Dave's children and Julia's new baby boy, Bjorn. "Are you getting any *ideas*, kids?" she asked Flan and her son Joe, sitting nearby. She ate nothing but drank something out of a sipper cup ("hundred-proof rye whiskey," she claimed) and laughed as hard as anyone when Beau walked over to her — on his hands.

"He used to be the star of our neighborhood circus," she explained to the Wahlbergs, the couple who had bought Grant's house. "Well, next to me."

"You used to put on a neighborhood circus?" said Regina Wahlberg.

"Yeah," piped in Portia. "And they were the funnest thing *ever*." She glared at her mother. "At least that's what my sisters say."

Merit smiled, patting her daughter's wild, dandelion-colored hair. "It's her deepest regret that

624

they were pretty much over by the time she came along."

"You would like to be in a circus, wouldn't you, Matt?" Regina said to her wriggly baby who was trying to climb over her shoulder. "You could be an acrobat."

It was a perfect day (except for the mosquitoes and a crop of bees that wanted to pollinate the potato salad), and when Slip's son Gil and Merit's daughter Jewel announced their engagement — well, stars exploded in the sky, nightingales sang, Dean Martin reunited with Jerry Lewis.

"You'll be Jewel's mother-in-law!" Merit said to Slip.

"You'll be Gil's!"

"We'll be related!"

But night falls on perfect days, and less than a week after the reunion, Slip was in the hospital again, and for what we knew would be the last time.

"Jerry wants me to come home," confided Slip to the Angry Housewives, "but I'm only going home when I know I'm going to die. And ladies, that time is not *now*."

Slip, for all her practicality, was not willing to concede her battle and thought that if victory was possible, it was in the hospital, near doctors and drugs that might offer a last-minute medical miracle, a stay of execution.

There was a steady stream of visitors: work friends, protest friends, Habitat for Humanity friends, and Slip's family — her kids, her parents, and her brothers.

"Fred?" I said, running into a red-haired,

bearded man in a hallway.

"Faith!" he answered, holding his arms out.

"You hug hard," I said after our embrace. "Just like Slip."

Fred laughed. "Well, as she always says, if you're gonna hug, *hug*."

A pregnant woman emerged from the rest room and took Fred's arm.

"Honey, this is one of my sister's good friends," said Fred. "Faith, this is my wife, Paula."

"You're one of the Angry Housewives?" asked the petite, dark-skinned woman, who was at least twenty years younger than her husband. When I nodded, she said, "Fred's told me all about you. In fact, we met in a book club he started at our local library."

"You guys turned me on to the power of book discussion," said Fred. "I even wrote a letter to the president, telling him he should start a monthly book club with all the other world leaders. The only catch is, I get to choose the books for them. The first one would be *The Feminine Mystique*, the second would be Krishnamurti's *Think on These Things*, and the third would be *Huckleberry Finn*."

"Interesting selection," I said. "Have you heard back from him?"

"Not yet," said Fred. "But I'm hoping he'll recognize a good peace plan when he sees it."

One night Wade and Mr. Paradise spirited Jerry off to a nearby bar ("You need a change of scenery and you need a drink," Wade told him), leaving us Angry Housewives alone with Slip.

"How's the scrapbook coming, Faith?" asked Kari.

"Great," I said, pulling a packet of photographs from my purse. "Look at this one."

I handed her a picture of Slip taken at one of Kari's Christmas parties, unwrapping a hugely padded bra.

"Let me see that," whispered Slip, and Kari leaned toward the bed, holding the snapshot out for her to see. Slip smiled. "I think you all got a perverse pleasure in being my Secret Santa."

"Oh, that's good," I said. "That'll be my caption."

I had gotten the idea of making a scrapbook of the Angry Housewives after I had made a scrapbook of my family for my sister, Vivien. I know she got it because her signature was needed for delivery, but so far I hadn't heard anything back from her. And that was back in March.

Looking through all my photographs, I'd come across a lot of the Angry Housewives, and it had made me want to document our history (or *herstory,* as Slip would say) too.

"Hey, pass those around," said Audrey, and when I handed her the stack of photographs, she laughed. "Oh, you guys, look at this one — it's from our California trip."

In this picture, all the Angry Housewives are standing in front of this little roadhouse, next to a big, bearded guy wearing a Hell's Angels T-shirt. He looks wild, and so do we.

"I wish I were a founding member," said Grant. "Look at all I missed out on."

"Yeah, but think what's ahead in the next thirty years," said Kari.

"I can just imagine," said Slip. We all grew quiet; Slip could command our complete attention with one word. "You know what I've been thinking?"

"What, Slip?" Merit asked.

"Let's ask Regina Wahlberg to join the book club," said Slip in the slow, whispery voice that was so unlike the way she usually spoke. "I know she likes to read — I always run into her at the library. Plus she's worked for Wellstone's Senate campaigns."

Leave it to Slip to try to ensure that her replacement (if that's what she was trying, in her sneaky way, to do) not only liked to read but was a liberal Democrat.

None of us had anything to say after that, but even if we had, Slip didn't stay awake to hear it.

"Man, she can fall asleep fast," said Audrey.

"With all the drugs she's getting, I'm surprised she stays awake as much as she does," said Kari, her blue eyes misting with tears. She stood up and, yawning, stretched with her hand at the base of her back. "Anybody else ready to call it a night?"

Everyone else was, in fact, but me.

"I'm so wired from coffee," I said, "I'm just going to stay here a little longer and work on the scrapbook."

"Be careful out in the parking lot," said Grant.

"On my honor," I promised.

Even with the clicking and whirring of the hospital machinery, the room was doused in a certain peacefulness, as if the molecules themselves had settled down after the departure of the other Angry Housewives.

Chuckling, I studied a snapshot taken the summer we had first gotten together. I loved coming across a photograph that could immediately take me back to a memory that had long been tucked away in an inactive file.

On a hot, sunny summer's day, Audrey had told us to pack up our kids and our swimsuits; she'd been invited to use the pool at a friend's house, and we were all invited too. While the host's teenage daughter kept the kids busy (not hard to do on a three-acre property with a playground, a playhouse, and three friendly dogs who were willing to fetch as many balls as the kids threw), we spent a luxurious, lazy afternoon in the swimming pool.

We had lolled around it in floats, all the while drinking martinis and smoking cigarettes.

"What's so funny?" said Slip now.

"Oh!" I said, my heart knocking. "I thought you were asleep."

"I was," she said, her voice raspy. "Till you started laughing. Now let me see that."

I handed her the snapshot and watched as a whisper of a smile crossed the sunken planes of her face.

"That's the day we taught Merit how to play poker."

"Yeah, remember how Audrey won all those pennies but they got knocked off that floating table?"

"And later we had the kids dive for buried treasure." Slip squinted. "My God, look at those hats. Not even Shriners would wear hats like that."

I laughed. "Hey, that's why we look so young now, Slip. Because we wore hats like that in the sun."

Slip looked at the picture for a moment more

before handing it back to me.

"Do you think I'm going to die, Faith?"

Heat pumped to my face. "I . . . we all are going to die, Slip."

"Good answer," said Slip, her eyes half closed. "But I mean soon, as in do you think I'm on my deathbed?"

"I . . . I don't know, Slip. I'm not a doctor."

"You *are* crafty with your answers, Faith. But if you were a doctor, you know what I would tell you?"

I shook my head.

"I'd tell you that you don't know everything. I'm going to surprise everybody." She waved her hand weakly. "Not only am I going to walk out of here, I'm going to *walk on my hands* out of here." A scowl creased her forehead. "I've got kids to see married, grandchildren to see born!"

She barely moved, but it seemed to me exhaustion pushed her back into her pillow. Her eyes were closed, and I assumed sleep had once again overtaken her, but then she said, "Still haven't heard anything from your sister?"

When I heard the words "your sister," tears sprang to my eyes. I barely spoke of Vivien anymore, so hurt was I at her rejection.

"No."

"Do you think you ever will?"

My heart thumped again. "I . . . I *have* to. Some way or another, I have to figure out how to get her into my life."

The shadow smile appeared again on Slip's face.

"Good old Faithy. Just like me — you never give up." She leaned forward, as if given a sudden injection of adrenaline. "And why should we? Why shouldn't the story end the way we want it to? I always hated when a book had a lousy ending. I'm gonna make damn sure my own life doesn't."

Her cackle turned into a cough.

"Slip," I said, taking her hand. "Don't. Don't wear yourself out like that."

She nodded, and I sat holding her claw hand until her breath evened out and she fell back asleep. One of the monitors clicked and another made a sound like an amplified gulp.

Shivering, I buttoned up my cardigan, feeling that panic was a thing ready to jump into my lap and that if I let it, I wouldn't be able to stop screaming.

Turning back to my photographs, I picked one up with shaking fingers.

It was the one of us posed with the bearded biker, and in a second the panic was batted away, far across the room.

I opened the acid-free (posterity demanded it) pages of the scrapbook and nestled the snapshot into those little corner thingies. Staring at the picture and into the past it represented, I finally put my pen to paper.

The Angry Housewives tame a Hell's Angel, I wrote. *Next stop: world domination.* I laughed, even though I was a breath away from bursting into tears. I looked at Slip, but my valiant, true friend did not stir, and I stared at the photograph for a moment more before adding, *We're still working on that one.*

631

About the Author

Lorna Landvik is the bestselling author of *Patty Jane's House of Curl, Your Oasis on Flame Lake, The Tall Pine Polka,* and *Welcome to the Great Mysterious.* She is also an actor, playwright, and proud member of her own book club.